ACCUMULATION

Also by Aimee Pokwatka

The Parliament

Self-Portrait with Nothing

Aimee Pokwatka

G. P. Putnam's Sons
New York

ACCUMULATION

PUTNAM
— EST. 1838 —
G. P. Putnam's Sons
Publishers Since 1838
An imprint of Penguin Random House LLC
1745 Broadway, New York, NY 10019
penguinrandomhouse.com

Book design by Laura K. Corless
Title page art: spiral strokes © Marusoi/Shutterstock

Library of Congress Cataloging-in-Publication Data

Names: Pokwatka, Aimee, author.
Title: Accumulation / Aimee Pokwatka.
Description: New York: G. P. Putnam's Sons, 2025.
Identifiers: LCCN 2025025640 (print) | LCCN 2025025641 (ebook) |
ISBN 9798217047628 hardcover | ISBN 9798217047635 ebook
Subjects: LCGFT: Fiction. | Horror fiction. | Fiction.
Classification: LCC PS3616.O5566 A64 2025 (print) |
LCC PS3616.O5566 (ebook) | DDC 813/.6—dc23/eng/20250604
LC record available at https://lccn.loc.gov/2025025640
LC ebook record available at https://lccn.loc.gov/2025025641

Printed in the United States of America
1st Printing

The authorized representative in the EU for product safety and compliance is Penguin Random House Ireland, Morrison Chambers, 32 Nassau Street, Dublin D02 YH68, Ireland, https://eu-contact.penguin.ie.

For Jason,
again

I don't like it that way. I want it my way.

—Louise Bourgeois,
Louise Bourgeois: The Spider, the Mistress and the Tangerine

ACCUMULATION

PART 1

I don't believe in ghosts, but I'm afraid of them.

—EDITH WHARTON,
Ghosts

1

When Ward found the doll, Tenn was in the backyard, pulling weeds nearly as tall as she was. They'd been in the house for less than a week, and this was the first time they'd turned their attention to the yard. The previous owners had let it go wild, and there was no telling what might be hiding in the overgrowth. The house was still teeming with boxes, but it was important to Tenn that she knew the yard was safe, that there were no dangers lying in wait for the kids.

As Ward approached from behind, Tenn's attention was focused elsewhere. She was prone to fixating on details, and she'd just discovered a cluster of symbols carved into the worn brick of the patio—a flower inside a circle, a cross with a backslash cutting across its bottom. This house was old—the main part built in the 1750s. The bricks of the patio were likely not as old, but running her fingers over the etching, Tenn was flooded with a sense of camaraderie that felt tethered to a different time. Then something spidery brushed against her shoulder, and she screamed.

"Welcome home, Tennessee," Ward said, making the doll do a dance on her shoulder. "I've been waiting for you."

Tenn swatted at both her husband and the doll, wiped a filthy hand across her sweaty forehead. It was hot even for August. They hadn't expected New York to be as hot as the South. Rivulets of sweat trickled down her torso under her overalls, over the crest of her hip, and down her thigh.

"You scared the shit out of me," she said, and snatched the doll away. It was small—the length of Ward's gloved hand—and bald, wearing a nightgown that had once been pink or blue but was now a dingy gray mottled with grass stains.

"Where'd you find this?" she asked. The doll looked up at her with soft, pursed lips, its blue eyes expressionless inside its plastic head. From one sleeve, a tendril of dead grass sprouted like an arm.

"Up front in the ivy," Ward said, and pulled Tenn close. "I like making you scream." He'd been like this since the move, despite the tenuousness between them that had preceded it. Even the day they'd moved in, after sixteen hours of carrying boxes in ninety-five-degree heat, they'd collapsed into bed and, as if magnetized, melded into sticky, exhausted sex. He bit off a glove and slid a hand inside Tenn's overalls, just in time for the kids to come running.

"Unhand her, beast!" Anders yelled, waving a stick that Tenn tried not to worry he'd impale himself on.

Ward kept his hand inside her overalls, roaming.

"Never!" Ward said, and kissed Tenn so deeply Anders shrieked and covered his eyes.

Aisling wasn't far behind, her small arms cradling one of the giant Nerf guns Tenn had bought, as promised, for their cooperation during the move. They'd never been allowed toy guns before. Tenn had never needed an outright bribe before, but it was hard to leave everything you've ever known behind, nearly impossible.

"You're not shooting at cars, are you?" Tenn asked.

She hadn't been paying enough attention to the kids, the work ahead of her in this ancient house so overwhelming she'd allowed herself to fall into a trancelike state. The kids had been on the roof of the detached garage, which was situated at the rear of the property. The garage roof had been a favorite hangout spot of the previous owners' daughter—they'd built a ladder onto the side for her to climb, nailed in so it couldn't slip.

"What's that?" Aisling said, and reached for the doll in Tenn's hand. Tenn extended her arm in offering, but her hand didn't open, the doll firmly in her grip.

"I found it up front," Ward said. "It was buried under the leaves."

Aisling prodded the doll but didn't take it. "I don't like it," she said.

"That's too bad," Ward said. "One of the selling points of this house was that it came with its own possessed baby doll. Your mother has been dreaming about this her entire life."

Tenn set the doll inside her gardening caddy, positioning it so its head peeked out the top. It was probably crawling with ticks. She listened for Gogo but didn't hear her. Also probably buried in the leaves, crawling with ticks. The doll gazed up at Tenn, dirt smudged across its dimpled cheeks. "At last," Tenn said. "Our family is complete."

"When I heard you scream, I thought a bear was getting you," Anders said. He still had the stick in his hand, ready to fight.

"I'm sorry to disappoint," Tenn said. "Maybe the doll is warding off the wildlife."

"You couldn't fight a bear," Aisling told Anders.

Anders whapped her in the side with the stick.

"Absolutely not," Tenn said, and yanked the stick from Anders's hand—too hard, she realized, when Anders balled his hand in pain. She reached out for him, to assess the damage, but he shrank from her grip. She hadn't meant to hurt him.

"Whatever!" he yelled. Anders had always been a little volatile, but the move had undone something inside him, his impulse control left behind in North Carolina. "Let the bears eat you!"

He ran back to the garage before Tenn could respond. She turned her attention to Aisling.

"Are you okay?" she asked. Anders hadn't hit her very hard, but Aisling, too, had been different since the move, floating around the yard, detached. Before, Aisling had been a burrower. She liked to nestle in the nooks, under blanket forts, inside closets. She liked to be tucked away, inside of things.

"That doll is creepy," Aisling said. Her curly hair was knotted at the back of her head, and she'd already made up her mind not to let anyone comb it. She raised her gun at the doll, its blank, worn face. "Don't you try anything," she said. "I'm watching."

Then she followed her brother, climbing the ladder to the garage roof with a lack of caution that surprised Tenn. Maybe the move would be good for them, eventually. They would learn to be adaptable. Tenn closed her eyes and willed them not to throw anything into traffic.

Gogo appeared from the front yard and deposited a splintered bone at Tenn's feet. The previous owners had also had a dog, judging by the scratch marks at the base of the back door. Tenn tried to snatch the bone before Gogo ate it and made herself sick, but Gogo was faster and disappeared into the woods with her prize.

Ward slid his hand back inside Tenn's overalls, cupping her sweaty ass. Tenn's underwear was soaked with sweat, but she liked it, liked Ward like this, liked the small hope growing inside her that the move would fix what they were both terrified was unfixable. She was still holding Anders's stick and was suddenly aware of its potential as a weapon.

"We should get you out of these," Ward said. He kissed her, and she felt his erection through his Carhartts. "These overalls are filthy."

"You're filthy," Tenn said. She dropped the stick and kissed him back, and the kids groaned from the garage. "What's gotten into you?"

"I must be channeling a demonic spirit," Ward said, tilting his head in the direction of the doll. It had been months since he'd been like this—unburdened. "I'm all wound up."

"I don't care if the doll is full of ticks, then," Tenn said. "We're keeping it." She would keep Ward like this, free from the strife of the last year. They could start fresh here, remember how they used to be. Ward slid his tongue inside her mouth.

On the street behind the house, a mulch truck honked, the sound resonating through Tenn's body. The kids were pumping their arms at every passing vehicle.

"The neighbors are going to love us," Tenn said. She went back for another kiss, aware of the doll in her peripheral vision, its face pointed upward from the caddy.

"And if they don't," Ward said, working his hand into Tenn's flesh, "we'll hex them."

Tenn felt his hand on her slick body, his nose against her cheek, his desire bending her back, like he might pin her down right there, in the yard. He only stopped at the sound of screeching brakes, and they looked up to see the unmistakable orange of a Nerf dart in the street, and the kids flinging themselves off the garage roof, forgoing the ladder, and slinking into the woodpile to hide.

× × ×

The house was on Harmes Way—that was the first thing. When Ward had told Tenn the name of the street, she hadn't believed him.

"Maybe we should see if there's anything available on Murder Lane first," she'd said. "We don't want to limit our options."

The second thing was that the house, thanks to a number of additions patchworked on over the years, was confusing. The living room connected to both the dining room and the extra bedroom; the sitting room upstairs connected to both the bathroom and the primary bedroom. Tenn got lost a lot, those first weeks, always walking through a doorway and arriving someplace unexpected. She couldn't remember which stairs led to which rooms. She couldn't remember where any of the light switches were. The house predated the use of electric lights by more than a hundred years, and when it had been wired, all the switches were installed in unintuitive places. The switch for the dining room chandelier was in the kitchen. The switch for the kitchen light was inside the back staircase, behind a door. Tenn put Post-its on the doors and the light switches, on the cabinets so she could find the silverware and dishes, but it was humid, and the Post-its kept curling and dropping to the floor, where Gogo would find them and squirrel them away. Sometimes Tenn walked from room to room and imagined that the house was changing around her, manifesting new halls and doors to seal her in. It felt like the kind of house that might absorb people.

Ward was six feet tall, and he had to duck through the doorways, and the doorframes were all crooked, giving the house a Wonderland vibe. The floor in the living room was so pitched that if you stood in socks at the north end, you would slide down to the south. If you went up to the attic, you had to prop the door open; otherwise it would slam itself shut. Many of these quirks were due to the way the house had settled, the real estate agent had been quick to add. Not because it was haunted, she said with a laugh. Apparently it had concerned one family enough that they'd moved on. People chose not to buy houses for all kinds of reasons.

Probably people had died there, statistically speaking, but the light was good.

The third thing about the house was that it was a gift—from Ward to Tenn. He was trying to make something up to her, though this went unspoken between them. They'd been together forever,

Ward and Tenn, fourteen years now. Not everything needed to be said out loud. And they both knew as soon as they saw it that this house—with its crooked floors and nonsensical light switches, with its kitchen window seat and big screened porch, with its wide plank floors scratched and worn by the many occupants who'd survived worse here before them—was Tenn's dream house. Buying Tenn her dream house—Tenn understood without Ward having to say it—was Ward's plan to get them back on track. And Tenn wanted it. She wanted it, too. She wanted it so much she was willing to overlook a lot.

* * *

Tenn pulled the doll from her robe pocket and hid it behind Ward's coffee mug in the cabinet beside the microwave. Ward was upstairs, in theory preparing for his first day at his new job but really just chasing the kids around with tickle fingers, his attempt to soften all their first-day jitters. Tenn's own new job didn't start for another two weeks, but Ward was going to help more, he'd told her that morning, holding a wide-tooth comb and steeling himself for battle with Aisling's newfound stubbornness about her hair.

Tenn started a batch of eggs on the stove and opened the drawer labeled *utensils* in search of the spatula. In the drawer, she found a box of foil, a handful of rubber bands, and three wilted dandelions, a dubious gift from one of the kids. She opened another drawer—a drawer that actually contained utensils—but the spatula was not inside. Tenn tried to remember unpacking the spatula but instead remembered opening this drawer and pulling out a long, thin fillet knife. She'd never put knives in a drawer at all, though; they had a knife block for that. And Tenn had never filleted anything in her life. But it happened to her sometimes, because—like the house—she was absorbent. She picked up strangers' accents and mannerisms without meaning to; she picked up their gaits and their moods. She was like that with images, too—after years of studying and working in film, her brain absorbed scenes that didn't belong to her, braiding them into memories of her own life. Sometimes it was hard to distinguish what was hers and what wasn't.

Ward was partway down the stairs when Tenn heard him. "Fuck!" he yelled, just as Anders entered the kitchen.

"Language," Anders scolded, mimicking Tenn's tone.

The door by the pantry opened, and Ward appeared, clutching his forehead. He'd come down the back staircase, which descended from his office, off their bedroom, to the kitchen. The back stairs were unusually narrow and steep—Tenn had fallen down them already, their second morning in the house, awake before sunrise, undercaffeinated and wearing socks that were too slippery. They'd made it a rule—no socks on the Murder Stairs. Her tailbone was still sore from the fall; her body hadn't felt right since.

"Did you slip?" she asked him. She leaned in for a kiss, but Ward went straight to the microwave to examine his reflection.

"Hit my forehead," he said. "These fucking ceilings."

"I thought you loved the ceilings," Anders said. Anders had gone on a brief hunger strike when the move had been announced, which meant he refused to eat at home while steadily emptying his cafeteria e-wallet, filling his backpack with pretzels and cookies at school so he wouldn't break in front of Ward and Tenn. "What about all the *character*?"

Ward had countered the kids' protests with a hard sell on the house—it would be a big change for all of them, but change could be good. The kids didn't care that Ward had been offered an executive position, a six-figure salary for the first time in his life. They didn't care that he'd be able to work from home two days a week, that his commute to the office would be a breezy fifteen minutes, that he'd be more flexible, more present. But in New York, he told them, there were better schools than in North Carolina, with cooler playgrounds, and they'd be only an hour from New York City and all its museums and musicals and restaurants. In the new house, they no longer had to share a bedroom, and there was a big flat yard where they could play. Gogo, too. That, and it was their mom's dream house. The kids were still soft enough that this last bit moved the needle.

"Is it bleeding?" Ward asked.

Tenn cupped his face with her hands and blinked away an image of a body crumpled at the bottom of the stairs. She was the only person who'd fallen down the stairs, but she wasn't seeing herself. Ever since her own fall, she couldn't stop imagining the rest of them, maimed in various ways by her dream home.

"There's a line where you hit it," she said. She traced a finger across the red mark, already puffy. "You're going to have a bruise."

"Perfect!" Ward said. "Nothing says VP of incident response like a visible head wound!"

Tenn reached past him for the skillet of eggs on the stove.

"Are those for me?" Ward said.

"The kids," Tenn said. "But I can't find the spatula."

Ward took the skillet and, with the flick of a wrist, flipped the eggs into the air. The yolks broke immediately upon landing. "Welp," he said. "Yeah, that's on me. I'll eat these ones. I can make a new batch for the kids."

Tenn found the plates on her third try. "I'll do it," she said. "Your days of having a stay-at-home wife are almost over. Take advantage while you can."

Tenn would make a new batch of eggs, because the kids would not eat eggs with broken yolks. The kids would not eat cereal if there was too much milk in the bowl, or if there was too little. Anders would only eat off blue plates this week, and Aisling would only use spoons, never forks. The kids had invented new rules and restrictions every day since the move, and Tenn was too worried the move had fucked them up to argue about the small stuff.

"I'll be in charge of breakfast tomorrow," Ward told her, holding his plate with the yolks bleeding out.

"You can get your own coffee," Tenn offered. She could feel the doll, crouching behind his mug, waiting for him.

Ward pressed into her from behind and kissed her neck. The image returned to Tenn's mind—the drawer full of knives, a hand reaching in, fingertips searching for the knife with the sharpest blade. "I'm going to grab some on the way in. I want to check out that place by the office."

Tenn rinsed the skillet, and the water came out of the tap so cold she thought there must be something wrong with it. She'd have to put it on her to-do list, later. Now she started the new batch of eggs, fully aware of the doll, still in the cabinet, as if the doll had X-ray vision and was watching her. Ward sat at the window seat, the window seat in this house he'd bought to make her happy. She returned her attention to finding the spatula.

"Aisling hid it," Anders said. He'd poured an entire box of Lucky Charms into a mixing bowl and was separating the marshmallows into a smaller one.

"Hid what?" Tenn said. She poured most of the contents of the mixing bowl back into the cereal box. Upstairs, Aisling was throwing a toy for Gogo. Gogo was a mutt the size and shape of a dachshund but with the musculature of a pit bull. The old floors amplified the sound of her bounding down the hall. Tenn hadn't gotten used to the sounds the house made yet. She kept thinking there were people walking around upstairs.

"The spatula," Anders said. "And the rolling pin. And a bunch of other shit."

"Language," Tenn said.

Anders smirked. He was nine, about to start fourth grade at a school where he knew absolutely no one. Tenn had tucked encouraging notes into the lunch boxes, accompanied by Hershey's Kisses. She couldn't stop Anders from swearing. All she could do was make him feel loved. She took a serving spoon from the utensil drawer and used it to gently turn one of the eggs. The yolk broke immediately.

"I'm not eating that," Anders said.

"On that note!" Ward said. He stood and wrapped Anders in his arms, a hug so tight Anders's first instinct was to fight. Ward released him, forgetting his plate on the table. "Have the best first day, kiddo. You're going to kill it."

Gogo entered the kitchen ahead of Aisling like a herald, carrying in her mouth a pink Post-it that said *sharp objects*.

"I don't want to go to school," Aisling said. "I want to work on a farm like in the old days. I want to milk a cow."

This town had once been primarily dairy farms, a fact they'd learned on their first visit to the library. In the 1800s, when mass production started putting family farms out of business, many of the farms were sold to wealthy New Yorkers who wanted weekend homes outside the city.

"I'll make you a deal," Ward said. He picked Aisling up even though, at seven, she disliked being held. "If you get through this week of school alive, I'll find a place for us to milk cows this weekend."

Tenn gave him a look, cautioning him not to promise something he wasn't sure he could deliver. They knew each other. She didn't need to say it out loud. He gave her a look back that said he'd figure it out. Ward was a problem-solver, though he faltered, sometimes, when the problem was of his own creation.

"I don't want to milk a cow," Anders said, and threw his comic book at Aisling's head. "Thanks a lot, jerk!"

Aisling squirmed, and Anders chased her from the room the

second her feet hit the floor. Ward ignored the commotion and folded Tenn in his arms.

"Your employees are lucky to have such a sexy boss," she told him. "Are you sure you don't want coffee?"

Ward looked to the cabinet, but before he could respond, there was a yelp across the house.

"I'll go," he told Tenn, and left the room as Aisling began to cry.

Tenn lingered for a moment in the kitchen before she followed him, leaving the doll in the cabinet behind.

2

Ward was supposed to meet Tenn at the school for Curriculum Night, but he texted at the last minute that he was stuck at work and wouldn't make it. The kids were with a sitter for the first time since the move, and Tenn was already irritated that she was wasting a sitter on an obligatory school event instead of something she might actually enjoy. Michaela was a high school girl from down the street, who'd come to introduce herself the day they'd moved in after hearing the kids shrieking in the yard. She played lacrosse and volunteered at the hospital, but other than that she was available if Tenn needed her.

Inside, Tenn followed the crowd to the cafeteria, where she took a seat in a sea of parents who were already deep in conversation. Most of these kids had been together since preschool; the parents would've known each other for years.

The principal started the presentation, which was a relief, though Tenn had not expected the curriculum here to be so different from that at the kids' previous school. She and Ward had never realized what the kids had been missing. Now she worried about how they'd catch up.

The principal clicked on a slide about social-emotional learning, about books as mirrors and books as windows. Tenn checked her phone, still hopeful Ward might text that he'd be joining her after all. This would be easier if he were beside her, returning her meaningful glances and squeezing her hand.

But there were no texts from Ward. Tenn was on her own.

* * *

The school was warren-like, with so many turns on the way to Aisling's classroom, Tenn worried she wouldn't find her way back. At Aisling's desk, she flipped through the parent packet: the daily schedule, a reading list, bullet-pointed activities for reinforcing the math curriculum at home.

"She's very sweet," a woman said. Tenn raised her head to find Aisling's teacher, Mrs. Simmons, looking down at her. Mrs. Simmons had a pet rabbit named Fido, and she loved saltwater taffy and hiking and mandatory dance parties, all of which Aisling was against. "So affectionate."

Tenn stood and introduced herself, trying to imagine Aisling being affectionate with this woman. Aisling could be prickly; like Tenn, she was often particular to the point of frustration. When she knew what she wanted, she wanted only that—nothing else would do. A spoon and not a fork, the purple cup and never the red, pants that were soft but not too soft—the list went on and on.

"She's very fond of you already," Tenn said, though Aisling had told her she didn't like the way Mrs. Simmons smelled. She smells like a rabbit, Aisling said. Like she eats hay all day.

Mrs. Simmons smiled graciously, because of course Aisling was fond of her. She had a plush, huggable quality, and she probably never put in earplugs to muffle the sound of her kids eating, as Tenn did. She was trying to make Aisling feel welcome, which meant if Aisling wanted to sharpen her pencil eighteen times a day, Mrs. Simmons would accommodate her.

"It's a difficult transition," Mrs. Simmons told Tenn, as if Tenn weren't fully in the middle of it. "And who knows, maybe the ghosts will help her."

"The ghosts?" Tenn said. The image of the doll's face rose, unbidden, to the surface of her mind. It was still tucked in the kitchen cabinet, waiting for Ward.

"She's got quite an imagination!" Mrs. Simmons said. She did smell like hay—her perfume was strong with notes of cut grass and rose. Tenn could feel the fragrance as pressure in her own skull. "It's always good to have an outlet. Maybe she'll be a writer! You could be a team!"

"A team," Tenn repeated. She had no idea what Aisling had told this woman about her. A few floaters encroached on her vision from the outer corners of her eyes. A migraine on the way, triggered by the inescapable clouds of perfume wafting at her from every direction.

"Aisling told me you're a filmmaker," Mrs. Simmons said. "Maybe she can write, and you can direct."

"Oh, a filmmaker!" said a woman patiently waiting to talk to Mrs. Simmons. The dark floaters in Tenn's eyes dilated. Tenn only got ocular migraines—the aura divorced from the pain—which wasn't so bad except that when she got one, she couldn't see for the next hour. She took medication to prevent them, but sometimes they broke through anyway. "Anything I'd know?"

Tenn's first documentary was about a poet named Eloise Borden, the widow of Jerome Borden, whose career as a revered literary critic had eclipsed her own. Eloise's eyesight had been failing as she aged, and a young woman in college read novels to her each week. Tenn was fascinated by the long tail of Eloise's failed ambition, two decades after her husband's death, and her young reader's reaction to it, especially as she grappled with her own relationship, a boyfriend who was anxious to get married and start a family. The documentary was Tenn's film school thesis, which had been accepted by a prestigious festival and earned her funding for a longer project about two women artists. There was a time when people admired Tenn's work, when they admired her vision and her mind. That was a long time ago. Tenn hadn't made anything noteworthy since then. Besides kids.

"Probably not," Tenn said. The window of her vision narrowed. She didn't know this woman or Mrs. Simmons—she didn't know anyone within hundreds of miles—well enough to ask for help.

Mrs. Simmons took Tenn by the hand. "Still," she said. There were other parents waiting to talk to her, listening. "So exciting. Your husband must be proud. Are you—"

"I'm sorry," Tenn interrupted. Mrs. Simmons's face was occluded by pulsing dark spots, so Tenn could no longer read her expression. "It's so nice to meet you, but I really need to leave."

* * *

The floor in the hall was covered with decals: logs for jumping, a winding path of numbered leaves. Tenn could barely see the hall ahead, but she could follow the logs, and stepped from one to the next toward the parking lot free of noise and light.

"Excuse me," a voice called from behind her.

Tenn turned despite the shimmer zigzagging across her eyes. This woman was much younger than her, wearing a jean jacket and rainbow-stripe tights, a favorite accessory of Anders's new teacher.

"Are you Anders's mom? Are you leaving?"

Anders had needed a family photo for a class project, which he'd informed Tenn about the morning it was due, which meant she'd been forced to send him with a blurry printout from their misaligned printer. Apparently, Tenn was recognizable from the photo anyway. She introduced herself, and the teacher held Tenn's hand with both of her own. Tenn could smell sulfur, like the chemical plant in her hometown in Pennsylvania. Sometimes migraines affected her sense of smell.

"I'm sorry," Tenn told her. She couldn't remember the teacher's name. "I was planning to stay longer, but I have a migraine."

"Oh, no," the teacher said. Tenn blinked, and when she looked again, she could read the apple-shaped sign on the teacher's door: *Ms. Lindorf*. "I really just need a minute."

The hall around Tenn looked like the inside of a kaleidoscope. "Of course," she said. "Anders said you share a hatred of socks. You wouldn't believe how excited he was about it."

Anders was excited that his teacher shared his distaste for socks, but that was the extent of his excitement. By the third day of school, he'd tried to fake a stomachache, which Tenn did not find credible since he followed the complaint by eating three Eggos.

"I have a lot of strong opinions," Ms. Lindorf said. "It gives the kids an opportunity to work on their debate skills." She was probably smiling, but Tenn was keeping herself steady by focusing on the paper apple on the door. "I was going to email you, but I figured I'd see you tonight. I just wanted to make sure there's nothing special we need to do for Anders's thirst."

"His what?" Tenn said. She was standing on a log with a little green worm peeking out of it.

"We're refilling his water bottle throughout the day," Ms. Lindorf said. "Multiple times. But even then he's still so thirsty. I thought it must be a medical issue, but there's nothing listed on his health forms."

Tenn could only look at the logs on the floor. The next one was home to a perky blue bird, who was eyeing the worm on her own log.

Her phone buzzed in her pocket. Anders drank a normal amount of water at home. It certainly wasn't excessive. Sometimes she had to remind him to drink when it was hot outside.

"I'm not sure what to make of this," she said. "He doesn't drink like that at home. He had blood work done recently, and everything was fine. Did he complain about anything else? Did he see the nurse?"

"I sent him to the nurse the first day," Ms. Lindorf said. "But his temperature was normal, and he was otherwise fine. He just can't get enough water. He always wants more."

"This is all news to me," Tenn said, shaking her head. She'd taken Anders for a checkup just before the move because he'd been so sick at the beginning of the year—Tenn had a hard time shaking the worry that something was wrong. "Thank you for telling me. I'm going to make an appointment with his new pediatrician first thing tomorrow. I'll let you know what we figure out."

"Of course," Ms. Lindorf said. "I mean, it's probably nothing. It's normal for kids to act out during a big transition. Moving sucks, you know?"

Tenn asked no follow-up questions because, before her, the hall grew increasingly dim. She shouldn't drive home like this, with her field of vision distorted. But if Ward couldn't get her, she didn't have anyone she could ask for a ride. Her phone buzzed again.

"It does suck," she said, and smiled wanly as Ms. Lindorf returned to her classroom. Outside, Tenn called Ward, whose phone went straight to voicemail. On the screen, she saw three missed texts from the babysitter, then two missed calls. The last text said, pls come home.

* * *

Tenn called Ward one more time, even though she knew he wouldn't answer. The babysitter's phone also went straight to voicemail—the new house was in a black hole of cell service. Tenn didn't like to drive in the best of conditions, let alone at night, on unfamiliar roads, when she could barely see. The roads here were similar to those in North Carolina, winding and poorly lit, with speed limits that were too high unless you knew every curve like you'd been driving them forever. Tenn drove slowly, focusing on the yellow lines, trying not to imagine Ward in the comfort of his office, playing a matching game while he listened to men talk on the phone. The car behind her followed too close, and its headlights made the spots in her vision angry. She pulled over to let them pass. Sometimes she had to pull over even when she didn't have a migraine, but it had been a while.

Tenn's trouble with driving had started the year before, after the death of her childhood best friend, Crystal. Crystal had been two years older than Tenn, and when they were kids, she'd been like a sister in a neighborhood full of boys. Tenn's parents fought a lot, and Crystal's house had been her refuge.

When Crystal died, it had been years since they'd spoken, not because of a falling-out, but because Tenn had gone to the public high school while Crystal's parents had sent her to a private school. Crystal died in a car accident, which Tenn's mother had described to her in too much detail. A single-car accident—Crystal versus a tree near the skate park in their hometown. She'd had a fight with her husband that afternoon. She'd left their baby at home. She hadn't been wearing her seat belt. She probably wouldn't have survived the accident anyway, but it was the lack of seat belt that Tenn couldn't evict from her mind.

Two days after Crystal's death, Tenn was driving the kids home from the library and felt a sudden tug at her car. It was as if something were pulling it—a sideways gravity—and the car wanted to succumb to that power. The car, not Tenn, was giving in to this tug, drifting shoulder-ward despite her efforts. The car behind her passed over double lines, and Tenn pulled onto the gravel shoulder.

Now, as she had then, she sat on the side of the road with her flashers on. She'd pulled over in front of an equestrian school, because this was a town where people owned horses, where people sent their kids to learn to ride. It was a cool night, and the horses were wearing coats. Across the street, there was a field, empty but for a ring of skeletal trees, which looked as if they were convening a meeting. Tenn turned on the air conditioner even though it wasn't warm. She wondered now, as she always did when she sat in her car on the side of a road, what Crystal was thinking just before she died. She wondered if she'd convinced herself that her husband and daughter would be better off without her, if hurtling through the windshield was a relief. The condolence messages online had all conveyed shock, but to Tenn it was clear: anyone could do anything at any time.

Sometimes, in the year since Crystal's death, Tenn had thought about driving into a tree herself. Sometimes, when she cut a piece of cake and licked the frosting off the knife, she thought about ramming the knife down her throat. When she was standing on the balcony of a hotel room far above ground, she thought about diving over the railing, headfirst, how she would experience the sensation of flight for a few seconds before her body was pulverized. She thought about the many things that might make her leave her body—tree, knife, pavement—though she had no real desire to do so. But she was capable of doing them. Anyone was capable of doing anything at any time.

Tenn's phone buzzed—another text from the sitter: Are u on yr way??? Tenn needed to get home, to her children. She needed to go home now. She blinked against the aura; she checked her seat belt to make sure it was secure. She turned off her flashers, pulled her car back onto the road. The road was dark and winding, and Tenn gripped the wheel to maintain control. A horse kicked in her direction as she drove away.

* * *

Michaela was on the porch with Aisling when Tenn got home. A wraparound porch, screened to keep the bugs out. Ward had bought the porch swing before they'd even closed. Tenn had rocking chairs and ferns, twinkly lights still in their boxes—the hanging was on Ward's list. Tenn could barely see now, through the migraine, but she reminded herself that she wanted this. The porch swing, the ferns—this was her dream. Even if the porch's rotten wood needed replacing, which would cost a fortune. Ward had bought her this house to make her happy.

Michaela was out the gate before Tenn closed the car door.

"Okay, so I was not really prepared for what this was going to be," Michaela said.

Upon seeing Tenn, Gogo shot from the porch and jumped wildly at the gate, frantic to greet her. Aisling stayed on the swing. She was holding a large segment of bone, hollow in the middle, running her fingers around its gnawed circumference. Like the doll, another relic found in the yard. Tenn didn't see Anders.

Across the street, the white horse whinnied—they had horses for neighbors, another check on the list of dream-home qualities. Tenn could sit on her porch swing and watch the horses, except right now, when she had a migraine. Gogo scrabbled at the gate, trying to get to Tenn, as if she could sense something was wrong with her.

"What happened?" Tenn said. "Where's Anders?"

"He chased us with scissors," Aisling said from the porch.

"Scissors?" Tenn said. Anders had a habit of throwing things when angry, but he was nine, and it was normal for children to struggle with impulse control. Tenn wasn't the parent who thought her kids were perfect angels. But scissors?

"Maybe he thought he was being funny?" Michaela said. She looked down the street, toward her own house. "But still."

But still. Tenn took out her wallet and paid Michaela double what she'd promised. There was a time when they couldn't afford a sitter at all, not so long ago. For years, she and Ward only went out when she could trade childcare with friends. She reminded herself that she was lucky; she could afford this. She could afford to pay the sitter her kid chased with scissors.

"I'm so sorry," Tenn said. "I swear nothing like this has ever happened before. I think we've all lost our minds a little, with the move." The explanation was pointless—this girl would never sit for them again, and she'd tell all her friends, who wouldn't sit for them, either, and Tenn would be stuck at home every time Ward worked late, which seemed, already, to be often. Michaela would tell her mom, who'd tell all the neighbors, whom Tenn hadn't even met yet. "Where is he now?"

"In his room, I think," Michaela said. "I held the door to the porch closed so he couldn't get to us, and eventually he gave up."

Tenn tried not to imagine what Anders was doing up there with scissors, unsupervised. Then the door to the porch opened. Tenn's vision pulsed with splotches, bright and dark at the same time. She touched Michaela's arm to steady herself and smelled gingersnaps, the scent emanating from either Michaela or the misfiring neurons in Tenn's brain. Tenn pressed her way through the gate, and Gogo clawed at her shins. She hadn't been gone long, but Gogo was like this with Tenn. When Tenn left, Gogo always thought she was gone for good.

Anders stood on the porch, holding a sheet of paper.

"Anders," Tenn said. She had no idea how to handle the situation. It was the first time one of her children had chased a babysitter with scissors. "Can you explain to me what happened tonight?"

Anders came sheepishly into the grass, his cheeks soft and round, dimpled. Michaela stared at her shoes, waiting to be released. Anders offered Tenn the sheet of paper, on which he'd written an apology and drawn three stick figures joined at the hands, holding balloons shaped like hearts.

The apology letter of a sociopath, Tenn thought, the taste of bile at the back of her throat. She handed the apology to Michaela.

"Again, I'm so sorry," she said. "Do you need a ride home?" Michaela's house was down the street, but it was dark, and it was the least Tenn could do.

"I'm fine," Michaela said. She pocketed both the drawing and the cash and started walking. "This neighborhood is safe."

* * *

It was after eleven when Ward got home. Tenn had put the kids to bed, but they kept getting up—Anders wanted water; Aisling couldn't sleep. The migraine had abated, but Tenn could still feel it, lingering in the doorway of her brain. Sometimes it was hard to tell when they were over. Sometimes she thought one was over, but it came back.

Tenn was alerted to Ward's arrival by Gogo growling, which did not stop when Ward entered the living room. Gogo remained on Tenn's lap, baring her teeth at Ward, whom she loved. Like the house, Gogo was a gift from Ward to Tenn, adopted just after Tenn lost funding for the film that was supposed to be her first feature, about two women artists painstakingly creating domestic installations, examinations of the unrelenting tedium of domestic life. She'd been slow in cutting together footage as proof of concept, in part because she was pregnant and couldn't stop vomiting, but also because the work she was documenting was slow, intentionally time-consuming. One artist was crafting a life-size nursery in which every surface was embedded with small, sharp pins, and the other a house the size of a garden shed, woven from donated skeins of women's hair. Gogo seemed to understand right away that her role in the family was to keep Tenn safe. Gogo was perfect except for the fact that she ate her own shit and wanted to kiss people on the mouth immediately after. She didn't usually growl, but she was part Chihuahua. Maybe, Tenn thought, the move had dislocated her, too.

"It's just me," Ward said, extending a cautious hand. Gogo sniffed it like it belonged to a stranger as Ward bent to kiss Tenn's brow. "I'm so sorry. You wouldn't believe how much some people love the sound of their own voices."

Tenn tried to imagine what it would feel like to come home to the house lit up, with the kids asleep in their warm beds, after a day of being paid well for work that fulfilled her. But she couldn't. She hadn't experienced anything close to that in years.

"Did you eat?" she asked him. She was too nauseated to eat, but if Ward was hungry, she would make something. She was trying to tamp down her anger at having been left to deal with the night's ordeals on her own, which was not Ward's fault. He worked hard to pay for this house, for this life.

"Johann ordered food," Ward said. Deliberately vague, Tenn understood, because the food had been good and he didn't want to rub it in. Johann was the CEO of IntelliVision, a company quickly rising in the field of video surveillance. He fed his employees well when he made them work fifteen-hour days. When Tenn had met him at a party at his country club, he'd been wearing an expensive sweatsuit and set off the taste of salted licorice in her mouth. Johann did intermittent fasting and swam with sharks once a year, and he loved Ward, a problem-solver who kept his cool no matter what Johann threw at him. Ward fed off the praise even if it was the praise of a morally bankrupt narcissist who was making a fortune putting cameras on every street corner in America. "How was Curriculum Night? Do we have to relearn math again?"

Tenn closed her eyes and listened as Ward walked from the living room to the kitchen and back again. Other people had creaked across these floors, other people with lives harder than hers.

"Not only do we have to relearn math again, Anders might have diabetes, and I came home to find he'd chased the sitter out of the house with a pair of scissors." She didn't tell him about the migraine, because she shouldn't have driven home in that state, and she didn't know how he'd react if she told him. Tenn knew Ward well, but there were things she'd unlearned about him in the past year.

"So, uneventful then," Ward said.

"I'm not kidding," Tenn said. Ward slid a glass of cold wine into her hand, then lifted her feet and sat beside her, and she let him, because this was their fresh start.

"Like, real scissors?" he asked.

Tenn held the glass against her cheek. She worried that if she opened her eyes the spots would be back. Every time she got a migraine, she panicked that the medication had stopped working, that she would have to go off it and try something else.

"Do you think we made a mistake?" she said. She opened her eyes, and the spots were lurking at the periphery. She thought she saw one of the kids in the doorway, but when she turned her head, no one was there. "Moving. What if we broke Anders?"

"People move all the time," Ward said. Ward had moved a lot as a kid, so moving was simultaneously no big deal and a source of deep-seated resentment.

Tenn herself was named after the state her mother had left just before Tenn was born, ripped away by her husband's work from the place and people she loved most when she most needed them. Tenn thought about it a lot these days, when she was overwhelmed by her newfound isolation. Her mother had held on to her bitterness, which only increased as the years went on, and Tenn was determined not to fall into the same trap herself, though she didn't know how, exactly, to avoid it.

"We'll talk to the school about it," Ward said. "Didn't you tell me they have extra support for transfer students? We should follow up with the teacher on that. Is that new?"

When Tenn sat up to see what he was pointing at, Gogo decided it was playtime. She brought Ward a stuffed duck and wriggled at his feet, waiting for him to throw it, all suspicion forgotten. Ward was pointing at a crack in the wall above the couch. When he said *we* should follow up, what he meant was Tenn should follow up.

"How could we tell?" Tenn said. There were a lot of cracks in these old plaster walls. Tenn would have to fix them as she painted.

Ward tossed the toy duck, then rubbed Tenn's feet, which suddenly felt raw. "When you say he chased the sitter with scissors," he said, "do you mean in a murdery way?"

Tenn sipped her wine, held the coolness in her mouth before swallowing. "He told me he was pretending to be a monster who cuts off people's skin to make dolls."

Ward almost spit out his beer.

"Because the monster has a sister, and he wanted to give her a present. But apparently he forgot to tell Michaela and Aisling he was playing a game."

"Good thing we moved to a school district with fancy psychologists," Ward said.

"On the plus side," Tenn said, "once word gets around the neighborhood, we'll never have to worry about a break-in."

Gogo barreled through the room with a Post-it in her mouth and jumped into Tenn's lap, spilling wine down her chest. "Fuck," Tenn said, rising. The Post-it said *kid bullshit*.

Ward was up, too, tugging at Tenn's shirt. "We better get this in the laundry right away," he said. Across the room, Tenn saw a kid, looming in the doorway.

"Wait," she said, and smoothed her shirt back over her bra. But again, when she turned, there was no one there. An aftereffect of the migraine—she was still seeing things. And the kids had been up so many times already. "Aren't you tired?" she said.

She thought about asking Ward to get her a cup of tea to help her sleep, so he'd open the cabinet and find the doll, finally. It was killing her that the doll was still in there. She couldn't get the doll out of her mind. But she didn't ask him for tea, just as she didn't tell him about the migraine. Instead she slid his hand back under her shirt. They were starting over now.

Ward licked a stray dribble of wine off her chest. "I am tired," he said. "I think you should put me to bed immediately."

3

Ward found the doll in the kitchen cabinet and hid it in the dog food bin in the pantry. Tenn found the doll in the pantry and hid it in the console of Ward's car. Ward found the doll in his car and hid it in Tenn's underwear drawer. The air conditioner broke, and they had sweaty sex with the windows wide open, not worrying about who might be listening. Tenn dealt with the broken air conditioner, met with the school psychologist, arranged an evaluation and counseling for Anders. In the mornings, Ward brought her coffee. Tenn took Anders to the pediatrician, who found no medical cause for his unquenchable thirst. Tenn bought sliced turkey until Anders would no longer eat it; then she bought pepperoni instead. She asked Ward to install cameras in the kids' rooms so she could see if they were getting up at night, if they were thirsty, if they were sick. Ward installed the cameras, found the doll in the toolbox in the garage, and brought it to Aisling's room, where he made it dance in front of the lens for Tenn to see later when she reviewed the footage.

At night, side by side, they watched the kids together, in the brief lulls between Johann's manic texts. The kids didn't care about the cameras; Tenn had filmed them constantly when they were small. And Tenn loved to watch anything on a screen. She loved, especially, watching live feeds—it was something that connected her work to Ward's, their mutual affinity for the calming power of surveillance. When Ward was stressed, he submerged himself in videos for work; when Tenn was struggling, she watched the hippo cam at the zoo, a live feed of the northern lights, a wedding chapel in Vegas. There was a bald eagle nest in Pittsburgh she watched every morning, though the nest was currently empty. When she was anxious or disappointed, she watched feeds for Abbey Road, for Old Faithful, for the Loch Ness monster—Ward could tell her mood by how much time she spent watching.

These days, since the move, Tenn watched a lot.

* * *

Ward stood by the bed as Tenn opened her eyes, saw the doll on the pillow beside her, and screamed.

Across the house, Gogo—always the first responder to Tenn's distress—started running. But Ward was at the bedside, ready.

"Good morning, Mommy," he said. He leaned across the bed and made the doll's arms open and close. "I've missed you."

Tenn clutched the doll to her chest and rolled onto her back. "I thought it was going to take you longer to find it this time," she said.

Ward lay beside her and touched her face. He was trying to touch her more, to be aware of how much he touched her. "I'm getting used to the rush of finding it," he said. "You're going to have to do something more extreme if you want to scare me."

Tenn smiled and set the doll on the nightstand. "Don't worry," she said. "I know how to make you scream." She fondled his freshly shaved chin. She was particular about his face—she liked it with exactly three days' growth, or freshly shaven, like this. Her particularity was foreign to Ward; the strength and specificity of her preferences wasn't something he experienced. He didn't understand where those preferences came from, how one option could feel completely right and another absolutely wrong. But he liked that about her, how getting something right for her made him feel like he'd cracked a code. "What time is it?" she said.

Then Ward watched her take him in—the shaven chin, the dress pants, the coffee delivered as an apology.

"A little after eight," he said. "I have to go in."

"Go in?" Tenn said. It was the weekend, and they had plans—they were going to explore the nature preserve today. They were going to pack a picnic and take the kids' bikes. "For what?"

"There was an accident at a roadwork site last night," he said. "Johann needs me to review the footage, and I have to sit in on some calls." He got up and dug through the hamper so he didn't have to face her. He felt like shit, but this was what he'd signed up for—a job that came with a boss who flooded his inbox with stream-of-consciousness emails between two and six a.m. but also a salary that allowed them to afford this house, this house she loved. "Have you seen my gray button-down?"

Behind him, he heard Tenn slide the coffee across her nightstand.

"No," she said. "I haven't seen your gray button-down. I also haven't seen the spatula, the checkbook, Gogo's leash, or the cuticle scissors. Everything keeps going missing in this house." Including Ward, which she didn't say. "Did I tell you I found a ring yesterday?"

"A ring?" Ward said. There was no sign of the gray button-down in the hamper, in the closet. There was no sign that Tenn was upset, which meant she was.

"It has the tiniest little diamond in it. I'm assuming it's a diamond. If it were fake, it'd be bigger. It was between the floorboards in Aisling's room." There were a lot of things between the wild gaps in the ancient floorboards; Tenn had started removing them, room by room, with tweezers. Popsicle sticks, cotton swabs, the backs of many earrings. Pills, all shapes and sizes. "Someday another family will find our spatula. All the things we've lost, or that Aisling has hidden."

"Though Aisling denies having hidden anything," Ward said. The kids were still in bed—Tenn would have to file a new missing item report with Aisling when she got up. Ward put on a button-down riddled with wrinkles as Tenn finally sat up and sipped her coffee. "What's that?" he said.

Tenn blinked her tired eyes and saw it—her right forearm, covered in scratches. Or not scratches, actually. More like welts, rising out of her skin.

"Maybe something bit me?" she said.

Ward knelt on the bed and took her hand. It didn't look like bites. It looked like she'd gouged her skin with her nails.

"Did you do that?" he asked. He tried not to sound accusatory, to sound concerned. He had to leave her; he couldn't stay.

"I don't know," Tenn said. She wasn't fully awake, but she would have to be. Ward didn't know what she'd do with the kids now, since he had to work. Maybe she would take them to the park by herself, but lugging the bikes around was exhausting, and she was so tired already. "Maybe I was scratching in my sleep?"

She ran her fingers over the welts, the look on her face one of genuine confusion. If she had scratched herself, she didn't remember doing it.

"Does it say something?" Ward asked her. It looked like a word, but he couldn't read it. The letters were still emerging. He took her arm gently and turned it to face him.

"It does look like writing," Tenn said.

Together they waited as the welts bloomed into letters, a word. "What does that mean?" he said.

"I don't know," she said.

Tenn took her arm back and held it stiff in front of her, and Ward watched her study it as if it were a part of someone else's body. Ward's phone buzzed—Johann's name on the screen. They were waiting for him. The welt on Tenn's arm said *DOGHOUSE*.

4

There was a reason Ward didn't want to leave Tenn, which she could see on his face when he then did leave, despite his effort to conceal it. Eight months before their move, Tenn had gone off the medication she took to prevent migraines. She'd been on it since Aisling was a toddler, and it still left her groggy in the mornings, even after all that time. But her migraines were hormonal, and her hormones were changing—she felt it in the length of her periods, her metabolism. And she'd only had two migraines the entire previous year. It was possible, she thought, she didn't need to be on the medication at all anymore. And she was tired of having to do check-ins with her family doctor every three months to renew a prescription that wasn't even controlled. She'd sit in the waiting room for forty minutes, and then the doctor would spend two minutes asking how she was doing—the answer to which was always the same as the last time—and she'd pay her thirty-dollar co-pay and leave. She didn't talk to anyone before she stopped taking it. It was a tiny dose—ten milligrams of a tricyclic antidepressant that, when prescribed as an antidepressant, was used at a dose of three hundred milligrams. She just wanted to see if life without a daily medication was possible.

There was a lot going on then, when Tenn went off the medication. Anders caught a virus and lost too much weight, and then there were endless visits with doctors trying to find the underlying cause of his inability to gain it back. In the end, no one found anything wrong, and Anders did gain back much of the weight once Tenn started adding butter to all his meals and instituting Ice Cream O'Clock every day after school. But it was stressful. And Ward hated his job then and was looking at other options, which added financial uncertainty to the mix, and Tenn was doing videography part-time to pay for after-school activities, which meant there was never enough time to do all the things their lives required of her. A beloved friend, the same age as Tenn, was diagnosed with cancer and went downhill fast. Tenn was anxious, more than usual, but their lives were anxiety-provoking, more than usual. And she was sad. But it was winter, and she was always a little seasonally affected.

Then a classmate from film school invited Tenn to the premiere of her first feature—a gritty revenge thriller about domestic violence. Tenn rented a dress and got a blowout and shrank with embarrassment every time someone asked about her own work. It was too painful to say out loud that she worked weddings on the weekends, the only way she could stay connected to her camera.

Tenn knew she was doing her best with the kids and the weight of knowing that her creative work, which had made her no money, had by necessity stopped being a priority. But it was getting harder and harder for her to believe anything would ever come of her early promise. She must have been kidding herself to think she'd ever make anything of real value. She was approaching the point where she'd have to stop pretending there was more waiting for her beyond wedding videography. She would never be a real filmmaker. The thought was almost unbearable, but the more she made herself think it, the more numb to the idea she became.

During this time, Tenn often woke in the morning feeling nothing, because she had nothing to offer the world and nothing to look forward to. And each day that she woke numb, it took longer and longer to get out of bed. She did get out of bed, though, because she had to, because the kids were already up and fighting, and they needed to be fed, and they needed their lunches packed, and she needed to make sure they were dressed for the weather, which was something they never, ever did on their own, and they needed to be taken to the bus stop, and then she needed to clean up the breakfast dishes and wipe the counters and get the laundry going and run to the store for the three things she'd forgotten on her weekly grocery trip, because there were always three things she'd forgotten, and then three more things she'd remember tomorrow. Then there'd be some other bullshit she'd forgotten about, because there was always some other bullshit she'd forgotten about, and Tenn would have to explain why she'd missed the parent-teacher conference, why she hadn't sent Aisling to school with the craft supplies she'd signed up for, why the library books were so late, again, as she paid the fine.

When he could, Ward took the kids out of the house on the weekends, so Tenn could sit on their bed—her workspace—and dream about making a film of her own. She'd been hoping to document the life of Ward's aunt Vera, a nun who left her convent in the late '60s, along with tens of thousands of other women radically overthrowing their lives in pursuit of love or children, or because their faith had changed in ways they hadn't anticipated. All choosing for themselves something outside of what was accepted—in Vera's case, a bookstore owner named Sadie, with whom she'd lived in boisterous and steadfast partnership until Sadie's death three years ago. Vera had not been doing well in Sadie's absence, but she was different when she told

Tenn stories, because storytelling was a way to give presence to the absent, to keep them near. For his part, Ward worried about how the project might affect his father, who was deeply ashamed of his family's rejection of Vera, and who wasn't doing great these days, either.

But sometimes Tenn thought about telling those stories anyway. Sometimes she still felt like herself.

One morning during that time, Tenn woke thinking about how she might die. The thought was generated by a part of her brain separate from the one that usually did the thinking. It was so separate that the thinking part of her brain provided commentary on the other part, as it formulated a plan, the nuts and bolts of a death that would minimize trauma to Ward and the kids.

The thinking part of her brain observed: *That's not good. That's not good at all.*

It was a Saturday. Tenn lay in bed, afraid to get up, afraid even to move, to put something in motion. Ward had plans that morning to take the kids to a children's museum, where they could fly pretend spaceships, where they could cast magnetized lines to catch wooden fish and punch numbers into a pretend cash register at a pretend store. He came into the bedroom, already dressed, and sat to kiss her good morning.

"I have to tell you something," Tenn said. It was the thinking part of her brain that said this. The thinking part of her brain was still in charge, for now.

"Is it that I'm sexy?" Ward said. He slid a hand under her T-shirt and cupped a sweaty breast. She was cold but she was sweating, her body extremely a body, her blood loud inside her head.

"You are sexy," Tenn said, because she thought it might be easier if she was funny about it. Her voice was already shaking. "But that's not what I have to tell you."

Ward kissed her neck, and she thought then she might just let him leave. One part of her brain wanted Tenn to get in the car and drive fast without wearing her seat belt. But the thinking part of her brain prevailed. "I'm having these thoughts," she said. She knew he'd noticed that she'd been anxious lately. That she'd been sad.

"What kind of thoughts?" Ward said. He was still holding her breast. He still had his lips against her neck, just resting there. Ward was a problem solver; he'd take over, do the rest, find a fix for whatever was wrong with her, the part of her brain that was malfunctioning. She just needed to tell him.

"I've been thinking about dying," Tenn said. Her voice was shaking, but she explained as best she could. "Like, I don't actually want to die. But there's this part of my brain that's . . ." Ward had gone stiff. He wasn't moving; Tenn could no longer feel his breath. "It's like there's a separate part of my brain that's making plans."

In the hall, Aisling and Anders were battling with magic wands that made noises that someone who worked at a toy company had decided were how magic wands sounded. Like little explosions, with chimes inside.

"Okay," Ward said, and straightened himself like a totally different person, one Tenn had never met before, a stranger. He wasn't looking at Tenn, a flat panic in his eyes. Tenn wasn't sure what he was going to do. Call a doctor, maybe. Call someone. Force her out of bed, out of the house. She didn't know what to do. There was still a part of her brain that was thinking, though. She didn't want to hurt herself; she didn't want to abandon her kids. It was just that this other part of her brain was so loud. It was telling her the kids wouldn't miss her, specifically. That anyone could fill her role, get them dressed and fed and on the bus every day. Ward could pay someone to do it, and it would be exactly the same.

Tenn waited for Ward to say something.

"I'm taking the kids to the museum," is what he then said. His face didn't look right; he didn't know what to do with his face. "Why don't you rest? Just take the day and rest. You don't have to do anything for anyone else. I'll keep the kids from bothering you."

Tenn nodded, unable to process Ward's reaction, and lay back down while he gathered the kids and their water bottles and snacks and hustled them away, leaving her alone. He'd decided the solution to the problem was to give Tenn peace, to free her from the noise and responsibilities of their daily lives. And he left her there.

Tenn stayed in bed for a long time, until her friend Helen texted to see if Tenn wanted to grab a coffee. Helen had a pie plate Tenn had left at her house. Tenn didn't put on makeup or brush her hair. The thinking part of her brain pulled jeans over her hips, made her fingers fasten her seat belt.

"You look like shit," Helen said when she saw her. "Did you already order?"

Tenn had not ordered. Tenn had arrived at the coffee shop and sat at a table, unable to think about coffee. She hadn't even brought her purse.

"Are you sick?" Helen said.

Tenn shook her head. She didn't want to tell Helen the whole story, but the thinking part of her brain, the thinking part opened her mouth and told Helen everything. Partway through, the barista brought Helen a paper cup of mint tea. Helen didn't drink it. She listened to Tenn, attentive but not panicked. She wasn't looking at Tenn the way Ward had. Ward's expression was permanently etched in Tenn's head.

When Tenn finished, Helen sipped her tea, finally. "This is antidepressant withdrawal," she said. "Do you want coffee? I can order it for you."

Tenn shook her head, but Helen got up and ordered Tenn a latte, then returned to the table and took out her phone. Helen had been a psychiatric nurse until her brother's death from an overdose two years prior, after which Helen had unceremoniously quit. She'd recently completed her yoga teacher certification, a hard reboot. Later, just after Tenn moved, Helen took a job teaching at the stables of a horse rescue. There were miniature horses there, during the classes, which Helen had told Tenn in a sheepish voice as Tenn sat in a fortress of boxes. Nothing had made Tenn cry harder than knowing she was missing the opportunity to do yoga with miniature horses.

"I'm going to pretend to be you and make an appointment, okay?" Helen said. She didn't wait for Tenn to answer; she was already looking up the number. She knew Tenn couldn't make the call herself.

"What's antidepressant withdrawal?" Tenn said. "I've never heard of that. Is that a thing?"

"Your migraine medication is an antidepressant, right?" Helen was still scrolling.

"But it's a tiny dose," Tenn said. "Way less than what they use to treat depression."

"You're practically comatose if you take a single Benadryl," Helen said. "You're sensitive to drugs. This is a brain chemistry issue. Your brain chemistry is all fucked up."

She found the number and showed Tenn her phone, waiting for approval. Tenn nodded, and Helen called and said her name was Tennessee Cherish and she was experiencing suicidal thoughts after going off her antidepressant, was there someone who could see her today, right away, please?

* * *

The doctor put Tenn back on her medication, because it worked to prevent her migraines, which had come back but which, at that point, she'd considered to be the least of her problems. If she wanted to go off this particular medication, the doctor told her, she should first talk to her neurologist to determine a new treatment plan for her migraines, and then they would taper the antidepressant slowly, under supervision. But Tenn didn't want to do that now. She started taking the pills again immediately, and the anxiety and the sadness, the thoughts about dying, went away, just like that. As fast as a person could leave their body.

That night after dinner, as the kids created deranged compositions on a hand-me-down keyboard, over the cheery, preprogrammed beats, Tenn explained to Ward what had happened. Ward's relief was visible, though Tenn wondered as he picked at his salad if he was chewing on something else. It went without saying that the whole ordeal had been a product of a whim on Tenn's part. How could she stop taking a daily medication without talking to anyone? He didn't say this, but Tenn could see him stabbing at the question with his fork. And she didn't say anything about his reaction, about how he'd left her there, alone, with her thoughts. She knew that he'd been terrified, that he hadn't known what to do. She knew he felt awful about it. He started bringing her coffee in bed every morning. He found a job that paid a lot more money and bought her the house of her dreams. But even then, Tenn could still see the look on his face in the moment when she told him. She couldn't stop thinking about how he'd left her, like it was fine if she died.

Like maybe that's what he wanted all along.

x x x

Ward had been gone for hours before Tenn realized Aisling was missing. She'd scrapped the plan for the park as soon as he left to meet Johann—it was too cold that morning anyway. Through the window, she could see frost on the grass, a surreal sight on the heels of early fall's intense heat. Maybe it was the sudden shift in weather that was making her so tired, a drop in barometric pressure, something like that. The kids were still quiet, and Tenn lay in bed with her coffee and enjoyed the peace. The chaos in their lives had been unrelenting for weeks—the packing, the unpacking, the newness of every trip out of the house. They'd earned a lazy day. On her phone, Tenn checked the feed from Anders's room and saw the lumps of her children, piled together in Anders's bed, under the covers. She closed her eyes and fell back asleep.

It was nearly lunchtime when Anders appeared in her doorway, holding something in his fist. He was tentative, afraid to enter. Tenn had been dreaming but could only remember the dream's urgency—like a crisis had been unfolding around her, and she'd been failing in her attempt to avert disaster.

"Morning, kiddo," Tenn said. "What do you have there?" She motioned for Anders to come to her, and he did, climbed into the bed and nestled against her body. The kids were little, soft and small even with their gangly limbs and sharp elbows. Tenn remembered the weight of them as newborns on her chest, the peace of it. One day they would stop climbing into bed with her, stop seeing her body as a source of comfort. For now, they still did.

Anders opened his hand. "I found this in my room."

In his palm was a single earring—a black enamel oval set with a small pearl.

"Last night I had a dream," he told her, "a monster was chasing me up the stairs, and the stairs kept going and going, and I knew I was dreaming and I tried to kill myself in the dream, but I didn't die so I just kept running and running."

When he put the earring in Tenn's hand, she remembered her own dream—she'd been standing on a wet sidewalk, watching men in suits unload a small, pearly blue coffin from a hearse. The memory was both visual and visceral—a blazing rent in her chest, an all-consuming compulsion to open the coffin and hold the child's body in her arms. She ran her fingers through Anders's hair.

"That's so scary," Tenn told him. She set the earring on her nightstand where she'd left the doll, which she now realized was gone. "What happened?"

"I ran and I ran and then the stairs turned to marshmallow, and I sank through to the downstairs and it was a different house," he said. "And Aisling was gone, and I couldn't find her."

"What about the monster?" Tenn said. She knew she needed to get up, but her body resisted, as if she were under a weight, anchoring her in place. Maybe she was coming down with something. Aisling, too, hadn't gotten up yet. But Tenn always told the kids to listen to their bodies, and their bodies were clearly telling them they needed rest.

"The monster was gone," Anders said. "You know how in dreams everything goes different?"

"I have dreams like that," Tenn said. Tenn rarely remembered her dreams, but she'd dreamed of Aisling before she knew she was pregnant with her. In the dream, Tenn had been holding Anders, a toddler at the time, and then he was gone and she was sitting across from a little girl. It was hard for her, at first, to hold two children in her mind at the same time. She'd grown used to giving Anders her complete attention. She had to learn how to split that attention between two people, and the result always felt halved, inadequate. In Tenn's dreams, she only had one child at a time, never two. Anders rolled so his elbow went into her side, which hurt.

"Is there something that's been scaring you?" she asked him. Maybe seeing the pediatrician had dredged up unpleasant memories of the many jabs and scans during his weight loss ordeal.

Anders shook his head, his arms around Tenn's neck tightening, which amplified the desperation still lingering from her dream. "Is it better when you sleep with Aisling?" Aisling had fallen asleep in Anders's bed last night, after a brief skirmish involving a Nerf gun.

"Yeah, but then she left," Anders said.

"For her room?" Tenn said. Tenn had checked the cameras before she'd fallen back asleep, and the kids had been together. "When?"

"No," Anders said. "Last night. She left."

Tenn sat up with a suddenness that woke Gogo, who'd dug herself all the way under the covers. Anders lay so Gogo could lick his face as Tenn grabbed her phone, checked the feed from Aisling's room, where the bed was empty. In Anders's room, the lump was still there, which did not reassure Tenn as it had earlier. Gogo abandoned Anders and followed Tenn as she rushed down the hall.

At the edge of Anders's bed, Tenn paused. She touched the lump, and it squished under her fingers—Anders's stuffed shark, not Aisling at all. She pulled the comforter off in one sweep. The entire bed was full of stuffed animals.

"Aisling!" Tenn yelled. She stormed into Aisling's room, holding a fist-sized hope that Aisling might be in there, curled with a blanket just out of the camera's sight. The bed was empty, as was the rest of the room—the closet, the hiding places under the bed and desk. She wasn't in there.

She also wasn't in the living room or the dining room, the kitchen or the pantry, the downstairs bathroom, the guest room, the half bath in the hall. Tenn walked the house at a brisk pace, trying not to alarm Anders but not wasting time, and in each room, she was met with Aisling's absence. She wasn't in the game closet under the stairs or in the last of the packing boxes Aisling had saved from recycling to make a time machine. She wasn't on the porch or in the front yard, the backyard, Tenn's car. She wasn't on the garage roof or hiding in the woodpile. Outside, Tenn filled her lungs with air so cold it stung. The weather had turned suddenly, without warning.

"Aisling!" she yelled. She yelled it through the house, out the front door, down the street. What the neighbors must have thought crossed her mind and vanished. She opened the game closet again, shook the empty cardboard boxes, fully aware she'd already looked there but unable to stop repeating these actions. She felt her phone in her hand. Ward was going to have questions. He was going to want to know why it had taken her so long to notice Aisling was gone.

Ward's phone went straight to voicemail, so Tenn sent a quick text—call asap—and moved on. She knew better than to waste time waiting to rise through the ranks of Ward's priorities.

Anders had put on his astronaut helmet and was searching the house with a magnifying glass, looking for clues.

Tenn returned to the front porch and the bite of the cold. If she stood there long enough, it would make her numb. She called Ward again, and again the call went straight to voicemail. She returned to the house and rechecked every closet. Back in the front yard, she opened the trash can and recycling bin, even though there was no way Aisling could've climbed inside on her own. She got on her hands and knees and looked under the porch. She didn't know how Aisling could disappear like this. Maybe she'd sensed Anders's fear in his dream and wanted away from it. She was like Tenn—she took other people's shit and internalized it, made it her own.

"Anders!" Tenn yelled, because she heard Anders on the porch.

"I found more mouse poop," Anders said. "Under the heater."

"When was the last time you saw her?" Tenn asked. She did the math—it had been fifteen hours since she'd seen Aisling in Anders's bed. She hadn't even tucked her in last night. She'd been so tired, and Aisling had wanted to argue about combing her hair after her bath. "Fine," Tenn had said, opting out of the battle. "Grow a birds' nest if that's what you want."

"Are we still going to the park?" Anders asked. He was holding the binoculars he'd set out. Anders, like Ward, craved the comfort of a plan, wanted to know exactly what each day would hold. They were supposed to be riding bikes right now. They were supposed to be having a picnic.

"Did you see her this morning?" Tenn asked him. She went back inside, checked the game closet again, the cardboard boxes. She couldn't stop herself.

Anders scanned the room through the binoculars. "I don't think she likes it here," he said. "This house."

"Why do you say that?" Tenn asked. She crawled across the room and knelt at his feet. "Did she tell you where she was going? Do you know where she is?"

Anders shook his head without moving the binoculars from his eyes. "I only know she's gone."

Tenn stood and listened to the house, to a childlike cry she followed to find it came from a radiator. She didn't hear anything else, not even Gogo, who'd gone missing, too, she now realized. When Tenn was upset, Gogo would stop at nothing to comfort her—she would have burrowed inside Tenn's body if it were possible. Tenn had felt similarly about the kids when they were little, like their bodies were meant to nest inside her own.

"Gogo!" Tenn yelled, in the backyard now, yelling at nothing, at the trees. She crossed the patio, barefoot, and swept her arms through a flower bed overrun with weeds, conjuring a spray of yellowjackets from the ground. One stung her on the ankle, and she flicked it away. Beyond the patio was a small slope, the fence, the garage. To the right, the empty field. They'd been planning to put a playset there, something they'd never had space for in North Carolina. Aisling had always wanted one shaped like a pirate ship. To the left of the patio, a strip of woods separated their property from the neighbor's. Aisling wasn't anywhere that Tenn could see. "Gogo!" she yelled again.

Another yellowjacket stung her leg as Tenn tried to remember the previous day. Aisling had protested the move, but she hadn't registered any complaints about the house, specifically. No one complained about Tenn's dream house, least of all Tenn, who hated it.

No, she didn't hate it—this wasn't about the house; it was about her. She hated everything right now. She stared at her phone. She didn't know a single person here she could call. She could get in the car and drive around, ask neighbors to help look. She could drive to Ward's office and drag him home. But if Aisling was here, close by, and she came back to the house to find it empty, what would she do? She was seven; she'd never been home alone before. Tenn dialed 911, but something stopped her from making the call. She didn't even know how long Aisling had been gone. There was a gnawed bone on the ground, and she picked it up. She didn't know what she was doing.

"Anders, get Gogo's treat bag," she told him, and Anders disappeared through the back door and returned moments later, holding a bag of jerky. Tenn shook the bag as another yellowjacket stung her armpit. The sting on her ankle was already swelling.

Gogo tore across the yard from the wooded strip, carrying in her mouth a shaggy clump of dead grass that would almost certainly lead to vomiting. She dropped it, ran two circles around Tenn's feet, and took off back toward the trees. Tenn watched her, unsure if she'd found something in the woods other than decay. But then Gogo was back, running another lap around Tenn. And again—into the woods and back to Tenn, back and forth. She was trying to get Tenn to follow.

Tenn wasn't wearing shoes, and the yellowjackets were still stinging her—a thought of Benadryl floated across the surface of her mind—but this didn't slow her, nor did the sharp rocks, nor the sticks cutting into her cold feet. The wooded strip wasn't wide, just thick enough that she couldn't see all the way inside it, through the wiry tangles of brush and weeds. Gogo was going bananas, frolicking in the rot. The house disappeared from view, and Tenn found a deflated kickball and small orange flags, warnings signs left by an exterminator. And then Tenn saw it. In the back corner of the wooded area, all the way against the fence, Gogo zoomed past what looked like a doghouse. Two doghouses, Tenn realized, as she approached, but one had collapsed in on itself.

Aisling was asleep in the other one, bundled in a thin fleece blanket, her head on Anders's robot backpack. The doll from the yard was tucked beside her. Tenn touched her forearm where the word *doghouse* had been, welted into her skin, hours ago. She gave Aisling a light shake, for one seizing moment fully terrified her eyes would not open.

Aisling's eyes were puffy and red. "I've been here so long," she said, and pulled the blanket tighter around her. She'd been crying. She'd been waiting for Tenn to notice her absence and find her. "Why did it take you so long?"

Tenn wrested Aisling from the doghouse and held her against her chest as Aisling wormed her cold fingers under Tenn's shirt. Tenn could see a tiny tick, embedded like a mole in the crease of Aisling's neck.

"Why were you hiding?" she said. "Were you playing a trick? Like Daddy and I do with the doll?"

Aisling turned her head against Tenn's chest to wipe her running nose on Tenn's shirt. "It doesn't feel good in there." She motioned toward the house.

"Why not?" Tenn asked. "What's wrong with the house?"

Aisling sniffled into Tenn's shirt. Tenn offered her the doll from the doghouse to hold, but Aisling wouldn't touch it.

"Sorry," Tenn said. "I thought you wanted your baby."

"It's not my baby," Aisling said. "And I didn't bring it with me. It came out here on its own."

Tenn felt the buzz of her phone in her pocket. Ward was finally calling her back.

* * *

In the kitchen, someone had left the faucet running. Tenn loaded the dishwasher, wiped the counters free of crumbs, scrubbed the saucepan left soaking in the sink. The water from the tap took too long to get warm. By the time Tenn was finished, her hands felt like ice.

Gogo snuffled her ankles, and Tenn knelt and let Gogo lick her chin.

"You did good today," Tenn told her.

She could hear Ward coming down the stairs from his office, but he took longer than she expected to reach the bottom, like he was walking very slowly, taking his time so she might be gone before he entered the room. He'd come home late—just before dinner—unable to leave work early despite the crisis. He was back on the phone before they'd finished eating, leaving Tenn all the cleanup, leaving Tenn to put the kids to bed. Aisling had gone without fuss, having spent the day sedate, curled by Tenn's side. Movies and hot chocolate had been all Tenn could manage after dosing herself with Benadryl, other than checking and rechecking Aisling's temperature, her fingers and toes. The cold wasn't what had hurt her, though. Tenn stood by the door and waited. Ward had stopped walking, but the door was still closed.

"Hello?" she said. She'd been waiting for him all evening; they'd barely talked on the phone. He'd gone quiet when she'd told him where Aisling had been, the word *doghouse* hanging between them, like a rope. Now she opened the door.

On the other side, Ward stood with his phone in his hand. He looked up at her, surprised.

"Hey," he said, "I didn't hear you there."

"I was just cleaning up," Tenn told him. The sponge in her hand smelled like mildew, but all the fresh ones had gone missing. There was something red and sticky on the counter, though no one, as far as she knew, had eaten jam.

"I have to be on another call in a few," Ward said. "It's a legal thing. It shouldn't take long. I just came down for some water."

He didn't look up from his phone when he said this. Then he reached for her, and Tenn was relieved until she realized he was actually reaching for the cabinet, for a glass. Tenn moved out of the way and kept going, all the way to the living room, where she sat on the couch, twisting to study the cracks on the wall behind her. They were getting bigger, maybe. It took a minute before Ward followed.

"Are you mad at me?" he asked. His eyes grazed her leg, the skin taut over the stings. He leaned in the doorframe, not sitting.

"You have to be on a call," Tenn said. The cracks on the wall were fine but distinct. They looked to Tenn like a map to someplace else.

Ward checked his phone again, then laid it screen-down on the side table. He sat at the far end of the couch and faced her. "I'm really sorry I had to work today," he told her. She could hear the guilt in his voice; she knew he felt like shit. "You have no idea how I felt when I saw your name on my screen. I would've done anything to come home to you."

"But you didn't do anything to come home to me," Tenn told him. "You didn't do anything at all."

Ward looked at his phone but didn't pick it up. There was only one place for him to hide, but his phone remained silent. "I can't just leave work when we're dealing with an accident," he told her. "What do you want me to do?"

The question was a question, but Tenn felt it like a weight around her neck. She was too tired to do the work for him tonight, to figure out how Ward could make her feel less alone.

"How did the doll get in the doghouse?" she asked him. She watched his reaction closely—she could tell when he was lying. They'd been together since college, and they knew each other, knew each other's tics and tells, their medical histories and family stories, every inch of each other's bodies. They knew each other's preferences and acted accordingly. He knew the household task she despised most—taking out the trash—and so did it himself before the trash got too full, just as she always emptied the dishwasher, because it was his most hated chore. They also knew how to make each other miserable, how to inflict small cruelties, and they avoided doing those things, for the most part.

"What about the doll?" Ward asked. Tenn could see he was confused by the question. But she didn't understand what had happened that morning—how the doll had gotten to the doghouse when she'd left it by the bed, how the word *doghouse* had been etched on her skin.

"You didn't hide it out there?" she asked. "And scratch the clue on my arm? Aisling must've seen you do it. I don't know why else she would've been out there."

Ward now looked at the cracks behind Tenn, and Tenn wasn't sure what he saw in them. Not a map, she thought. Another problem that needed solving.

"You think I let our daughter sit outside and freeze all morning?" he asked.

"That's not what I said," she told him.

"I didn't move anything," Ward said. "The doll was on your nightstand when I left. And I didn't touch you at all until you were awake."

Tenn could see that he was watching her the same way she watched him, except he wasn't suspicious, as she was, about a prank gone wrong. He was looking for evidence that the wrong thing was her brain.

Tenn turned over the possibilities in her mind. Aisling could have crept in and taken the doll from the nightstand; Anders could have scratched Tenn's arm after seeing Aisling leave. But Anders had been worried about Aisling's disappearance, too. The only other alternative was that Tenn had done it herself, somehow, in her sleep. She'd never sleepwalked before, though, and there was no evidence that she'd started now. If she'd wandered out of the house and into the woods in her sleep, her feet would've been dirty. She would've gotten dirt in the bed.

"Maybe Anders did it," Ward offered, walking through the same process of elimination as Tenn. "Maybe he saw Aisling leave and scratched your arm, then took the doll out to her. He chased a babysitter with scissors. Maybe it was like that, and he thought he was being funny."

Tenn closed her eyes and listened to the house, a radiator emitting a whine she could feel in her chest.

"Maybe," she said.

Tenn didn't say she would've woken if Anders had grabbed her arm and started scratching it. Ward had asked what she wanted from him, and what she wanted was to feel different, to feel valued, as he was, for her mind, for her insight and skills. She could still remember how it felt, sitting on the floor of Eloise Borden's room at the nursing home, chatting as they always did, small talk while Tenn checked her audio to allow Eloise time to reacclimate to the camera. Eloise had been telling Tenn about her granddaughter's birthday, about the surprise cake that spilled candy when sliced open. Tenn had asked a simple question—did she ever want to write about it?—and Eloise's answer surprised her.

Of course she wrote about it. She always had.

Eloise directed Tenn to a box in her closet, where Tenn found sheaves of poems, decades' worth, all unpublished. Eloise had never stopped writing, not in the years when her kids were little and she stayed up late typing Jerome's essays, nor in the years after his death, when her work shifted to preserving his legacy.

She hadn't given up writing. She'd given up writing for others.

Tenn had sat on the floor and read the poems, which were so different from Eloise's early work. Motherhood had stripped her of time but bestowed upon her an unmuzzled clarity. These poems were thorny, full of wild beasts and bodies in pain, of metamorphosis and mewling and key changes, laid eggs and lost hair, red wolves and secret cigarettes and a desire for annihilation, of all the dishes in the world, which needed washing.

Marriage and children hadn't stopped Eloise from being an artist. Instead, she'd created life and at the same time reached the height of her artistic power. The issue wasn't that Eloise had stopped writing but that her husband had written *what does this mean* too many times in the margins, that she couldn't attend readings given by other woman poets because she was stuck at home with the kids. At a time when literary magazines would publish only one woman at a time, when a poem about washing dishes—even a poem replete with rage and longing—was seen as better suited for *Ladies' Home Journal*, the bigger problem was that Eloise was married to a critic who didn't understand her work, and that she allowed his voice inside her head.

All that time, Tenn had thought she'd been making a documentary about the sacrifices this woman had to make to enable her husband's career, about the way the world makes it impossible for women to be more than one thing at once when motherhood is considered the pinnacle of womanly achievement. But in that moment, Tenn recognized that her understanding of Eloise had been wrong, limited. She'd been making a film about a failed poet when she should've been making a film about her poetry, a film about resisting erasure. What she'd thought was a tragedy should actually be a celebration of Eloise's work, a rebirth of it into the world, for which Tenn could act as midwife.

Later that night, sitting with Ward in their tiny apartment, she'd told him how her understanding of the entire film had changed as she read the poems, like she'd been toiling in a small room and a doorway had appeared, and she'd walked through it into a vaster space. All in one moment, she could see the whole film come together, but differently than she'd imagined. She saw a new way to assemble the puzzle pieces, to create a richer and more challenging picture. It felt like there was a well inside her, and she hadn't known how thirsty she'd been until she drank from it. The water was clear and cool, and there was more and she could share it; she could ladle this water out so others could drink, too.

Ward listened while she spoke, and then he told her she'd never been wrong about the documentary.

"You were only wrong about yourself, what you're capable of," he'd told her. "But it's always like that for you. You doubt yourself and doubt yourself, but the answer is always there, inside you. You just have to find it."

Tenn could feel herself beaming, like Ward was shining a light on her. She wanted to stay in that light with him, together, to remind each other of the light's existence.

Now, Ward watched her, the light nowhere to be seen.

"Are you feeling better?" he asked her.

"What do you mean?" she said, though she knew what he meant. He wasn't talking about the yellowjacket stings, which felt now like something was trying to hatch through them. He meant that she'd been tired, so tired she'd fallen back asleep after he'd woken her. If she'd gotten up when he'd left, she would've realized Aisling was missing sooner.

"Did you take your temperature?" he asked.

"It's fine," she said. "I'm fine."

"You don't seem fine to me," he said.

"What's that supposed to mean?" Tenn asked. She didn't like fighting; all she wanted to do now was go to sleep. Sleeping didn't require light, only a darkened room. "I've been tired. Of course I've been tired. I've had to unpack the whole goddamn house by myself."

"Are you sure that's all it is?" His phone buzzed on the table, and he ignored it. That's how Tenn could tell he was really worried. Not worried she was getting sick. Worried she was *already* sick, that it was happening again.

"Why don't you just say what you want to say?" Tenn told him. She knew him; she knew what he was thinking.

"Say what?" Ward said, his voice raising. Ward never raised his voice at Tenn, and it turned a dial inside her, a pressure that was building, that needed release.

"Why don't you just say you don't believe me?"

Ward stood and turned away from her, and Tenn felt something brush her shoulder. Her mind went straight to the yellowjackets, the anticipation of a sting. She swatted at it before realizing it was plaster.

"The fuck?" Ward said. He was looking past her now, all his anger and concern replaced by disbelief.

"What?" she said.

She turned to see the wall above her had split as they argued. In the middle of the fine lines, a fissure had rent the map in two.

"Fuck," she said, reaching up to feel it, more plaster crumbling at her touch.

Ward moved closer, knelt beside her on the cushion, put his fingers next to hers, then on hers. "I'm sorry," he said. He pressed his face into her neck and left it there.

"It's not your fault," she said. Then she realized she wasn't sure what he was apologizing for. They stayed there for a minute, together in front of the wall, as if they were waiting for it to get worse. Ward's phone continued to buzz. He looked at her.

"Go," she said. It would cost money to fix the wall, so she shouldn't keep him. "I'll call someone about this in the morning. But can you take out the trash when you get a chance?" If she didn't ask now, she'd forget. Whatever else was going on, the trash still needed emptying. "I've stuffed it down as far as it'll go."

"I'll do it," he said. He was already moving; she followed him to the kitchen. "And while I'm thinking about it, we're out of little spoons. I don't know what the kids were doing with spoons tonight, but they're all dirty."

Tenn only liked to eat with the little spoons, Ward knew. The big ones felt wrong in her hand.

"I'll run the dishwasher," she said. She'd just run it yesterday. Sometimes it felt like a shadow family was using their dishes, filling the dishwasher every time she looked away.

In the kitchen, Ward touched her elbow, a tentative touch, like a stranger trying to get her attention. They hadn't resolved anything, and they wouldn't, again. Ward opened the freezer as he put his phone to his ear. "Hey, did you get my email?" he said. Before he went upstairs, he handed her an ice pack, directed it to her ankle with his eyes.

5

Because Ward answered his phone after six p.m., Johann's nightly calls became so regular that Tenn saved home projects for after dinner so she'd have something to do other than stew.

"Did you watch it yet?" Johann said on this particular Wednesday night. Johann never bothered with greetings.

Ward opened his email to discover the reason for the call—there'd been an incident on a cruise ship while the ship was docked, and an IntelliVision camera at the port had caught it.

"Watching now," Ward said, downloading the file. "Hold on."

In the bedroom next door, Tenn was on her hands and knees, removing relics of past owners from between the floorboards. Ward could hear her humming, a simple melody on repeat. He didn't recognize the song.

Tenn continued humming as the video began to play. On-screen, Ward saw the cruise ship, anchored at the end of a long concrete dock, massive against the surreally blue sky. The water, too, had an unreal quality, the sky and water so blue they looked photoshopped. He didn't know what he was looking for, at first—he scanned the decks, the balconies, the lifeboats. Then he registered it—a blur of motion from a balcony near the center of the ship.

"What was that?" Ward said. "Did something fall?"

"A passenger," Johann said. "A passenger went overboard."

Ward could hear the wind against Johann's phone—he went walking on his sprawling estate any time he got wound up, a daily occurrence. They'd been through similar incidents before, but he still needed Ward to talk him through it.

"I'll check with the port's lawyers about their contract with the cruise line," Ward told him, "and have a tech pull the raw video from the camera. Once we have the uncompressed file, we should be able to see more detail. I'll call you back once I've watched it, and we can go from there."

The wind whipped against the phone; Johann was breathless. "Right," he said. "Good."

"The passenger," Ward said. He already knew the answer, apparent in Johann's agitation. This was a legal matter—police would be involved; it was international. "Did they survive?"

"No," Johann said. "The guy died."

Ward made his calls, then replayed the compressed video while he waited. The passenger fell from the second of five decks of balcony rooms, situated near the top of the ship, which had fifteen decks in total. Ward replayed the footage again, zoomed in this time, but the fall was fast and the figure on his screen only a few pixels wide. Ward had watched terrible things caught on camera before—car crashes and construction accidents, muggings, worse. It was easier to shake off when he couldn't see the victim's face. He could still picture the last one, a thirtysomething adjunct professor at a community college who'd died from a heart attack, alone, in an alley behind a hospital. He'd gone in with chest pains but left out of concern for the cost of the tests. He was feet from the ER when he slumped against a dumpster. A custodial worker had passed by, and the dying man had turned his head, as if he were ashamed of his illness. He reminded Ward of his father, the way he recoiled from help. With the adjunct, Ward coped as he always did when he watched something disturbing—he imagined the victim's face as a photo in an album, and he allowed himself a long look before turning the page, for good. It was an effective visualization. It usually worked to keep the images at bay.

In the next room, Tenn was humming. Ward watched the video again. His role in this was managerial—he oversaw the processing of data and ensured it was handled in a way that was unimpeachable if needed in court. His job was not to grieve the dead, only to preserve evidence. On his screen, a blurred figure streaked down the white ship, all the way to the water. Ward felt a sudden urgency, even though the danger had passed—the passenger was already dead. He scanned the water in the minutes after the fall, but the passenger did not break the surface. The water temperature at the port that day, according to a quick search, had been cold, and the passenger had likely sustained serious injury upon impact. Tenn hummed, and Ward realized the source of his discomfort. Her proximity was the issue—she was too close, too close to this man and his fall. He knew how her brain worked, how it devoured images. He was afraid she would walk in on him and see it.

Ward paused the video and pulled up a sumo wrestling forum so there'd be something else on his screen while he waited for the uncompressed footage. Ward liked watching sumo because the bouts were so short—he couldn't stand the tension of sports that took longer.

When the footage came through, Tenn went quiet. The detail was there; Ward could now see the passenger—his clothing, his hair, his face. He watched the fall again, his whole body aware of the closed door behind him, ready to hide the video if it swung open. On his next pass, he slowed the footage—the passenger was middle-aged with white-blond hair, and he was wearing blue shorts and a floral shirt, unbuttoned down his chest. Before the fall, he'd been leaning over the rail on his balcony, looking down at the water below. At first, Ward thought the man had lost his balance—he jerked back before pitching over the rail, as if destabilized by the movement of the ship. But the ship was docked, the water around it still. Ward considered the possibilities: He could've had a seizure, or seen something in the water and leaned out too far. Ward watched again, with each watch becoming surer. The passenger leaned out, as if considering what awaited below. When he drew back, he was gathering momentum. He went over the rail with more force than seemed possible from an accidental fall. From the room attached to the balcony, a woman in a yellow sundress appeared and folded over the rail in horror. There were people on the balconies around her, knotting into clusters as the woman wailed. In the next room, Tenn hummed, the same tune over and over. On the video, the woman's mouth was open in a silent scream. Ward watched her lean too far over the rail and worried she would follow, even though he knew she hadn't.

What do u think, Johann texted.

The cruise line would be looking for any evidence that might thwart a lawsuit from the victim's family. This video would change the shape of people's lives.

Not sure, Ward replied. Could be he fell. Could be something else. He knew better than to put anything beyond that in writing.

There would be meetings in the next days and weeks and months, meetings with authorities, with lawyers—Ward saw his carefully planned agenda blow to pieces in his mind. When he could be driving the kids, when he could be helping Tenn extract pills from these old floors—he'd be in meetings when they were supposed to be picking apples or carving pumpkins. He made a few calls to ensure the data was being handled according to protocol and returned to the bedroom, to Tenn.

"Everything okay?" she asked. In one hand, she held a pair of tweezers, in the other a shard of amber glass. Ward should have told her about the ship right then, but something stopped him. He could still see the passenger slipping down his screen, but in his mind the man's body was replaced with Tenn's.

"Okay for now," he said. "What can I do to help?"

Tenn handed him the pick from their nutcracker, which she'd been using to excavate two hundred years of caked dust.

"You know, we could be doing something else on this floor," Ward said. Tenn wouldn't go for it—he was just trying to make her smile.

"Not going to pretend I don't enjoy seeing you on your hands and knees," Tenn said.

"Baby, if cleaning is what does it for you, I'm going to empty the dishwasher so hard later."

Tenn smiled and returned to her tweezers, and Ward took the pick to a gap she hadn't attacked yet. There was a whitish pebble lodged inside, but the pick wouldn't budge it. In his mind, Ward saw a blur against a ship, so he lay on his belly and focused on this work. The photo album was closed now; the pebble was all he would allow into his mind. It was yellowed and lumpy, wedged into the subfloor. Ward didn't think it was anything of value, but he knew it was there—it would drive him crazy to leave it. He scraped at the subfloor, shaving tiny splinters until the stone gave. Ward stuck a wad of putty on his pick—Tenn's technique—and used it to extract the mystery object. Tenn was now vacuuming, going over the same spot again and again.

"What the fuck?" Ward said. He turned the object over in his palm.

"What now?" Tenn said, switching off the vacuum. She was tired even though she'd slept late that day—he hadn't seen it before, the hollowness under her eyes.

"Mommy!" Aisling yelled, her voice faraway, muffled by the plaster walls. The kids had been watching a movie in the living room. The room shook as she charged up the stairs.

When Aisling came into the bedroom, she was grinning, one hand clenched in a fist. Ward showed Tenn what he'd found—a human tooth—and felt a pain in his own mouth, in his molar. He probed it with his tongue and tasted blood.

Aisling extended her hand. "I lost a tooth!" she said, excited, and opened her hand to show them—the tooth wet with her blood.

* * *

Ward had to sit in on a call with some lawyers, leaving Tenn to put the kids to bed on her own. He could hear her downstairs, begging Aisling to comb her hair, asking Anders why he was back in the kitchen, a full hour past bedtime. Anders was hungry but only for one peanut butter cracker at a time, in twenty-minute intervals. Aisling was concerned that the Tooth Fairy would take her tooth, which she wanted to keep, and insisted upon writing a letter to plead her case. Tenn dealt with the ongoing stream of requests with more patience than Ward would have.

The cruise line's outside counsel was a woman in her seventies, who joined the video call from her Manhattan apartment, where she chain-smoked while stroking a weepy-eyed Pomeranian. Ward walked the lawyers through the video of the incident, and the lawyers nodded along, none of them seemingly disturbed by the footage. The passenger in question was visible on his balcony, alone, looking down at the water below, several times that morning before his fall. It wasn't Ward's job to speculate about what he'd been doing there.

The cruise line would offer the family a settlement, Ward knew, but there was always the possibility of a lawsuit. The lawyers asked a few more questions from the comfort of their homes and thanked Ward for his time, and Ward exited the call, the passenger's falling body frozen on his screen.

Downstairs, Tenn was fielding questions about the Tooth Fairy—where she came from, what she looked like, what she did with all those teeth. Some people thought the Tooth Fairy looked like a mouse, Tenn explained, but Tenn had never seen her, so she couldn't be sure. Ward didn't want to interrupt—Tenn was a better architect of childhood mythologies than he was. He'd once told Anders the reason they never saw the Easter Bunny was that rabbits are prey to everything from hawks to dogs, so the Easter Bunny had to be careful.

Ward didn't think he'd find anything when he started searching—it was too soon for the family to have written an obituary. But with the right combination of keywords, Ward landed on a Facebook post from a Christian bookstore in Georgia, announcing an early closure due to the death of one of its owners while on a cruise. The Tooth Fairy took the teeth to a magic cave, Tenn told Aisling, where the teeth were ground to make fairy dust. In the bookstore's timeline, Ward recognized the passenger by his hair—chin-length and white blond. The man's name was Daryl Shepherd, though most knew him as "Shep."

In the kitchen, Tenn banged a hand against the faucet—the water pressure dropped at random and neither of them had called a plumber yet. Shep appeared to be around the same age as Ward and Tenn, and he was married with two kids not much older than their own. Ward clicked through to the About page on the bookstore's website. Shep had worked as a youth pastor before opening the inspirational bookshop with his wife, Roxy, so they could spend more time with each other and their kids. Roxy had been a wild child before finding Jesus. Shep was from Utah but had settled in Georgia, in his wife's hometown, where they had an English bulldog named Skynyrd.

Downstairs, Tenn told Aisling that some people thought the Tooth Fairy took children's teeth to protect them from witches, who might use the teeth to cast spells against them. He knew he should go downstairs and help with the kids, but the photo album in his mind wouldn't close as neatly as usual. If he had a little more information, it would be easier for him to sweep Shep out of his head. He didn't want the image in his mind as he lay next to Tenn while she slept, as if the image might seep from his subconscious into her own. Shep had jumped, and Ward needed to know why. He needed to know if there'd been signs. In the aftermath of Tenn's antidepressant withdrawal, Ward had started reading, late at night, a forum for people who'd lost loved ones to suicide. There was a man who'd lost his wife, who pinpointed the beginning to the moment when she'd told him about an appointment that didn't exist. *That's when she started lying*, he'd written. Ward was always on the lookout now. His worry was like a little candle, burning in the back of his mind. The candle lit up things he hadn't seen before. The candle was still holding Tenn in its light.

On the bookstore's Facebook page, people were posting tributes. Shep loved gardening, and a neighbor shared the recipe for Shep's famous garden pesto, made with pecans and chard. Ward read every comment on the bookstore's page, then did the same on Shep's personal profile. Shep had survived thyroid cancer ten years prior, a transformative experience, and began cruising as a way to live more fully in the aftermath. One person wrote that Shep was playing slots in heaven, that he was on the big cruise ship in the sky. There were no euphemisms that suggested a struggle with mental illness; Shep had not lost a battle or come to the end of his suffering. Downstairs, Tenn told Aisling that in Nepal they believed that if you kept your own baby tooth, a bird might eat it and then a new one wouldn't grow in its place. Ward wondered what people would post in the case of his death, or Tenn's. But he'd thought about how people would react to Tenn's death before.

Tenn knocked on the door, and Ward closed his browser.

"Yeah," he said.

Tenn was carrying a basket of laundry, and Ward could smell it, detergent on clothes still warm from the dryer. She'd folded all the laundry while he sat there, stalking a dead stranger.

"Are you going to be much longer?" she asked him.

Tenn looked more tired than he'd seen her since the kids were newborns. The memory of that exhaustion was slippery these days, but when it found him, it was visceral—his eyes burned, his limbs turned to stone. It had been worse for Tenn, with the nursing. When Aisling was a few weeks old, she'd avoided driving; she was so tired she worried she might drive into a tree. That's how she looked now, though sleep deprivation was no longer the cause.

"We've got a bunch of uncompressed video transferring," Ward said. The pain in his molar returned then, and he prodded it with his tongue, even though it hurt. "I'm just catching up on email while I wait."

"I'm going to put this away and go to bed," she told him. "How's your tooth?"

"It's fine," Ward said, though the pain suddenly sharpened to the point he worried it would affect his speech. If he told her it felt like there was a screwdriver wedged in his tooth socket, she'd worry. "I'll be there as soon as I can. Can I do anything to help?"

Tenn looked past him to his screen, empty save for the meaningless geometry of the IntelliVision logo. "I cleaned up downstairs," she said.

"I'll get the lights before I go to bed," Ward said.

"Thanks," Tenn said.

Ward watched her leave the room, anxious for her to be away from his computer, from his office, from a man plummeting to his death. But Tenn was back before he could open a new window.

"Shit," she said. She set the laundry basket on the floor, having remembered some task left undone.

"What?" he said.

"The fucking Tooth Fairy," she said. "Do you have cash? I gave the kids all mine for the book fair."

Ward slid his wallet across the desk and opened it. "Is twenty too much?"

"Twenty dollars?" Tenn said. "For a tooth?!"

"It's all I have," Ward said, which was a lie. He had two ones, but two ones didn't seem like enough. He wasn't sure why he didn't just say that, but he didn't. In the back of his mouth, the pain intensified, a live wire sending out sparks.

"Fuck," Tenn said.

"We can afford it," Ward said. His computer screen in front of him glowed, a source of danger.

"We're not paying twenty dollars a tooth," Tenn said. "If we pay twenty dollars for this tooth, they'll expect it for every tooth."

"So what then?" Ward said. "The Tooth Fairy doesn't show tonight?"

Tenn turned away from him, but barely. She was so tired; Ward wondered if something was seriously wrong with her, an undiagnosed illness, if it was eating at her invisibly as they spoke. He remembered his mother, when the cancer began to spread. Tenn turned back to him, her mouth creased with resignation. "Anders has ones in his wallet," she said. "I'll slip a few out tonight and replace them tomorrow. He won't notice."

"What if he does?" Ward said. He glanced at his screen for just a second, even though there was no work open, no emails coming through to review.

He could tell Tenn noticed by her tone. "Don't worry about it," she said. "I'll take care of it."

"I'm sorry," Ward said, and felt in his jaw as if the bone had cracked in two, the pain radiant. "I'll go to the bank tomorrow and take out a bunch of ones. I'll put an envelope in my sock drawer so it's not an issue in the future. I should have done it a long time ago."

Tenn picked up the laundry and walked through the doorway without a good-night kiss. "Thanks," she said, and closed the door behind her.

Ward opened his email, opened his Slack, opened a spreadsheet tracking one of a million projects. He opened them not because he intended to work, but in case Tenn came back. Ward stared at his email, eyes unfocused, until he heard Tenn get in bed and switch off her light. Then he returned to Daryl Shepherd.

* * *

From the dentist's chair, Ward listened to the hygienists as he held his tooth in a little Tupperware full of milk. He'd woken on a bloody pillow, the tooth loose and lumpy in his mouth. Tenn had not been flustered—by the blood, by the tooth, by the coincidence of both Aisling and Ward losing teeth in a twelve-hour span. She was tired but competent, as she always was. In the bathroom, he'd stood before the mirror, staring at his bloody chin, his face unfamiliar. He stayed in front of the mirror until Tenn told him to get dressed while she put the tooth in milk and made an appointment.

The dentist's name was Dr. Doyle, and he introduced himself and held the Tupperware up to the light even though the milk was opaque, the tooth hidden from sight. "So how long had this tooth been bothering you?" he asked.

"It wasn't," Ward said. "It didn't bother me at all before last night."

Dr. Doyle put on gloves and fished out the tooth, milk pooling on the latex. "It's a nice tooth!" he said. Dr. Doyle was a pediatric dentist, but he was the only one available for emergencies that morning. He was younger than Ward by a decade, and he appeared to have an extra decade's worth of energy.

"Thanks," Ward said. "I've never lost a tooth as an adult. Is that something that just happens?"

"Well, people lose teeth," Dr. Doyle said. "Certainly."

"But without warning?" Ward asked. "Teeth can just fall out of your head?"

"A healthy tooth isn't going to fall out on its own," Dr. Doyle said, "if that's what you're asking. There was no trauma that precipitated the loss?"

Ward retraced his day before the tooth began to hurt, but at no point could he remember anything happening to his mouth. He'd helped Tenn excavate the floor; he'd watched a video of a man falling to his death. His mouth had not been involved.

"Popcorn kernel?" Dr. Doyle asked. "Were you chewing ice? Opening a bottle with your teeth?" Ward shook his head, and Dr. Doyle continued. "Soccer game? Recent car accident?"

"Nothing," Ward said. The tooth had vacated his mouth of its own accord. He didn't even know how long ago it had happened—one hour, five hours, seven. The blood was dry on his pillow when he woke.

Dr. Doyle peeled open a set of sterile tools. "Let's take a look."

Ward closed his eyes as his chair reclined and Dr. Doyle adjusted the light. There had to be something wrong with him, for a tooth to fall out of his head. There had to be something wrong for him to find a tooth in the floorboards just as Aisling lost a tooth just as his own tooth began to ache. People had lost teeth in their house before; maybe contamination was to blame for Tenn's tiredness, the kids' behavior, all of it. Radon, arsenic—Ward considered the possibility that the house he'd bought Tenn to make her happy might be killing them.

"Your gums," Dr. Doyle said, "are immaculate!"

"Thank you," Ward said as best he could with someone else's fingers inside his mouth.

Dr. Doyle probed Ward's gums, then removed his gloves and performed an external exam of Ward's neck and jaw. "Do you smoke?" Dr. Doyle asked.

"Not for a long time," Ward said. "Do I have the mouth of a smoker?"

"You do not!" Dr. Doyle said. "Just checking! How's your diet? Any nutritional deficiencies that you're aware of?"

"I eat reasonably well," Ward said. "I take a multivitamin."

Dr. Doyle abandoned Ward's mouth and turned to his chart, faxed from Ward's previous dentist, with a look of deepening concern. "I don't see any medical issues here. Diabetes? Arthritis? Hypertension? Are you on any medications?"

"No," Ward said. "Nothing."

Dr. Doyle put down the chart, and Ward saw then the reason for his concern—he was stumped. "Huh," Dr. Doyle said.

"Is that bad?" Ward said.

"You've got a healthy mouth!" Dr. Doyle said. "I'm not sure what's going on here! Let's do some X-rays!"

"Okay!" Ward said. He didn't feel cheery about the situation, but he couldn't help but match Dr. Doyle's enthusiasm.

The hygienist left the room and returned with a lead drape and thyroid shield. Their weight was a comfort against Ward's mind, which spun increasingly far-fetched explanations. Maybe he had cancer and it had already spread; maybe his entire body was shutting down. Maybe one of the kids had pried his mouth open in the night and performed an extraction. Ward focused on the weight of the lead drape, craving the heavy certainty of an answer. Across the room, his phone buzzed in his jacket pocket. Was it Johann, he wondered, or a call from the school, a call from the police, a disaster unfolding? Every time his phone buzzed, which was a lot these days, he prepared himself for news, bad news, the worst. Was it work, or was it a stranger calling to inform him that his wife had fallen from a great height? The lead drape held him down, and it was a relief to be immobilized, to be relieved of the burden of solving whatever problem waited at the end of the line.

The phone stopped buzzing; Ward pulled himself together as the hygienist instructed him to open and close. It was improbable that he had cancer and losing a tooth was the sole symptom. There would be a logical explanation for his tooth, and for everything else. There was nothing strange about any of it.

"Well, this is strange!" Dr. Doyle said, when he returned to the room with Ward's films.

"What's strange?" Ward said.

"No sign of inflammation or decay. No sign of anything, really!" Dr. Doyle said. "I can't find a single reason this tooth came out. There's no cavity, no apparent trauma or disease. Nothing!"

"So what, then?" Ward said. "It just fell out for no reason? How is that possible?"

"Good question!" Dr. Doyle said. "It's not, really. I'm going to recommend you see your family doctor for blood work." He took out a prescription pad and scribbled a note for Ward to take with him. Then he stopped. "There's not anyone who wants to hurt you, is there?"

Ward laughed, and it sounded desperate, because he was increasingly desperate for an answer. "I haven't lived here long enough to make enemies," he said.

Dr. Doyle nodded. "If you were in the middle of an acrimonious divorce or a lawsuit, I might suggest someone was trying to poison you, but that's all I've got! Let me know what your doctor finds, because this is going to drive me nuts!"

Ward took the note, his mind turning over the possibilities. He wasn't like Tenn, didn't think in images, but now his mind's screen played a scene: Tenn carefully dosing his morning coffee with a glass dropper from a blue bottle labeled with skull and crossbones, looking guiltily toward the door. It was ridiculous. It was so ridiculous Ward could only imagine it in a ridiculous way.

Dr. Doyle put Ward's tooth in a plastic treasure chest and started talking about implants. It was a good thought to save the tooth in milk, but there was no salvaging it at this point. An implant was Ward's best option to avoid problems in the future.

"Think of it like taking a book off a bookshelf," Dr. Doyle told him. "Eventually the other books on the shelf will slump to the side."

Ward accepted Dr. Doyle's brochure. There was a hole in his mouth—that was the problem. And the solution to the problem was to fill it. Ward allowed this to be a comfort, instead of thinking about what it would cost. Instead of thinking about how, that morning, after Tenn had calmly deposited his tooth in the Tupperware, Ward had opened the refrigerator to find the doll inside, next to the milk.

6

"Hold on," Helen said. "Matt got me a glass of wine, but I'm clearly going to need the bottle."

Tenn sat with her phone inside the bedroom closet, empty dresses hanging around her, disembodied. It was quiet in the closet; in the closet, she was contained. There was more rustling as Helen got comfortable. When Tenn and Helen got on the phone, they could go for hours, even when they lived five minutes apart.

"Okay, so: Have you been to a doctor?"

"Do you think I'm hallucinating?" Tenn whispered. "Do you think I have a brain tumor?" She'd been texting Helen about the household objects going missing, Aisling's disappearance, her unceasing exhaustion. It wasn't until teeth started falling out of people's heads that Helen insisted on a call.

"Did you know most of the time when people think their houses are haunted it ends up being carbon monoxide poisoning?" Helen said. "I read that somewhere."

"Who thinks the house is haunted?" Tenn said. She hadn't told Helen what Aisling's teacher had said about ghosts.

"I'm not trying to put thoughts in your head," Helen said. "It's simply the facts that your house is very old and dolls aren't capable of moving on their own."

"You think we're huffing fumes," Tenn said. She didn't want to talk about ghosts with Helen, who was more open to possibility than Tenn. Helen had been dabbling in essential oils when Tenn met her. Whatever the differences between Ward and Tenn, they were united in their lack of belief.

"I don't think you're huffing fumes," Helen said. "But weird shit usually has a mundane explanation. I've seen people who were convinced there were angels or demons talking to them, and it was just like . . . a UTI, or schizophrenia."

"Do you think I'm schizophrenic?" Tenn said. "Could that make me scratch my arms in my sleep?" She asked despite the fact that Ward had already installed a camera in their bedroom at her request, and the footage did not reveal nocturnal scratching. But if Helen told her she might have schizophrenia, Tenn would believe her. They'd been friends since their kids were babies; they'd sat with each other through their ugliest moments for years.

"I'm not trying to diagnose you over the phone," Helen said. "And you know if I thought there was something wrong with you, I'd tell you."

Tenn now realized she *wanted* something to be wrong with her—a clear diagnosis, a named illness that could be treated. But she'd been to the dermatologist, who'd diagnosed her with dermatographia—a condition in which even light pressure can leave marks on the skin—and referred her to an allergist, who'd found she was allergic to orris root and *Cladosporium herbarium*, a type of mold. They'd had the house checked for mold (none present). They'd had the furnace serviced, checked the house for carbon monoxide (none present), installed new carbon monoxide detectors throughout the house anyway.

"I swear I didn't move the doll from my nightstand," Tenn said. "And I really don't think I could scratch a legible word into my arm in my sleep! But what else could it be?"

"Did the allergist check to see if you're allergic to yourself?" Helen asked. "That's a thing that can happen. You can get sick and be allergic to your own antibodies."

"I'm pretty sure they didn't check for that," Tenn said. She could call and ask, but she couldn't handle another appointment right now. She was tired of appointments. Sometimes it felt like her sole job was appointments. But she had a real job now, and it started tomorrow. She would have to juggle work and appointments at the same time.

Tenn listened to Helen breathe, a long, slow exhale, and imagined her in an improbable yoga pose, a foot behind her head.

"The job will help," Helen said. "It's good to have something to think about other than your life. It's good to be reminded of your own competence."

Downstairs, there was a thud, followed by a yelp. Ward's pace to meet it did not indicate an emergency. Tenn should've put more thought into the job before now, but she'd wasted all her time unpacking boxes and making sandwiches. But maybe it was better she didn't have time to think. If she had time to think, she'd get mired in what the job symbolized—a laying to rest of her dream that she would make another film of her own. The job was in production with a luxury real estate developer in the city, not exactly a field that sparked her creative interest. But maybe she would grow to like it. Luxury real estate was about details, and there was nothing she loved more than details.

"I don't even know what I'm going to wear yet," Tenn said. A jumpsuit leg brushed her unmanicured nails, her hair months overdue for a trim. "I don't remember what it feels like to look professional."

"You'll remember," Helen said. It wasn't always on Helen to give pep talks, but she was good at them. "You'll remember a lot of things. You'll make friends and fix your walls, and the kids will adjust and stop trying to kill their babysitters. You're in the worst of it now. All you have to do right now is survive."

Tenn closed her eyes and imagined herself in Helen's room, which was painted a lush green and had a four-poster bed whose posts looked like trees. It felt like being swallowed by a forest, Helen's bedroom. Tenn wanted to be there, not here, in her dream house.

"Are you sleeping?" Helen asked. "Maybe you're waking up at night and you don't realize it, and that's why you've been so tired. Maybe you're like everyone else in society and you just need more sleep."

"I'm sleeping," Tenn said. She would have been happier if she weren't, if there were an easy explanation for her exhaustion. She would take a sleep disorder or an allergy to her own body so long as the mysteries of her life could be explained.

"Make another doctor's appointment," Helen said. "Sometimes you have to keep going back until they take you seriously."

Tenn told Helen she would, and Helen started a story about a miniature horse at the rescue stable. The horse was named Cinnamon, and he could catch a Frisbee and shake hands. Tenn tried to pay attention, but her mind kept returning to Helen's advice. How long had it been since anyone had taken her seriously, she wondered. At this point, what would being taken seriously even mean?

* * *

Tenn's first day of work did not start smoothly. First Anders spilled a full cup of milk on the kitchen floor, then Aisling decided the only pants she could tolerate were ones that were dirty, so instead of getting dressed she ran screeching through the house in her sweater and underwear. Tenn sopped the milk, pulled the pants from the hamper, washed grass stains in the sink and used her hair dryer to blow them dry. As they left for the bus stop, Gogo busted out the door behind them, and Anders fell on the sidewalk trying to herd her back inside. Ward was supposed to be helping that morning, and Tenn imagined him in a conference room, glistening pastry in hand, because Johann had an idea, which constituted an emergency. Anders had skinned his knee, which meant Tenn had to capture Gogo, take the kids back inside, clean the wound, apply a bandage. The bus came and went while Tenn was providing first aid. Undeterred, she charged into the street, waving her hands wildly. She'd never make her train if she had to drive the kids to school. Miraculously, the driver saw her and waited while she ran with the kids and their backpacks down the street. Tenn thanked the driver, kissed the foreheads, and stood for a moment watching the bus carry them away. A messy start, she thought, but Tenn had spent the past decade of her life dealing with messes. Messes, she could handle.

Tenn left her phone on the kitchen counter when she ran up to the attic, aware of but too rushed to check the itching on her arm. She'd set out everything she needed before she'd gone to sleep, but she'd forgotten about her viewfinder. She wouldn't need it this first day—dedicated to paperwork and orientation—but she wanted it anyway. The viewfinder had been a gift from Ward upon her film school graduation, bought used and even then too expensive. Tenn had carried it with her on every job she'd worked since, a reminder that someone once believed in her.

Gogo was hot on Tenn's heels, as she always was, and Tenn paused at the attic door to put Gogo in a stay. Gogo was a good girl—obedient even though she could smell the mice. The mice in the attic had evaded Tenn's traps, and Ward had escalated to rat poison after they discovered the mice had eaten through a box into Anders's baby blanket. Tenn had her objections, but they could hear the mice at night, running and running, which set Gogo into barking fits. They'd lectured the kids about keeping Gogo out of the attic—Gogo would eat anything, even things that could kill her. Tenn propped the attic door open with the rock and watched dog and rock, ensuring both were still before ascending the stairs.

The attic door slammed shut as soon as Tenn reached the top, and Gogo broke her stay and clawed at the wood. Tenn stood in the dim light, letting her eyes adjust. She just needed the viewfinder; she knew which box it was in. There was a window at the attic's far end, so it wasn't completely dark. Tenn made her way past a sea of old paint cans to the boxes that contained her equipment. The viewfinder was where she expected it—safe in its Bubble Wrap, its weight and ridges familiar in her hands. She ran back down the stairs, mentally listing the things she needed to grab on her way out: bag keys phone, bottle of water. At the bottom of the stairs, Tenn turned the doorknob, which came off in her hand. On the other side of the door, the knob's mate fell to the hardwood with a *plunk*. Gogo barked at the knob like it was an intruder. Tenn pressed the door, but it didn't open.

The light switch was at the bottom of the stairs, which Tenn remembered once her heart settled. She reached up, found cobwebs first, then the frayed string. She examined both the doorknob in her hand and the hole in the door. The knob was shiny black, heavy metal coated with chipped enamel, and at the end there was a square-shaped opening. The peg that fit into it was on the knob that had fallen on the other side of the door, in the hall. The knob in Tenn's hand couldn't turn anything on its own. It was just a receptacle. Tenn gave the door another shove, but it had already latched shut. In order to open the door, she'd have to find something she could fit into the hole that would engage the latching mechanism.

Tenn sat on the stairs for a minute to gather herself. She'd always wanted a house with personality, and now she had one. She'd miss the first train, take a slightly later one. She would call her hiring manager, and they would understand. Later, she and Ward would laugh about it. It would be fine. Her arm was itching, and she was hot, so she shrugged off her blazer. On her left forearm, raised in welts, she found the word *PAINT.*

Tenn touched her arm, closed her eyes, looked again. The letters were distinct but the spacing irregular; it was possible she was reading too much into it, a sequence of meaningless lines she'd scratched, absentmindedly, while stressed. But there were a lot of paint cans in the attic. She'd been planning to haul them down, but that meant she'd have to figure out how to dispose of them. Now Tenn walked back up the stairs, to the collection of faded cans, most of the lids welded shut with orange paint. The previous owners had loved orange, every room painted a different shade. Tenn didn't know what she was looking for—it wasn't like the word *paint* held a clue to her escape. There were a lot of paint cans in the attic, enough to paint the whole house three times over. And there, amongst the paint cans, Tenn found the doll.

Tenn knelt before the doll but didn't touch it. She'd walked right by it before without noticing, even though it was clearly visible, plain as day. But the light had been off, the attic dim. She examined its face, as if its expression might have changed since the last time she'd seen it. But of course it hadn't changed. The welts on her forearm were already fading. She didn't know how the doll had gotten up here and tried to supply an answer—a deepening of Aisling's kleptomania, Anders's questionable sense of humor. Except neither of them could have scratched the word *paint* on Tenn's arm through her blazer, without her noticing. Tenn was the only person who could've done that.

Tenn looked at her arm as if another word might appear, instructions for turning the latch and freeing herself. But the skin on her arms was uncooperative, mottled pink with a few freckles, a mole. She put the doll in her hip pocket so she wouldn't lose track of it, and the doll peeked out, along for the ride.

First Tenn looked for a paint can opener—an obvious answer—but despite the profusion of cans in the attic, there was no opener to be found. Next Tenn surveyed the boxes: mementos, photo albums, out-of-season clothes. Somewhere in this mess was something useful. Beach toys, foldable lawn chairs, their tent. The doll gazed out over the boxes, placid, as Tenn's rummaging became more frantic. Downstairs, Gogo barked. All the tools were in the garage. There were board books and mouse-chewed blankets, finger-painted art projects. There wasn't anything long and skinny that could fit into a square-shaped hole.

Tenn sat on the floor speckled with mouse shit and thought. She had a job to get to; she couldn't just not show on her first day of work. Tenn was a resourceful woman. She'd navigated permit applications, booked locations, adjudicated arguments over which crew members could touch which sandbags on set. She took a deep breath. Now was not the time to panic. The doll looked out from her pocket in the direction of the tent.

Tenn opened the tent bag and pulled out a stake, and when that proved too big, she smashed a plastic tent clip with a board book into a smaller piece that also didn't fit. She dug through boxes until she found a hex key—all their furniture was cheap; of course they had a hex key—which also didn't fit.

On the air-conditioning unit, she found a tag from its last inspection, dangling from a thin metal wire. She twisted the wire and inserted it into the latching mechanism, but the wire was too flimsy to catch. She rummaged through the bag of beach toys and pulled out a purple plastic shovel, the end of which was thin and flat, like a credit card. Back at the door, she wedged the shovel between the doorframe and the door, trying her best to jimmy it open, until the plastic snapped, sending Gogo into a frenzy on the other side.

Tenn imagined the time passing as a series of trains, train after train leaving her behind. She turned and faced the stairs, still determined. She could salvage the day if she got out soon enough; her employer would be reasonable when she explained why she was late. The floors in this house were riddled with loose nails, which worked their way out due to settling. She scoured the stairs until she found one protruding, which she yanked at with her hands, doing nothing but taking off skin. She wound her hand in a cast-off sweatshirt and continued, until her bleeding palm made her stop.

Even then, Tenn kept trying. Brute force was next—she kicked the door as hard as she could, repeatedly, until pain pierced her knee. The door remained closed. Tenn sat on the steps and bashed the doll against the floor.

Bashing the doll against the floor didn't help; the skin on Tenn's forearms remained smooth. She had to get out of there, to keep the job she needed to stay sane, to show Ward her brain was fine, no cause for concern. The attic had a window. The window was small, but not too small for Tenn to fit through, three stories above the ground. Anyone could do anything at any time. But Tenn wasn't trying to die. Tenn was doing the opposite of trying to die. The window faced the back of their property—the patio, the strip of woods. The sill was full of dead spiders and moths. Tenn gripped the frame with her bleeding hand and wrenched it open.

"Hello?" she yelled. All Tenn could hear was traffic, the road that ran along the back of the house. There was a big truck idling, the blare of a horn. "Hello?" she yelled again. All the neighbors probably knew about the babysitter incident, or had heard Tenn yelling for Aisling when she went missing in the cold. What difference did it make if they found her now, trapped in the attic? Maybe they'd think

Ward had locked her up there, his mad wife, like a woman in a nineteenth-century novel. *My wife*, he'd tell them, *she sleepwalks and scratches words into her skin. It's better for everyone if she stays where she can't hurt anyone, where the only person she can hurt is herself.*

Tenn spent ten minutes yelling out the window, another hour listening, still hopeful, for the sound of a neighbor walking down the street. There weren't that many houses on this street, though. The day had begun, and her neighbors, unlike Tenn, were at work. She tried the door again—kicked it, punched it, asked it nicely, then not nicely, to open.

The door didn't answer. The door remained closed.

Finally resigned to her failure, Tenn took a bucket from the beach bag and peed in it. She checked on Gogo, worn out from scratching and barking, asleep now against the attic door. Tenn was getting hungry, which is how she knew it was close to noon. Only four more hours until the kids got home. The front door had a smart lock, so they could let themselves in with a code. They'd open the attic door when they heard her yelling. And then she would deal with the aftermath.

Tenn organized boxes, sorted through photos and clothes. She was trapped, but she could still be productive. Everything would be fine with the job, with her life. She was just having a rough day. She told herself this every time she heard a noise, every time she saw movement in her peripheral vision. There were mice in the attic, and she was on edge. She considered getting out her camera and documenting her slow descent into madness—she'd always loved found-footage horror—but she knew the batteries were long dead.

With nothing left to do, Tenn let her exhaustion overtake her body. Her body had been telling her she needed rest, but she never had time to listen. It wasn't that uncomfortable on the attic floor. She felt then that maybe she'd never leave it—this attic floor, this house, this place that was keeping her where it wanted her. There was a faded towel amongst the paint cans, also left by previous owners, printed with a map of the Hawaiian Islands. Tenn balled it under her head. She could remember experiencing this heaviness before—a slow descent through dark water, the yearning of her body to find the bottom. Tenn couldn't stop the heaviness from taking over, even when she reached for the doll in her pocket and discovered it was gone.

* * *

It was Ward yelling that woke her. Tenn had fallen asleep on the plywood floor under the window, all worries washed away in her sleep. Ward was moving through the house calling her name; the intensity of his distress came through the door. Tenn sat up at the sound of metal against wood, the long peg of the doorknob being refitted into the hole. Her right arm was asleep, her left foot full of needles. When the door swung open, Gogo charged up the stairs, and Tenn remembered the rat poison and called to her.

"Tenn?" Ward said. He ran up behind Gogo, who was smothering Tenn's face. Tenn could see it in his clenched jaw—he hadn't expected to find her asleep. "Jesus Christ," he said, doubling over before rushing toward her. He knelt and put a hand on her forehead, checking for a fever. "Are you okay?" For a moment, Tenn thought he might carry her away, like a fireman. "What happened?"

Gogo, overexcited, gnawed on Tenn's hand. The kids climbed a few stairs, then stalled. Anders asked permission to come up. Ward had told them, Tenn now realized, not to follow. When Anders reached the top, he took Tenn in with spooked eyes.

"The doorknob fell off," was all Tenn could say at first. She shook her sleepy arm and gazed out the window, where the quality of sunlight had changed. "What time is it?"

"What time is it?" Ward said, and shook his head. "For fuck's sake, Tenn, how long have you been up here? You didn't go to the city?" He spotted the bucket of urine, and his face went sour.

"Since morning," Tenn told him. Her sleep had been heavy, like a blanket; an entire lifetime could've passed while she was out. "I came up . . ." She stopped and looked at the paint cans, realized there were parts of the story she couldn't tell. "I was on my way out the door. I just ran up to get my viewfinder. I left my phone in the kitchen because it was only going to take a second. But then the door slammed shut and the doorknob fell off, and I couldn't get it open."

"Anders, take Gogo downstairs," Ward said. "It's not safe for her up here."

Anders actually listened for a change, ran down the stairs and reappeared with a squeaky caterpillar. Gogo ceased her licking and followed him down, eager to play.

"I don't like it up here," Aisling said. "It's too crowded."

Tenn scanned the attic—it wasn't crowded at all. She'd stacked the paint cans and moved all the boxes to the periphery. This attic was so spacious that when Tenn and Ward had first seen it, they'd joked it would take years before they filled it with enough junk to render it unusable.

"You can go down, honey," Ward said. "Get your snack. I'll be right there."

Aisling looked at Tenn with concern. "Are you coming, too?" She asked like she was worried Tenn might stay, like she may have decided the attic was where she lived now.

"Right behind you," Tenn said.

Ward turned toward the stairs as Aisling descended, so Tenn couldn't see his face, couldn't read him. She could usually tell what he was thinking, but not right now. Then Ward sat on the floor beside her and put his head on his knees, his movements slow, like his body was arthritic, hurting.

"The kids got home and couldn't find you," Ward said. He was talking to his knees. "Only your phone on the counter. Anders called me from it. I didn't answer the first time, but he kept calling and calling. I was pissed that you kept calling me. I was in a meeting with a client and couldn't leave. When I finally answered and it was Anders, I nearly puked."

Tenn imagined Ward driving home, terrified of what he'd find, not yet awake to the anger she could hear now in his voice. "I'm sorry," she told him. "I tried everything to get the door open. I tried a tent stake; I tried to pry up a nail." She showed him her hand, the gouge in her palm, her blood dried in the lines like it was telling her future. "Wire, a shovel. I nearly climbed out the window."

"Why didn't you prop the door open?" he asked.

It was Tenn's fault she got trapped. Of course it was her fault. The kids had been alone; Ward was scared and needed someone to blame. It was all because of Tenn's carelessness. "I'm not stupid," she told him. "I did prop the door open."

"Where's the rock?" Ward said. "It's not by the door."

"Did you actually look?" Tenn said. Ward could never find anything, even when what he was looking for was right in front of his face. "I put it in front of the door. I put it there."

Ward shook his head. "I don't think you did, Tenn," he said. "The rock isn't down there."

"I obviously didn't want to spend my entire day trapped up here," Tenn said. She couldn't explain any of it—the rock, the door, the doll. "I have no idea what's going to happen with the job now. They're going to think I'm deranged when I tell them I got trapped in an attic."

Ward took her hand and held it to his chest. He was angry because he was scared, and he was scared because he loved her, which she knew even though he didn't say it. For Ward, fear and anger were intertwined. He resented what scared him; what scared him most was the unfixable. "Maybe you can make up an emergency," he offered. "Something with the kids."

Tenn didn't say what she was thinking, which was that inventing a fake emergency might conjure, for their children, a real one. She wasn't superstitious; she didn't really believe it. The bigger issue was that the last thing an employer wanted was a mother with needy kids.

"I guess I should get the kids going on their homework and make dinner," Ward said. He hesitated. It was Tenn's first day of work, in theory, and he'd promised to help. "What were we having again?"

"Tortellini with ham and peas," Tenn said, one of the few dishes the kids would always eat. Ward had never cooked it, though. "I'll take care of it." She stood unsteadily, retrieved the plastic bucket that held her piss. She would make dinner, help with homework, explain to her employer why she'd failed to show. She would keep going, as she always did.

Ward started down the stairs, but Tenn stopped him.

"I'm really sorry," she said, though now that she thought about it, she wasn't sure why she kept apologizing. She hadn't done anything wrong. She was just doing it out of habit, because she didn't want him to be upset.

Ward pulled her in, held her against his chest. He held her so tightly it hurt.

7

The head of HR greeted Tenn in the glass-walled foyer of a mirrored skyscraper in the Financial District and asked with sincere concern about her accident. Tenn put one hand on her neck, lied, and said she was lucky. She'd made it to the city without drama this time, taken a train that arrived an hour earlier than necessary. The head of HR was a heavily contoured woman named Lori, who wore a leather vest and stilettos of terrifying height. When Tenn took her hand, she was reminded of rhubarb pie—a tartness zinging her tongue. Something about Lori's perfume.

Lori led Tenn to the elevator, where they shot up thirty-seven floors to the real estate firm's suite. The lobby was industrial and expensive—polished concrete floors, chairs with sharp angles, everything made from leather and chrome. The receptionist was a tall Black woman who looked like a model. Tenn followed Lori to a corner conference room with floor-to-ceiling windows looking out over Wall Street and New York Harbor. The sight of the city below made

Tenn feel unstable, as if the glass might give way and she'd fall. Lori had Tenn's paperwork ready on a glass table and offered Tenn a riveted chair.

"Derek is on location at a new listing in Chelsea," Lori explained. Derek was the company's director of content, and he'd hired Tenn on the recommendation of a mutual friend from film school. "He won't be in the office until Wednesday, so that gives us the day to get your paperwork sorted." When Tenn had met Derek for her interview, Derek hadn't been familiar with her work and hadn't asked about it. Instead, he'd shown her an example of what they produced, video tours of multimillion-dollar real estate listings in the tristate area. He had long silvery hair that fell in loose waves over his shoulders.

"Kiki said you have a great eye for detail," he'd told Tenn. "I assume you know Premiere Pro?"

Lori presented Tenn with a stack of paperwork and a pen that did not write when she tried to use it, after Lori left the room. The conference room was freezing, so cold Tenn's fingers were stiff, uncooperative. She was still skimming the first page in her stack of papers when her phone began to buzz, the school's number on the screen. Lori had left to get a camera, to take a photo for Tenn's badge. Tenn declined the call and continued writing, her mind spinning out over the possibilities. Both kids had been fine that morning, but a call from school during the day usually meant someone was sick. Tenn was too far from home to be the parent who dealt with it. Ward would have to be on sick duty today, for a change.

Tenn got through one full page before Ward texted her: Can u talk to school? Called twice but I'm on job site

can't talk now, Tenn replied. JUST got to work.

Lori returned with a camera, and Tenn stood against a wall and forced a smile. Lori studied the image on her screen and deleted it. "Let's try that again, shall we? Say *money*!"

"Money," Tenn said as her phone on the glass table audibly vibrated. The muscles in her cheeks were as stiff as her hands. Lori made an evaluative face at the camera's screen.

"No one really looks at your badge anyway," Lori said. She turned her attention to Tenn's phone on the table, unavoidable. "Is everything okay?"

Tenn's body went hot even though the room was cold. She couldn't field a call from school right now; she'd barely had time to sit. She couldn't afford to be seen as more of a liability than she already was. Her phone quieted but not her worry about the kids.

"I'm sure it's fine," Tenn said. She willed Ward to call the school, as if her mind were actually powerful, capable of creating change. But he hadn't told her he was visiting a jobsite today. Maybe there'd been an accident. Her phone resumed vibrating.

Tenn approached the table slowly, as if her phone were a cursed object, something she knew she should not touch. She could hear the music that would be playing if this were a horror film, the strings taut, the tension about to snap. The sight of the school's name on her screen conjured a thousand disasters in her mind. Anyone could do anything at any time.

"Excuse me," she said, fumbling the phone as she picked it up. "I actually have to take this."

Lori eyed the paperwork. "Take your time," she said, a patronizing edge to her tone. "I'll get your badge going."

Tenn smiled politely as Lori left her.

"Hello?" she said. She walked to the windows and looked down on the street, filled with people who were unconcerned about her life.

"Hi, this is Dr. Lin from Odell Elementary. Is this Mrs. Trevino?"

Outside, Tenn spotted a woman in leather and wished for armor of her own.

"This is Tennessee Cherish," she said. "Aisling and Anders Trevino's mom." She didn't say *I kept my name*, because her name was clearly written on the million forms she'd filled out for the school. But they didn't know her yet. At the kids' old school, Tenn knew everyone who worked in the office, brought them peonies from their yard in the spring.

"Of course," Dr. Lin said. Tenn was waiting for her to say everything was fine, but she didn't.

"Is everything okay?" Tenn said. "Did something happen?"

"Oh, everyone's safe," Dr. Lin said. Tenn could hear women's voices in the background, someone laughing. She hadn't met a Dr. Lin at the school. She'd met the principal and the assistant principal, and the psychologist working with Anders, whose name was Dr. Jarrell. Dr. Jarrell played cards with Anders while they talked, so when Tenn asked about their meetings, Anders would only say *I won at Uno* or *Dr. Jarrell was surprised I know how to play Texas Hold'em.*

"I always panic a little when I see the school's name on my phone," Tenn said.

"Of course," Dr. Lin said again, which didn't ease Tenn's anxiety. "I was starting to worry no one would answer. Is now a good time?"

Tenn stood facing the window and did not turn to see if Lori was watching. It was not a good time, but it fell on her anyway because Ward was busy. "Yes," she said.

"I'm calling about both kids, I'm afraid," Dr. Lin said, "but Aisling is my immediate concern."

"Is she sick?" Tenn asked. Aisling had seemed fine that morning, though they'd argued because Aisling wanted to bring her stuffed *Lactobacillus bulgaricus* to school and Tenn had said no. The teacher had already sent a note discouraging stuffed animals in the classroom, though Aisling had pedantically argued bacteria was not an animal. Tenn had relented when Aisling started to cry. She didn't have the bandwidth that morning. "Is this about Aisling's stuffed bacteria?"

"Bacteria?" Dr. Lin said. "No, it's not about bacteria. I don't believe Aisling is ill, but we've had a concerning incident this morning."

"An incident," Tenn said calmly, though she wanted to scream at Dr. Lin's vagueness. Had Aisling scraped her knee or broken her fucking neck? "What does that mean?"

"Aisling asked for permission to leave PE to use the restroom this morning," Dr. Lin said. "But she didn't go to the restroom."

"Where did she go?" Tenn said. She could still see Aisling in the doghouse, Aisling in the cold. But Aisling couldn't have left the school without someone noticing.

"She went to the custodial closet, where she removed a large jug of floor cleaner. Then she took the jug to her classroom, which was empty at the time, and tried to put the jug in her backpack to take home. But the jug was too big to fit, and it was also heavy, and it spilled all over the floor just as Aisling's class returned from the gym."

Tenn stood in the cold conference room with the impervious city before her and felt a tug, like she was being pulled through the glass like a ghost toward the ground. "I don't understand," she said. "Why would she want floor cleaner?"

Aisling had stolen a lot of shit, but as far as Tenn knew she hadn't stolen anything from school before. Maybe there wasn't a reason she'd chosen floor cleaner, specifically. Maybe it was random, like a spatula or a leash.

"According to Aisling," Dr. Lin said, "she took the cleaner because ghosts don't like places that are clean."

"Ghosts," Tenn said. The word was already in her mind, hovering.

"Yes," Dr. Lin said. "According to Aisling, there are ghosts in her new house, and—" She paused, considering her wording. "According to Aisling, the house is old and dirty, and it doesn't smell clean the way it does here at school, so she thought if she brought the cleaner home, it might get rid of the ghosts."

Tenn sat again at the glass table and looked at her bare legs through the glass, the flesh raised.

"Are you still there?" Dr. Lin said.

"I'm here," Tenn said. "I'm sorry. Both kids have struggled with the move, and I know she mentioned ghosts to her teacher, but I thought she'd forgotten about it. She hasn't said anything about cleaning before." Tenn cleaned the floor sometimes by pushing a damp washcloth around with her foot, which probably didn't help, but she didn't say that. "Where is Aisling now?"

"Her socks and shoes were soaked by the spill, and she didn't want to go back to class, so she's in the nurse's office," Dr. Lin said. "With Anders."

"Anders?" Tenn said. She'd barely talked to Anders that morning, concerned only with herself, getting herself out the door. Ward had been in charge of the kids. He'd even given her a pep talk—her career was a priority, for both of them.

"Anders fell asleep during math today," Dr. Lin said, "which, I'm sure you're aware, is not the first time."

"Not the first time?" Tenn said. Was it possible, she wondered, that she'd been living in a different reality than the rest of her family? "This is definitely the first time I've heard about him falling asleep at school." How many times could she be clueless about her kids before this woman tagged the situation as neglect? "I've spoken with his teacher about water consumption but not this. Is he okay?" She imagined Anders asleep at his desk, his hair stuck to his forehead with sweat, his classmates looking on. "Does he have a fever?"

She turned just enough to see Lori in conversation with a deeply tanned man, both looking between Tenn and a document.

"He doesn't appear to be sick, no," Dr. Lin said. "Just very tired. We let him sleep, of course. School policy is that if a child falls asleep in class, Mr. Delgado, our PE teacher, carries them to the nurse's office, where we have a cot for them to finish their nap. If a child falls asleep in class, their body is telling us something. It's usually kindergarteners, who aren't used to the full day, but sometimes our older students, too. Was this something that happened regularly at Anders's previous school? I don't see any notes about it in his records."

"Anders has never fallen asleep at school before," Tenn said. "As far as I know." She hadn't had time to check last night's footage and was afraid now what she'd see. "What did he say? Did he say why he's so tired?"

Outside, Tenn watched a parade of nannies with strollers crossing the puddle-filled street. She wondered where the babies' mothers were, how they managed to buy this time.

"He's still asleep," Dr. Lin said. "And Aisling is curled up beside him now. It's very sweet, actually. They're sweet kids."

On the other side of the glass, Lori was speaking with a different man now, who wore a pristine suit and a frown. The call was going on for a long time, Tenn was aware. She flashed an apologetic smile.

"I know Anders has mentioned to Dr. Jarrell that sometimes he has scary dreams. Is that something he's expressed to you as well?"

Tenn wanted to bash her head through the glass table but thought she probably shouldn't on her first day. "Yes," she said. She saw him sometimes, in the footage, sitting up in his bed at night, frozen, like there was a wild animal in his room, tracking him. "He wakes up sometimes, though usually he goes right back to sleep. He hasn't seemed more tired than usual at home."

Now that she thought about it, Tenn wasn't sure if this was true. Anders had been spending more time in his room lately, but on the footage, he seemed perfectly happy, building with Legos or drawing. For all her flaws, Tenn kept the kids stocked with art supplies, so they were always making something—bracelets, paper bag puppets, monsters covered with googly eyes and pom-poms.

"Well, I think we can agree that ensuring Anders gets enough sleep is a priority," Dr. Lin said. "Right?"

"Of course," Tenn said. The man in the suit was standing at a desk in an office across the hall, signing something. Lori stood beside him looking smug.

"At this age, most children still need nine to twelve hours of sleep," Dr. Lin said. "I'm going to send you some literature on ways you can create a soothing sleep environment, and a script you can use for talking about bad dreams. I'm also going to give you a few names—one is a pediatric sleep specialist; the other is a neurologist. I don't think we need to go down that road yet—the first step should be a conversation with your pediatrician. There's not necessarily cause for alarm, but it's important to rule out potential medical causes for insomnia, and it's possible your doctor may suggest something like melatonin to help Anders with this transition. And again, this is very common, especially in kids who are going through a big change. And let's set Aisling up with a counseling meeting, too."

"Okay, yes, that all sounds helpful," Tenn said. "We'll read everything, and I'll schedule an appointment with Anders's doctor right away."

"Great," Dr. Lin said. "I also wanted to mention something else." In the background, the bell rang, and Dr. Lin paused.

"Sure," Tenn said. The man in the suit stood near the door like he was waiting for her. She realized he was shoeless, the kind of man who was as comfortable at work as at home, because he lived there. She turned back to the window and pretended she hadn't seen him. Her anxiety was replaced now by a familiar resignation—this was where *she* lived, in a bubble in which everything fell on her, forever. On the street, umbrellas were popping open in black bursts. It had started to rain, pretty hard. Tenn hadn't brought an umbrella.

"I don't want to overstep any boundaries," Dr. Lin said. Her voice lowered to a more intimate tone. "But I wanted to let you know that if there's something going on at home, if you're dealing with a medical diagnosis or a chronic illness, for example, you can always talk to us here at school, and we're here for you and the kids, to help them process what they're feeling."

"A diagnosis," Tenn said. She and Ward had talked about her allergy testing at the dinner table, but the kids had been arguing over a game at the time. "I don't understand."

"Anders's art teacher tells me he's been drawing gravestones," Dr. Lin said. "Gravestones with your name on them. Sometimes when kids know a loved one is sick, they can process that in unusual ways. If they aren't certain someone will get better, or very rarely, when we have a parent with a terminal illness, a child will explore ways to prepare themself for what's to come."

Tenn couldn't speak for a moment. Hands on the glass table, she could remember lying in a dim bedroom with a quilt draped over her lap. She could see the quilt clearly—each square contained a sun. It wasn't a quilt she owned; she'd seen it in a catalog or on a TV show. "I'm not . . ." The school thought that she was dying, that Anders was preparing for Tenn to be dead. "I've been dealing with allergies, but I don't think we've given the impression that it's serious. Certainly not terminal. But I suppose Anders could be sensitive about appointments. Or maybe he's just entering a goth phase." It wasn't the appropriate time for a joke, but Tenn coped the way she coped.

"I'm sorry," Dr. Lin said. "I didn't mean to imply . . ."

"No, of course," Tenn said. "I'm glad you mentioned it. The neighbors have—" She stopped. She imagined the teachers, gathered around Anders's drawings, speculating. "The neighbors have these stones in their front yard, like graves. Old houses, you know. I'm sure that's where the image came from. I just don't know why he's putting my name on them. We'll talk about it. I'll let you know what we figure out."

There was a house at the end of the street—a colonial like theirs but with better landscaping—with two stones in the yard. Anders had pointed them out one afternoon as he and Aisling rode their bikes up and down the street.

"Dead people," he said when Tenn caught up. She'd been lagging behind and worried, when he'd stopped, that he was hurt.

"Oh," she said. The stones were rounded and gray, the etching too worn to read from the street. "Maybe it's not people," she told him. "It could be pets. Or sometimes really old houses have mile markers."

"Then why are there two of them?" Anders asked, and pedaled away.

"Do you want to come get them now?" Dr. Lin asked. "Aisling has been asking for you."

Both Lori and the man in the suit had disappeared, the hall now empty. They'd left Tenn alone like she'd ceased to exist.

"I'm in the city at the moment," she said, "at work. But I'll head back." Her stomach turned as she said this, her body revolted by her decision. But Aisling was asking for her, and Ward wasn't answering his phone. Tenn knew how it would go—she'd hang up and call him, and he would text that he was busy. It was clear now that she was the one who had to get the kids.

"No worries," Dr. Lin said. Tenn pictured Anders on a cot, and Aisling beside him, her feet wrinkled and astringent, pressing her *Lactobacillus bulgaricus* to her brother's chest. "They're safe here. I'll tell Aisling you're on your way."

"Thank you," Tenn said. "And thank you for calling. It's been a challenging time for all of us, and we appreciate the support. Hopefully things will settle down soon."

"Hopefully," Dr. Lin said, and hung up.

Tenn looked out the window for a minute, gathering the nerve to go in search of Lori. The rain was coming down hard with no sign of letting up.

⁎ ⁎ ⁎

When Tenn got home with the kids, she made snack plates of fruit and cheese and put a set of modeling clay on the table for the kids to play with while they talked. It was easier to talk if you had something in your hands. She put her phone in Do Not Disturb mode, because she was certain that if Ward called now, she would lose it on him.

The kids sat at the table and stuffed their faces with cheese.

"So who wants to go first?" Tenn asked, knowing full well that only Aisling would talk.

"Anders fell asleep, and Mr. Delgado carried him to the nurse like Sleeping Beauty," Aisling said. She took a few colors of clay from the kit and opened them with a sense of purpose. "That's what Mrs. Grecco said." Mrs. Grecco was the school nurse, which Tenn knew because she had also called Tenn, on Tenn's train ride home, to tell her Anders had been talking in his sleep. "And I told Mrs. Grecco *Sleeping Beauty* is not a good story, because princes shouldn't kiss people while they're sleeping. If you're asleep, you can't give consent."

Anders squeezed his own clay like he was trying to compress it into something smaller.

"Dr. Lin told me you were tired because you've been having bad dreams."

Anders didn't look up from his clay, from his strawberries. Aisling was already making something—she shaped a lumpy middle and two appendages that looked like arms.

"Did you have any dreams during your nap today?" Tenn asked. She knew Anders had because of the nurse's call, but it was possible Anders didn't remember.

Anders shrugged and ate a strawberry, squeezed his clay.

"The nurse told me you were talking," Tenn said. "You were saying, *They're getting you.* Do you remember?"

Tenn wanted to ask who was being gotten, who was doing the

getting. But Anders squeezed his clay so hard it squished between his little fingers. He was just like Ward—he got angry at the things he couldn't fix. Tenn was angry, too, at Ward, at the unfairness of the situation. At the fact that she was left to do the fixing, again. Anders said nothing.

"That's okay," Tenn said. "What's important is that we find a way to help you sleep better. We're going to see the doctor about it on Thursday. But is there anything else you can think of that might help? Is there anything we can do to make your bedroom feel more cozy?"

On the train, Tenn had googled ways to help kids through nightmares. She'd already ordered a few picture books; she'd downloaded a meditation app they would use before bed. She would limit screen time in the evenings; she would hang a dream catcher and give Anders a special bracelet, a talisman to protect him in his sleep. But all the articles advised caregivers to deal with the source of fear directly—to talk through it, to write a new ending for the dream. Which only worked if Anders remembered his dream, and was willing to share it.

Anders wasn't answering, so Tenn asked again. "What do you think, buddy?"

Anders took a sharp breath and threw his lump of clay at Tenn from across the table. The clay hit Tenn in the chest, a misshapen fist that broke apart in her lap.

"I don't want to sleep! I don't want to go to the doctor! I don't want to do anything!" Anders stormed off, up the stairs, and the house shuddered when his bedroom door slammed shut. Gogo, who'd been sitting under Aisling in case she dropped a piece of cheese, planted herself on Tenn's feet.

Tenn sat calmly, watching Aisling shape her clay. This was Tenn's job today, her job every day. Aisling was making fingers; she was making toes.

"He doesn't want to talk about it," Aisling said.

"What about you?" Tenn said. "Do you want to talk about it?" She didn't specify a subject, because it was better to let Aisling get there on her own. Aisling knew what was coming; Tenn could tell by the intensity with which she focused on her sculpture. She'd shut down if Tenn pressed too hard—this was a trait she'd inherited from Tenn.

Aisling shrugged, focused on her work. Her creation had taken shape—a figure the same size as the doll from the yard. "I already talked to Dr. Lin," she said.

"I understand you talked about cleaning," Tenn said. She was afraid to say too much, to betray Aisling's trust in Dr. Lin. She was afraid to mention ghosts, because she wanted to hear Aisling's language for her fear, to see its shape in her mind. "Is that right?"

Aisling nodded. She was shaping the figure's face, giving it the same dull expression as the doll. The clay she'd chosen for the face was red.

"If you want, we can work on that together," Tenn said. "We can have a cleaning day and get everything how you like it. Do you think that would help?"

Aisling was deeply absorbed in her figure, using a plastic carving tool on its face. Aisling was like Ward, too—she had no patience for talking when there was work to be done.

"Is that a doll?" Tenn asked. Aisling took a wooden dowel from the clay kit and used it to hollow out the figure's eyes. "Does it have a name?"

"It's not really a doll," Aisling said.

Tenn thought she was going to make eyes for the sockets, but Aisling left them empty. "Oh," she said, "what is it then?"

Aisling looked at her work, satisfied. The doll's hands were open, the fingers long and wormlike.

"It's a container," she said. "Don't touch it."

* * *

Ward didn't get home until after the kids had finished dinner. Tenn was washing dishes, and the water was freezing, because something was wrong with the well or the sink. Neither of them had called whoever they were supposed to call yet.

"Russell is leaving," Ward said unceremoniously, forgoing greetings or questions about Tenn's job or the kids. Tenn had no idea who Russell was. He didn't mention the incident that had tied him up all day. "So Johann wants me to take over his accounts."

"His accounts?" Tenn said. Ward handled incident response, not client accounts.

"The clients already know me, and they like me better than Russell apparently." Tenn could hear the pride in his voice—it was good to be valued, to be needed. "And that means I'll also be taking over Russell's team."

Ward was already managing a team of his own, and he was barely around to help as it was. But he wasn't asking if she was okay with it. He wasn't thinking about how much more would fall on her.

"Is it a big team?" she asked him.

"Bigger than mine," Ward said.

Tenn fixed Ward a plate of tacos—Anders had refused leftover pasta, so Tenn had been forced to cook again. In the living room, the kids were pretending the floor was lava, leaping from pillow to pillow to keep from being burned. Every pillow and blanket would be on the floor now, and Tenn would be the one to pick them up.

Ward ate his tacos, unworried, it seemed, as Tenn was about the demands on his time. "I'm getting a raise, too," he said. Sauce dribbled down his chin as he grinned.

"Already?" Tenn said. He'd just started the job, and it paid well as it was. She sat in the chair across from his, her hands cold but her face hot with the memory of standing in the conference room, nodding through a lecture from a broker at her firm about the importance of reliability.

Ward looked up from his taco and saw that Tenn was not okay. "I'm going to take you on a very nice vacation next year," he said. A year was a long time away, though, a long year of Tenn leaving work early every time one of the kids had a cold. Another year of being the one to help with the homework, of both cooking dinner and doing the cleanup. Ward read her face. "You could go away yourself. You should go somewhere with Helen."

"That's a nice idea," Tenn said. "What about the kids?"

"Maybe my dad can come stay," Ward offered. "He always says he wants to spend more time with them."

Ward's dad never stayed with the kids because Ward's dad sometimes fell asleep with a cigarette in his mouth. Tenn's parents never stayed with the kids, either, because Tenn's parents screamed at each other constantly and were usually on vacations of their own. They'd never had anyone to help them with the kids besides friends, who were far away now.

In the living room, a body hit the floor, which shook the dining room.

"Jesus, they're going to destroy this house," Ward said.

"Is everyone alive?" Tenn yelled.

"I fell," Anders said. "But nothing's broken."

"You're burned to death by lava," Aisling said.

"I'm not burned to death," Anders said, "because I cast a cold and light spell on my body, so lava can only burn me if I touch it for more than thirty seconds."

"There's no spell," Aisling said. "You can't just make things up. You can't make a new rule to save yourself after you're already dead."

Ward took another bite and gave Tenn a look. She hadn't told him what the nurse had said, about Anders calling out in his sleep. She hadn't told him, and he hadn't asked.

"So let's make a plan," Ward said. "For the next time this happens. Because it's really not ideal for me to get a million calls in the middle of the day like that. And it's not fair to you, either. I know that. We need to have a plan."

"A plan," Tenn said, and felt like an animal was trying to claw its way out of her, an animal that was dangerous, that she had to keep penned in. Ward was concerned about her work now, though it was still on Tenn to make the plan. It was on Tenn to make the plan and to take Anders to his next doctor's appointment. It was on Tenn to set up Aisling's counseling sessions and to make the dinner and wash the dishes and get the kids in bed, while Ward sat upstairs dealing with Russell's accounts. Ward made more money than Tenn did, by a lot, so his job was the priority. She didn't say any of this. It was understood.

"That thing happened again," is what she did say. She'd be the one to make the plan; it was the solution that made sense. Ward was eating late—he hadn't had a free minute all day. The kids wouldn't be young forever, and they needed her now, which wasn't anyone's fault. She started clearing the table. The kids had left it littered with junk from their backpacks—dead leaves, an eraser shaped like a pumpkin. Aisling was working on a school project with the theme How We Spend Our Days Is How We Spend Our Lives, and she'd been cutting out representations of her days from magazines: Pop-Tarts, an easel, a dog, a bed. Tenn tried to think of what she'd put in a collage of her own life, but all she could imagine now was dirty dishes and the kids. "With my car."

Ward tipped a bottle of hot sauce over a taco and the sauce flooded out, way more than he'd expected. "Fuck," he said. He tried to scrape off the excess, but the sauce was too thin. "Where it feels like the car is pulling to the side?"

"Yeah," Tenn said. They'd had this conversation before, but she brought it up now because she was angry. She was angry that he didn't believe her when she had said something was wrong. They'd had it checked, the tires and the alignment, and the mechanic hadn't found anything. It was Tenn's anxiety, Ward had told her, a statement of fact—she felt unsafe in her car because of Crystal's death. Tenn had let Ward convince her it was all in her head. But today a light had come on. "I had to pull over on my way home from the train station."

"Is that why it took you so long to get the kids?" he said, and wiped his brow. The hot sauce was making him sweat.

"No, it took me so long because I was getting reprimanded on my first day of work for being unable to stay in the building long enough to do my fucking job," she said.

Tenn went to the kitchen and returned to the dishes, the freezing water. If she held her fingers under the tap long enough, they would go numb. She was hot in the face; she shouldn't have brought up the car at all. Everything felt wrong to her—her work, Ward's work, the house, the kids. Everything. It felt like the room was tilting, too, like the whole world wanted her to fall off its edge. She was barely keeping herself from falling. From the living room, there was another crash.

Ward appeared behind her, carrying his plate. His eyes were watering; the hot sauce was too hot. There were still cups on the table, his dirty napkins, crumpled in a wad. Tenn moved to walk past him, to finish cleaning, but he stopped her.

"We'll hire someone," he said. He was different now; he'd remembered himself. "That's what people here do. They hire it out. We'll hire someone to get the kids off the bus, to help with their homework. My raise will cover it. It doesn't all have to be on you."

"We can hire a sitter for after school, but that doesn't cover emergencies like today," Tenn said. "It was my first day." She could feel her voice breaking. "Do you have any idea how humiliating that is? I didn't even finish my paperwork."

Ward pulled her in and held her against him, and she let herself sink for a moment into his warmth. He was trying to solve the problem, but not every problem had an easy fix.

"I'm sorry," he said, and stroked her hair. "I'm sure they'll understand. People have emergencies with their kids all the time."

"Would Johann understand?" Tenn said into his shoulder.

Ward didn't answer the question. "I'll take the car," he said. "I'll have it checked again." She could tell by the way he was still holding her tight that she'd worried him, and then she felt bad for making him worry. "But you know what happened to her isn't going to happen to you." Tenn could hear as he said this that it was partly a question: Was it possible she might drive her car into a tree? "Even if you were in an accident. It wouldn't be the same."

"What do you mean?" Tenn said. She knew what he meant, but she wanted to hear him say it out loud.

"She wasn't wearing her seat belt," Ward said, which Tenn knew. She'd told him all the details. The viewing had been closed casket for a reason. It was Crystal's fault, was what he meant. "But I know you'd never do something that stupid."

Tenn pulled away, no longer able to stand Ward's touch. "I don't know," she said. "Sometimes I feel pretty fucking stupid."

There was a shock of noise then, like the sound of a falling tree. It had happened in North Carolina when the weather was violent—trees came down in their yard. Tenn moved fast while Ward lagged behind.

In the living room, the kids were both on pillows, standing still on their islands amid the lava. They were staring at the wall above the couch. Aisling had her hands pressed over her ears.

"We didn't do it," Anders said. "We weren't doing anything bad."

"It was really loud," Aisling yelled, unable to judge her own volume. "Why was it so loud?"

On the wall above the couch, the crack had split apart, leaving a rough gap in the plaster. The couch was coated with dust, like ruins.

"I believe you," Tenn said.

She and Ward looked at each other, so much hanging in the air with the dust. They stayed that way, each waiting for the other to take charge, until Tenn took the kids by the hands and led them away through the lava so she could clean up.

8

Ward didn't wake at the sound of the doorbell, and when Tenn shook him, he blinked but didn't move to get up. Gogo was already gone, barking her way across the house. Tenn grabbed her phone from the nightstand, a flush of adrenaline propelling her, and followed. She was wearing one of Ward's old shirts, and though it didn't cover her underwear, she did not stop for her robe. She was moving so fast she tripped on the stairs, three from the bottom, and toppled forward onto the hardwood, landing on her left knee. She stayed there a moment in the dark, stunned by the pain, a familiar dread in her body. Gogo raced to Tenn, a loving creature with a vicious bark, and licked Tenn's leg. Tenn didn't understand her own terror, there on the floor at the bottom of the stairs. They lived in a town with a nonexistent crime rate. Her children were safe in their beds. The doorbell rang again. It was 2:47 a.m.

When Tenn opened the door, Gogo ran outside, and Tenn stood there in her underwear, in the dark, in the cold. Aisling was on the sidewalk, an unfamiliar blanket around her shoulders like a shawl, and Gogo snuffled her feet before moving on to the older woman behind her, dressed in scrub pants and a chore jacket, a gray braid down one shoulder. She stood several feet back from the house. Tenn stepped fully outside and pulled Aisling against her body, then returned to the foyer to turn on the porch light. The strange woman looked down at Gogo, and Gogo sat as if receiving wordless instruction.

"Frankie," the woman said, by way of introduction. She pointed down the street. "From the house with the graves."

"Graves," Tenn said. She called Gogo, who came but snarled when Tenn captured her and shoved her inside, behind the door. Tenn's knee burned, her legs bare and exposed, but she knelt before Aisling anyway. Aisling was wearing rain boots and holding her green T-ball shirt with filthy hands. "What happened?" Tenn asked her. "What are you doing out here?"

"I thought she was a raccoon," Frankie said. "I heard noise out front and sent Frank to make sure they weren't getting in the trash." Frankie was calm but did not come closer to the house as she spoke. "Frank's my husband. He came in with her and said, 'I'm pretty sure this isn't a raccoon.'"

Gogo was barking and barking inside, throwing her body against the storm door. Aisling put her hand on the glass to calm her, but Gogo was increasingly distressed that she could see but not lick them.

"What was she doing?" Tenn asked.

Behind her, lights began to flick on as Ward made his way toward the commotion.

"She was digging," Frankie said. "She didn't have a shovel, but she was digging her little heart out."

"In your yard?" Tenn said. She thought of the gravestones and tried to make sense of it, but she couldn't. She was cold with a sense of urgency, like in her dreams where there was something she was supposed to do to avert disaster but didn't know what it was. "Why were you digging in their yard?"

Aisling extended the T-shirt with filthy hands. Inside the shirt was the red-faced clay doll. "It needs to be buried."

Tenn reached for the bundle, but Aisling pulled back. "Don't touch it!" she warned. "You can only touch the shirt."

Tenn gently took the bundle in her arms, then peeled back the fabric to examine the doll. Aisling snatched it away and pinned it to her chest.

"I don't understand, sweet pea," Tenn said. The pain in her knee was insistent, a shout. "Why do you want to bury your doll?"

Ward appeared at the door then, bare chested but wearing a pair of sweat shorts. He looked at Tenn through the glass, standing outside in the cold with her whole ass showing. He held Gogo back as he opened the door, and Gogo bucked against him, trying to get free.

"Can you take Aisling inside?" Tenn asked him.

Ward didn't ask questions, just obliged Tenn's request. He nodded to Frankie with confusion.

"Do you want to come in?" Tenn asked her. She took the blanket from Aisling's shoulders as she went in and wrapped it around her waist, then finally introduced herself. "I'm so sorry about this. I don't know what's gotten into her. She never did this before we moved. I can't believe she was digging in your yard. We'll cover any damage, obviously."

"Oh, nonsense," Frankie said. "It's just some grass and dirt; no one's getting bent out of shape about that. I just worry about the kids. We have a pond in the back. I hate to think of someone falling in."

A pair of eyes flashed across the street, a stray cat or a fox, hiding in the shrubs. "Are you sure—"

"My daughter sleepwalked," Frankie said.

Tenn looked inside, but Ward had taken Aisling away, into the warmth of the house. "I'm not sure Aisling was asleep," Tenn said. "It sounds to me like she knew what she was doing."

"Oh no, I don't think she was asleep," Frankie said. "I'm telling you about the bells."

"Bells?" Tenn said.

"When my daughter was little, we put bells on the doors. So we could hear if she was moving around the house at night. I threatened to put one around her neck, like a cat, but I didn't want to strangle her. But the bells were good. We caught her before she got too far, most of the time."

"Bells," Tenn said again. "Yes, that's a great idea. We'll have to put something on the doors so we can hear her."

Tenn would hang bells; Tenn would hire someone to install alarms. In that moment, she could already feel it happening again—Aisling slipping away from her, over and over, into the cold. If Tenn made a collage of the days of her life, warning bells would be included.

"I'm so sorry about everything, really. I know the kids have been curious about the stones in your yard. We should've come by to say hello before this."

"Home burials were more common in the past," Frankie said. "Still legal in most states. Just not done anymore."

Tenn tried to imagine burying someone she loved in her own yard, unsure if proximity to their unbreathing body would bring comfort or madness. "I can grab my keys and drive you back down the street," she offered.

Frankie took one step back and then another, creating distance between her and Tenn, between her and the house.

"I'm not going to get lost," Frankie said. "Don't you worry about me. You have enough to worry about already."

* * *

Tenn was on the train to the city when she got the call that her position had been eliminated. Derek was the one to call her, and she pictured him tousling his silver waves as he told her in a pained voice that the decision had not been his. She was sitting with her viewfinder in her lap, dressed in her most professional jumpsuit, ready to prove her competence, the value of her eye. Tenn thanked Derek for the opportunity and watched the world blur by—gray rocks against gray sky—while the train carried her toward a job she'd lost before she started. When the conductor came down the aisle, she wiped tears from her neck and showed her ticket on her phone. The conductor was a small man with a baby face, and he put a tentative hand on her shoulder. Tenn smelled cigar smoke, the sour sweat of a drunk. The train was crowded—she could smell everyone around her. At Grand Central, she stood under the ceiling, staring up at the constellations, Orion raising his club. She'd read once that the mural had been painted backward, the image reversed by a projector, so that east was west and west was east. Tenn read the schedule and found the train home, which she boarded without bothering to leave the station.

In the lot of the train station, Tenn sat in her car for a long time before driving, unsure she was capable of keeping it on the road. The dashboard light had gone off; Ward would forget he'd said he'd take it in. She made it only a mile before she felt the tug and pulled off into the nearest parking spot, in front of the library. She couldn't drive herself home; she couldn't call Ward to come get her. She got out of the car and entered the library, where she could sit until the world felt less sideways.

Inside the library, it was chaos. One preschool story time had just ended; another was about to begin. There was a toddler face down in the hall, screeching, and several more chasing each other with paper-plate noisemakers, filling the hall with the rattle of dried beans. Their mothers stood in a cluster, ignoring the noise. In an adjacent room, there was a baby crying, multiple babies crying. Tenn felt the wailing in her breasts.

Upstairs, Tenn went straight to nonfiction, in search of a biography. She could anchor herself that way, with the details of some other woman's life, the hardships she'd overcome. She could remind herself that her own life was comparatively good, survivable. The tug was still with her, a gravity pulling her disasterward. If she got too close to a window, her body might simply pass through. She walked the rows of books without direction. She couldn't read right now. She couldn't even read the titles. She let her fingers graze the spines until the tug subsided and bent to look at the book on which she'd landed: *Local Spirits and Their Haunts* by Dahlia Beckett. Tenn pulled it from the shelf and paged through—a compendium of local ghost stories plus a chapter called "The Homeowner's Guide to Ghosts: Practical Tips for Living with Your House and All Its Occupants." She tucked the book under her arm. Maybe she would find something inside that would help Aisling.

"Ghost problems?" a voice said, startling Tenn out of her misery. She turned to discover a woman with luxuriant curls wearing a sweater knit in the pattern of a Ouija board. *Yes*, the sweater said. *No. Goodbye.*

"Ghosts," Tenn said, and smoothed her hair, worried she had taken on the appearance of someone with a ghost problem.

The woman gestured toward the book. "That's my aunt," she said. "She's the town historian for South Bouton. She does ghost tours, so I've been a ghost every year since I could walk."

"Oh," Tenn said, "that sounds fun." Maybe she and Aisling could read the book and go on a ghost walk together. Maybe she could turn it into a bonding experience, a new family tradition.

"I'm Senna," the woman said, extending a hand. Tenn smelled mango and sunscreen—Senna was wearing a small vial around her neck that appeared to be made to hold potions. "It means 'brightness,' but it's also a laxative."

Tenn couldn't help but laugh, and introduced herself. Senna was holding a book about the anthropology of witchcraft. She looked younger than Tenn, but not by much. Tenn had a sudden urge to grab on to her. She missed Helen. She missed eating chips and watching bad TV with someone who only judged her when she needed judging.

"I like your sweater," Tenn said. She wondered if Senna had a planchette tucked inside her pocket.

"Thanks, but listen"—Senna leaned in close—"no Ouija boards if you actually have ghosts."

"No?" Tenn said. She wasn't sure if this woman was serious, but she considered asking, what if your whole body was a Ouija board—what then?

Senna shook her head. "I've done enough house calls with my aunt," she said. "You have to know what you're dealing with." She offered Tenn a card from her bag, which was not for ghost-related services. *County Clerk, Land Records Division*, the card said. "Always start with the records." She gestured again to the ghost book. "There's a chapter in there about researching your house's history. Let me know if you need any help. I love a good haunting."

"Thanks," Tenn said, wishing she could float, ghostlike, out of the building, to a place where she was not in need of the services of a county clerk / ghost hunter. "I'll let you know."

Senna raised a fist in solidarity and disappeared behind a shelf marked *Metaphysics*. Tenn checked out the book and returned to her car, no more certain she could keep it on the road.

* * *

In the kitchen, someone had left the faucet running. Tenn loaded the dishwasher, wiped the counters free of crumbs, scrubbed the casserole pan left soaking in the sink. The water from the tap took too long to get warm. By the time Tenn was finished, her hands felt like ice.

Gogo snuffled her ankles, a scrap of Post-it hanging from her mouth. When Tenn tried to take it, Gogo swallowed it greedily, then stuck her tongue all the way up Tenn's nose.

"Stop eating things," Tenn told her, scritching Gogo's butt.

Ward was coming down the stairs from his office, but he was moving slowly, a glacial pace. She hadn't told him about her job; they'd barely talked since he'd gotten home. He'd stayed upstairs in his office through dinner, ate at his desk. There was a problem, Tenn had gathered—his phone voice quieter than usual, his dinner plate mostly untouched. What his cameras captured was worse some days than others, and he tried not to burden her with images that couldn't be unseen. They both knew Tenn's mind worked differently than his. She stood on the other side of the door and waited. The sound of Ward's footsteps stopped.

"Hello?" she said. She'd been waiting for a good time to talk to him and wondered if she'd ever find one. She opened the door.

On the other side, Ward stood with his phone in his hand. He looked up at her, surprised. "Hey," he said. He was happy to see her, as if, in her absence, he'd forgotten about her. "I didn't hear you there."

"I was just cleaning up," she told him. There was a film on the counter, like seawater that had dried into a lace of salt. "I wanted to talk to you."

"I have to be on a call in a few," Ward said. "This guy curled up and died outside a hospital."

"Again?" Tenn said.

"What?" Ward said.

"Didn't you tell me about a professor who died outside a hospital?" She was pretty sure he had, but maybe she was misremembering.

"Oh," Ward said. "Yeah, that was different. This guy was homeless; the video is awful. But it shouldn't take long. I was just coming to get a drink."

He continued looking at his phone while he said this. He reached out toward Tenn, and she was relieved until she realized he was reaching past her, to the cabinet for a glass. She moved out of the way and leaned against the sink. She should have told him about the job then, but instead she took the sponge and started scrubbing the counter.

"Can you take out the trash when you get a chance?" she asked him. It wasn't a good time; she couldn't burden him with her own problems now. He'd watched someone die and would have to over and over. "I've stuffed it down as far as it'll go."

"I'll do it," he said. He was typing on his phone, responding to a message. "And while I'm thinking about it, we're out of plastic cups. I don't know what the kids were doing with cups tonight, but they're all dirty."

Tenn watched him fill his glass, first with ice, then with bourbon. Somewhere that day, a man had died alone, with only a camera as his witness. It took a toll on Ward, though he tried not to show it.

"I'll run the dishwasher," Tenn told him. She'd just run it the day before.

"Thanks," he said. "You're okay?" He was still looking at his phone; Tenn could see a rim of grief around his eyes.

"I'm fine," she said.

When he looked up at her, she realized it was the first time he'd really looked at her all day. There was a fleck of tomato sauce dried above his lip, and she wiped it away with her thumb. "Are you?" he asked.

She wasn't sure what he'd seen—maybe he could tell she'd been crying. She'd worn an eye mask to counter the swelling before he got home. "Do you think I'm not?" she asked.

Ward leaned against the counter, and Tenn could see it, briefly suspended—this one moment, one chance for them to reconnect if they both grabbed it at the same time.

"I don't know," Ward said. His phone buzzed, but he pressed it against his leg. "Just asking."

Tenn wanted to tell him everything, to sink against his body and let him hold her so she didn't slide all the way off the world's edge. She didn't like carrying her failure around inside her. But she was used to it.

Then Ward's phone began to ring. "I'm so sorry," he said, and kissed her on the brow before pressing the phone to his ear. "Hey," he said, "did you see my message?" He paused at the bottom of the stairs and blew her an air kiss, both of them knowing their moment had come and gone. Tenn blew a kiss back and closed the door.

In the bedroom, Tenn found the doll, waiting for her on the bed, propped on her pillow, her sole companion. The last she'd seen it, she'd hidden it in the bag of beach toys in the attic, which she hadn't expected Ward to open again until summer. She checked the footage of the kids' rooms on her laptop and found them both asleep. The footage from the primary bedroom camera wouldn't load.

When Tenn turned back to the bed, the doll was no longer on her pillow—somehow it had been moved to Ward's. Her forearm tingled, and she raked her nails down its length rather than see what it said.

9

Ward positioned the skeleton behind the hedges so it looked like it was climbing from the yard into the street. Tenn had gone to the store, and he was trying to get the decorations in place before she got home. She'd seemed off last night, but she loved Halloween—the storytelling, the art direction, the costumes. She loved creating a world where the dead could return to life. In North Carolina, all their friends would come to their house for Halloween, and the kids would trick-or-treat around their neighborhood while the adults drank cocktails from a smoking cauldron in their yard. One year, Tenn and her film school friends made a giant Louise Bourgeois spider from wire and papier-mâché, and the local news came to film it. Ward imagined the look on Tenn's face when she came home and found the skeleton, waiting for her. He'd duct-taped an umbrella to its hand, because the forecast called for rain.

Anders came running with the box of spiders, small ones they'd hung every year from the magnolia at their old house. Tenn had wept over the tree the day they'd left it—they'd carved their initials into its trunk; they'd laid a blanket under its branches and attempted to christen it after they'd moved in. Aisling had been a baby then, and they'd brought the monitor out with them into the yard. She squawked awake just as Ward got Tenn's pants off, and Tenn ran inside in her underwear as an elderly neighbor drove by. The tree had been her favorite thing about the old house; as soon as they'd seen it, they'd both known it was home.

The new house had its own special tree, a gnarled buckeye out front that a neighbor in the garden club had told them was more than two hundred years old. Aisling had taken one look and announced she could see a face in the gnarls; she said there was a witch inside who could look out but never leave. Tenn had lit up when Aisling said this, because she knew Ward had found this house for her—a house where they'd make myths together, a house their kids would always remember. Their childhoods would be tied to it, memories of skating the pitched floors in their socks. Ward was giving them something his own parents had never managed—a sense of home. He braced his ladder against the trunk, gave it a good shake to make sure it was stable. The ground was dry—he was reasonably sure he wouldn't slip. He cut a length of fishing line and threaded it through a spider's loop.

Now Aisling appeared on the porch.

"When is Mommy coming home?" she asked.

They were out of yogurt again, because yogurt was all Aisling would eat this week. They'd been out of coffee that morning, too, which was strange because Ward had made coffee two days ago, and the bag of grounds had been nearly full. They'd run out of ketchup, which he'd discovered when he went to put some on his scrambled eggs, the giant bottle in the fridge empty, as was the produce drawer, only a few shriveled grapes left in the plastic tub. Tenn had just been to the store the day before. It seemed like a lot to forget, but they went to the store so often, it was easy to conflate trips.

"She should be home soon," he said. He climbed the ladder, because he needed to get this done before Tenn caught him. Tenn didn't like it when he climbed ladders, because he'd fallen off one in front of her once while installing a ceiling fan. He looped the fishing line over the nearest branch. "Do you need something, kiddo?"

Aisling didn't answer, and when Ward looked back to the porch, she was gone. Anders, too—presumably sneaking screen time while Ward was occupied. He adjusted the spider's height and tied a knot in the line. Tenn would be so happy when she drove up and saw her spiders, when she saw the skeleton, peeking over the hedge. Ward had been hiding the skeleton in his car all week. They could make it do something new every day—hold a beer, rake the leaves, wield a set of clippers. Tenn would have more creative ideas. They would pose the skeleton together; they would create elaborate tableaus involving lawn chairs and flamingos. Tenn loved that kind of shit.

It wasn't so much that Ward slipped but that the ladder moved out from under him. He had one hand on a crooked bough when the ladder jerked away, and Ward held on tight, trying to kick the ladder back in place with dangling legs. When he looked down, he saw a streak of movement—a rabbit or a squirrel, already gone. He reached out for another branch, but he was too far away, and he went down hard and fast into the ivy.

The ivy was damp and green-smelling, and Ward let himself be enveloped as he lay there, empty of breath. It would've been worse without the ground cover. He looked up at the tree, its branches nearly bare, only a few dead leaves holding on. He didn't think anything was broken, though it was hard for him to breathe. It seemed like a bad idea to try to move.

He yelled once, but the kids were playing video games inside, where they couldn't hear him. Gogo appeared from the porch and licked at his face, until she found something dead beside him and began eating it. Ward reached over to stop her, and when he turned, he saw it—the doll in the ivy, in the same spot where he'd found it back in August. He was still looking at the doll when Tenn pulled up to the house, seeing only the skeleton, the spider dangling by a thread, and got out of her car whooping with delight.

* * *

In the car, Anders suggested an invisible man had moved the ladder.

"What?" Tenn said. She was calm in the driver's seat; she checked her blind spot and changed lanes. When she'd found Ward on the ground, she hadn't hesitated, just loaded him and the kids into the car and started driving. They were already halfway to the hospital.

"Maybe the invisible man took our spatula," Anders said. "Maybe an invisible man broke the living room wall."

"Cow!" Aisling yelled, and slapped a hand against her window. If you saw a horse or a cow on your side of the car, you got a point. If you passed a graveyard, all your points were dead and gone. The kids hated coming home because they lost their points every time they passed Frankie's house. From the passenger seat, Ward listened to the kids count cows. He couldn't make sense of anything else. Maybe the invisible man had locked Mommy in the attic, Anders suggested. Ward had been careful on the ladder, because he'd fallen off a ladder once before. He'd checked it for stability; he hadn't made any sudden moves. He'd been trying so hard not to make the same mistake twice.

In the waiting room, Tenn put Ward in a chair and told him to stay, so he did. His neck hurt, and he was still thinking about the invisible man. He'd been careful with the ladder; he couldn't explain how it had fallen. When Tenn sat, both kids climbed into her lap, arms around her neck like they were strangling her. Aisling asked

Tenn what would happen to the doll. When Tenn had found Ward, on his back in the ivy, he'd been holding it. He'd picked it up because he thought seeing the doll might make Tenn laugh instead of panic when she found him. After Tenn had put him in the car, she'd taken the doll and marched it across the street, where she stuffed it in the neighbor's mailbox.

When they got home hours later, Ward watched Tenn check the mailbox to find it empty.

× × ×

Ward stopped fighting when Tenn said she was going to tie him to the bed.

"Is that a threat," he asked, "or an offer?"

Tenn shook her head and pulled extra pillows from the closet to prop him up. The doctor at the ER hadn't found signs of internal bleeding, concussion, or spinal injury, but Tenn was enforcing bed rest for the remainder of the day.

Tenn perched at the edge of the bed and took Ward's hand. He could see the exhaustion in her eyes, now that the adrenaline had worn off. She'd been scared for him the way he was scared for her. They were bound together by their fear of each other's mortality, creeping closer every day.

Tenn pulled back and looked out the window, toward the hedge.

"What is it?" Ward asked. "Are you mad about the ladder?" Ward didn't like it when Tenn was upset and he didn't know why. He needed to know the reason so he could fix it. She hadn't seemed upset with him, specifically, at the hospital, but if he was stuck in bed recovering, everything else fell on her. When he'd fallen off the ladder before, Aisling had been a baby, Anders a toddler. It had been a lot of extra work for Tenn, and for no reason. *Look, no hands*, he'd called to her, before falling and breaking his arm.

Tenn was watching something outside, and Ward followed her gaze, expecting to see an animal—a turkey, a deer. What he saw was the skeleton perched over the hedge, no longer holding the umbrella. The skeleton was holding a shovel instead. Ward hadn't seen Tenn reposition it when they got home. When he looked back at Tenn, all he could see in her face was worry.

"Did you put it like that?" he asked her.

"Did I put what like that?" she said.

She looked out the window, confused. He wanted her to look out and see what he saw—the skeleton in the yard, the spiders hanging from the tree—all these things they'd wanted, together.

"The skeleton," he said, and pointed. "I set it up holding an umbrella." He'd posed it that way because of the forecast, but the clouds had cleared, and now the sky was blue.

"You don't remember getting the shovel?" Tenn asked, going for Ward's water on the dresser.

There was no time after his fall when Ward could have moved the skeleton; it could only have been Tenn. "Must be my head injury," he said. "Maybe I'll remember better once you nurse me back to health." When she returned with his cup, he took her hand and pressed it against his chest, and she let him. "I'm really sorry I fell. I know it's harder for you when I'm out of commission. What if we watch a movie tonight, and I rub your feet the whole time? I won't even try to seduce you."

Tenn kept her eyes on the skeleton, as if now she didn't trust it. Next he would have to point a camera out the window, to record what was happening in the yard.

"You can seduce me," Tenn said. She was someplace else, even with her hand on his chest. "If you want."

"I do want," Ward said, and pulled her down to kiss her neck.

"The groceries," Tenn said, suddenly straightening. "God, the fucking milk! My car is going to smell like vomit."

Ward lay back against the pillows and listened to Tenn cross the house to the front door. Through the window, he watched her empty her trunk, her arms loaded with more bags than she could comfortably carry. She was halfway down the sidewalk when she stopped and set the bags on the ground. Ward had to get up from the bed to see what she was doing, a pain shooting through his side. Tenn bent over, one arm elbow-deep in a bag on the grass. When she stood, she was holding the doll.

10

"Fuck," Helen said. "Fuck ladders. Fuck real estate. Fuck all of it."

Tenn hadn't told Helen about the job before now, because they hadn't found a good time for a phone call. Helen was always at soccer, at hockey, at a cello lesson. It was hard and getting harder to find an opening in her schedule.

"Yes," Tenn said, in the nicest house she'd ever lived in, inside of which she could fit three of the house where she grew up. "Fuck real estate."

"What are you going to do?" Helen asked. "What did Ward say?"

Tenn smelled the closet around her, the amalgam of old carpet and laundry soap. Sitting in this closet always made her crave apple butter. "He didn't say anything, because I haven't told him yet."

Helen choked on whatever she was drinking. "What the fuck? Why not?"

Tenn lay on her back and looked up at the walls, her eyes adjusting to the dark. This closet had more cracks in its plaster than anywhere else in the house. Upside down, they looked like vines, alive and growing.

"He was all wound up," Tenn said, "after we got home from the hospital. Yammering on about how life is for the living. I didn't want to spoil the mood."

"Hm," Helen said.

Tenn knew what *hm* meant, which was that Helen thought Tenn's answer was bullshit.

"I just haven't found the right time," Tenn said. "First a guy died, then Ward fell off a ladder. I'm going to tell him, obviously."

"Tenn," Helen said.

"I will!" Tenn said. She couldn't tell Helen the real reason she couldn't tell Ward, which was that something was happening around her, with the doll and the skeleton and her skin, that she couldn't explain. She couldn't say the idea of an invisible man was becoming less and less ridiculous to her, that she'd bought sage to secretly smudge the fucking house. She'd been trying to come up with an explanation for the various objects in the house that seemed to be moving around on their own, and she'd been failing. Perhaps one of the kids had developed telekinesis, which could be fun. "I just need to have a plan first. A plan that doesn't involve me fully losing my mind."

"Could one of your neighbors be fucking with you?" Helen said. "If this were a horror movie, weird shit would keep happening until you and Ward were so paranoid you tore yourselves apart, and then it would turn out a creepy neighbor had been watching you through a hole they drilled in your siding and getting off on it the whole time."

Tenn missed watching scary movies with Helen. When Tenn had to put her hands over her eyes, Helen would narrate.

"We've barely met the neighbors," Tenn said. "And the lady with the graves wouldn't come within twenty feet of the house. I can't imagine she has a motive."

"Maybe she wants your house," Helen said. "For the land or something. And she's trying to scare you out of it. There's always an explanation."

"Maybe she thinks the house is cursed, and she's trying to scare us out to save us," Tenn said. "Or maybe I have a brain tumor." She thought she saw a crack grow in front of her—there was only so much pressure a wall could take. She could hear mice scratching, too close. "I could accept that my brain is at fault. Yesterday a woman bumped into me at the grocery store, and I had this moment where, in my mind, I was standing in some European plaza on a hot day. There were tourists; I could smell BO, everything. It's like twenty degrees here, and I swear I started sweating."

"What plaza?" Helen said.

"No idea," Tenn said. "But it was so real to me. There was a herringbone pattern to the brick and a tower with a clock at its base, and I could smell horses. I must've seen it in a movie."

"You're dissociating," Helen said. "Your brain is trying to protect you from despair." She paused. "Knock it off!" she yelled. In the background, Tenn could hear Helen's boys arguing, their pubescent voices, on the cusp of change.

"Ward said we should go on a girls' trip together," Tenn said. "Do you want to run away with me?" In the closet, it was easy for Tenn to imagine herself disappearing, a game of hide-and-seek in which she was never found.

"I'll be right there," Helen said. "I'm teleporting to a European plaza in my mind. Hold on." Helen put the phone down, and Tenn listened to her patiently resolve the nonsense conflict. "For fuck's sake," she said when she came back. "Like we don't have enough problems as it is. Let's argue over fictional characters." There was another burst of whining, the sound diminishing as Helen walked away. "Let's do it," she said. "For real. I'll buy tickets today. The week before Thanksgiving? We're getting drunk on a beach."

"I'll do anything," Tenn said. "I need something to look forward to."

Helen closed a door, and her tone softened. "You have a lot to look forward to," she said. "We're going to run away together. And in the meantime . . ."

The line went quiet as Helen thought about it. In the closet, the scratching came closer, so close Tenn could believe it was coming from inside her head.

"In the meantime?" she asked.

"Talk to Ward," Helen said. "And then you rally because it's not going to feel like this forever, and you know that. Nothing stays the same forever."

"Right," Tenn said. "Sometimes it gets worse." Tenn touched a crack, and the taste of cooked apples flooded her mouth.

"Sometimes," Helen said. "But in your case, I have a hard time seeing how it could get much worse."

* * *

First the contractor came, then the structural engineer. The contractor's name was Edgar, and he was midtwenties, wearing a T-shirt advertising a brand of energy drink, which allowed Tenn to believe that maybe he didn't know what he was talking about. She'd lied to Ward and told him she could stay home for this because Derek was on vacation, and there were training modules she needed to complete.

Edgar measured the fissure in the living room wall as Tenn and Ward looked on.

"I told my wife these old houses get cracks for all kinds of reasons," Ward said. Ward had told Tenn that morning that the contractor would look at the cracks and tell her it was just the house settling, and then she'd feel better. Ward told her this, she knew, because this is what he told himself, because he couldn't admit he worried, as she did, that buying this house had been a mistake.

Edgar ascended the stairs to the bedroom, where Tenn had already pulled the bed from the wall. The cracks were worst behind the headboard, which Ward had decided was a result of vigorous fucking and thus a problem they could not possibly resolve. They would get used to the cracks; you could get used to anything.

"Walls do get cracks for all kinds of reasons," Edgar explained, more to Ward than to Tenn. "Settling is a big one. Sometimes if a house is left vacant for a long time, the lack of climate control can get cracks going. In newer houses, it can be fresh lumber with too much moisture or faulty taping over the drywall."

"But . . ." Tenn said, because a *but* was coming.

"Do you have trouble opening doors and windows?" Edgar said.

"Is that a metaphor?" Tenn said, a joke that didn't land. Then: "The back door sticks. I've had trouble with some of the windows, which at first I thought was because they were painted shut, but they're stubborn." She didn't mention the attic door, the doorstop Ward did not believe, as she did, had disappeared.

Edgar nodded. "Do you have mildew in the basement?" He crossed the room and put a hand on the wall opposite the bed. "You see how this is bowed a little? You have nails popping out?"

Ward stood in the room and stared at the camera over the door, capturing all of this. "We had a thorough inspection before we bought the place," he said. "The previous owner was an architect. He had the house raised and put on a concrete slab. So I suspect some of what we're seeing is signs of an older foundation issue that's already been resolved."

Edgar left the bedroom, studied the angles of the doorframe, opened and closed the attic door. Tenn and Ward followed him back down the stairs to the living room, where he remeasured the fissure in the wall.

"Horizontal crack, over an inch wide," he said. "Cracks on the second floor, cracks extending diagonally from the doorways." He shook his head. He wasn't the owner of the company; he was just the owner's son. Maybe he didn't know what he was talking about. "Yeah, I don't think your issues are resolved at all."

"Is that a metaphor?" Tenn said, even though it wasn't funny.

* * *

The structural engineer had a last-minute cancellation and arrived the same afternoon. Tenn entered a dissociative state as he talked about the foundation. The engineer was into equipment: adjustable joists and jacking, underpinning and hydraulic piers. Ward nodded along, eager to get started. They had a problem, but it was a problem that could be fixed.

Tenn tried not to think about the cost, how they would pay for it. There was only one thought in her mind, and it replayed over and over: they were stuck here now; they were stuck. Tenn hadn't realized until then, standing coatless in the cold as the engineer measured the concrete slab, but she'd been harboring a fist-size hope that everything would fall apart, that Ward would hate his job or Johann would sell the company, and then Ward could cash in his stock options, and they could sell this house and go home. But there was no selling an old house with a fucked-up foundation. The engineer recorded his measurements of cracks that hadn't been there during the inspection. Every option he outlined cost tens of thousands of dollars.

"I'll send a full report," the engineer told them. "With all the recommendations." He had a white mustache that was stained yellow above his lip. "It's a big job, but you'll be preserving a piece of history and all that's in it." He could see the sticker shock on their faces. "It helps to think of it as an opportunity rather than a disaster."

Tenn and Ward stood in silence as the engineer drove away. Tenn had been reading the town historian's book, the one about local ghost stories, about ghost lore. If you had ghosts in your house, the foundation could be an issue. Granite, especially, was a stone that retained energy. If the foundation was leaking, getting rid of excess water could help. Water was a conductor of energy and thus of ghosts. On the flip side, any work on a haunted house could be dangerous. Renovations were known to trigger ghosts, who were notoriously change-averse. You never knew what might happen once you started digging.

"Good thing we have two incomes now," Ward said.

"We don't, actually," Tenn said. She could say it here, outside in the cold, where she felt numb. "I got fired."

"What?" Ward said. She could feel him beside her, studying her in disbelief. She'd been lying to him for days, and he hadn't seen it. "When?"

"A few days ago," she said. "Tuesday." He'd asked about her puffy eyes the day before, and she'd blamed allergies. "All Derek would say was that the position had been eliminated, but it's not hard to figure out why."

Ward turned his attention to the skeleton in the yard, which he'd posed yesterday in the hammock with a fedora over its face. He'd made a list of poses, one for every day of October. His expression was familiar, his face locked.

"Oh," he said, and Tenn braced herself for the argument, for Ward to demand that she explain herself. But he didn't. "We'll have to finance it, then," he said. He couldn't fix Tenn getting fired, nor could he fix her reticence to tell him. But he could fix the foundation. He lifted the skeleton like a bride and carried it to the trash bin. "I'm sure we can get a home improvement loan with my salary. We have good credit."

Tenn watched Ward position the skeleton's hands around the bin, as if it were pushing the trash to the curb. Many of Ward's ideas involved multiple skeletons, a whole skeleton family, which Tenn had not agreed to because of the expense. There was only so much left every month after they paid the mortgage, all their bills.

"But what about the monthly payments?" she said.

Ward walked into the street and shaped his hands into a frame, an auteur composing a shot, then returned to the skeleton and adjusted its position. He couldn't fix their marriage, but he could arrange an aesthetically pleasing tableau. "It's not like we can ignore the problem and hope it goes away," he said. "We'll have to find the money in our budget. What can we cut?"

He asked Tenn this question, because Tenn was the one responsible for their budget, because Ward was too busy with work to manage the bills. But Tenn had tightened the budget to the point where she could barely breathe. They didn't eat extravagant meals or buy designer clothes; Tenn rarely bought anything extraneous at all. She didn't want to pull the kids from their after-school activities. The only frivolous expenditure in the budget was her trip with Helen.

"I can skip the beach," she said. A trip to the beach wasn't necessary; preventing the collapse of their house was.

"No," Ward said. He took one of the skeleton's hands and positioned it over its chest, the place where its heart would be if it had one. "We'll figure something else out."

But Ward didn't know the budget the way Tenn did. It was the only solution that made sense. Ward was posing the skeleton, but Tenn could see he was thinking about something else. Whatever it was, he didn't say it out loud.

"I'm going to look for another job," she said. "Obviously. I can't go on a trip now; it doesn't make sense. And Helen's busy anyway. It was bad timing for her. She just didn't want to say it."

"Tenn," Ward said.

She braced herself again—she hated fighting, but she wanted to have it over and done with. She hadn't told him about the job because she'd been afraid of his reaction, afraid he would minimize it the way he did everything else. "Yes," she said.

"I'm sorry about the job," he said. He was talking to the skeleton, as if there were no difference between Tenn and the dead. "You should still go with Helen," he said. This was what he could give her; he was trying. "You need a break. We can put off the repairs."

"Ward," Tenn said, "there are cracks in our foundation."

Ward turned to Tenn as if he might finally say something real, but the bus pulled down the street, its doors opening with a hiss, to release the kids, who were already fighting.

"Is that a metaphor?" Ward said.

* * *

It was so cold in the bedroom Tenn's first thought when she woke was that the furnace must've died. The ensuing anxiety yanked her out of her dream, leaving the afterimage of blanched wood behind. The dream had been vivid—she and Ward had been together in the backyard, and it was early morning, cool but not cold, wet tongues of grass flicking at her ankles. The yard was strewn with driftwood, like on a beach. She and Ward wandered the bare limbs, tangled like the remains she'd seen in a documentary about elephants, their graveyards of enormous, bleached bones. The driftwood was like that, skeletal, and she and Ward climbed through it together, because they were trapped there. They were there in the yard, and they could never leave.

Tenn closed her eyes and saw the branches more clearly, the limbs imprinted on her vision like a photo negative. Downstairs, the kids were pouring cereal, spilling it on the floor. It was the morning of Ward's appointment for his implant, which their dental insurance would only partially cover. Outside, men unloaded equipment in the yard; she could hear the heavy rumble of the excavator. All they needed was a busted furnace on top of everything else.

The door at the bottom of the stairs opened, and Ward came up quick, without coffee. "Do you know where the gloves are?" he asked. "I checked the coat closet, but they're not in there. It got below freezing last night, and Aisling said they're not allowed to go outside for recess if they don't have gloves."

Tenn sat and held her stiff fingers under her armpits to warm them. "I didn't realize it was going to get so cold," she said. She wanted Ward to touch her, and he did, leaned down to kiss her eyebrow. He could still be familiar, as he had been last night, holding her, his arms all comfort. They could pretend everything was fine, even when it wasn't, over and over.

"Just wait until it snows," he said. He lay next to her on the bed, the tenderness between them their sole source of warmth. "The kids are going to lose their fucking minds."

"You're going to have to buy a snow shovel," Tenn said.

Ward took her hands in his own, and the warming of her fingers registered as pain. "We can get sleds," he told her. "There's a big sledding hill at the town park. That's where people from work take their kids."

"We can make a snowman," Tenn said. In her mind, she could still see the driftwood, caging them in. "We can make a whole family of snowpeople and dress them up."

Tenn eased into the warmth of Ward's body and let the jagged edges of her life soften. They had come here, to this place and this house, for a new start, and it was still happening. Then Ward pulled away.

"What?" she said.

He gave her a second to remember, and when she didn't, said: "Gloves."

Tenn knew she needed to get up, but the cold made it hard to move. The cold and something else, the same fatigue that had been plaguing her, deepened into her joints. She wanted to move, but her body wouldn't cooperate. Then she remembered the end of her dream: just before she woke, she'd realized she was free from the spell, and she walked out of the backyard, leaving Ward and the driftwood behind.

"Are you okay?" he asked her.

Tenn forced herself up, trying to mask the difficulty. Maybe it was a virus brought home by the kids, or a side effect of the antihistamine the dermatologist had prescribed for her dermatographia. "Is there something wrong with the heat?" she asked him. "It's so cold in here."

"I thought we ran out of heating oil at first," Ward said. He opened his dresser and began rummaging, looking for something to pull over his T-shirt. Tenn had unpacked his clothes for him, and he didn't know where his sweatshirts were. "But it's just the radiators. The valves were turned all the way to the right so no steam could get out."

"That's weird," Tenn said. "Did you turn them off?"

"No," he said. He looked up from his dresser. "Did you?"

"No," Tenn said. He moved on to the closet, avoiding her gaze as if she might see something in it. "Did you ask the kids? Maybe they did it because of the noise." Anders had complained that he could hear the radiators at night, that they kept him awake. They sounded like a child sometimes, crying. He could have done it, or Aisling, with the intention of helping him sleep.

"They both swore it wasn't them," Ward said. He was looking at Tenn's wrist. The skin was puffing up in the place where he'd rubbed it, as if she were allergic to him. "Fuck," he said. "Is this still happening? Even with the new prescription?" He pulled on a sweater, still avoiding her eye. "Maybe you're allergic to something they didn't test for," he said. "Something in the dust on the radiators. Something old."

Tenn didn't answer, because she'd vacuumed the radiators, and if the issue was allergies, shouldn't the antihistamine help?

Ward sat again at the edge of the bed, an expectant look on his face. When she didn't respond, he asked gently: "Do you remember where the gloves are?"

"I'll get them," she said. "They're in the attic."

* * *

Tenn found the box of seasonal clothing quickly because she'd organized all the boxes the morning she'd been trapped. Opening the box, she half-expected to see the doll inside. Maybe Ward had known the gloves were there the whole time; maybe he was still playing with her, despite everything. But the doll was gone—she hadn't seen it since the day after Ward's fall, when she'd shoved it in the trash bin just before pickup. Inside the box, Tenn found hats and gloves, swim trunks and water shoes. She gathered the winter gear just before the door at the bottom of the stairs slammed shut.

Tenn stood for a moment in the dim attic and reminded herself that Ward was downstairs, and that she'd removed the latching mechanism from the doorframe. She wasn't trapped, and yet she felt trapped, felt suddenly like someone was in the attic with her, even though she'd come up alone and no one had followed. As she moved toward the stairs, she was gripped by a fear as if by a pair of hands—a fear that when she reached the bottom, the latch would be reaffixed, the door would be closed, and she would be unable to open it. Both the thought and the fear were fleeting. The thought, Tenn knew, was irrational. She couldn't help the way her brain reacted, conspiring against her. But she could ignore it. The door would be unlocked because it was unlockable. A latch couldn't reinstall itself on its own.

Tenn was on the first step when she saw it. Not the doll, but a silhouette—a crisp, black silhouette in front of the attic window. The silhouette was unmoving, head and torso, nothing below. Tenn's heart began to pound—her body reacting before she could think. She could see a silhouette, a shape her brain tagged—immediately and undeniably—as *ghost*.

Tenn froze in place and blinked hard, twice, trying to reset her eyes, her brain. She was free from migraine symptoms—no aura, no pain. But she hadn't had coffee yet, and she'd woken with limbs of driftwood seared into her vision. The silhouette had the same quality, like the darkness that stained your vision after you stared into a light. Tenn turned her gaze to the opposite wall, but the silhouette did not follow, fixed in place in the center of the window frame. She chanced a step forward, and the silhouette did not move. Her brain, once again, supplied an identification—*ghost*. This was a ghost. Tenn couldn't shake the thought, even though this was not how ghosts looked in her imagination, in movies, in books. But that's what it was. A ghost.

Tenn held the gloves and hats in her hands and felt the texture of the yarn, the pilling at the seams, the realness of what was happening. She wasn't afraid, exactly, her mind taut with curiosity, like when she uncovered the first threads of a story she wanted to tell. The silhouette was as stationary as a piece of furniture, and from it Tenn felt no sense of threat. She scanned the room in search of an object blocking the light, a source of shadow or projection. Maybe a previous owner had left a dress form she'd somehow missed. But there was no trick, no mannequin casting a shadow. The silhouette was simply there, in the attic with her. It was revealing itself to her for a reason. She'd read the ghost book from the library with Aisling, the focus of which was on communication. Sometimes a ghost needed to be told that it could leave.

"Hello," Tenn said, keeping her voice low in case Ward was within earshot. She understood instinctively that her volume was irrelevant to the ghost. "Is there something you need?" She looked to her forearms as if the skin might raise in response, but it had calmed in the absence of Ward's touch. Tenn blinked again. She wasn't hallucinating. She didn't have a migraine. She felt more awake and clearheaded than she had in years. She continued, "If you need help with something, I'm here. I'm listening. But if not, you can move on. There's a new family here now. You can go."

The silhouette did not move from the window.

"Can I do something for you?" she asked. According to the book by the town historian, when a ghost did not move on, it was because it had unfinished business. Tenn didn't like the idea of having to exact revenge on a ghost's behalf, but if that's what it took to get their lives back on track, she would become an avenger.

The silhouette provided no answer. It remained before the window as solid as a tree, like it might stay in one place for a hundred years.

"Tenn?" Ward said.

He was walking through the bedroom, and she looked to the bottom of the stairs, to the door, which was still closed. When she looked back to the window, the silhouette was gone. She heard Ward turn the doorknob, the door rattle in its frame.

"Tenn?" he said.

"I'm coming," she said. "I have the gloves."

"Is this locked?" he said.

"There's no latch on the door," she said, which he knew.

"The bus is going to be here any second," he said. "Aisling needs her gloves."

Tenn looked back at the window one last time, even though she could feel, with a twinge of disappointment, that the presence was gone. At the bottom of the stairs, she pushed the door, but it didn't give.

"Let go," Ward said.

Tenn removed her hand from the doorknob and watched it twist from side to side. "I'm not holding it," she said.

"Tenn, come on," Ward said. "It's not funny."

"Do you hear me laughing?" Tenn asked, a panic fluttering in her chest.

Tenn pressed her body weight against the closed door, against a resistance. Wood doors could expand and stick in the doorframe, but she didn't think it could happen this fast. It felt more like someone on the other side was holding it shut. She thought about the silhouette, but it was gone now; she could feel its absence just as she'd felt its presence. The word *presence* stuck in her mind. "Just move," she said. "I'm pushing as hard as I can."

"For fuck's sake," Ward said. "Let go of the door."

From downstairs, Aisling yelled that the bus was outside.

"Tenn!" Ward said.

"I'm trying!" Tenn said. She rammed her shoulder against the door, trying to unstick it, but it didn't budge. "What are you doing?"

"Daddy!" Aisling yelled.

"Come on, Tenn," Ward said, in his voice the same annoyance as when she called him at work. "It's not funny. Open the door."

Tenn hadn't been scared before, but she was now, her whole body suddenly alight with terror. She rammed into the door again, pain jolting her shoulder, but the door was unrelenting, holding her in. Something was keeping her in the attic, and she needed out, away from it, immediately.

"He's leaving," Aisling yelled.

Tenn heard Anders run up the stairs. She couldn't breathe.

"How are we going to get to school now?" Anders said.

The door rattled once more in its frame and then went silent with Ward's resignation. Tenn was unable to imagine what he was thinking, unable to form a single thought against her body's frantic need to escape. She threw herself against the door one more time, and it flew open into Ward's face. Tenn bounced back from the impact and buckled onto the floor.

"Fuck!" Ward said, both hands clutched to his face. A thin stream of blood ran down his chin onto his work pants. "Are you kidding me?"

Tenn looked at Anders, crouched at the top of the stairs. She could hear Aisling, creeping up behind him.

"Go get your backpacks," Tenn told them, "and wait by the door, both of you. I'll drive you to school in a minute."

Anders hesitated, but obeyed once Ward reassured him, through bloody fingers, that he was okay. Ward stared at Tenn with disbelief, like he didn't know her, hadn't believed her capable, until now—just now—of hurting him. Tenn walked swiftly to the bedroom, where she retrieved the box of tissues. Back in the hall, she tried to press one to Ward's nose, but he snatched it from her hand.

"That fucking hurt, Tenn," he said, his voice muffled, nasal. The blood flowed steadily, soaking the tissue. There was no way he'd be able to sit in a dentist's chair now, mouth open, breathing through his nose.

Tenn closed her eyes and replayed what had happened. She'd told Ward she was pushing the door; he'd heard her ramming into it. It had felt like someone was holding the door shut.

"I'm sorry," she said, and she meant it, but she was also angry, furious that Ward could even think that she'd done it all on purpose. "The door was stuck, and I panicked. I was just trying to get out."

"Are you serious?" he said. "The bus was outside. Aisling needed her gloves. Why were you holding the door closed in the first place?"

"Do you think I'm stronger than you, Ward?" Tenn said. She'd been tired for weeks; yesterday she'd needed Ward's help with the groceries, which she'd struggled to lift onto the counter. "I wasn't holding the door closed. I was trying to push it open. You could hear me the entire time." Ward's blood soaked through another tissue, so Tenn reached into the box and conjured a thick pad. Ward flinched when she brought it to his face. "That contractor said doors can stick when there are foundation issues. I don't know what else it could have been. Do you think I was trying to make the kids miss the bus? Do you seriously think I was trying to hurt you?"

Ward turned away from her and looked at the camera in the hall, as if considering what its footage might reveal. Tenn could hear the kids milling around at the bottom of the stairs in their squeaky sneakers. When Anders got anxious, he paced. Tenn tried to walk past Ward, but he grabbed her arm.

"Where are you going?" he said.

Tenn felt a calm settle over her body, as it did in an emergency. She almost liked emergencies—their immediacy soothed her, her cluttered mind. In an emergency, there was a clear order of operations. "I'm taking the kids to school," she said. She wasn't going to fight with Ward right now, when she was so angry. If they fought now, one of them would say something they'd regret. "If I don't take them now, they'll be late."

Ward kept ahold of her arm, and she knew, despite the lightness of his touch, that he was leaving a mark, that her skin would rise in welts the exact shape of his hand, his thick fingers. She would have to keep her arms covered in the school office when she signed the kids in.

Then, from downstairs, across the house, Anders screamed. Tenn's body began to move automatically, as it always did at the sound of a child in distress.

"What happened?" she yelled, rushing down the stairs.

In the living room, Anders was on the floor, clutching his foot, his shoes nowhere to be seen. Aisling knelt beside him, a little hand on his shoulder.

"My foot's bleeding," Anders said. "I stepped on that."

On the floor a foot away, a dulled nail protruded from a floorboard. Anders had stepped on it, the nail puncturing the sole of his foot.

"What happened to your shoes?" Tenn said. He'd been wearing them a minute ago; Tenn had heard him pacing.

"I didn't put them on yet," Anders said, and curled into himself. He was so small still. So small and easily hurt.

"It's okay, baby," Tenn said, kneeling beside him, smoothing his uncombed hair. It was important, when kids were hurt, to model calm. "It doesn't look too deep. We'll get it all cleaned up, and it'll feel better in no time."

Ward circled Tenn to where the nail protruded from the floor. "How could you leave this sticking out in here?" he said. He was trying to suppress it, but Tenn could hear the anger, brimming over in his voice.

She kept her attention on Anders, hugged him upright. She wanted to scream but she couldn't, not in front of the kids. "I didn't leave a nail sticking out of the floor," she said.

"You've been over these floors a thousand times now," Ward said.

"Exactly," Tenn said. "The same floors in this house where you live, too. The same floors you've never checked once for nails. Did you know they can keep popping up after you pound them back in? Of course you don't, because I'm the one responsible. I'm the one responsible for the nails and the gloves and every-fucking-thing else."

She scooped Anders up, even though she was so tired, and carried him to the bathroom, to the toilet seat. From the closet, she took the peroxide and antibiotic ointment and gauze, because this, too, was her responsibility. She poured the peroxide on a cotton ball and gently pressed it to Anders's foot. She'd have to check the date of his last tetanus shot.

"The contractor said sometimes nails pop out when there are foundation issues," she reminded Ward. It wasn't just her; a *man* had said it. "You were there," she said. "You heard him, too. Do you really think I would leave a nail sticking out on purpose?"

Anders was in pain, and he was looking to her for reassurance. Tenn kissed his forehead and told him he was brave, which he was.

Ward stood in the doorway, shaking his head, unspeaking. He didn't cope well with situations that didn't come with easy answers. The pipes gurgled, a human noise, because every part of this house that carried water felt entitled to speak.

"Mommy!" Aisling said.

Tenn looked to the sink, where the faucet trickled gray-brown liquid that smelled like shit. The pipes gurgled again, and putrid water began to rise from the tub drain.

Ward stood in the doorway, wad of bloody tissues pressed to his nose. He looked at Tenn as if this, too, were somehow her fault.

"What do we do?" she said. They'd never had a septic system before. Maybe they needed a plumber, but she didn't know.

Ward shrugged, a problem-solver at a loss as to how to solve the problem. "Call for help," he said.

* * *

Tenn texted Senna, the woman from the library.

> Hi, this is Tenn. We met at the library.
> This is probably weird
> but I need to research my house
> with some urgency

Oh boy, Senna texted.

I'm ALL OVER this
I'm at the land records office like all day every day
Come see me?

Yes, Tenn texted.
Sounds like a plan

* * *

In the kitchen, someone had left the faucet running. Tenn loaded the dishwasher, wiped the counters free of crumbs, scrubbed the lasagna pan left soaking in the sink. The water from the tap took too long to get warm. By the time Tenn was finished, her hands felt like ice.

Gogo licked Tenn's ankle and spotted something under the stove, out of reach. She whined at it until Tenn knelt, used a finger to free the prize—a piece of popcorn—bringing with it a sticky clump of hair and cereal. It was filthy under the stove—Tenn was sorry she'd looked. Now she'd have to move the whole thing so she could clean under it, the mess she couldn't unsee. Gogo rolled to her back and wriggled expectantly, and Tenn rubbed a circle on her soft belly.

"What a good belly," Tenn told her.

She could hear Ward coming down the stairs, but it took him longer than she expected to reach the bottom, like he was walking very slowly, taking his time to avoid her. When she'd come home that morning, after bandaging Anders's foot and taking the kids to school, Ward had been gone. He'd come home after dinner with bruises under his eyes, hugged the kids, and shut himself in his office. Tenn had handled the gurgling pipes herself, called around until she found a plumber who referred her to a septic service. The most likely scenario was that the foundation work had damaged the septic line, which would need to be replaced as well. When Tenn texted Ward this news, he'd responded: k.

Tenn stood in the kitchen facing the door and felt as if she'd done this before, waited for Ward in the exact same spot in the exact same way. Ward had stopped walking, but the door was still closed.

"Hello?" she said. She opened the door.

On the other side, Ward stood with his phone in his hand. His eyes lifted, but he wasn't looking at her.

"Hey," he said, his tone normal, as if nothing out of the ordinary had happened between them. "I didn't realize you were there."

"I was just cleaning up," Tenn said. She'd hurt Ward and she was sorry for it, but she was also furious with him. She was furious and exhausted and heartsick. She turned to the counter, which she'd already cleaned. But when she tilted her head, she could see an oblong spot on the quartz. She took the sponge from the sink and wiped it, again struck by the feeling that she'd already done this.

"I have to be on a call in a few," Ward said. "With the chain-smoking lawyer. I'm going to drive to the gas station and buy a pack of cigarettes if I can't find something to put in my mouth."

He disappeared into the pantry and returned with a tub of pretzel rods, his attention already back on his phone. Tenn studied his face, the bruises blooming under his eyes. There was a problem between them that needed solving, but Ward had opted out this time, choosing instead to avoid it.

Tenn put a hand on the cool counter and felt as if the kitchen were contracting around her. What would happen, she wondered, if she told Ward what she'd seen in the attic, if she tried to explain to him that the silhouette in the attic was tied to the door, to the nail? It was possible she could tell him. She could drive her car into a tree; she could take a knife from the knife block and plunge it into one of their soft stomachs. Anyone could do anything at any time. The oblong spot remained on the counter even though she'd just wiped it. She went back for the sponge.

"I keep wiping this spot," she said. "I feel like I keep doing the same things over and over."

Ward pulled out a pretzel rod and scraped the salt with his teeth, avoiding Tenn's eyes. She wanted him to say something and worried for a moment that his silence would be permanent, that they'd stay there forever, quietly avoiding giving voice to anything real. The trash was overflowing, and Tenn almost asked him to take it out just to have something to say. But she decided to do it herself, an apology. She hated fighting with Ward. She hated knowing he thought the worst of her, but she was so tired, too tired to be the one to make it right.

Ward's phone lit up with a notification, but he didn't touch the screen. Tenn felt suspended, as if they were both trapped in this moment where everything was wrong.

"Can you take out the trash when you get a chance?" she asked him, because she didn't want to be trapped; she wanted to be free. "I've stuffed it down as far as it'll go."

"Yeah," Ward said, distant, on autopilot. "And we're out of little forks. I don't know what the kids were doing with forks today, but they're all dirty."

Tenn tried to remember what they'd eaten for breakfast or dinner, but she couldn't remember any food at all. She looked to the counter, to the spot on the quartz, and when she looked back, Ward was gone.

Tenn stood still in the kitchen, which was quiet for a moment before the footsteps resumed, though it sounded like Ward was coming down the stairs instead of going up. She waited, but it took longer than she expected, like he was walking very slowly, taking his time to avoid her. Tenn stood on the other side of the door and waited. The kitchen felt like it was pulsing, but it was probably just Tenn, her exhausted brain awash with drugs.

"Hello?" she said. She listened, but Ward was quiet. She opened the door, and there he was, standing at the bottom of the stairs.

"Are you okay?" she asked him. She remembered her dream in which they were trapped in the damp, cool yard with the driftwood. There was an early morning feeling now, too, even though it was night and they were inside with the heat on.

"I have to be on a call in a few," Ward said. "The chain-smoking lawyer. I want a cigarette. I haven't wanted a cigarette in years. I need something to put in my mouth."

He disappeared into the pantry and returned with a red box of toothpicks.

"What happened to the pretzel rods?" Tenn asked him.

"What pretzel rods?" Ward said.

Tenn entered the pantry and found the pretzel rods on the shelf. She was pretty sure she hadn't bought multiple tubs.

"Why are you doing this?" she asked. Ward was in the kitchen, staring at his phone. Either he was fucking with her, or he was having a stroke. But his face looked the same as usual, his speech unslurred.

"Doing what?" Ward said.

"Can you take out the trash?" she said, even though that wasn't what she wanted to say. "I've stuffed it down as far as it will go."

"Forks," Ward said in response.

Tenn turned away to the spot on the counter, which she'd wiped, which was still there. When she looked back, Ward was—once again—gone.

Tenn closed her eyes and breathed. She bent her fingers, wiggled her toes. She didn't think she was dreaming. She was awake and her hands were very cold; they felt like ice. She heard Ward on the stairs and waited, but he was slow. She felt trapped in the moment the way she'd felt trapped in the attic, as if she were pushing hard against a resistant force. The stairs creaked.

"Hello?" Tenn said. She listened, but Ward was quiet. She opened the door, and there he was, standing at the bottom of the stairs, looking at his phone.

"Fuck," Tenn said.

"I have to be on a call," Ward said. "Do you have a cigarette?"

"No," Tenn said. "Neither of us has smoked since I got pregnant with Anders."

Her hands were very cold, and she rubbed them together, as if warmth was what she needed to break the spell. In her dream about the driftwood, she'd escaped the yard and left Ward behind. But now she couldn't remember how she'd gotten herself free.

"I need something to put in my mouth," Ward said. He headed for the pantry, but Tenn blocked his path with her body. She didn't know what to do. They couldn't keep replaying the moment over and over. In the attic, she'd escaped by force, hurting Ward in the process. Ward was staring at his phone, so she snatched it away.

His eyes lifted; he was in a daze. "I have a call," he said. "With the lawyer."

Tenn went to the sink, filled a mixing bowl from the drainboard, and submerged Ward's phone.

Ward stood watching but did not move to stop her, to retrieve his phone, to turn the water off. The water was running even though it wasn't supposed to be, with the septic line damaged. The water to the house had been turned off. Tenn didn't know what to do. It felt like some force was trying to pin her there, in the kitchen, to keep her in place. She didn't know how to break free.

"We keep doing this," Tenn said. "We keep doing the same things over and over."

Ward looked at his hand as if it were still holding his phone and tapped at his palm, his wedding ring.

"I have a meeting," he said.

"What's the meeting?" Tenn said. It occurred to her that she'd already broken free of the spell because she was aware of it. She walked out of the kitchen, through the living room, opened the front door and stood out in the cold. Back in the kitchen, Ward was fixed in place, tapping his palm. Tenn could leave if she wanted, but Ward couldn't. She could walk away, but only if she left him behind.

"Tell me what the meeting is about," she ordered.

"You know," Ward said.

"Tell me," Tenn said.

Ward looked at her for a moment, confounded. "A cruise ship," he said, finally.

"What about a cruise ship?" Tenn said. "What happened on the ship? Tell me."

Ward looked like he'd just woken and was trying to remember a dream. "Someone fell," he said. "Someone died?"

"Who fell?" Tenn asked. Ward had told her what had happened; she knew it had affected him more than he let on. He'd watched the footage many times now; she'd heard him on the phone, walking lawyers through it. And now he was stuck in a loop, like the man falling in his video. "Who fell from the cruise ship?" she said.

"It was you," Ward said, his voice like a child's, naming colors or shapes. The water was still running; Ward jabbed at his empty palm. "But you didn't fall."

"No?" Tenn asked, confused.

"No," Ward said. "You didn't fall. You jumped."

The kitchen pulsed but did not get smaller. Tenn listened to the rush of water in the sink. She could feel the counter behind her, pulling at her attention, but she didn't look away, at the spot. Her hands went hot, her palms sweating.

Ward blinked at her. "Why is the faucet on?" he said. "I thought the water was off." He crossed the room to the sink. "Is this my phone?" he asked. He turned off the tap, pulled his phone from the bowl, looked to Tenn for an answer. "What just happened?" he asked.

"We keep doing the same things over and over again," Tenn said. "It's like we can't stop."

PART 2

No feeling is final.

—RAINER MARIA RILKE,
"Go to the Limits of
Your Longing"

11

Ward was at work when the school called. They'd called Tenn first, more than once, but she hadn't answered. Ward didn't have time to deal with the school, because he had four new camera installations in progress, and he'd been in back-to-back meetings all morning. There was a lawsuit involving a fall—black ice—and the insurance company wanted footage from weeks ago. Ward couldn't leave work, not today, not in the middle of everything.

Tenn didn't answer when he called her—not the first time, nor the second, the fourth. Ward sent a text—Pls answer—then stood and paced his office. Tenn had been making two separate breakfasts that morning when he left—eggs and soldiers for Aisling, buttermilk pancakes for Anders, because those were the only breakfast foods they'd eat this week. He didn't think she had plans for the day. Maybe she'd decided to paint the living room—she had a tendency to lose time when she was working, forgetting appointments and meals, forgetting the date, though she hadn't done that in years. He returned to his desk and opened the app for their home cameras only to find all the feeds gone black. The cameras had been taken offline, one by one, just before noon.

From his office, dead feeds on his screen, Ward watched his colleagues—an account manager stirring sugar into an afternoon coffee, a UI engineer leaning in the doorway of a back-end engineer, asking a question. Tenn had been tired; Tenn had been lying. Last night she'd been spooked, claiming he'd been saying nonsensical things he didn't remember. She'd put his phone in a bowl of water, and he'd had to waste part of his morning replacing it. The receptionist was on her phone, a devious smile on her face, glancing up to survey the room. It seemed impossible to Ward that people could be going about their days while he teetered on the edge of a cliff.

At the school, Ward was greeted by the security officer, who asked after Tenn, which surprised him. Inside, he was met by bustling women preparing for dismissal, including a middle-aged secretary whose hair was cut in layers that pointed in every direction, like a signpost.

"Mr. Trevino," she said warmly.

Ward didn't recognize her, but he smiled as she led him to the principal's office. Through the glass wall, he could see Anders, small in a chair made for adults, reading a book with a picture of a door on the cover. On the cover, the door was cracked open, an inhuman hand wrapped around the knob, preparing to reveal what was inside.

* * *

Ward told the kids to wait in the car while he went inside so he could check the state of the repairs. There was a backhoe in the yard behind the house, and Ward could hear it grinding, clawing at the ground, as he walked past Tenn's car, parked out front. One of the workers in the side yard offered a wave.

"Have you seen my wife?" Ward asked him.

The worker shook his head—he didn't understand.

When Ward opened the door, Gogo did not come running to greet him. The house was quiet and still, stuffy, the way it felt coming home after a weeklong vacation.

"Tenn?" Ward said, trying not to play out possibilities in his mind. He was afraid to leave the living room, afraid to take a single step farther into the house. He'd been harsh when she'd hit him with the door, when Anders had stepped on the nail. He'd been harsh, and she'd been lying. If she could go days without telling him she'd been fired, what else could she be hiding? "Tenn?" Maybe she was trapped in the attic again, he thought, before remembering he'd come home yesterday to find the door off its hinges, a baby gate in its place.

Ward advanced slowly through the living room, pausing at the spot where Anders had hurt his foot. Tenn had hammered the nail back into the floor with so much force she'd dented the wood. She'd left the hammer on the adjacent bookshelf, as if she expected it to happen again. The only sound Ward could hear was the backhoe, scraping away at the yard like a gravedigger.

"Tenn?" Ward called again. He needed to look for her but felt rooted in place, unable to move. Tenn was the one who was good in emergencies, who didn't get bogged down by panic. Behind him, the front door swung open, and the kids ran into the living room.

"I told you to stay in the car," Ward snapped.

"But I need to pee," Aisling said.

Anders dropped his coat on the floor, and Aisling her backpack, from which a handful of buckeyes spilled out and rolled across the hardwood floor. At the sound of the commotion, Gogo came running, but instead of greeting the kids, she snatched a stray buckeye and ran off with it.

"Pick those up," Ward said. He needed to keep the kids there, in the living room—this was all he could think. There was still no sign of Tenn, no footsteps in the upstairs hall. "Gogo will get sick if she eats one."

The kids scrambled to retrieve the scattered buckeyes, and Ward left them, his panic overridden by a need to find Tenn before they did. Gogo raced with her buckeye to the kitchen and back again. This time Tenn was just behind her.

"What does she have in her mouth?" Tenn asked him. "Leave it," she told Gogo. Gogo leapt onto the back of the couch like a cat, and Tenn caught her, pried the treasure from her jaws. "Gross," she said, and carried the wet buckeye to the bathroom trash. Ward followed. "You're home early," she said. "And you got the kids?" She paused, tuning in to the kids arguing in the living room. "What time is it?"

Ward watched Tenn turn the water on only to be met with a dry faucet, then wipe her slobbery hands on a towel. She looked the same as she had that morning, only her cheeks were rosy with exertion and she'd put her hair up.

"Where have you been?" Ward said. "I called a million times."

Tenn was looking past him, toward the kids, whose argument was escalating.

"Give it back!" Aisling shrieked.

Tenn shook her head and slipped by him to the kids, entering the living room just as Anders threw a remote at Aisling's forehead. Upon impact, Aisling screamed like she was exorcising something from her body.

"Anders!" Tenn said. Anders bolted up the stairs to his bedroom and slammed the door.

"I hate you!" Aisling yelled, and began to sob.

"Good grief," Tenn said, kneeling before Aisling. All Ward could do was watch. He was relieved—of course he was relieved—but there was also something else, an undercurrent of anger he couldn't reason away. They'd done this before—she'd made him worry like this over and over—and he was so sick of his fear for her. "Let me see,"

Tenn said. She prodded Aisling's forehead, and Aisling flinched. "What was that about?"

"He was taking all my buckeyes," Aisling managed between sobs. "I spent so much time collecting them."

Tenn held Aisling's face in her hands, and Aisling calmed at Tenn's touch. "I'm sorry," Tenn said, and kissed her hair. "We'll get them back; don't worry about it. Let's get something cold for your forehead, okay? And maybe a little treat, too. Would that help?"

Aisling nodded and wiped her nose on her wrist, and Tenn led her by the hand to the kitchen. Again, Ward could only follow, as if everything were normal, as if everything were fine. Everything but Ward's body, awash in adrenaline, which would dissipate and leave him shaky and exhausted.

In the kitchen, Tenn took a bag of edamame from the freezer and handed it to Aisling, who set it on her head like a hat. That's when Tenn noticed the clock. "You *are* home early," she said, turning to Ward. "What happened?"

Ward sat at a bar stool at the counter and watched Tenn go to the pantry and return with a little pink cake wrapped in cellophane. Aisling grabbed the cake and ran off, all misery forgotten.

"The school called you first," Ward said. "You didn't hear your phone?"

Tenn felt her pocket and, failing to find her phone inside, scanned the room. "Shit," she said. "I didn't realize."

She looked to Ward, apologetic, and Ward felt the shame of sitting in the principal's office, as if he were the one who was in trouble. *He clearly needs more support than we've been giving him*, the principal had said.

Now Tenn began searching the kitchen for her phone. "The backhoe," she said. "You wouldn't believe the noise. I can barely think." Outside, the backhoe was still at it, creating a chasm in the yard. Tenn lost her phone a lot; she could never keep track of it. Ward shouldn't have been surprised. And he wasn't surprised, not really. But he was angry.

"I had to leave a meeting to go to the school," he said. He didn't say that she had scared him, that he'd been terrified. "Anders got in a fight."

"A fight!" Tenn said. "What do you mean, a fight?"

Tenn checked the window seat, the pantry, the guest room—her phone was nowhere to be seen. Maybe it was with the spatula, disappeared into the ether, along with the checkbook, the doll.

"What were you doing?" Ward asked her. Tenn opened the refrigerator, as if her phone might be inside. Then he saw it, on the ceiling above the window seat: a camera that hadn't been there before.

"What did the school say?" Tenn asked. "Did you talk to Ms. Lindorf? Did she tell you what happened?"

Ward didn't know who Ms. Lindorf was—a counselor, a teacher. Tenn was the one who usually dealt with the school. She'd installed a second camera over the window above the sink—two cameras positioned to cover the entire room. On the counter, Ward now spotted Tenn's laptop, the drill, a plastic container full of screws.

"Some kid made a joke about his creepy drawings, so Anders threw his thermos at his head."

Tenn sat in the window seat and put her head in her hands. "His thermos?" He'd come home and done the same thing to Aisling. He was doing the same things over and over, which neither of them said out loud. "Is he okay?" Tenn asked him.

"Anders?" Ward said.

"The kid," Tenn said. "Who did you talk to?"

"The principal," Ward said. He couldn't remember her name. "The kid's okay. A goose egg, she said. She gave me a referral. We have to get a diagnosis if we want the school to provide more services."

"A diagnosis for what?" Tenn said.

Ward wanted to ask about the cameras, but Tenn was focused on Anders. By the recycling bin, he now noticed an entire stack of camera boxes, extras from his office he'd brought home for testing.

"The principal was vague about it," Ward told her. "The school can't diagnose kids themself. She just kept saying, 'It starts with a conversation with your doctor.'"

"I'll make an appointment," Tenn said. She reached for her pocket, her phone's disappearance already forgotten.

"Fine," Ward said. He pinged her phone with his own. "I actually have work to do." He was shorter than he meant to be, and Tenn looked up at him with surprise. She didn't ask if he was mad, because she didn't have to. But she hadn't expected it, because in her mind she hadn't done anything wrong, which made him madder. If her phone was making noise, neither of them could hear it.

"Fine," Tenn said, with more hostility than he expected. But it wasn't Ward's fault she hadn't answered her phone.

There was a timid knock on the back door, and Ward opened it to find one of the workers, offering Tenn's dinging phone. He thanked the man and returned the phone to Tenn, who took in the missed calls on the screen. She shook her head. "I thought it was in my pocket," she said. Then she was quiet. There was something else, but Ward didn't know what it was.

"What's wrong?" he asked. He knew that he shouldn't be so angry, or that his anger wasn't really about the phone.

"I wasn't in the backyard today," Tenn told him. "I don't know how it got out there."

Ward looked again at the pile of camera boxes, but Tenn's gaze was on the window, the chewing machinery in the yard. Then she turned abruptly, as if she'd remembered something, and returned to Aisling in the dining room, where she gently stroked the lump rising from Aisling's forehead.

"I'm sorry," Tenn told her. "You didn't deserve that."

In the corner of the dining room, above the china hutch, Ward saw another camera, its shiny black eye.

* * *

Ward was at the bottom of the stairs when he felt Tenn's hand on his forearm. It was cold in the kitchen, but his T-shirt was damp. Across the house, the doorbell was ringing, and Gogo was barking herself hoarse.

"Ward," Tenn said. Her hand was freezing; her fingers felt like ice. "Ward!"

Ward tried to remember what he'd been doing, but his mind was an empty field, populated only with skeletal driftwood. He was holding his phone in his hand. A phone call, he thought. He was supposed to be on a call now, because someone had fallen.

Tenn released her grip but kept watching him.

"Again?" he said. He hadn't believed her the first time, when she told him what had happened, like he'd been sleepwalking. Ward had never sleepwalked before, not once. He skimmed the footage from the bedroom camera most mornings, focused on Tenn rather than himself. He never got up at night, not that he'd seen. He didn't think it was possible to sleepwalk while awake.

"You were talking to me," Tenn said.

"About what?" Ward asked her.

The doorbell rang again; Gogo was going wild. Tenn took a sharp breath and started across the house. This house was spread out—it was a long way to the front door. Delivery people would knock and be back in their vehicles before anyone made it to the door to greet them.

Ward was slow to follow, his body oddly stiff, like he'd just woken from a bad night of sleep. But it was afternoon, and he'd been at his desk. When he reached the front door, Tenn was already outside, talking to a man from the septic company. He looked to be in his fifties, and he was wearing muddy boots, but his hands and coat were fine and clean. This was not a man who'd been digging. This was the man the diggers called when they hit a problem.

Ward grabbed his coat from the hook. Tenn hadn't bothered with hers even though it was freezing.

"If you follow me," the man was saying, "I'll show you what we're looking at."

In the backyard, there was a trench, dug the length of the septic line. But the man was leading them past it, down the hill toward the fence and the garage, where the backhoe was parked. By the backhoe, they met another man, younger, holding paperwork.

"Here's the documentation we have from the town," the older man said, "that shows the leaching field."

Tenn and Ward looked at the map, which showed a line leaving the house, a box the line fed into, then a series of longer lines extending outward from the box. The lines appeared to extend through the field to the right, not this slope where they were standing.

"As you can see, the diagram shows the leaching field over in this flat area," the man said. He pointed in the direction of the field. "Not here."

"Right," Tenn said. She gazed up at the house, at the window in the attic. She looked perfectly comfortable standing in the cold, whereas Ward, in his warm coat, felt his teeth chatter.

"But it turns out," the man said, "the leaching field isn't mapped correctly. You can tell because the ground here is soggy. See?"

He walked them closer to the trench, where another man stood in knee-high boots, smoking a cigarette. The ground was wet, swampy.

"What does that mean?" Tenn said. Ward watched her breath hang in the air and wondered how she wasn't shivering.

"Do you want my coat?" he asked her. Tenn was always the cold one of the two.

Tenn shook her head, barely registering the question, her attention focused on the man, the map of lines.

"It means the leaching field is here, but no one knew about it. And so they drove a backhoe over it, repeatedly, which is probably the reason for the damage."

Tenn looked to the attic again, and Ward followed her gaze. Maybe the kids were up there, playing with the blinds.

"The leaching field is damaged," Tenn said. "So what does that mean? It has to be fixed now, too?"

The man began to outline the process of repair, which boiled down to a lot more digging. Tenn nodded along, her face unreadable. Ward was too cold to be still anymore; he had to move. He walked out into the field, which is when he remembered his dream. Or not a dream, really. He didn't think it counted as a dream if it happened while he was awake. He walked a brisk loop around the empty field until his body began to generate heat. When he returned to Tenn, the man was on his phone.

"Are you okay?" Tenn asked him. She'd been worried about a stroke the previous night, and she studied his face now the same way.

"Are you?" Ward said. He didn't need to hear details to know the work would be expensive. There was no way Tenn wasn't freaking out about the expense, but it wasn't her calm that bothered him most. It was her lack of awareness of the weather.

"What do you mean?" Tenn asked him.

"It's so cold," he said.

Tenn shrugged, as if she didn't mind, as if she was already numb and couldn't feel it. All Ward wanted was to break her out of it, to make her feel what he felt, to feel the same thing at the same time.

"I had a dream," Ward told her. It wasn't really a dream, but he didn't know what else to call it. "We were in the yard, but it was like a beach or something, with all these dead trees washed up, like driftwood."

Tenn began to shiver then, as if the cold had finally penetrated her shell. Ward took her hands in his own to warm them.

He continued, "It was morning, and it was cool and wet, and we were out here, in the yard with the trees. And then I realized we couldn't leave. We were trapped out here. And I said to you, 'We live in the yard now.' And then I woke up."

Tenn turned away from him, and Ward took off his coat and wrapped it around her shoulders. But she was shivering harder now, so hard Ward thought he should take her inside. The septic guy was giving instructions to the man with the papers, trying to mitigate the damage.

"That's weird," Tenn said. She wouldn't look at him.

Then Ward remembered Tenn said he'd been talking to her. "Hey, what did I say to you at the bottom of the stairs?"

Tenn stared up at the attic like she expected to see something, the source of all their problems, but the window only reflected the gray sky. "Did I say you were talking?"

Ward's body buzzed with the same unease he felt when Tenn told him she was fine when she clearly wasn't. He didn't understand why she couldn't just be honest with him. He wrapped her in his arms, to warm her. Despite everything, he still wanted her, warm and in his arms. He wanted her to be familiar again.

"I would live in the yard with you," he said into her hair. "I would build you a tree house. We could live in the yard, in a tree house, and be happy."

Tenn didn't answer, only stood in Ward's arms and shivered.

12

Anders never asked for playdates, so Tenn said yes to the request without question. In North Carolina, they'd had playdates all the time, but Anders had struggled to make friends since the move, increasingly since developing a reputation for launching projectiles at people's heads. Tenn was trying harder now, though, trying her hardest to set their house right. She'd opened every window, vacuumed cobwebs from every corner, scrubbed the floors with scalding water until her hands were raw. Together, she and Aisling had read all the books, poured salt around the property, even though Ward thought it unwise to indulge Aisling's fear that way. Tenn had installed sensors on the doors, which sounded an alarm if one opened in the night; she'd bought amethysts for the kids to keep under their pillows. She'd taken Anders to the pediatrician, again, and to the sleep specialist. She'd bought reams of paper so he could draw what he dreamed, and when he drew monsters, they gave the monsters names that rendered them ridiculous, like Blue Tit McGee and Sunshine Farts-a-Lot.

She was trying.

Now Tenn tidied the house in case Anders's friend's mom wanted to stay, directing herself in the role of good hostess. She made a spread of strawberries and cubed cheese and pretzels; she set out juice boxes in three different flavors. Anders was going through enough—now the anticipation of a visit with a pediatric neurologist who would likely diagnose him with some behavioral disorder, which in turn would mean being pulled from class by new specialists, something his classmates would surely notice. If Anders had a friend, she was determined to help him keep him.

The boy's name was Carter, and his mother appeared at Tenn's door carrying a pigtailed toddler who squirmed in her mother's arms. The mother had left her car running in the street.

"You have my number?" she said, looking back at her car, the driver's-side door wide open. "We have a music class."

Tenn's disappointment was met with an equal relief—she needed to make friends, and yet the thought of socializing made her want to lock herself in the attic.

"I have it!" Tenn told her. "You can text me anytime. I'm going to let them play video games for a bit, and then we're going to make hot chocolate."

She'd already asked about dietary restrictions; she'd made sure Carter's mom knew they had a dog. Carter ran past Tenn without greeting. Behind her, Gogo bleated like a goat, overexcited by the introduction of a new face to lick.

"I'll be back around noon," the mother said with an exhausted smile. She set her daughter down but held tight to her hand as the girl tried to wrench it free. Tenn stood in the doorway until the mother had driven away.

"How do you like fourth grade, Carter?" she asked him.

Carter was fully absorbed in the stack of game discs by the TV. "What?" he said.

"Do you like school?" she said. "What's your favorite subject?"

Carter dropped the discs to the floor, one by one, rejecting them. "PE," he said.

"Mom," Anders said. He gave her a look that felt teenage, that felt like a harbinger of things to come.

"Okay, okay," Tenn said. "I'll be in the other room. If you need anything."

Anders rolled his eyes as Tenn settled in the dining room, close but not too close, hoping only to make it through the next two hours without disaster.

* * *

The playdate was disaster-free right up until Carter's mother texted that she was on her way to pick him up. Tenn had lured the boys away from the game console with a bag of marshmallows for hot chocolate, and then she'd supervised as they ran off the sugar in the torn-up yard. After that: snacks, an attempt to play a board game Carter deemed stupid, then the boys disappeared into Anders's room to look at Pokémon cards.

Tenn sat briefly at the table and took in the crumbs they'd left behind, the game pieces on the floor, the empty mugs and their sticky rings on the tabletop. Ward had delivered coffee to her bedside that morning before reporting that he had a dinner meeting and would be late tonight. But she was so tired. Her doctor had checked her thyroid, tested for anemia and Lyme. She was trying. But either nothing was wrong with her, or something was wrong that hadn't been detected yet. She closed her eyes and listened to the boys yelling at Aisling to stop looking at them.

Then, from upstairs: a crash that shook the house's old bones.

Tenn's first thought was Anders's bookcase, secured to the wall, a wall in this house that was deteriorating around them. She was up the stairs quick, racing through the hall—that's why it seemed like a blur, why she ignored the black blur of a silhouette by the hall window. Her mind registered its presence, but it seemed insignificant, dwarfed by her fear for Anders, for his friend.

In Anders's room, the bookcase was upright, but the contents of the shelf above it were on the floor—board games, several puzzles, a basket of magnetic building tiles, the bin of Pokémon cards.

"You have to help!" Anders was saying. He was red-faced and teary, looking to Tenn in frustration. "He knocked everything on the floor, and now he won't help me clean it up. We have to clean up our own messes in this house!" he told Carter, repeating words Tenn had uttered a thousand times. In the doorway of her adjoining bedroom, Aisling toed the threshold, clutching her stuffed *Lactobacillus*.

"Carter, did you knock these games onto the floor?" Tenn asked. She was aware of her breathing, keeping it controlled, because a fear stirred inside her of what might happen if she got mad. The silhouette in the hall was there for a reason, a reason that was unclear to her. She turned to the window, but nothing was visible now other than a bare tree on the other side, a hawk on a branch in the cold sun.

"This isn't my bedroom," Carter said. He avoided eye contact with Tenn. He knew his mom was on her way, knew exactly what he could get away with. "I don't have to clean someone else's bedroom."

Tenn thought of the meditations she did with the kids and imagined herself sitting on a rock in the middle of a stream. She visualized her frustration floating past her, dead leaves on the water. The exercise felt necessary, as if anger on her part might have unintended consequences. She wasn't sure where this feeling came from—she wasn't a yeller; she rarely lost her temper. Aisling looked past her, through Anders's room into the hall, where the light flickered.

"Still," Tenn said, "if you made the mess, the kind thing to do is help clean it up." She got down on her knees, showing Anders she was helping. "We can all work together until your mom gets here."

Tenn felt an outsized urgency for Carter's mom to arrive, to take this kid out of her house and away from her. She swept Pokémon cards into a heap with her hands.

"I don't want to help," Carter said.

Anders slid an empty puzzle box across the floor. "What if we race?" he asked, a trick he'd learned from Tenn, making cleanup fun. "Look, this one's my favorite." The puzzle was one he'd picked himself—a five-hundred-piece broccoli floret.

"God, you're such a freak," Carter told him. "Leave me alone!"

Tenn took the puzzle box and watched Anders, who was visibly trying not to cry. But he hadn't thrown anything at Carter's head, an unexpected but welcome show of restraint.

"Well," Tenn said, "we all make choices, and I don't think you're making the choice to be a good friend right now." She locked her most loving gaze on Anders. "I'm going to help you with this," she told him. "I know you didn't make this mess, and you don't have to clean it up on your own."

"Whatever," Carter said, and nudged an island of Pokémon cards with his foot. Tenn gathered more puzzle pieces—hornet's eye, scorpion's tail—tamping down her disgust.

Then Anders said, "What's wrong?"

Tenn looked up to see Aisling, frozen between bedrooms, staring past them at the hall.

Carter lifted his gaze from the floor. "What is that?" he said, and barked out a laugh full of terror.

Good, Tenn thought, a petty impulse rising, at the sound of fear in Carter's voice. She didn't know what had scared him and allowed herself the small hope it was a plastic skeleton, a decorative spider Aisling had dragged down from the attic as a prank. When she turned to look at the hall herself, she saw nothing other than a beam of sunlight streaming in, and Gogo, lying in the pooled light like a cat. Carter backed away toward Aisling's room, and Aisling stepped aside to let him through. Once in Aisling's room, though, Carter screamed.

"Carter?" Tenn said, up and off the floor so fast it felt like levitating. The lights in the bedroom flickered. She didn't know what was happening, only that she was responsible.

But Carter was faster, running from Aisling's room back through Anders's, through the hall and past the window, through Tenn's room and Ward's office, and then she heard the sickening thumps as he fell down the Murder Stairs, like a pumpkin plopping step by step. In the presence of a true emergency, Tenn's fear fell away, and she followed to the top of the stairs. There were silhouettes packed around her—lining the hall, crowding her bedroom—an audience gathered to watch this accident unfold. Tenn kept her back to these onlookers, as if they'd been there all along, as if their presence was inconsequential. Carter lay at the bottom of the staircase, whimpering.

He was still conscious, at least, Tenn thought, floating in a cloud of calm, staying inside it lest she found another feeling that made things worse. The doorbell rang, and Gogo barked, and Tenn descended the stairs and knelt by Carter's side.

* * *

When the paramedics had gone, Tenn texted Senna, loaded the kids in the car, and drove to the town historical society, located in a former meeting house once used by state delegates in the aftermath of the Revolutionary War. She was afraid to be in the house now, afraid to keep the kids there. A small woman in her seventies wearing a fleece vest and neon running shoes greeted Tenn at a table with a cash box awaiting her donation. Tenn never carried cash but opened her wallet to find a twenty, which she handed over with something approaching abandon. If twenty dollars could buy her an answer to what was happening in her house, it would be a bargain.

Tenn had already researched, with Senna's assistance at the land records office, the house's line of ownership, just after she installed cameras in every room that didn't already have them. She hadn't told Ward about the visit, just as she hadn't explained about the cameras. Ward seemed determined to ignore this particular problem, so Tenn would have to solve it in his stead.

Senna wasn't far behind, wearing a pink sweater with a bouquet of knit flowers sprouting from the breast pocket. When she hugged Tenn hello, Tenn smelled sunscreen and mango again, and remembered sitting on a vinyl car seat on a summer afternoon. Or not remembered, maybe. There was a specificity to it that didn't belong to Tenn, the happiness and longing, the quality of the sunlight and the color maroon. A coming-of-age film she'd seen once, but a tragic one—Tenn's memory of it surrounded by a catastrophic aura.

Tenn introduced Senna to the kids as Aisling roamed the room. On the meeting house walls, there were stained photographs: a stone chapel, cows in a field, the largest mound of hay Tenn had ever seen. A row of men in dark shirts standing close but not touching. From across the room, she'd mistaken them for silhouettes.

"We read her aunt's book," Tenn told Aisling as she curtsied before Senna. "The ghost book?"

Aisling beamed, starry-eyed at the mention of her new favorite author. Aisling was especially interested in the part of the book on banishment spells. But spells, the book cautioned, should only be used if you were sure what kind of spirit you were dealing with.

"What's a meeting house?" Aisling asked.

Aisling had been the one to let Carter's mom inside, while Tenn knelt beside him, already on the phone with 911. Tenn was good in emergencies, good with other people's pain. Carter's mom wanted to drive him to the ER herself, but Tenn convinced her to wait for the paramedics, because they didn't know if he'd hurt his spine and shouldn't move him on their own. Carter cried when he saw his mom but settled as they waited, as Tenn iced his visibly broken arm, as she pressed a dish towel to his hip where it was bleeding. He asked for a cookie, but she explained that he might need anesthesia and therefore shouldn't eat. There was an ease to it, as if Tenn had played out the scene before, as if she were rehearsing to do it again.

"A meeting house is really just a church," Senna explained. Worn benches lined the room, like pews. "They called them churches first, at the beginning of the eighteenth century, but then people were afraid of ascribing sacredness to a building."

"You don't want a building getting ideas," Tenn said. Senna raised an eyebrow.

Tenn pulled out her notebook, which contained the names on the deeds to her property going back to the mid-1700s. If ghosts were real—and Tenn was proceeding now as if they were—then she needed to know who'd lived and died inside her house. "Elbert and Cornelia Fountain," she said. "Are those names familiar?"

"The Fountain family was prominent in town for a long time," Senna said. "Do you know Fountain Street?" Tenn shook her head. "Near the library? We've had a couple Fountains as town supervisors." Senna made a face, searching her memory. "I don't think I've heard of Elbert and Cornelia, though."

Senna crossed the room and began paging through a clothbound book with a broken spine.

Tenn followed and pulled her own dusty book off the shelf. This book was about graves—there were two cemeteries in town housing Revolutionary War soldiers—including photos and inscriptions from the headstones. *Death is a debt to nature due*, Tenn read, *which I have paid and so must you*. Sitting beside Senna, the aura returned—Tenn could taste mango, feel hot vinyl under her thighs, and then an intense pressure broke across her nose, like she'd been hit.

"Jesus," Senna said. She put down her book and rushed for a box of tissues as Tenn touched her face, brought her fingers away wet with blood. Across the room, Anders watched without moving, as if he was afraid anything he did would make it worse. Aisling sat beside him and put a hand on his, the two of them knit together by their impotence and fear.

"What happened?" Senna said, returning with the tissues.

Tenn took a wad and held it to her nose. She didn't know how to make sense of anything happening around her. The room went murky, like during a migraine, though she had no other symptoms.

"I don't know," Tenn said. She looked down and read: *Remember you must shortly be / Laid in the dust to sleep with me.* "I had this weird memory of sitting in a car in the summer, and I could taste sunscreen and mango, and then it felt like something slammed into my face."

Senna's demeanor changed—she moved back through the pews, putting space between her and Tenn. She was looking at Tenn the way Ward had when she'd hit him with the door, like he was accusing her of something.

"Can you still taste it?" Senna asked. "The mango?"

Tenn searched her mouth, but both the sunscreen and the mango were gone. She shook her head. Maybe there was something in their well water, untested for by the lab, eating holes in their brains. Maybe Carter had drunk the water, too. "Sorry," Tenn said. She swapped out her tissues; the bleeding slowed. "I don't know where that came from. I can't even eat mango. I'm allergic."

"Has that happened to you before?" Senna asked.

"I never get nosebleeds," Tenn said.

"That's not what I meant," Senna said.

"What *did* you mean?" Tenn said, though it was clear in Senna's expression that she didn't want to say in front of the kids.

Senna returned to her book with renewed interest. "Okay, the Fountains, the Fountains. Here we go. Elbert and Cornelia Fountain."

She read for a minute, her expression changing from intrigue to concern.

"I'm optimistic based on the faces you're making," Tenn said. *Were they silhouette artists?* she wondered. *Did they have a gruesome accident in the attic?*

"Elbert Fountain was the black sheep of the family," Senna said. "His father and brothers were all dairy farmers, but Elbert wasn't into cows, I guess, and instead started his own cobbling business, which wasn't uncommon for farmers at the time. In the winter, they'd go from house to house, staying long enough to make or repair whatever shoes people needed."

"Shoe repair," Tenn said. It wasn't what she'd imagined, but a cobbler could die inside his house as easily as anyone else. Aisling had found a candy bowl and offered Anders a mint, which seemed to ease his anxiety. Tenn was filling Ward's role as problem-solver, and now Aisling was filling Tenn's role, doing the mothering. Maybe next Anders would take over for Gogo and shit on the rug. All of them were outside themselves, playing someone new. Even Ward, who'd taken the role of a stranger.

"Huh," Senna said. She was quiet as she continued reading.

"Did they die?" Tenn asked. She couldn't ask what she really wanted, which was did they die in a manner that would require them to walk her attic for eternity as silhouettes, communicating with the living through skin writing and a decrepit baby doll.

"They definitely died," Senna said. She looked at Tenn like she was about to deliver bad news. "Elbert Fountain got caught in a historic blizzard," she said. She turned the book around to show Tenn the photo: a barn with snow blown in a drift to the top of its door. "He was on his way home from a cobbling job. Cornelia went out looking for him. They were found a week later, a few hundred feet apart, frozen to death."

Tenn imagined her and Ward that way, trapped in the yard in the snow, searching for each other blindly even though they were nearly close enough to touch. They'd already done it, in their dreams, only Tenn had escaped and Ward had not. She could almost feel it now, the cold in her body, a painful cold that gave way to a comforting numbness.

"She'd left the kids alone," Senna said. "The oldest was eight, the youngest an infant. The kids survived by eating salted pork and jars of apple butter. After Elbert and Cornelia were found, the kids were sent to live with Elbert's brother, Jeremiah, a gentleman farmer. His farm eventually became the town park."

Senna turned the page to a photo of Jeremiah Fountain, sitting in a rocking chair with a toothless grimace. His hat hung off a hook behind him, but at first glance, it appeared to be hovering, worn by an invisible companion. In her own book, Tenn read another epitaph, this one for a four-year-old girl: *It is pretty, she exclaimed / Before her spirit took flight.*

"That's not what you wanted to hear," Senna said.

Tenn considered the fact that people not dying in her house was bad news. She'd already read about the subsequent owners on an ancestry website—Thad Crawford, the son of a Revolutionary War sergeant, who owned land all over town, and his wife, who was referred to only as "Miss Kate," a schoolteacher. They eventually relocated to one of their other properties, where two of their children died of smallpox. After the Crawfords, the house was owned by a couple named Mr. and Mrs. Poor who'd ironically sold their dairy farm for a bajillion dollars as the town began to transition from a farm community to a weekend getaway for wealthy New Yorkers. Tenn hadn't found any indication that the Poors or anyone who'd owned the house after them had died there.

"How can no one have died in the house?" Tenn asked. She'd never believed in ghosts, and the fullness of her conversion scared her. It would be easier if she were crazy, but she'd been to the neurologist.

The neurologist's name was Dr. Khan, and he looked like an aging movie star—floppy hair and a boyish smile. He asked without judgment about drug use, about head injuries and carbon monoxide. He asked about Tenn's memory and tested her hand strength and reflexes, observed her gait. Amongst the tests he ordered was an MRI, and the technician who performed it talked to Tenn in soothing tones as she lay inside the giant washing machine, trying not to move.

She'd been in the school parking lot when Dr. Khan called with the results. When he told her that her brain was beautiful, she'd put her head on the steering wheel and cried.

Tenn wasn't having a stroke or developing a brain tumor; she'd simply learned a new fact about the world and its workings, a concept she couldn't comprehend before she experienced it herself, like the love she felt holding each of her children for the first time. It was like discovering the never-endingness of the universe. Even if she couldn't comprehend the physics, the universe still went on and on.

Aisling had sidled up to Senna and now stood by her side, waiting to be called on.

"Yes?" Senna said.

"Have you ever seen a ghost?" Aisling asked her.

Senna shook her head. "I wish," she said. "You know how some people have super-sensitive noses?"

Aisling looked at Tenn, whose sense of smell was so keen there was no lying to her about brushing your teeth or washing your armpits. They both nodded.

"It's like that," Senna said. "Most people can't see them. My aunt has, but only a few times, and she's spent a lot of time looking. It's a rare sense, plus they have to want to be seen, my aunt says. According to her, it takes a lot of energy to be seen, which means they flicker, so even if they *do* want to be seen, you have to look at the exact right time."

Aisling seemed satisfied with this answer, but she wasn't done with her questions. "Have you ever felt one in a room? Have you seen one move things?"

Tenn jumped in before Senna could answer, because no one in her household needed additional reasons for nightmares.

"Ghosts don't have bodies," she told Aisling. "So they can't hurt you." She didn't believe this was true—her silhouettes had already hurt a child, after trapping Ward at the bottom of the stairs. It was spreading. But she couldn't put that fear on Aisling.

Aisling rolled her eyes and moved closer to Senna, her ally. She trusted Senna to tell her the truth. "Do you believe that?"

Senna looked at Tenn, asking permission, which Tenn granted with a nod, realizing in that moment that she trusted Senna, too.

"Here's what I believe," Senna told Aisling. "Spirits are a form of energy. Sometimes spirits are in bodies"—she gestured at her own body like a game show model demonstrating a prize—"and when we die, our spirits leave our bodies and continue on. But a spirit outside a body is still a form of energy, and energy is defined by its ability to affect matter. Heat, for example. Heat is a form of energy, and it can change water to steam. Right? And spirits are the same."

"I'm a spirit, too?" Aisling said. The idea seemed to cheer her. Across the room, Anders curled over a map, his mouth so full of peppermints Tenn worried he'd choke.

"You sure seem like a spirit!" Senna said, and Aisling, in response, performed a spirit dance, twirling around the room.

Senna put a hand on Tenn's knee, and the taste of mango returned to her mouth, intensified. It reminded her of her grandmother, the scent of her lotion, the sweetness of it. Maybe everyone was haunted, in a way, by memories, by fragments of songs and books and films they saw once and thought they'd forgotten.

Or maybe Tenn was different, a possessor of a rare sense.

Outside, the world was darkening—it was getting close to dinnertime; Tenn would have to take the kids home and feed them. She would have to explain Carter's fall to Ward. She thanked Senna and gathered their things. On the wall by the door, there was a photo of two trees, growing so close their branches were intertwined.

"They're called Mr. and Mrs. Trees," Senna told her. "Those ones are at the top of Post Road. They were planted to mark a wedding. They're almost three hundred years old. People still do it sometimes, but it seems like a bad idea with the divorce rate, you know? Do you really want to live in a world where your wedding trees grow and grow while your own marriage fails and then you die?"

Tenn studied the trees. One of them looked like it might have the same blight that took out their birches in North Carolina.

"I'm wary of anything that goes on past death," Tenn told her.

* * *

When Ward got home, Tenn was on the couch, alone with a hefty glass of scotch. The scotch had been a gift from Johann, expensive enough that Ward had been saving it for a special occasion. Ward didn't say anything when he saw her, just passed through the living room and went upstairs to unload his bag. He hadn't responded to Tenn's initial texts about Carter—he'd been in a meeting—finally answering the third time she called. There wasn't anything he could do, though, and they both knew it—Tenn was alone with the paramedics, alone to deal with Carter's mom, their homeowner's insurance. Ward had a meeting, then more meetings, a dinner. She could smell cigar smoke on his clothes as he passed through.

"How bad is it?" he asked when he finally joined her with his own glass.

"One arm is broken," Tenn said. She'd been texting with Carter's mom all day. "The other is sprained at the wrist. Concussion and a lot of bruises. No internal bleeding, though. No spinal injury."

"Thank God," Ward said, and drummed his fingers against his glass. "What did his mom say?"

"She was pretty shaken up," Tenn said, "when she first got here."

"I mean, to show up for your kid and find them crumpled in a heap at the bottom of someone's stairs . . ." He looked at her like he was waiting for her to explain, but she couldn't tell Ward that Carter had made her angry and, as a result, the ghosts had punished him. She was too depleted to translate her experience into something believable.

"She's calmer now that she knows he'll be okay," Tenn said. "She's mostly confused. I guess Carter keeps telling people he got scared because the house was full of Black people."

"Black people?" Ward said. He took a big drink of his scotch, drummed his fingers against the glass.

The lights in the living room flickered, as they had in Anders's room, when Carter made her upset. Tenn had played dumb when his mother asked about what he claimed to have seen. Ward drummed his fingers again, a repetitive action.

"Something spooked him," Tenn continued. "The kids can tell you. He ran in one direction, turned around, ran the other. We were all in Anders's room, and then he was gone." She paused, considering her language. "He looked like he'd seen a ghost."

"A ghost," Ward said.

Tenn drank the scotch, which was making her relaxed and warm, which was good, because she was afraid now of what would happen if Ward upset her. She'd been upset with him, too, the night he'd gone looking for a cigarette, returning over and over to the bottom of the stairs. She'd been upset because he believed her capable of hurting him.

"What do *you* think scared him?" Ward asked her. Tenn could tell as he asked this he suspected someone in the house was to blame.

Had Anders been a creep? Had Tenn graduated to terrorizing fourth graders? The light in the living room flickered, and Ward craned his head toward the lamp, as if the source of the problem might be external, visible.

"It's been doing that," Tenn said.

"That doesn't answer my question," Ward said.

Tenn imagined herself turning ghostly, translucent, disappearing into her surroundings. It was the only way she could think to keep the ghosts at bay—if she disappeared.

"There wasn't anything on the footage," she said. She'd watched it twice before sending it to Carter's mom. The cameras hadn't captured the silhouettes, only a terrified boy running full speed at a staircase.

"That also doesn't answer my question," Ward said.

"What's the question?" Tenn asked.

"What do you think scared him?"

Tenn's forearms were uselessly quiet, the ghosts leaving her to clean up their mess on her own. If she told Ward the truth, he'd think she was crazy and she'd get upset, and who knew what would happen. But she saw the way he looked at her, when he left her in the mornings, when she repositioned one of her cameras. When she wielded a knife, slicing apples for the kids.

"I can't tell you what I think," she told him.

"Why not?" Ward asked. He drummed his fingers, and Tenn wanted to slap them.

"Because you won't believe me," she said.

Ward looked at the wall, not at Tenn. It was covered with a plastic sheet to keep the dust from getting everywhere, and it was billowing slightly, as if, inside the wall, something were breathing. "What does that mean?" he said.

Ward playing dumb made Tenn even angrier. She took a slow breath, tried to cool the simmer in her chest.

"It doesn't matter," she said. She could tell him the truth, but she'd still be alone with it. Nothing she said would change that.

"It doesn't matter that a kid nearly died in our house today?" Ward asked. "It doesn't matter?"

Tenn refused to meet his eye, refused to accept another accusation. Ward would watch the footage and see for himself—what spooked Carter wasn't visible.

Ward shook his head. "Black people." He was already distrustful of Tenn's mind—whatever she said now would only reinforce that. It was liberating, in a way, to be doubted, to know anything she said would be subject to the same filter.

"They're not people," Tenn said. She knew she shouldn't have said it, but she was so tired of Ward's derision. "I've seen one before, in the attic. But there were more this time."

Ward watched the wall like something might emerge from the rift.

"I researched shared hallucinations after I got the kids to sleep," she told him. "They call it folie à deux."

"'Madness of two,'" Ward translated.

"Apparently shared psychotic disorders are only a thing when you have a close relationship with someone," Tenn said. "Like if I thought aliens were real and hallucinated being abducted, you might have the same experience."

"Or not," Ward said. Ward hadn't seen any ghosts, which he didn't need to say. Maybe they weren't close enough, Tenn thought, but also didn't say.

"We should have the well checked again," she said. "And the house, for carbon monoxide."

Ward drummed his fingers, shook his head, his disbelief playing out the same way, over and over. "Sure, Tenn. Carbon monoxide."

Tenn finished her scotch, rose from the couch.

"Where are you going?" he asked her.

"Why bother talking if you don't believe anything I say?"

"How am I supposed to believe anything you say when you're saying things that sound crazy?" Ward said.

Tenn burned with fury and needed to get away from it, to sit in the upstairs closet where it was quiet and dark, where no one could upset her and make the house more dangerous. But she couldn't disappear now. It wasn't about her alone.

"Aisling saw them, too," she said, and felt as if there were an elevator inside her, descending. "Aisling saw them, but Anders didn't." She didn't mention what Aisling had told her, after they'd left the meeting house and come home.

She watched Ward take this in—one hand clenched around his glass, the other knuckled against his forehead. Then he emptied his glass and drummed his fingers. Tenn imagined herself into a lake—calm water all around, her anger sinking through it, like a body. There was no way to convince Ward that what she'd experienced was real. The only thing she could do was protect him from the consequence of upsetting her.

"I want to go to Helen's," she told him. She hadn't talked to Helen about it, but Helen would say yes; Helen would put a pitcher of flowers by Tenn's bedside.

"Helen's," Ward repeated.

"For Thanksgiving," Tenn said. "For a break." It didn't have to be Helen's—she could go anywhere. She just needed to get away from Ward and the kids, so they'd be safe.

"I have to work Thanksgiving week," Ward said, which Tenn knew. They'd already ruled out the possibility of traveling.

"I know," Tenn said. "I can take the kids with me if you want." She offered though she had no intention of taking them with her, to soften what came next. "But I think it would be better for them to stay here with you. Their first Thanksgiving in the house." The lights flickered; Ward drummed his fingers against his glass. "The grocery store does a whole turkey dinner to go," she said. "I can order it for you. All you'd have to do is reheat it."

Ward drummed his fingers; the lights flickered, and Tenn tried not to see shapes in the hall. They'd been lurking all evening, in doorways, in corners, like cats that only came out when you stopped looking. She could feel Ward's resentment as he sat there, turning it over. He believed she was capable of hurting him, of hurting the kids. And maybe he was right. If she left or if she stayed—she would hurt them either way.

Ward drummed his fingers for so long Tenn almost shook him to make it stop. "Fine," he said, finally. The lights went out and stayed that way, and in the darkness, Tenn thought Ward might reach out and touch her. But they were too far apart. The lights came back on, and he gazed at her like she was a stranger. "Fine," he said again. "You clearly need a break. We'll fend for ourselves."

He got up and left the room, and Tenn wasn't sure if he was getting a refill or removing himself from the conversation until he didn't come back. She was content that the drumming had stopped. In the kitchen, she poured another scotch to blunt the impact of his easy agreement. Or maybe she drank the scotch because it made it more likely she'd lose control—she wasn't sure anymore. She drank and the lights went out again, and she stood there in the dark, alone, thinking about what Aisling had said.

After they'd come home from the meeting house, Anders had returned to his room, docile, to pick up puzzle pieces. That's when Aisling took Tenn by the hand.

"I saw them," Aisling told her quietly.

"You saw them?" Tenn said, and scanned the room. The silhouettes had gone, and with them taken Tenn's sense of safety. Whatever was happening to her couldn't happen to Aisling, too. "Have you seen them before?" Tenn asked her.

Aisling looked to the hall, as if she was worried about being overheard. She nodded.

"Was it that many?" Tenn asked her. "Have you seen a lot of them, all together like that, before?"

Aisling shook her head. "Not like that," she said. "They don't usually work as a group."

"What do you mean *work*?" Tenn said. "What were they doing?"

Aisling tugged Tenn's hand, and she leaned down so Aisling could whisper the answer into her ear.

"They were eating you."

13

On her laptop in the kitchen, Tenn paged through open tabs: the camera feeds for the attic, the primary bedroom, the downstairs hall, where the electrician and his assistant aimed flashlights inside the wall. If she watched long enough, surely something would reveal itself. The electrician had found knob-and-tube wiring in the living room, and now he was tracing it to see how far it went. It wasn't necessarily a hazard, knob-and-tube wiring, unless the wires had been spliced. Upon inspection, they discovered the wiring had been spliced at least twice over the years, which meant it would all need to be replaced. The wiring itself would cost over ten thousand dollars, not including the repair of the walls, which would cost thousands more. Tenn had come to accept that the house was the only thing they would ever spend money on, and that she would live there forever, her chance of escape dwindling with each new disaster. She could imagine herself as a ghost in her own home. It was the easiest thing in the world to imagine.

Tenn opened the schedule of flights to North Carolina, the live feed for the local wolf conservatory. One of the wolves had recently died, and his littermate now refused to come out of her den. In the attic, light came through the blinds in shivers. Tenn could remember the exact shape of the silhouettes, but she couldn't make them appear at will.

A notification popped up in her browser, a friend request from a high school classmate whom Tenn had never been friends with in the first place. She clicked on the profile—the man's name was Ricky Jefferson, and he looked like a meathead, shaved head, bare bronzed chest shiny with oil. She closed the profile, ignoring the request. All she wanted was to watch the world on a screen, to remove herself one big step from her life. This was the problem with her work, her filmmaking—her reluctance to let herself be part of the story. The filmmaker was always part of the story, whether they wanted to acknowledge that or not, but Tenn loved documentary because she was interested in other people's stories, not her own.

Tenn switched tabs, restless, landing on the live feed from a public library in Idaho, which touted itself as haunted. But there were no ghosts to be seen on the library's Ghost Cam. She closed the tab and switched to the local news website for her hometown in Pennsylvania. They had live cams around town for traffic and weather, and Tenn scanned the highways before clicking on the feed for the skate park. The skate park was on the same road as the high school, a long, flat stretch where the speed limit was too high, where late at night bored teenagers would race. Tenn watched traffic pass for a few minutes before she realized she was watching the exact spot where Crystal had died.

In the attic, the light softened, dampened by a cloud. In the hall, the electrician's assistant scratched his ass. So far, inside the walls, they'd found newspapers ranging from the 1920s through the 1970s, a tin of camphor hand cream, a snake skin, and a single black lace-up ankle boot, the leather's sheen hidden under a hundred years' worth of dust.

The electrician, whose name was Dan, had been eager to show her. In the olden days, he'd said, people hid shoes to ward off spirits.

At the wolf conservatory, a deer carcass was delivered over the fence, and the other wolf in the enclosure fell on it with snapping jaws. Feast or famine—that's how wolves ate, their survival marked by extremes. Still, the grieving wolf did not emerge. In Tenn's hometown, a car slowed by Crystal's tree, then sped up again.

There was a knock at the doorway between the dining room and the kitchen. It was Dan, the electrician.

"I'm going to need to cut the power," Dan said. "While we start removing the old wiring."

"That's fine," Tenn said. She needed to stop staring at her computer anyway. She needed to leave the house, to touch grass and call Helen and make plans.

"The wires in the wall," he told her, "now that the walls are open—you don't want to mess with them. You want to keep the kids from getting in there. Dog, too." Gogo had befriended Dan and had been following him around the house, though she was usually standoffish with strangers.

"Of course," Tenn said. "I'll make sure no one goes near the openings."

Dan stepped into the kitchen and retrieved the tissue box from the counter, which he handed to Tenn.

"Thank you," she said, and wiped her face. She didn't know how to explain. She couldn't tell Dan the world had gone sideways and she was slipping off its edge.

"This kind of work can take its toll on you," Dan told her. He had thick hands and a smoker's cough, and he always wore a ball cap with a whale on it. "It's hard to see your house ripped apart. It can feel like it's never going to be back together again."

"You're right," Tenn said. "I have this feeling that something's happened that's irreparable." It was a word that kept coming back to her: *irreparable*. The walls would be patched and painted, eventually, but something else had broken that was beyond repair.

"You ever see one of those Japanese bowls that broke and got put back together with gold?" he asked. "My daughter talks about them in her yoga classes."

"Kintsugi," Tenn said. She'd watched a film about it once, a love story with fractured pottery.

"That's it," Dan said. "I knew there was a fancy name for it. The idea is that the scars are what make something beautiful. Not really a yoga thing, per se. But you get the picture."

"Your daughter sounds very wise," Tenn said. She tried to imagine any part of her life reassembled, threaded with gold, but the image wouldn't gel in her mind. On her screen, the grieving wolf raised her head, then stood.

"She might be," Dan told her, "if she ever leaves her dirtbag boyfriend. She's a good teacher, though." He took a tissue from the box, balled it in his hand, and stuffed it into his pocket. "Okay, I'm going to kill the power now."

"Thank you," Tenn said, anxious about being cut off from her screen. But if there was a presence in her house now, it was uninterested in revealing itself. The grieving wolf circled the deer carcass, then returned to her den and lay back down in the dark.

* * *

Tenn woke to Ward sitting beside her on the bed, his hand on her arm cold, freezing. Her heart raced at his touch, a chemical rush in her body jolting her to sudden wakefulness. It was early, not quite seven.

"What's wrong?" she said.

"I can't find Aisling," he said softly. He wasn't carrying coffee. He wasn't dressed for work. His hand on her arm was cold and tight; he needed her arm to keep himself upright. "She's not in the house. She's not in the house. I can't find her."

Tenn sat up against the heaviness in her body, feeling pinned in place, as she had in her dream of driftwood, as she had in the attic. Bile climbed her throat, and she scrambled to the bathroom, where she vomited in the toilet.

Tenn had microwaved chicken soup for her dinner, and she retched the remnants of carrots and noodles until she was empty. Ward followed and stood over her, panicking. She knew he was panicking because he did nothing, which is what he did when he panicked. Her face was very hot, and sweat bloomed across her chest, a droplet sliding between her breasts down to her stomach. Ward turned on the sink and then knelt behind her, pressed a cool washcloth to her neck.

Tenn stared into the toilet, at the flecks of carrot in the water. She could feel Aisling's absence in her stomach, in her arms.

"Did you check the doghouse?" she asked.

"It's raining," Ward said, and Tenn heard it now, against the windows. It was November. It was cold outside, always cold when Aisling disappeared. She was out there somewhere in her skeleton pajamas, shivering in the storm. Gogo inserted herself under Tenn's armpit and licked at her mouth. "But I looked outside already. I searched the whole wooded area. She's not out there."

"I'll call Frankie," Tenn said, trying to think where Aisling might go to rid the house of ghosts. Maybe she'd found something new to bury. Maybe she'd found a shovel.

Ward disappeared and returned with Tenn's phone. She flushed the toilet, closed the lid, pressed Frankie's number on the screen. It rang several times before Frankie answered.

"I was just dreaming about you," Frankie said, dispensing with pleasantries. "What's happening?"

Tenn wasn't sure if Frankie knew who she was talking to. "Hi, Frankie. This is Tennessee Cherish, from down the street."

"I know who it is," Frankie said. "I just told you I was dreaming about you." Tenn heard rustling, the mumble of a male voice. "Go back to sleep," Frankie said. Then to Tenn: "What's wrong? Is it Aisling?"

The skin on Tenn's arms crawled, like a warning. There were no welts, though; new meds had stopped the skin writing, that channel for communication now closed. She hadn't looked around the house yet. She hadn't done anything except vomit. It was possible Aisling was perfectly safe, dreaming under a blanket on one of Gogo's many beds. Ward was bad at finding things that were missing.

"Have you seen her?" she asked.

"I don't think so," Frankie said. "But then, I've been asleep. Hold on."

Tenn laid her cheek against the cool porcelain of the toilet lid. Ward had left the bathroom and was talking to Anders in a soothing tone. The bus would be there soon. Tenn wasn't sure if they should send Anders to school. She couldn't bear the thought of being parted from him, too. She heard Frankie clear her throat, shuffle across her house. She heard a door hinge creak open or shut.

"I don't see her anywhere," Frankie said. "She's not in the yard. It doesn't look like anyone's been digging."

Tenn tasted bile again but swallowed it down. "Okay," she said. "I'm sorry to have woken you. Thank you for checking."

"It's not a problem," Frankie said. She paused. "I'll put on boots and check the pond, if you want."

Tenn's vision pulsed, the start of a migraine. "Yes," she said, because she had to. "Thank you."

"I'm going to put you down a minute," Frankie told Tenn.

Tenn could only listen as Frankie pulled on her boots, as she walked around the yard to the pond. Tenn was in the bathroom, but she could feel the cold, wet grass. She could feel the cold inside her. Frankie didn't narrate, so Tenn listened to the swish of fabric, a small splash, water stirring. Frankie pressed the phone back to her ear.

"Nothing in here but leaves," Frankie reported.

"What was the dream?" Tenn asked her. Tenn didn't believe that dreams held significance, that their meaning came from anywhere but the subconscious. But she needed to know.

"What?" Frankie said. She sniffled. It was early and cold, and it was raining.

"You said you were dreaming about me," Tenn said. "What was the dream?"

"You won't like it," Frankie said.

"Tell me anyway," Tenn said.

Tenn heard the door creak again, and more rustling, maybe a towel. "I dreamed you were hooked up to a machine," Frankie said. "And the machine was draining you into a bucket. And the bucket was nearly full, but the machine was still going at it, pumping you away."

Tenn didn't know what to say to that. "And what happened?" she asked.

"I woke up," Frankie told her. "Do you need help looking? She can't be far."

"I don't know," Tenn said. "Thank you. I don't know." She hung up and turned her head to feel the cool of the toilet lid on the other cheek, which didn't help her. Maybe Aisling was close. But someone could be close and still not be okay.

* * *

The day passed in quiet desperation. Tenn went door to door while Ward drove the surrounding neighborhoods; then they called the police. The electrician and his assistant showed up to find Tenn on the living room floor, searching a box for a recent photo. This year's school pictures hadn't come home yet. Tenn had photos on her phone, of Aisling dressed like a Ghostbuster for Halloween, of Aisling eating a slice of chocolate cake, the icing smeared down her chin like a beard. But she didn't have copies to give to the police.

Ward sent the electrician away and gently pulled Tenn to her feet.

"We can text it," he said.

They'd kept Anders home from school, where he didn't want to go anyway, and Tenn suddenly realized she didn't know where he was. "Anders!" she yelled.

Anders appeared from the hall, carrying Aisling's stuffed *Lactobacillus*. Aisling never left her *Lactobacillus*. She'd argued with Tenn a few days prior about taking it to school, and Tenn had threatened to hide it. It had been a bad moment for Tenn. All she could think of now were bad moments. The day before Aisling had asked about their plans for Thanksgiving so many times Tenn snapped at her. Aisling had upset Tenn, the same way Carter had. Was she able to see the ghosts, their reaction to Tenn's anger? Was she trying to get rid of them, Tenn wondered, or get away from them?

Anders knelt to let Gogo sniff Aisling's toy, which Gogo did before fervently licking Anders's hands. Tenn had told him he could have ice cream for breakfast, and he was covered in chocolate syrup.

"Text what?" Tenn said.

"Text pictures of her," Ward said. "To the police. Here, give me your phone. I'll do it."

Tenn handed Ward her phone, mentally paging through the ghost books she'd read with Aisling. They'd smudged the house; they'd ringed it with salt. She didn't know what Aisling might try next. Maybe she was wandering the streets in her pajamas, looking for a priest. There were two officers in the house, a woman who looked too young to be a cop, with damp hair in a frizzy ponytail, and an older man who seemed stimulated by this opportunity to exert his authority. He was asking Ward about identifying birthmarks and scars. He'd already instructed them not to touch anything in Aisling's room, not to delete files from their computers, not to put the trash on the curb for collection.

"Anything could be useful," he said.

He'd also told them they shouldn't have wasted time looking for Aisling in the first place; they should've called the police right away. As if those twenty minutes had been crucial, a critical mistake they would regret. They were doing everything wrong, as wrongly as possible. Again, the word *irreparable* stuck in Tenn's mind.

"And you say this has happened before?" the male officer said.

Tenn felt invisible; no one even looked at her. Ward was talking about the camera footage, about the woods, which they would search again, with a team. Tenn wandered from the living room to the dining room to the kitchen. The counters were clean, so she unplugged the stove and worked it away from the wall, inch by inch. There was so much filth under the stove they couldn't see. She couldn't do anything right now. She couldn't conjure Aisling into the room with her desperation. But she could clean. Anders sat at the counter over his bowl of melted ice cream and watched her.

When Ward came into the kitchen, Tenn was on her hands and knees, scrubbing at a warped piece of hardwood. The wood had been damaged by some long-ago spill and subsequently covered by the stove. Now Tenn knew it was there, like the filth, hidden from sight but visible in her mind.

Ward knelt beside her but didn't touch her, didn't move to stop her futile scrubbing. "They're putting out a bulletin," he said. "They're letting all the places know." Tenn knew there was more involved—she'd heard the names of agencies from the other room—but she wasn't capable of holding on to any details. "They said we should designate one person to be in charge of answering the phone. And put a notepad and pen nearby, so we can write down what people tell us. Otherwise, we might forget."

Tenn was still scrubbing the ruined wood, her fingers pink from the heat of the water. Ward put his forehead against her shoulder, and she could feel his frailness, as if the morning had aged him forty years, and they stayed there on the floor, sunken and sick, for a long time.

* * *

That night, after Ward fell asleep, Tenn sat up in the kitchen watching footage from Aisling's bedroom, Aisling leaving her room in the dark, over and over. It was the only video where they could see her—the camera that covered the back door had died not long before Aisling's disappearance. The other doors in the house all stayed closed, the windows locked, the footage offering no glimpse of Aisling leaving. In the footage from the day before, Aisling carefully removed the batteries from the motion sensor on her bedroom door.

In the attic, moonlight moved, revealing nothing. Tenn opened Facebook, though she hadn't posted there in years. In her notifications, she found the friend request from Ricky Jefferson, the meathead from high school. Tenn clicked it numbly, wanting only for the little red flag to go away. When Ricky's profile loaded, the first post was a tribute from a classmate, a photo of them together as pimple-cheeked teens. Ricky had died two weeks ago, before the request had been sent.

Tenn read the condolences on Ricky's timeline, written by people who addressed him directly as if, somewhere, he could read them. Half the posts were by his wife, tagging him in news stories about his death. He'd died from a stab wound sustained outside a bar. His attacker had previous convictions—he was smirking in his mug shot—and he'd fled the scene of the crime and hadn't been found. Ricky's wife was posting through it, begging family and friends to share. *No one just disappears*, she wrote. It must have been the wife, Tenn thought, who'd logged in to Ricky's account and friended her, friended anyone she thought might have known him and could help.

Tenn abandoned her laptop to walk outside in the cold, wet yard. A neighbor had brought a rotisserie chicken for dinner, which only Anders had eaten. There'd been a call from the school, handled by Ward, who'd recorded the gist on a notepad. Tenn had called her parents, called Helen, and everyone had tried their best to reassure her that Aisling would turn up fine, but Tenn was past reason now. Aisling's disappearance was her fault, the way Ward getting stuck at the bottom of the stairs was. These things happened when Tenn was unhappy, and she knew this, but she was still here, endangering the people she loved.

Tenn stood in the cold and stared up at the attic window. Aisling was gone, but Tenn could still feel her, a phantom limb, a presence. She wondered where Ricky Jefferson was now, if some part of him still lingered, a silhouette in the ICU hall. She wondered if her own silhouettes would soon return, rendered vivid by her distress. She wondered if it was possible to call upon them to help find Aisling, to bring her back to Tenn, safe and whole.

Tenn returned to the house, leaving wet footprints on the hardwood. She crept up the attic stairs as quietly as she could, not bothering with the light. She was halfway up when she remembered the camera in the hall.

Tenn stumbled down the stairs and over the baby gate; there was no door on the hinges to resist her. She could hear Ward in bed. He'd only been out for a few hours. They'd spent a long time lying there, in a room that felt too empty, holding each other without speaking. There was nothing to say. Neither of them could muster a hope that could be false, that could be dashed. Neither dared to think the worst, either, or not think it, but say it out loud, as if saying it out loud might make it come true. Tenn heard Ward's feet hit the floor as she raced back to the kitchen, to her laptop.

Ward was behind her, their minds synchronized by terror.

"We forgot the hall," he said.

Tenn slid the laptop to Ward, because her hands were shaking. He clicked through the footage, and they watched the hallway in reverse, the raw edges of the plaster. They hadn't checked the footage from the hall between the dining room and living room because there were no windows or doors in it. Tenn knelt beside Ward on the rug. She didn't pray, but she was in a position of prayer. *I'll do anything*, she thought. She wasn't addressing a higher power but the spirits, the ghosts—she didn't know what to call them, but she could feel them around her, their density in the house, drawn out by her anguish. They were there, filling the room; they were there with her. *I'll do anything*, she thought, and imagined herself being drained into a bucket. *You can have me.*

Ward stopped the video, went back. Together they watched Aisling slip into the hall, a little skeleton glowing in the dark. She took a few steps, lifted the tarp covering the opening in the plaster, and then, as if the house were absorbing her, Aisling disappeared inside the wall.

* * *

Tenn wrenched her arm from Ward's grip, ripped down the tarp, and plunged inside the wall despite his warnings. Inside, it smelled like the dust that cooked off the radiators, carrying the skin cells of the dead to your lungs. Tenn pressed on through the nest of wires, and though a shock radiated through her armpit into her limbs, she did not let the pain of it stop her. Aisling was unconscious at the end of the hall, like a little mouse in a maze, having reached a dead end or her destination. She'd been there the whole time, as Tenn called and called for her, obscured by a veil of plaster. Aisling was curled between two beams of wood, which did not form right angles but leaned toward one another like they needed the support.

Aisling was heavy in Tenn's arms and very hot, and Tenn was grateful for her body heat, grateful and afraid. Aisling murmured against Tenn's chest, but Tenn couldn't understand what she was saying. Everything was muffled, there inside the walls—it felt private to Tenn, this moment between her and Aisling, who'd peed through her pajamas, who was sticky and sick. Tenn knew where the live wire was and avoided it on her way out, her arms prickling, a gray headache creeping from the base of her skull.

Ward had the phone to his ear when Tenn emerged in the hall, and he took Aisling with one arm and touched Tenn's burned torso with another.

"Fuck," he said.

Tenn reached for Aisling, because she wanted her back in her arms, even though her arms were no longer working right. There was a spasm in her left biceps, a pain that felt like static, and her tiredness folded over and over her like a blanket. Still, she wanted Aisling back—she could bear anything but another separation. She reached for her, but Ward didn't hand Aisling over, his face frozen in an expression Tenn knew well.

* * *

In the car, Tenn sat in the back with the kids pinned against her body, watching the house grow smaller and smaller in the rearview. Inside her, memories jumbled—warm sand and rhubarb, chewing tobacco and mango, an immense and gaping loss. Tenn couldn't hold on to any of it for long, though, as soon all thought was subsumed by the growing crackle of her pain. It was cold in the car, and Ward turned the heat up high, the air vents muffling all other sound. Tenn felt like a child being driven home from her grandmother's, on those nights when her father had carried her to the back seat, when she'd pressed her forehead against the window's cold. She felt like a child, holding her own children. Aisling was more alert now, and she was asking questions. What time was it? Where were they going? Would Gogo be okay if they left her in the house all by herself?

At the emergency room, Ward put Tenn in a chair before hunching over the desk, his voice low but full of urgency, holding two clipboards at the same time. Tenn reached out a hand—she was the one who filled out the paperwork—but then a slight man with long eyelashes appeared and held her by the elbows to help her up.

Tenn resisted, because Aisling was curled beside her. Aisling was wearing different pajamas than before, a clean nightgown, though Tenn hadn't changed her. Ward appeared at Tenn's side and took over pulling Tenn to her feet.

"What are you doing?" she asked. She took Aisling by the wrist. "She's so hot. Feel her forehead. She's the one who needs to go."

"Look," Ward said, lifting the hem of Tenn's shirt so she could see the burn, the bubbled skin below her armpit. She could feel the pain, but her pain didn't matter. Her priority was Aisling, making sure Aisling was okay. She'd offered herself to the ghosts, and they could have her. As long as they left the kids alone.

"It's not that bad," she said, and smoothed her shirt back in place, though she could feel it in her teeth, like she was biting down on something dry and vibrating.

"We won't keep you apart for long," said the man with long lashes. Ward gently pried Tenn's fingers from Aisling's arm. "She can come, too. She'll be right behind you."

Then Tenn was moving down the hall, Ward by her side, Aisling and Anders behind him. Anders was pale with worry, so Tenn decided to cooperate. Someone had given the kids coloring books and stickers, and Aisling had a stuffed panda wearing a blue shirt with the hospital's logo, which she held by one paw, disinterested.

"Mr. Trevino," a voice said from the opposite direction.

On Ward's face, Tenn could see the war, his attention painfully split between her and Aisling.

"Go," she said. She gathered herself and nodded with resolution. The man with long eyelashes opened a curtain, showing her the way to her cot. "Stay with Aisling," she told Ward. "Don't let her out of your sight."

* * *

The scans were all fine—Tenn's brain, her heart—though the doctor cautioned the full effect of an electric shock was not always immediately apparent. The man with the eyelashes—a PA named Jeff who asked *Is this okay?* with every touch—bandaged Tenn's torso and disappeared to order her prescriptions. Ward appeared through the curtain in his absence.

Tenn attempted to stand, because Ward was childless, but Ward put a hand on her elbow and laid her back down.

"You don't need to do anything right now," he told her. He slid a chair from the corner and sat beside her, held her hand. "Just rest."

"Where are the kids?" Tenn asked.

"Aisling found a doctor who specializes in gut biomes," he said, "and they're deep in conversation about probiotics. Anders made a friend, too." Tenn closed her eyes and allowed herself the comfort of knowing her kids were safe, safely contained in this brightly lit building, with background-checked adults. "Those creepy pictures he keeps drawing at school are apparently based on some video game, and there's a nurse who plays it. I've never seen him so happy. All this time, he just needed a fellow gamer who loves melted demon-horse-people the way he does." Ward rubbed his hand over hers, lifted her gown to look inside.

"Are you checking out my bandage," she asked him, "or my side-boob?"

"Why not both?" Ward said, and pressed his lips to Tenn's hand. She'd scared him, again; she was always scaring him. "They said it should've been worse, but I guess you were moving fast to get to Aisling. It's a miracle she didn't get shocked, too, but the wire was too high."

"I thought the tarp would keep them out," she said. "I was more worried about Gogo than the kids."

"I didn't even think about it," Ward said. He'd been uninvolved in the process altogether."

Tenn tried to focus through the staticky pain of the burn. "Aisling was so hot," she said.

"Ear infection," Ward said. "That's the only thing the doctor could find. She must've already been feverish when she climbed in there. But her temperature's down now. They gave her fluids and antibiotics. She's going to be fine."

"She didn't seem sick," Tenn said. "What did she think she was doing?"

Aisling had never had an ear infection in her life, and she hadn't complained of ear pain before her disappearance. She'd eaten a big dinner the night before, talking excitedly about school, the parachute in gym class. *Ghosts*, was all Tenn could think, but that couldn't have been the explanation Aisling gave Ward.

Ward squeezed her hand as if he were in danger of losing her. "She heard us fighting," he told her. "She said she thought if she was missing, we'd stop."

Tenn's arm twitched, but Ward kept holding it. Aisling was right—they'd stopped fighting. But nothing else had changed. Now that Aisling was found, everything would continue as it had before.

"I'm sorry," Ward said.

"For what?" Tenn asked him.

Ward went quiet, considering the question. In the next cubicle, two people were speaking Spanish, which neither Tenn nor Ward understood. One of the pair, who sounded like an elderly man, began to cry.

"Do you remember when we first moved in?" Ward said.

"It wasn't that long ago," Tenn answered. She thought back to the day of the move—the oppressive heat, the endless stacks of cardboard boxes—but the painkiller was kicking in, and as her pain receded, the jumble of memory inside her resurfaced. Gingersnaps and sunscreen, a fingernail scraping the nape of her neck. Tenn wasn't sure which were hers and which were strays.

"I thought this house would be good for us," Ward said. "For you. I thought buying this house would make you happy. That's all I want, Tenn."

"I don't need a big house to be happy," Tenn said, though she knew that wasn't entirely true. In their little ranch in North Carolina, they'd always been on top of each other; Tenn could hear every word everyone said through the walls. She hadn't liked that, either. It wasn't that Tenn didn't want the space, but that the space wasn't worth what they'd traded for it.

"I don't want you to go to Helen's," Ward said. At the prospect of returning to the house, panic overrode everything else in Tenn's body. All Tenn knew was that she couldn't go back there; it wasn't safe for her to be there with Ward and the kids. "I think we should go away together, spend time as a family, alone. Away from work. Away from the house."

Tenn wasn't sure how to read what he was saying, how he thought the house fit into the equation. Maybe he'd seen something, too, she thought. Or maybe he'd just decided to humor her.

"What about Johann?" she said.

"Fuck Johann," Ward said.

Tenn turned her face away.

"Hey," Ward said, and climbed beside her on the narrow cot. Tenn laid her head on his chest and listened to his heart, accelerated. He was afraid—she could hear it in his body—but he still couldn't bring himself to say what she needed to hear: that he wanted her alive, that he did not want her dead. He would never say it, and she would never be able to stop thinking about it. He would say everything right, except that. "We're not too late to fix this, are we?" he asked. "This is just a rough patch. One day we're going to look back at this year, and we're going to laugh."

"Remember the time Aisling nearly died inside the walls and Anders made everyone at school think he was a sociopath?" Tenn said.

"Hilarious," Ward said. "Remember when I locked myself in my office and worked for so long you forgot why you loved me?"

"A fucking riot," Tenn said. She tucked her head into his armpit and smelled the seaside scent of his deodorant. He'd smelled the same way their whole adult lives, which they'd spent together. And maybe, if they wanted it hard enough, things would get better. They loved each other, still, and love was like a contract: you had to renegotiate it periodically, to renew it. Tenn could hear Ward's love for her through his chest.

"Where do you want to go?" she asked him.

"I don't know," he said. "Someplace warm? Someplace where we can get good biscuits but don't have to see our families."

"I do love biscuits," Tenn said.

"I know you do," Ward said. "New York is shit for biscuits. What about Georgia?" he asked.

"What about Georgia?" Tenn said.

"Warm and sunny," Ward said. "Spanish moss on the trees. And all the biscuits you can eat. Your Thanksgiving dinner could be an enormous pile of biscuits."

Tenn could eat biscuits; she could sit in the sun. She could hear in Ward's chest that he wanted her alive; she didn't need him to say it out loud. If the house was a source of danger, it was better for them to leave it together.

"Georgia," she said. "Georgia it is."

14

It wasn't until they crossed the Mason-Dixon Line that Ward started to recognize Tenn again. In Virginia, she rolled down the window and stuck her feet out in the wind. Half an hour later, she was singing. The farther they got from New York, the more herself she seemed—she played guessing games with the kids, gleefully took them on a candy spree at a gas station. When Ward swung through a drive-thru, she devoured a large order of fries before they made it back to the interstate.

In North Carolina, it was sunny and the trees were still green, and Ward held Tenn's hand in stopped traffic. At a picnic table outside Columbia, Tenn kissed him long and slow, and she felt familiar, her mouth a place Ward knew well. He began to think she was right to blame the house—in an unfamiliar place, they'd become unfamiliar, too, to each other, to themselves. But now they were starting over again. Ward didn't know how many times you could start over, but he would do it as many times as it took.

They crossed a bridge that felt endless and arrived at a resort Ward had found on an island off Georgia's coast. The only person who knew where they were was Gogo's pet sitter. On the island, they rode bikes and ate ice cream and visited a rehab center for injured sea turtles. They went on a dolphin watch piloted by a captain with two Labs, a yellow one named Shrimpy and a black one named Palmetto, who rode along as scouts. Aisling and Anders spent the entire ride rolling around the boat's deck alongside them, more excited about the dogs than the dolphins. Ward braided Tenn's hair to keep it from tangling in the wind, a skill she'd taught him on the baby doll they bought for Anders to help him learn to be gentle when Tenn was pregnant with Aisling, which he'd dragged around the house by the hair.

On their third day, Ward took Tenn to a beach covered with driftwood, dead trees bleached by sun and salt, a strange and skeletal graveyard. Ward climbed into the crook of a big bough and pulled Tenn beside him.

"I dreamed about this," he told her. It was how he'd found the resort—he'd been searching for the driftwood expanse from his dream, still so vivid in his mind, and it turned out it was real. The feeling on this beach was the same as in the dream. He'd dreamed them here together, cast out from the house. "Is that possible?"

Tenn put both hands flat against the wood as if she could sense something from it. "I don't know what's possible," she said.

In Ward's mind, a scene replayed on a loop—Tenn disappearing into the wall despite his telling her not to, despite his sharp warning about the live wires. Was it maternal instinct, he kept wondering, or something else?

Anders chased the tide out but leapt away, squealing, when it came back in. Aisling had already thrown herself, fully clothed, into the water, and continued to throw herself at every wave, no matter the size.

Ward set his hands alongside Tenn's, wondering if it was still possible that they could feel the same thing at the same time. The wood was warm and smooth, unsettling in its familiarity. The dream felt fresh, like it was still unfolding: their yard full of this driftwood—this exact dead tree. He didn't know how it was possible that he'd dreamed of this tree. Maybe he'd seen it somewhere, on a travel show, and forgotten it. He wondered if this was how Tenn felt when she remembered images but couldn't place them.

Tenn tugged at the bandage under her arm. "I keep seeing her in there, curled up, sweating. She was in there the whole time. What if we hadn't found her? What if we'd found her too late?"

Ward pulled Tenn close, and she tucked her face against his neck. He'd watched her charge through the wires without stopping her. He'd told her to stop, but he hadn't held her back. They breathed the same air together, dug their toes into the same sand.

"This is nice," she said. "It feels nice here, in the sun. Maybe I'm not crazy after all. Maybe I'm just a big, dumb leaf, and all I need is more sunshine."

"You know I don't think you're crazy," Ward told her, though it wasn't entirely true. They were there together, and it felt good, but it didn't erase the fact that she was seeing things, that she believed the things she saw were real. That her belief was so strong she'd passed it to their daughter.

Aisling went under a wave, and Ward felt Tenn tense until Aisling's head popped back up above the water.

"You just think I'm acting crazy," Tenn said. It was a statement of fact, no anger in it.

"I think you haven't been yourself," Ward said carefully, though that wasn't exactly true, either. Tenn had been different, estranged from the version of her he'd always known, but that didn't mean it wasn't her. It was possible to change and still be yourself.

"I didn't hit you with the attic door on purpose," she said. "That door really was stuck. And I didn't leave a nail sticking out of the floor on purpose, either. I would never do that."

"I don't think you want to hurt the kids," Ward said, which was mostly true. He didn't think she *wanted* to hurt anyone. But he was worried she was capable of it, one way or another. The little candle in his mind continued to burn, casting them in its light.

"But you think I might anyway," Tenn said. The effort of saying this warped her voice; she sounded like she was talking with her ears plugged.

Ward didn't know how to respond. He worried about her constantly, but telling her that would only make her feel worse.

"I worry . . ." he said. "I know it's not your fault. I know it was because of your medication." He was fumbling for the words; he couldn't get it right in his head. "It's just hard sometimes . . ." He stopped, started again. What he wanted to say wouldn't make anything better, but there was no way to start over if they couldn't be honest with each other. "I think sometimes—a lot of the time—about how you could've left us, how you could still leave us anytime. I don't want to have to worry about it, but I do."

Tenn stared out at the ocean, not at Ward. The ocean made her nervous—she didn't like that there was so much beneath the surface she couldn't see. "And you resent me for it," she said, which they both knew was true.

Ward could only nod and stare at the ocean, too.

"I'm really trying," she said. "I go to the doctor; I take all the pills. I'm trying to take care of my brain and everything else at the same time."

"I know," Ward said. "And I haven't been around enough to help. It's not what we discussed. I know that, too." They both knew this, but it was still hard, so hard to say it out loud. You could start a conversation without knowing its end, and the end could be different from what you wanted.

Aisling yelled something Ward and Tenn couldn't hear, standing with her back to the water. Behind her, a wave gathered force and knocked her flat. Tenn sprinted into the water and fished her out. Aisling came up laughing and coughing simultaneously.

"I love the beach!" she yelled.

Feet away, Anders was building something: not a sandcastle, exactly—more like a mound. He kept walking down the beach, filling his bucket with sand, and dragging it back.

"What are you making, buddy?" Ward asked him. He didn't understand why Anders went so far to get the sand. Ward could see the hole down the beach, deepening.

Anders shrugged and added another bucketful to the mound, before carefully flattening its top. "I'm not sure," he said. "But there's something inside it."

Tenn watched Aisling, who appeared unfazed by having the wind knocked out of her, before returning to Ward's side, where she melted against him. Tenn didn't usually relax on the beach, but today she seemed lulled by it. Ward, on the other hand, was increasingly anxious. His phone buzzed in his pocket, the phone he'd told Tenn he'd keep off.

"I don't want to hurt anyone," Tenn told him. "Not even myself." Ward couldn't tell, now that he thought about it, if she was relaxed or just tired. She seemed, like the beach itself, eroded. "But I don't know how to go on if you can't believe anything I say."

Ward wanted to believe her, and he did, in that one moment. The problem was his fear that the moment wouldn't hold, that next week, back at home, she'd feel differently. The problem was his inability to fix that problem, if it was fixable.

"I believe you," he said, because he wanted to, wanted her to believe him, too. "And when we get home, I'm going to carry you over the threshold, and we'll start over again. Again. I never carried you over the threshold when we moved in."

"I knew this was all your fault," Tenn said.

Ward leaned into her. It was familiar; she was familiar. They were happy together; they'd always been happy. They could find their way back, in time. In time, they'd forget this had ever happened. "I'm going to do better," he said. "Take more time for you and the kids." Ward knew it would take more than words, but words was where he had to start. "I just want you to be happy." This was, at last, actually true.

Down the beach, three gulls inspected Anders's hole, keeping their distance. Anders emptied another bucket, reflattened the top of his mound. He did it the same way every time, with the same technique.

"I am happy," Tenn said, nestling against Ward. One of the seagulls got brave and charged at the hole, but before it reached the edge, all three exploded into the air and flew away. "I'm happy right now. And I want to stay that way. I want things to be better."

Ward watched the tide go out and in, over and over again. This was why people liked the beach, he thought. It felt possible that the tide might take something away, bring what they needed in its stead.

"Then things will be better," he said, and decided to believe it. If you believed something hard enough, sometimes it came true.

* * *

On Thanksgiving, they went to a buffet at the resort, a biscuitless cornucopia of the worst Thanksgiving food they'd ever tasted. Tenn ordered a bottle of champagne—after a few glasses, the food hardly mattered. The kids would only eat dinner rolls and ice cream anyway, and Tenn returned from the dessert table with three slices of key lime pie for her alone, gazed down at them with pride as if they were her children. After the kids fell asleep, Ward turned on the shower, and they fucked on the bathroom floor, under the rattle of the fan, feet against the door, which did not lock. When they were finished, Tenn draped her chest over Ward's, both of them slick with sweat and steam. Her body was sharp, angular. Ward hadn't realized how much weight she'd lost since the move. He rested a hand over the crest of her hip, covering it.

Tenn rubbed his chin, his vacation stubble. He was two days of growth past how she liked it. "I'll shave tonight," he said.

"No," she said, into his chest. "I like you scratchy."

"You never have before."

"But I do now."

They lay there for so long Tenn's breathing began to slow, and Ward thought she'd fallen asleep atop him. He'd let her sleep late every morning of the trip, but she was no less tired here than at home. "You know," she said, not asleep after all, "I keep thinking it's so complicated, but it's not. It's not that complicated."

Ward's arm had gone dead, but he didn't want to move her. The turkey, the champagne—she was tired. "What isn't complicated?"

"Any of it," she said. "This is what's real, and the rest is bullshit." Her body on his dead arm got heavier. "All I need is this."

Tenn was wet and warm against him, and Ward felt it, too, the essence of their lives neatly contained in this hotel room—her body and his, the burned skin of her torso, the kids' delicate ears, their blood and their bones. This was what mattered. Not the house, not his job, not the work she had or hadn't done. Tenn held Ward tighter, and he held her back. Her breathing body was real, and he held on to it and gave thanks.

* * *

The next day they drove north toward Atlanta. There was a state park with Native American burial mounds on their route, which seemed like a necessary endcap to a Thanksgiving trip composed mostly of swimming and ice cream. In the back seat, the kids argued about who could hold their breath the longest. Tenn had her eyes closed, though Ward knew she was awake—they kept driving over bridges, which scared her. Her eyes were still shut when he parked, and then the kids were out quick, ready to move their restless legs. Ward followed them into the parking lot and waited for Tenn to join them.

But she didn't.

Ward corralled the kids and walked around to Tenn's side of the car, where he found her folded over in her seat, head to knees. He opened the door.

"What's wrong?" he asked her.

Tenn didn't have panic attacks, as far as Ward knew, but there was a look in her eyes—a helplessness, a searching. Ward thought she was going to ask for help, but instead she clenched her calf. "Cramp," she said, into her thighs. "You go ahead. I'm right behind you."

Ward stood outside the car, unable to move his feet from the ground. Tenn had been fine—she'd just been fine—everything had been good between them again. But now she was buckled, the back of her neck pale, blaming a cramp instead of telling Ward what was really wrong. He didn't want to leave her. He knew he shouldn't leave her.

Aisling pulled his arm. "I'm starving," she said. "I'm dying of starvation."

A car honked, and Ward turned to see Anders, frozen in front of it, in the middle of the lane. He took both kids by the hands and led them across the parking lot, to safety.

Ward felt his distance from Tenn with the same clarity he'd felt in the emergency room. And—he understood in a part of his brain beyond language—this feeling would return to him, again and again. It was exhausting to stretch yourself between so many people at once. Maybe this was why Tenn was so tired all the time. He bought the kids snacks, which they ate like feral animals before sprinting off toward one of the mounds. Ward stationed himself where he could see both the kids and the car until Tenn joined him.

"I fed them cookies," Ward told her, and pointed to the vending machine by the visitor's center. "Are you okay?"

"Yeah," Tenn said. Her shirt was damp with sweat, and she was holding an empty water bottle. "I was fine until you pulled into the parking lot. I don't know if I can even describe it. I just felt . . . overcome, somehow."

"Is it a migraine?" Ward asked, though he knew Tenn could recognize a migraine when she was having one. He didn't want to suggest a panic attack. "Or maybe this is from the shock? The doctor said there could be damage you didn't notice right away."

"Maybe," Tenn said. She was studying the closest burial mound, looming before them. "I'm probably just hypoglycemic." She said this the same way she said *I'm fine*, a lie told to make Ward feel better. "I'm too old to eat donuts for breakfast."

"I'll get you something," Ward said. He didn't want Tenn to think he didn't believe her. Hypoglycemia was a problem with a clear solution. He ran off to the vending machine, returning to Tenn at the same time as the kids.

"Mommy, did you see?" Aisling said. "The mounds are flat on top, just like Anders's sandcastle!" She ran off again, and Anders followed. Aisling was right—the mound Anders had made in the sand looked exactly like the burial mound in front of them.

Ward offered Tenn a peanut butter cracker, and Tenn took it and thanked him but did not eat.

15

In the kitchen, someone had left the faucet running. Tenn held her hands under the tap until they felt like ice. There was trash on the counter, fast-food bags from the car. The house had been put on hydraulic jacks in their absence, and Tenn thought she could feel it move beneath her, unstable. She unpacked the cooler but left the suitcases for the morning. From her purse, she retrieved her prescriptions, took her pills one by one so she could go to sleep. But the tap water had been cold, and her hands were numb, and she spilled the last bottle on the floor.

Tenn dropped to her knees to get to the pills before Gogo, before remembering that Gogo wasn't home. It was too late tonight to get her from the pet sitter's. Gogo was still there, safe from Tenn's clumsiness.

Tenn got a chopstick from a drawer and knelt to retrieve the pills that had slid beneath the stove. It was dirty under the stove, her chopstick bringing with it a sticky clump of hair and crumbs, despite the recent cleaning. She could see herself there, on hands and knees, scrubbing and scrubbing the warped wood. A strange feeling descended, like a cage dropping over her, the walls of the kitchen shrinking around her.

Ward started down the stairs, and Tenn stood, put the pills back in the bottle and into the cabinet above the stove. She couldn't remember if she'd actually taken one. The stairs creaked, but the door didn't open, like Ward was taking his time, walking deliberately slowly to avoid her. She'd slept on the drive home, woke sweating, her bandage soaked. It was after midnight when they arrived, and Tenn had carried the kids to their beds while Ward went to his office to check something for work. Vacation was unceremoniously over. Now she stood by the closed door and waited. Ward was no longer walking, but the door was still closed.

"Hello?" she said. She hadn't felt right since morning. All she wanted to do was sleep in her own bed. She opened the door to find Ward on the other side, holding his phone.

He looked up at her, surprised. "Hey," he said. "I didn't hear you there."

The kitchen again contracted, a pulse only Tenn could detect.

"The water was running," Tenn said. The septic repairs, too, had been completed while they were gone, but the issue with the water temperature had not been resolved. No one could explain why it came out so cold. Their water heater was fine, to Tenn's surprise.

"I have to be on a call in a few minutes," he told her.

"So late?" Tenn said.

"There's a problem with an install in Germany," Ward explained. "I'm waiting for the tech on-site to call me back. I was just coming down for a drink."

He disappeared into the pantry, returned with an art deco–style bottle Tenn hadn't seen before. He set it on the counter: brandy. Tenn skimmed the label. *50 Year*, it said, in gold lettering.

"Where'd that come from?" she asked, thinking it was a gift. Fifty-year anything would be expensive.

"The guy at the liquor store was raving about it," Ward said. "It's a blend of seven different vintages. This bottle has brandy in it that was distilled during the Civil War."

Tenn didn't know anything about brandy, and she'd never seen Ward drink it before.

"How much?" she asked him.

"Hm?" Ward said. He was reading his phone.

"How much did it cost?" she asked. She was too tired to walk up the stairs, just then. She was working up to it.

Ward took a glass from the cabinet and uncorked the bottle. "It was like four hundred. But people resell it for over a thousand. People hang on to this stuff and sell it years later to pay college tuition."

But not if they drank it first, Tenn didn't say. Ward poured his glass and went to the freezer for an ice cube.

"You bought a four-hundred-dollar bottle of brandy," Tenn said. She'd been out of it, but she was awake now. They'd spent more than they should have on the trip, all put on a credit card—the resort, the gas money, meals.

"Do you want a glass?" Ward asked. His face was so innocent, as if it had never occurred to him to discuss a large purchase that was wholly unnecessary. The week before at the store, Tenn had put back a package of smoked salmon because of the price. Fifteen dollars.

Tenn turned her attention to the counter, which looked like the scene of a spill someone had made worse while attempting to clean it. But the counters had been spotless when they left. No one had used the kitchen for a week.

Ward was midsip when Anders screamed across the house. Tenn was already running, her body moving automatically.

"What happened?" she said, stumbling through the luggage piled at the base of the stairs.

In the living room, Anders sat on the floor, clutching his foot. Aisling knelt beside him, a little hand on his shoulder, blinking at Tenn with alarm.

"My foot's bleeding," Anders said. "I stepped on that."

On the floor, the same nail Anders had stepped on before protruded from the wood, the hammer on the bookcase behind it.

"Why are you out of bed?" Tenn asked him. "Why are you up?"

"I was scared," Anders said, curling into himself. "I don't like to be all alone."

"It's okay, baby," Tenn said, and pet his uncombed hair. They had done this before, and now they were doing it again. She felt Ward enter the room behind her, slow to follow.

Tenn scooped Anders up and carried him to the bathroom. From the closet, she took out the peroxide and antibiotic ointment and gauze. She'd done this before, too, like a rehearsal. She kissed Anders on the forehead and told him he was brave. Aisling disappeared and returned with Anders's slippers. In the living room, Ward pounded at the floor with the hammer. Tenn waited for him to join them in the bathroom once he finished, but he didn't. She didn't know where he'd gone. She didn't think he'd go back to work without checking on Anders.

Tenn bandaged the foot and went through the elaborate process of getting the kids back in bed, this time together: sips of water, hugs and kisses, sleep stories and songs. She watched them both closely: Anders to make sure he was settled, Aisling to make sure she wasn't watching something invisible to Tenn. Tenn asked if she was okay.

"I liked it better when we were on vacation," Aisling said, then lay beside her brother and held on to him, as if she were trying to pin him in place. When he tried to take his slippers off, she insisted he sleep in them.

With the kids back in bed, Tenn returned to the kitchen, where she heard Ward, creaking on the stairs. It sounded like he was coming down instead of going back up. Maybe he'd gone up and realized he'd forgotten something. Tenn stood in the kitchen and waited for the door to open, the walls pulsing around her. Tenn was very tired, and the house was up on jacks. It would take some getting used to.

"Hello?" she said. She listened, but Ward was quiet. She opened the door, and there he was, staring at his phone at the bottom of the stairs. "Did you need something?" she asked him. Ward went up and down the stairs all day, she told herself. There was nothing strange about finding him here, now. She ran through a mental checklist of tasks to stay calm—she needed to check the doors, turn off the lights, find her toothbrush in the toiletry bag.

"I'm still working," Ward said. "I'm waiting for the tech on-site to call me back. I was just coming down for a drink."

He disappeared into the pantry and returned with a bottle of cooking sherry. The expensive brandy was on the counter, forgotten.

"Can you take out the trash?" she said, even though that wasn't what she meant to say. They hadn't been home for a week, and the trash was empty.

"Cups," Ward said in response.

Tenn turned away and looked at the film on the counter, and when she turned back, Ward was gone.

Tenn closed her eyes and breathed. This couldn't be happening now—she wasn't angry or upset. She was, however, recovering from a shock; the doctor had said it might have neurologic side effects. Her hands felt like ice—her whole body did, a numbness seeping through her. She heard a creak on the stairs and waited, but nothing happened.

"Hello?" she said. She listened, but Ward was quiet. She opened the door, and there he was, staring at his phone. "Ward," Tenn said.

"I'm waiting," Ward said, "for the tech to call me back. Do we have anything to drink?"

He walked past Tenn into the pantry, and Tenn followed him. There was more liquor on the shelf, but he reached instead for a bottle of champagne vinegar.

"Let me get that for you," Tenn said, taking the bottle from his hands. Ward followed her to the kitchen, obedient.

Tenn set down the bottle, her hands so cold she could barely feel them. She rubbed them together as if warmth might break the spell. They'd done this all before, and Tenn hadn't been stuck then, but now she was so numb she wasn't sure she could move. The kitchen felt like it was getting smaller by the second.

"God, I'm thirsty," Ward said. Instead of going to the pantry as Tenn expected, he stooped to open the cabinet under the sink. He pulled out the first bottle he touched: bathroom bleach.

Tenn didn't know what to do. She could hide the bottles of cleaner, but then what? Her only instinct was to flee, even though they'd just gotten home. But it felt like returning to a house on fire.

Tenn took the bleach just as Anders screamed again. The suitcases were still piled by the stairs, as if they were waiting to be loaded into the car. In the living room, Anders clutched his foot. Aisling knelt beside him, weary. The slippers she'd brought for him were gone.

"My foot's bleeding," Anders said. "I stepped on that."

On the floor beside him, the nail was protruding, the same nail Ward had just pounded back down.

"Where's your Band-Aid?" Tenn asked.

"What Band-Aid?" Anders said.

Tenn examined the bleeding foot. There was only one wound, no sign of previous injury. Ward stood in the doorway, detached from Anders's pain.

"Please help me," she pleaded. "I don't know what's happening. I can't do this on my own." She didn't know what to say to snap him out of it. She could no longer remember how she'd managed it before.

Ward crossed the room and picked up the hammer, but he stalled with it raised over the floor.

"Ward?" Tenn said.

"Daddy?" Aisling said.

Anders began to cry.

"It's okay, baby," Tenn said, the words automatic. "It doesn't look too deep. We'll get it all cleaned up, and it'll feel better in no time."

Tenn scooped Anders up, felt his weight in her lower back. She wanted to move toward the door, to get the kids out of the house, but her numb body disobeyed her brain's orders.

Ward picked up the bleach from the floor where Tenn had left it and carried it away, toward the kitchen.

Tenn followed Ward, Anders bleeding in her arms, Aisling trailing behind, wraithlike in her nightgown, now holding Anders's rain boots. The water in the kitchen was running; Ward stood at the base of his stairs, tapping at the bleach bottle like it was a phone screen.

Anders whimpered in Tenn's arms. He was so small—both kids were. They needed Tenn to figure this out. Anders snatched Ward's phone from his hand and threw it. It hit Ward in the head and slid across the floor, and Ward stood stunned for a long moment before crossing the room to retrieve it.

"This is my phone," he said.

The kitchen pulsed but didn't get smaller this time. Tenn listened to the water, running and running. She wondered how long you could leave it running before the well ran dry. She could feel the counter behind her but didn't look away, at the film. Her hands were sweating.

Ward blinked at her. "Why is the faucet on?" he said. He left the bleach on the counter and turned off the water. "What happened to my phone? What's going on?"

Aisling pressed against Tenn's side, silent and shivering.

"I don't know," Tenn said, "but we need to get the fuck out of this house."

* * *

The kids didn't argue when Tenn ordered them back into the car, or when she carried them from the car to a queen bed in a hotel two towns away. The only light she turned on was in the bathroom. The kids fell back asleep with ease—they were different outside the house—and Tenn watched them, Aisling sucking a lock of hair, Anders clutching Aisling's stuffed *Lactobacillus*, which Aisling had given to him as if, Tenn couldn't help thinking, it were an anchor. Ward sat at the edge of the second bed, unmoving.

Tenn knelt before him and tugged off his right shoe.

Ward looked at her. "We're at a hotel," he said. He'd been like this the whole drive, not fully present, unable to engage beyond simple narration. *We're in the car. The light is green. The light is red. There's a dead deer on the shoulder, and its eyes are open.*

"We're at a hotel," Tenn confirmed. She was starting to worry whatever the house had done to him was irreparable. Houses couldn't do things to people, but she couldn't deny that things happened to all of them inside the house. They'd had the water tested; they'd checked the gas line for leaks. Ward had been to the doctor, who'd deemed him healthy. But maybe the hydraulic jacks had created another problem—something new. There was nothing Tenn wanted more than a mundane explanation for what was happening. She wanted this problem to have a solution, so they could fix it and go back to the way things were before. "Do you remember why we left?"

"Where's my phone?" Ward asked. He'd run a finger over its cracked screen in the kitchen, set it on the counter, and left it there. He was starting to come out of it. He looked down at his feet—one shoe on, one shoe off—then around at the hotel room. The bathroom light created shadows that were long, dripping. "What are we doing here?"

"There was a problem at the house," Tenn told him. "We had to leave."

Ward reached down and touched her face, pulled her into his lap. It was familiar—she'd sat in his lap a hundred times before—but there was something off about it. Ward held Tenn tight, because he didn't understand. Then he stiffened, pushed her away. "The kids," he said.

He got up and rushed to the other bed, put a hand on each of the kids' foreheads. He kneaded his temples, shook his head at Tenn, and went to the bathroom, where Tenn heard the water begin to run.

Tenn lay on the bed, fully clothed, her exhaustion hitting like she'd fallen from a great height. A moment later, the bathroom door swung open, casting the room again in its light. "The kids," Ward said, and rushed to their bed, where he put a hand on each of their foreheads.

* * *

Tenn got Ward to sleep by dosing him with nighttime cold medicine, still packed in the caddy they took with them on trips. He passed out atop the covers and Tenn sat beside him with her laptop, fully dressed, drinking shitty coffee from a paper cup. She was afraid to fall asleep, lest Aisling wander out of the room, toward the highway, or Ward wake thirsty and drink the hand soap.

Leaving the house hadn't fixed Ward, and Tenn didn't know how to make sense of it. All she knew was that she needed to find someone who could. She typed the name *Amos Blum*—the architect who'd sold them the house—expecting to find a social media profile, a professional website, if not for him, then for his wife, who was a writer. Instead, she found an obituary.

Two obituaries, actually, rolled into one. Once again, Tenn couldn't make sense of things—both Amos Blum and his wife had been found dead on the same day, just over a month after closing on the house. There was no cause of death reported in the obituaries. They were dead, and they'd taken all their knowledge of the house along with them. Tenn wondered whether if she went to the place where they'd died, she might find them as silhouettes, swaying before the windows, and beg them for answers. She reread the obituary, searching for anything that might help her.

What she found was Amos Blum's daughter.

* * *

When Ward woke, he called the fire department, then the gas company, then the doctor. They'd already checked for a stroke, for a leak, for carbon monoxide, but Ward would check again. Tenn went straight to the train station after driving the kids to school. Ward was doing the same things over and over, but she was trying something different. Amos Blum's daughter, Neri Gerges, lived in Brooklyn, and she'd responded to Tenn's late-night message with an invitation to meet for brunch. Tenn wasn't sure what Neri would tell her, but she was ready to believe it. She'd wasted too much time stewing in doubt, but that was over now. Tenn would believe anything if there was a chance it might save her family.

Neri was already at the restaurant, seated outside in a plexiglass box strung with fairy lights, the twinkling magic neatly contained. She stood and took Tenn's hand, then released it as if Tenn had shocked her. Tenn took a seat, her feet suddenly aching, like she'd walked the whole way there instead of taking the train.

Neri unfolded her napkin, arranged her silverware beside her plate. She was petite with dark hair, pixie cut, and a slim gold hoop through her nose. She wore faded coveralls and a blue-and-white evil eye, strung around her neck on a leather cord. In the course of lightly stalking her online, Tenn had learned she was an architect, like her father, though her last name had come from her mother—Fatima Gerges, a Lebanese-born travel writer. On the train, Tenn had churned over the choice of name, wondering if the decision had been Neri's or her parents'. She wondered what exactly she'd passed on to her own daughter. She wondered if it was possible to undo it.

"I was so sorry to hear about your parents," Tenn told Neri, which she'd already written in her message. Tenn was desperate to know how they'd died but couldn't ask outright, first thing. "I only met your father briefly, but he left an impression." Amos Blum had arranged to meet Tenn and Ward at their closing, to give them his original blueprints for the addition he'd put on the house. "We had one of his blueprints framed," Tenn told Neri. "It's hanging in the living room, and we intend to leave it there if we ever move." Tenn almost said it belonged to the house, as if a house were capable of possession, but caught herself.

"They loved that house," Neri said. She picked up her spoon, turned it over, set it back in place. "My mother cried for weeks when they were packing. They stayed almost ten years after my sister and I moved out, even though it was much more house than they needed. But my mother couldn't bear to leave it. It was her dream house. When people came over, she used to tell them the house liked to absorb people."

Tenn tried not to overidentify with the dead, but she was struck by the similarities between her and Fatima, their relationship with the house. "Funny," she told Neri, "I use the same term—*absorption*." Tenn tried to remember if Amos Blum had planted the word in her mind, but her memory of their conversation was murky, as if she'd dreamed it. She'd had a sense from Neri's messages that she was eager to meet, but now that they were here, Neri would barely make eye contact. Maybe the memory of the house was more painful than she'd expected. The waiter arrived with coffee for Neri, who told

Tenn she wasn't hungry. Tenn ordered a bowl of soup. Outside their little booth, everyone was bundled in scarves. It was soup weather. Neri watched through the plexiglass, the plastic cloudy, distorting.

"Do you want to see what I brought?" Tenn asked her. The shopping bag was obvious, crinkling noisily against Tenn's legs under the table. It was her pretense for this meeting—to offer Neri the many things she'd found in the house since their arrival. Tenn pulled items from the bag, all found in the attic—old sheet music, a gnawed straw hat, a robot dog. The tiny diamond ring from the floorboards was zipped in her wallet.

"Was this yours?" she asked.

Neri's eyes skimmed the ring, but Tenn saw no light of recognition. Instead, she reached for the robot dog.

"I tried it with fresh batteries," Tenn told her. "But it still didn't work."

"I have these blank spots," Neri said. "There are so many things about my childhood I've forgotten." She pressed the button on the dog's head even though Tenn had told her it was dead. "Is that age?" she asked, then laughed, embarrassed. She was barely thirty.

"I'm afraid it gets worse when you actually start to get old," Tenn said, though she wondered if the blank spots were age at all, a cold worry for the kids taking hold. "There was a doll, too, that we found in the yard, but it's gone missing."

Neri took the straw hat and set it on the table a safe distance in front of her, as if an object could be charged, could be a vessel.

"My mother hated that doll," she said, "if it's the one I'm thinking about. Silky bow on the chest?" Tenn nodded, and Neri smiled and continued. "She threw it away twice, and both times I fished it out of the trash."

"Why didn't she like it?" Tenn asked. It was creepy as fuck now, but it hadn't always been.

"It had a serial number in the plastic of one of its feet that she thought was bad luck," Neri said. "She had superstitions, my mother. If you felt sick, it was never a virus but something amiss in the spirit world. Did you open and close scissors without cutting anything? Well, you've harmed a spirit that was floating around the room, and now you'll pay. Did you leave a nail clipping on the floor? Because an evil spirit probably collected it to use for black magic."

"I vacuumed like a hundred nail clippings from between the floorboards, so I don't think evil spirits collected them all," Tenn said.

Neri laughed, finally loosening. "My dad's," she said. "My mother would never. It went on and on. Shower at night? Bad spirits could come out with the water and follow you. I couldn't even leave my shoes upside down."

"What happens if you leave your shoes upside down?" Tenn asked.

"Bad events!" Neri said.

"Christ, my kids throw their shoes everywhere," Tenn said.

"There were more," Neri said. She brought a hand to the evil eye on her neck and rolled the glass with her fingers. "I know there were more, but I can't remember them. I have a hard time remembering certain things—mornings, meals. What bedtime was like. The everyday stuff we did over and over. It's all blank in my mind."

"Lots of people have trouble remembering their childhoods," Tenn offered.

Neri shook her head. "No, it's weird," she said. "I can remember other places from that time with perfect clarity. Friends' houses, elementary school classrooms. But the house is fuzzy for me." She put a hand on the straw hat, took it away. "I know this hat was my mother's because she's wearing it in photos. Some with us together. But I can't remember actually seeing her wear it." She held it finally, taking it in her hands with purpose. "I don't feel her, either. She was superstitious about objects, too. She thought objects could hold spirits. It was so fucking annoying to shop with her. She had to pick every single thing up and hold it."

"Did she think that about the house?" Tenn asked. She hadn't been sure how to ask the question, but Neri had led them there. "Did she think there were spirits there, too?"

"Why do you ask?" Neri said. She moved on from the hat to the sheet music, humming softly as she read it. She was avoiding Tenn's eyes.

"I'm sorry," Tenn said. She could see Neri's mistrust, not of Tenn but of herself. She didn't trust herself, her memories, her mother. It was hard to live in a world with so much mystery. "My daughter is convinced we have ghosts in the house," Tenn said, hoping to give Neri's childhood self an ally. "It seems like the kind of thing your mother would've noticed."

"Kids have vivid imaginations," Neri said, as if she was repeating something she'd been told. "Though if you asked my mother, imagination had nothing to do with it. She talked, and her invisible friends talked back."

Tenn felt hot in the little translucent box, trapped even though she was outside. "They talked to her?" she asked. "What did they say?"

"Well, I couldn't hear them," Neri said. "And she'd never talk about it if my dad was around. They must've fought about it at some point, though I never overheard anything." Again, she picked up her spoon and put it back in place. "Sometimes she talked to her sister who'd drowned, and then it was mostly complaints about my grandma. But not always. She told me once they were like characters in a play, and sometimes they showed up to do their scenes, and it was important we let them."

"What happened if you didn't?" Tenn asked.

Neri shrugged. Neither used the word *ghost*, but it lingered in the booth like the coffee's steam. "There was a man who was very tall, who stood at the kitchen sink and turned on the water. There was a boy who ran through the upstairs hallway, back and forth, which really aggravated her. When she got pissed about something, which was rare, honestly, she'd leave the house. Sometimes for days."

"She'd leave?" Tenn said. "What did she think would happen if she stayed?"

Neri looked like she was about to speak, then stopped abruptly, confused. "I was going to say something, but I already forgot it." She stopped and laughed at herself. "Christ, my brain! I don't know what she thought would happen. It had something to do with the addition Dad put on, but I was young at the time. I don't know the whole story."

"The addition," Tenn said. The addition, which included Aisling's room, was the only part of the house that wasn't falling apart.

"All I know is there were a bunch of big cracks in the old part of the house, and that's what started the reno. But Mom was convinced the problem was somehow her fault, and Dad couldn't convince her otherwise. Something like she thought her bad energy was to blame. I've always suspected that's why travel was so important to her. If she stayed in one place for too long, eventually her bad energy would catch up to her." Neri picked up her spoon again, a repetitive motion. "I'm sorry. I know how it sounds. But she believed it. It was real to her."

Tenn wasn't sure how to respond. She wasn't sure how it would affect Neri to hear that Tenn believed her mother. "It doesn't sound so odd to me," she told her. "People tell me all kinds of stories when they hear I live in an old house."

"Oh, it wasn't specific to the house," Neri said. She picked up her spoon, put it back in place.

Tenn held her own spoon, because she needed to do something with her hands. "What do you mean, it wasn't the house?"

"She was like that everywhere," Neri said. "At hotels, when we were visiting family. After they moved. Always chatting with someone no one else could see, refusing to come inside if something was bothering her. She spent a lot of time outside at family gatherings."

She kept talking, but the world around Tenn had gone sideways and she was slipping. The ghosts were in her house, safely contained there. Nothing bad had happened in Georgia, but the ghosts had been waiting when they got home. If the ghosts were in the house, Tenn could protect her family by keeping them away from it. She hadn't considered the possibility that they might encounter new ghosts elsewhere.

Neri was still talking. "You're not supposed to pay attention to ghosts if you see them, according to my aunt. It makes them stronger. My aunt had dementia, though, and my mother was on all kinds of medications. More as we got older. Every time I came home, there was another new vial of pills."

Tenn's soup came and she lowered her face over the bowl and closed her eyes. She hadn't come to see Neri expecting to learn all the secrets of the universe, but she'd thought she'd learn *something* about the house that might help. Neri seemed convinced the issue was all her mother.

"Someone can be sick and still be right," Tenn said, because she believed it. She'd passed through her disbelief, and now she was on the other side.

Neri drank her coffee. "My dad never bought it, of course," she said. "If she brought it up, he just sighed like he did when she was talking about her collections. She collected all kinds of things—owl statues, sea urchin shells, wind chimes. When I was little, I rolled my eyes along with Dad, but sometimes at night, I find myself watching the shadows like something's inside them. That's one thing I remember about the house—how the shadows looked like people to me. If ghosts do exist, I can see how they'd have been drawn to Mom, specifically. There was something about her, a curiosity, maybe, that attracted them. She was a storyteller; she was always interested in peoples' stories. It was like her ghosts sensed that about her and needed her as a repository or something. I know that's not why they died, but sometimes I wonder."

Tenn smelled her soup and tried to keep herself from asking the question. But she understood then that Neri was waiting for her to ask it, needed her to ask, to give her permission to say it out loud. Tenn put down her spoon. "I'm sorry," she said. "I don't actually know what happened. It wasn't in the obituary."

"Oh," Neri said. She'd finished her coffee and now dragged a finger through the condensation on her water glass, the writing as strange as the words on Tenn's skin.

"You don't have to tell me," Tenn said. "I don't mean to pry."

"No, I don't mind," Neri said. "My wife is tired of hearing about it. It's one of those things where I can't stop talking about it even when I know people don't want to hear it."

Tenn put her hands around her bowl because her hands were cold and the bowl was warm. Now that the answer loomed before her, she was afraid to hear how Fatima had died. She was afraid, she realized, that Fatima's fate was her own.

"They died of dehydration," Neri said, matter-of-factly. "In their own home, in their own kitchen, which had running water and a fridge full of lemonade and stupid sugar-free antioxidant drinks. They died four days apart, but both from the same thing. They just stopped eating and drinking."

"Holy shit," Tenn said.

"Yeah," Neri said. "My sister and I were traveling, and we called for a welfare check since neither of them were answering their phones. It's awful to say, but my first thought when I got the call was that it was somehow my mother, that she'd snapped or . . . I don't know what I thought."

Tenn understood. Anyone could do anything at any time, especially a woman whose mind wasn't right, a woman who believed in ghosts and bad energy.

"I couldn't make sense of it. All I could think was that if you listen to ghosts long enough, who knows what they'll say?" Neri continued drawing on her glass, the same pattern as before. "I still can't make sense of it. Neither could the police, not with both of them, days apart. Carbon monoxide doesn't explain it. Or dementia. And the footprints . . ."

Tenn sat quietly while Neri worked up to it, wondering if ghosts could leave footprints, if ghosts had feet.

"They were just . . . walking in circles?" Neri said, her voice breaking. "For days and days, even after their feet started to bleed. It was easy to see what they'd been doing, not that the footprints answered any questions."

"What do you mean, walking in circles?" Tenn said. Neri looked at her sharply because Tenn had lost control of her tone.

"Dad had been going back and forth from the kitchen to the patio, which is where he went when he was avoiding something. He'd say, 'I just need to breathe the world for a bit,' and that was the end of the conversation. Mom stayed in the kitchen, walking from sink to counter and back again. They found her with a sponge in her hand, the counters spotless. They were like toy trains on tracks, never leaving their courses. Even after Dad died, which was faster because of his kidneys, she kept walking around his dead body on the floor. For four days. They walked and walked and pissed and shit themselves, and eventually they collapsed to the floor and died."

Neri traced the pattern on her glass even though there was no condensation left. Tenn reached out and touched her hand to stop her.

"Sorry," Neri said, startled. "I do that sometimes."

Tenn wanted to keep her hand on Neri's, to keep her safe the same way she wanted to keep Aisling safe from harm. But she didn't know how. All she could see was danger—broken walls, bloody footprints, a woman at the center. But the woman wasn't Fatima—it was Tenn.

"Your mother was a beautiful writer," Tenn said, the only words of comfort she could find. Fatima Gerges was gone, but at least she'd left something behind. "I read a few of her pieces last night. The one about Petra. She made everything feel so alive."

Neri shook her head. "It had gotten too hard for her," she said, "with her arthritis. She'd stopped altogether, not long before she died." Neri made her hands into claws, as if her mother's pain had lodged in her own fingers. "I told her there was dictation software she could use, but she was wary of technology."

"Do you write?" Tenn asked. Had writing been a safeguard for Fatima? she wondered. Had she trained Neri to protect herself in the same way?

"She always encouraged me, but I didn't have the knack. Drawing was my thing, which I got from my dad. Once I started taking drawing classes, she got off my case. I think she just wanted me to have an outlet, you know? But maybe I should give it another try. She would've liked that."

"Maybe it'll help you remember some of what you've forgotten," Tenn suggested.

Neri touched a finger to her water glass but stopped herself. "Actually," she said, "I've been thinking about it lately. Writing down some of her stories. Sometimes I think I can hear her, whispering in my ear." She covered one ear with her hand, either holding something in or keeping it out. "Or maybe it's just tinnitus," she said, and laughed. "You know, I'm going to do it. I feel better just thinking about it. Thank you," she told Tenn, and took her hand, just for a moment, a quick squeeze.

Tenn felt her feet, as if they were raw, as if she'd been the one walking—a memory or a premonition, she wasn't sure.

* * *

Tenn didn't have much time before she needed to get the kids from school. She'd called Senna from the train, and Senna arrived at the house just after Tenn, walking straight into the dining room and ordering a pizza to be delivered two hours later. "As a safeguard," she said. "In case we get stuck."

At the table, she unloaded her backpack. Her aunt Dahlia, the family ghost expert, had stopped doing house calls, but Senna had assisted her enough to know the drill.

"Most so-called ghost hunters rely on a combination of pseudoscience and the fallibility of human perception," Senna told her. "There's an app that supposedly translates electronic voice phenomena into words, but it's all bullshit. There's a reason people hear things in EVP—it's called pareidolia. The tendency to find meaning in ambiguity, like a Rorschach test."

Tenn considered the possibility that she was being tested, that what she saw in the ink blots, over and over, was death.

Senna pulled from her bag a wooden bowl and three candles. "I stole these from my aunt," she said. Then she removed a small black cloth, onto which she set a crystal ball.

"What—" Tenn said.

"Hear me out," Senna said.

Tenn sat at the table, her laughter delirious. Had she become a person who consulted crystal balls? Maybe! She was beyond hope; she'd try anything—a crystal ball, a séance. This house had made her doubt everything she thought she knew about the world. It had made her doubt Ward, doubt herself, her treacherous brain. But maybe she'd spent her whole life seeing the world incompletely and her doubt was correct, a necessary step. Maybe it was impossible to truly know another person, even the person you thought you knew best. Maybe she didn't know herself and was capable of things she'd never considered. Fatima Gerges had considered her bad energy a source of destruction, and Tenn had allowed herself to become a person she didn't like anymore, her unhappiness bleeding out into her family. If Tenn didn't want to end up like Fatima, she would have to throw out what she thought she'd known.

Senna arranged the candles, lit them one by one. "Do you have a notebook?"

Tenn got the notepad by the phone and a Valentine's Day pencil whose end Gogo had chewed. Senna filled the wooden bowl with water, which she sloshed on the kitchen floor as she rushed back to the dining room. Senna was not wasting time. She didn't want to be in the house longer than necessary.

"What exactly are we doing here?" Tenn asked her. She needed to do *something*, but this felt like a summoning—the opposite of what she wanted.

"*Scrying* comes from the word *descry*," Senna said, "which means 'to catch sight of.'" She positioned the crystal ball, the bowl, the candles, fussing with the arrangement. "Some people use mirrors; some use fire. But the medium isn't what's important."

"What's important?" Tenn asked.

"What's important is that you stop thinking," Senna explained. "We want your conscious mind out of the way. So whatever's here with us has an opportunity to show itself."

Tenn watched thin plumes rise from the candles and saw nothing but smoke. "But isn't this the same as a Rorschach test?" she asked. "Whatever I see is rising up from my subconscious?" A message on her skin was one thing—externalized. But Tenn was constantly sifting through images that she'd absorbed from elsewhere but that felt like her own. She wasn't good at telling the difference between what was hers and what wasn't.

"Maybe," Senna said. "Or maybe you'll experience something you couldn't have on your own. It's happened to you before, right?"

"What do you mean?" Tenn said. In the crystal ball, she saw her own face, distorted. Even images she struggled to place came from inside her, some vault in her mind, filtered through her imagination. Like dreams, like art—it all came from somewhere.

"At the meeting house," Senna said, "when your nose bled. Did you really think that was just a memory?"

Tenn tried to remember what she'd felt that day at the meeting house, but it was faraway now, just out of her mind's reach. She checked the time on her phone. She'd have to leave soon to get the kids. "How do we do this?" she said.

"My aunt always does an introduction first," Senna said. "According to her, there are two rules. The first is to always be polite."

"And the second?" Tenn said. She'd stayed up all night, and she could feel it now, the hot creep of her exhaustion, as she watched the candles flicker and sway. She could smell motor oil and taste coconut and feel the skinlike cool of hydrangea petals. These strays were all within her, even though she couldn't identify their origins.

"Always say goodbye when you're done," Senna said. She cleared her throat, and Tenn tried to quiet her mind, let her thoughts sink away as if through water. Senna said a few words, introduced herself. She told the spirits they were listening.

"And now?" Tenn asked.

Senna sat tall in her chair, tense. "We wait."

Tenn waited. She waited and smelled motor oil, the scent bringing with it a heat to her thighs, the muscles squeezing. She could taste mango. She wasn't sure how to be blank when these sensations stirred inside her. She watched a candle, let her eyes unfocus as the flame danced, unpredictable. She slid the wooden bowl close and studied it, the water's surface reflecting back points of light from the flames. In her mind, she was standing in an air-conditioned room, at a counter where something sweet was being prepared for her. It was hard to hold on to, so she let the memory go, along with the dull awareness that it was hard to hold on to because it didn't belong to her. She tried to be blank and then she stopped trying to be blank because she didn't have to try because she was practiced at it. She could lose her identity for weeks and months and years; she could become a completely different person. She looked into the water and saw that it was a lens, like an eye or a camera, bending and refracting light. On the lens were reflections: the textured plaster of the ceiling above, the dark void in the doorway between rooms. The candle flame, upside down, dripping like a pale orange icicle, stretching like taffy. Tenn had never liked taffy, but Crystal had—the banana kind. Crystal had smelled like banana taffy and grape lip balm, and they'd practiced kissing with each other, tissue pressed between their lips. Tenn was the only one left to remember it, a memory that would someday be lost but for now, inside Tenn, was preserved. This was what the living did—preserve the dead. Tenn was just a receptacle, and she let the memories flow through her, first of Crystal, then of others, her hand picking up the gnawed pencil, bringing with it a new flood of fragments: a sudden splintering of a pencil's soft wood, its impressionability between her teeth. She remembered the way it felt to move a pencil across a sheet of looseleaf, the agonizing feedback of the pencil and its raspy scratch on the page, and then the scratch was all there was, scratch scratch scratch

until Senna's warm hand covered her own, pressing down hard, Senna's voice loud and high: *"Goodbye Goodbye GOODBYE."*

* * *

Senna pulled Tenn by the wrist, straight out of the house.

"What the fuck?" Tenn said. She tried to orient herself in her body, but she felt as if she'd walked into a hotel room already occupied by strangers.

Senna told Tenn to get in her car and disappeared back inside the house. Tenn didn't have her keys, so she climbed inside Senna's car, an old Cadillac that smelled new, which was unlocked. Senna returned more quickly than Tenn expected, her backpack unzipped, candles smelling of snuffed flames. Senna started the car and turned the heat up high, and they sat there in silence but for the shush of the fan. Tenn had no idea what she'd written, but Senna was doing breath work, hands clenched in her lap. Tenn tried to remember, but it was already out of reach, like a dream. Senna had stuffed the notepad under her shirt—Tenn could see the outline through her sweater.

"Are you going to tell me?" Tenn said finally. "What I wrote?"

"Absolutely not," Senna told her.

Senna looked at the house, her eyes wild. This was her aunt's area of expertise; Senna was just an apprentice. Tenn couldn't remember where she'd left her keys. She thought of Ward, waking at the bottom of the stairs, detached from his work, from everything. Tenn could feel objects in her orbit but was disconnected from the material world.

Senna took a napkin from the glove box and wiped her nose. Tenn hadn't even registered that she'd been crying.

"What's wrong?" Tenn asked. "What the fuck happened?"

Senna started the car, calmed her breath. "Careful," she said, motioning for Tenn to breathe with her. "I'm not sure we're alone."

* * *

Senna drove Tenn back to the hotel, quiet the whole ride, and Tenn stayed quiet, too. She didn't understand what Senna had meant, exactly, but it had tuned Tenn, like a radio, to a new frequency. It was time for her to listen. In the parking lot, Senna waited for Tenn to get out, then rolled down her window.

"I'll text you," she said, and pulled away.

Tenn lay on the hotel bed and considered the possibility that the only solution to the problem was to remove herself entirely from her family. It wasn't a new thought. Anyone could do anything at any time. In the next room, two people were arguing, and she couldn't understand what they were saying, only the hostility of the tone, escalating. Tenn imagined this argument, playing in a loop, her and Ward trapped in their own fight that got worse and worse until it started over again from the beginning. The woman in the next room began to sob; the man was muttering, and all Tenn could make out was his bitterness. She tried to picture what she'd written but she could only see the pencil, brought home in a Valentine's bag covered in paper hearts. Then Tenn remembered: the kids. She'd left her car at the house, and it was dismissal time.

Tenn went to the bathroom and splashed water on her face, then texted Ward that she was having car trouble. Could he run to the school and pick up the kids? Ward didn't respond. She called Senna, whose phone went straight to voicemail, but Senna called back almost immediately.

"Listen," Senna said, "can you disable the cameras inside the house?"

"What's going on?" Tenn asked her. "I need my car so I can get the kids from school."

"The cameras inside your house," Senna said. "Can you switch them off remotely? So they stop recording?"

In the next room, the woman had gone quiet; the door slammed shut, then opened, slammed again. Tenn's laptop was on the hotel desk, the camera app already open. "Sure," she said. She checked the feeds. In the upstairs hallway, afternoon light pooled on the floor.

In the living room, she spotted a single tube sock left by Anders. "Why?"

"The less you know, the better," Senna said. "I'm going to park in the back so I don't get caught on any doorbell cams. Go to the desk and talk to someone who'll remember you."

"Senna, wait," Tenn said. She tasted mango again, the flavor haunting her. "This is my house we're talking about. My *house*."

"I'm not going to burn it down," Senna said. "But you can't stay there. Go talk to someone. I'll text you later."

Tenn sat at the room's desk, above which hung a mirror, which reflected back the closed curtains behind her. On her laptop, the feed for the haunted library was open, but nothing happened other than patrons checking out books, because unlike Tenn's eyes, a camera lens could only capture the living. Tenn watched a woman pull a book off a shelf and put it back in the wrong spot, and then she disabled the cameras in the house and went to hotel reception, where she told the woman at the desk she needed to switch rooms.

16

Ward stood on the sidewalk, staring at Tenn's car, listening to her phone ring, unanswered. Snow fell over his hair, over his coat, dusting him. Tenn had been excited about snow, about snowball fights and sledding, about mittens and hot chocolate, when they'd made the decision, together, to move here. The Tenn he knew would've been thrilled by this sight; she'd have been outside prancing, catching snowflakes on her tongue. The third time he called, she answered on the sixth ring.

"Hello?" she said, as if she wasn't sure who was calling. She was breathless, like she'd run to get the phone. The tension in Ward's stomach loosened at the sound of her voice, replaced by a kernel of resentment that she'd made him worry, yet again. "Ward?"

Ward heard rustling, a car alarm in the background. "Where are you right now?"

"I'm at the hotel," she said. "I just texted you. I don't have my car. Can you get the kids?"

It was nearly four, past time for pickup. Ward wasn't sure he should leave the house. He stepped back inside, left the door open despite the cold.

"We're already late," he said. "Can you call and tell them I'm coming?"

Tenn huffed and puffed; Ward heard a door open and close. "I'll call," she said. "How long till you can leave work?"

"I'm not at work," Ward told her.

The background noise quieted, and Ward tried to read the silence. He could hear Tenn breathing more slowly now, like she was making an effort to sound normal.

"Where are you?" Tenn asked him.

"Something happened," he said. He crossed the house to the dining room, where a wooden bowl sat on the table, filled with water. "Brady called me." Brady was a tech bro who lived two doors down, whose favorite pastime was blowing leaves. Sometimes he blew leaves from Ward and Tenn's yard when he ran out of leaves in his own. "He came home early and saw our front door open. He was worried something happened to you."

"I didn't leave the door open," Tenn said. "What happened? Was it a contractor?" The question was genuine—he believed Tenn hadn't done it herself.

"It looks like someone broke in," he told her. "I'm trying not to touch things too much, but the doors are all fucked up."

"What do you mean the doors are fucked up?" Tenn said.

Through the window, Ward watched the snow and tried to remember what she had planned that day, why Tenn's car was here and she was not. Ward had come to the house that morning to let in the fire department, who'd found nothing that indicated the house was unsafe. He'd been preoccupied with his own schedule, rearranging it to make time to see the doctor, again. Maybe Tenn had told him her plans and he'd forgotten.

"As far as I can tell," he said, "they came in through the back door in the kitchen. The glass is broken, and Brady didn't see anything suspicious on his doorbell cam. They seem to have gone through the house and bashed all the knobs off the exterior doors." The house had a lot of doors—the front door, the porch door, the kitchen. There was even one in the dining room, which led to the side yard—the real estate agent had called it a coffin door.

"What do you mean they bashed the doorknobs?" Tenn said. Her confusion seemed sincere—she didn't sound like she was acting. "Did they take anything?" she asked, which was the right question.

"Not that I can tell," Ward said. He walked through the dining room to the kitchen, which was already cold. "They weren't practiced, whoever did this. It looks like a gang of possums with sledgehammers came through. But none of the doors will latch closed now. Which isn't ideal," he said, "in December."

Ward carried a bar stool from the counter to prop the door closed, which was the best he could do for now. He didn't have time to sweep the glass and cover the window, not if he was going to get the kids.

"Did you call the police?" Tenn asked him. It was the right question to ask; she was asking the right questions.

"Not yet," Ward said. "I just got here." He walked back to the dining room, where he sat at the table and studied the bowl of water, the drips of wax on the tabletop beside it. "Tenn, why is your car here?"

Tenn didn't hesitate. "I told you this morning I was going to pick up a few things from the house," she said. He didn't remember, but it was plausible she'd told him. He didn't remember much from the night before, after they got home. He'd sat at his desk, responded to a few emails, and the next thing he knew they were in a strange hotel room. He could remember her terror but not what caused it. She continued: "And I told you I was having coffee with my friend Senna this afternoon, remember? So she picked me up from the house, but when she saw what a mess I was, coffee became wine, and then one glass became three." Tenn rarely drank before the kids were in bed, but this, too, was plausible. Tenn *was* a mess; maybe Senna had thought wine might take the edge off. "So she brought me back to the hotel, because obviously I couldn't drive. She was going to take me to get the kids, but she got a call from work and had to deal with it."

"So you left your car," Ward said. He was upstairs now, walking through the bedrooms. Tenn's jewelry was on her dresser, seemingly untouched.

"Yeah," Tenn said. "And when I got back to the hotel, these people were screaming at each other in the next room." It was all plausible, but Ward could hear it, the way Tenn had rehearsed this story, the way she'd thought through his inevitable questions. "It was really bad, so I went to the front desk and asked if they could put us in a different room, because the last thing we need is the kids in here listening to the breakdown of a marriage. So that's what I've been doing. I didn't hear your call because I left my phone when I was moving all our luggage."

"Did you call the school?" he asked her. "When I didn't answer, what was your plan for the kids?"

Tenn was quiet for a minute; she had no prepared answer for this question. "I don't know," she said. "I thought you'd call back. I'm sorry. I never drink during the day. And I'm so used to getting the kids off the bus—I forgot I had to drive."

Maybe it was all true—the wine, the noisy neighbors—but Ward didn't think so. Tenn was a lightweight, and she didn't sound like she'd had three glasses of wine, for starters.

On the bed, there was a pile of kids' clothing—Tenn hadn't been lying about that part. But Ward realized she'd been packing for another week when they'd only discussed one more night, time Tenn had insisted she needed to make sure the house was safe. "How long were you planning to stay at the hotel?"

"We have no idea what happened last night," she said, and he could hear the terror in her voice, the same terror he'd heard that morning. The fear wasn't fabricated—he could feel it through the phone. Tenn wasn't usually the one who panicked. "I don't want the kids sleeping there until we have some understanding of what's going on."

Ward didn't think what had happened was much of a mystery. He'd been tired last night—he'd driven all the way from Georgia with few breaks. But Tenn refused to believe he'd been sleepwalking despite his doctor's assessment that a sleep disorder was likely the cause. Ward would have to do a sleep study to confirm, but there was no time for that now. He didn't know how to convince Tenn the house was safe if she'd made up her mind otherwise.

"Well, we can't sleep here tonight anyway," he said. "None of the doors will stay closed, and it's going to get below freezing." Back downstairs, he dragged an armchair from the living room to barricade the front door. "And Brady had a bear in his yard two nights ago."

"Oh, perfect," Tenn said. "A bear is all we need."

"I don't even know who to call about the doors," Ward said. "If there's someone who can replace the knobs or if we'll need whole new doors. And we have to deal with the glass in the kitchen."

"I can call the wall guy," Tenn said. "He knows everyone. He'll know who we should call."

"I guess I'll get the kids, then," Ward said.

"Yes," Tenn said. She waited a second before she continued. "Do you want me to call the police?" There was rustling again and then the sound of people talking—a lot of people talking, like in a lobby. Tenn walked through the crowd. Maybe she was still moving their things, Ward thought, or maybe she just wanted to make sure she was seen. "If someone broke into the house, we should call the police, right?"

Ward listened to the commotion—the hotel was busy. He imagined all that noise coming through the walls while they were trying to get the kids to sleep.

"You know, I would, Tenn," he said, "but I think once they come inside and see that we have surveillance cameras all over the house, they're probably going to ask about the footage." There was a camera pointed directly at the back door, which Tenn had installed herself. "But since you disabled all the cameras less than an hour before Brady called, I'm guessing that'll create some questions you don't want to answer." He opened the coat closet and took out the kids' hats and gloves. Maybe they could play in the snow in the hotel parking lot. "But do you want to call anyway? Do you think that's a good idea?"

Tenn said hello to someone at the desk, and Ward listened as the noise dimmed, as she left her witnesses. She hadn't thought about how to explain the cameras. Ward waited for her answer, no longer trying to discern truth from lie but rather what the lie meant, how scared he should be.

On the street, a man got out of a car, carrying a pizza box.

"No," Tenn said. "I guess not."

* * *

The hotel had been taken over by a college lacrosse team, and the night was punctuated by the sounds of young women running through the halls, knocking on doors to adjacent rooms. Tenn read to the kids, something she rarely did now that they could read on their own, to drown out the pounding, a high-pitched voice saying, "*Let me in, you little bitch.*" At one point, there was an ice fight in the hall, stray cubes bouncing off their door, left to melt on the carpet. Ward didn't want to ask Tenn about the house in front of the kids. Maybe, he thought, he could trace his fingernail along her forearm and let her skin ask the question. But he was unsure what to ask now to sort this out. The only question he could form was *Have you lost your fucking mind?*

Ward left the room to take a call from Johann, and when he came back, the kids were asleep and Tenn was on her laptop, headphones over her ears. Ward sat beside her, put his AirPods back in, and opened his own computer. There was a sumo tournament underway, and he watched a few bouts while Tenn watched the live feed of the house, the cameras back on, fully functional. There was a new virus going around Japan, so spectators were banned from making noise beyond clapping. If they opened their mouths, they risked spreading disease.

He texted her: Do u want to talk about it

Tenn texted back: talk about what

Ward stole a glance at Tenn's screen as he watched his own, wondering what she was looking for in the house—an intruder, a bear. But then he saw bookshelves and realized she wasn't watching their house at all. It was a library, and not one he recognized. Live feeds usually soothed her, but she was tense now as she watched, as if she expected to see something in a library, past closing.

The house, he texted. He couldn't just ignore it, but if Tenn had her way, they'd sit there the whole night without saying a single word.

On Tenn's screen, the library remained empty, the rooms dimly illuminated by red exit lights. On Ward's screen, a new bout was starting, and a wrestler reached into a basket of salt and flicked a pinch across the ring, like he was seasoning it. His opponent, an unusually hairy man, responded by taking an enormous handful of salt and throwing it flamboyantly into the air.

not really, Tenn texted back.

Then she slipped off her headphones and nudged Ward's arm. "Why do they do that?" she whispered.

Ward pulled out one of his AirPods. "It's a purifying ritual," he said. "To ward off bad spirits." On his screen, the two men faced each other and squatted. One put a single fist on the floor, then the other. "And it helps absorb sweat from their hands."

Tenn scooted closer and watched as the men exploded up and into each other, their bodies melding together as they fought. The hairy man went for the other's throat.

We can't just not talk about it, Ward texted.

"What's the wizard saying?" Tenn asked.

"That's the gyōji," Ward said, about a man inside the ring wearing a pointy hat and an elaborate silk robe. It was easier to talk about sumo than their problems. "He's like a referee. He says *still going still going* until it's over." From the corner of his eye, he saw movement on Tenn's screen. "What's that?" he said. He pointed to the library, a room lit with red light.

"What's what?" Tenn said.

"That," Ward said.

Tenn saw it then, too, a person-size shadow in the doorway. On Ward's screen, the hirsute man picked his opponent up by his mawashi and carried him out of the ring while the opponent helplessly kicked his feet. Tenn and Ward were both captivated by this development, and when they looked back to Tenn's screen, the shadow was gone.

"You saw it?" she said. "Where'd it go?" She toggled through the other rooms, but the intruder was no longer within the cameras' sight. An intruder—that's what the figure looked like to Ward.

"Should we call the police?" he said.

"It's in Idaho," Tenn said, as if that answered the question.

"Why are you watching a library in Idaho?" Ward asked her.

Tenn picked up her phone. it's haunted, she texted, as if *haunted* were a word she couldn't say in front of the kids. She resumed whispering. "Or it's supposed to be. I've never seen anything, before now."

"But it's a setup, right?" Ward said. Tenn kept her eyes on the screen. "They stage it, like a publicity thing?"

Tenn shrugged.

On Ward's screen, the wrestlers returned to their sides and bowed. Tenn clicked through the library's rooms again, but there was no movement, no more shadows to be seen in the halls. Then she opened a new tab in which a giant panda climbed a tree after a cub.

Tenn, Ward texted.

i'm trying to protect you, she typed. it's not safe there

Protect me from what, he typed. Maybe he could have the fire department come back and walk through the house with her, or a home inspector. If Ward couldn't convince her the house was safe, he would find someone who could.

Tenn watched her screen, though the pandas were no longer visible, having climbed outside the scope of the camera's vision.

there's no point, she finally typed.

No point to what??? he asked. Talking?

not if you're not going to believe me

Ward sat with this for a minute, the possibility that what she believed might be so far from what he believed that there was no way to bridge the difference. Tenn had never been prone to magical thinking. Her parents hadn't even been able to sell her on Santa when she was a kid.

What are we supposed to do then? he asked her. It was so stupid to argue over text when they were sitting an inch apart, but he was worried if he asked aloud she'd shut down. I genuinely want to understand what you're thinking here.

Tenn clicked another tab: a digital mandala shaped like a lotus, casting the room in shades of purple and blue. Tenn breathed along as the petals unfolded, then returned to her phone. i can't do this tonight, she typed. not with the kids here. i need to protect my energy.

On Tenn's screen, the mandala shifted, from purple to pink, the dark stamen at its center expanding like a black hole drawing its viewer nearer. A new sumo bout started, and one wrestler threw another off the dohyō into the spectators. Tenn switched tabs to a feed of sporadic traffic, then abruptly closed her laptop and lay down facing the wall. Ward followed suit and switched off the light, to the sound of women cackling in the hall. In the room next door, a hairdryer started up. Neither Ward nor Tenn spoke, side by side in the dark, as if they were far apart, their connection severed.

* * *

Ward woke atop the desk, his right elbow burning with pain. Tenn was below him, scrambling into sweatpants.

"What's going on?" he said. His vision was dull, and he cradled his hurt elbow against his chest, the pain insistent. "What happened to my arm?"

"I have to leave," Tenn said. She had one shoe in hand, and she was looking for the other. She knelt beside the bed and swept a frantic arm across the floor.

Ward dropped to his knees, and Tenn popped up by the desk to spot him. She offered a tentative hand, then retracted it as if she'd thought better of touching him. Her eyes were spooked, glued on Ward. He climbed off the desk, and Tenn eased him into the chair.

"Leave?" Ward whispered. The kids were in their bed, still asleep, oblivious. He tried to extend the arm, but the pain made him shudder. The room was dark, but he could see the glow of morning around the drapes. "What time is it?"

Tenn watched like she didn't trust him, like he might do something unpredictable.

"Early," she said. She stuffed the wrong foot into the sneaker, not bothering with the laces. "I have to go." She got back on her knees and crawled across the floor, searching. She was moving fast, like something was chasing her. Ward got down beside her, dumbfounded by the intensity of her terror.

"What happened?" he said. "What's wrong?" He tried to remember how he'd gotten on the desk, but his mind was blank. The last thing he remembered was Tenn's fingers, their hands close but not touching as they fell asleep.

Now Tenn crawled away from him, still looking for her second shoe. He grabbed her by the ankle, and she yanked it free but stopped crawling and knelt on the carpet to face him.

"It happened again," she told him.

Ward held his elbow, which was swelling, which was hurt. "The sleepwalking?"

Tenn shook her head. "It's not sleepwalking," she said. "That's not what it is."

"What is it, then?" he asked her. He scanned her body—for bruises, for marks. He'd never seen her like this, purely desperate to escape, like a character in a horror movie fleeing a monster. He didn't think he could hurt her, even in his sleep, but maybe it was beyond his control.

"You were hanging spiders in the tree," she told him. She turned her head, spotted the shoe, grabbed it, and shoved her foot inside. Ward reached out and took her hand, because he was certain if he didn't, she would get up and run.

"What tree?" he said.

"The tree," Tenn said, and waved her free hand. "The tree in the yard. I woke up and you were on the desk, and I asked what you were doing, and you said you were hanging spiders in the tree. You said, 'I'll do anything to make you happy.' And then you fell, but you didn't wake up. You just started the whole thing over again."

Ward didn't remember, not the climbing, not the falling. He didn't remember having a dream. He didn't think it should be possible to stay asleep through a fall, through this pain. "Did you try to wake me?"

"Of course I tried to wake you!" Tenn said. She wrenched her hand away and crawled to the dresser, where she'd left her purse. She was wearing sweatpants and a T-shirt—no bra—and red Chucks on the wrong feet, the laces wild. She was leaving. "I shook you, I talked to you, I tried to put you back in bed. I sat on your lap, but you pushed me onto the floor. I'm trying so hard to protect you and the kids, but you never listen. You never believe a word I say!" She ran into the bathroom, and Ward heard the rattle of pill bottles, which she stuffed inside her purse. "What else am I supposed to do? If you have any ideas, I'm all ears!" Ward could only watch her, his wife, fully unraveled, giving each of the kids a solemn kiss on the forehead. "But of course you don't have any ideas. You're completely checked out, so it's all on me, as fucking always. And now I have to go, Ward," she said. "Right now. This is happening because of me."

Ward stood and blocked the door with his body. Tenn was rummaging through her purse for her keys. He never should've taken her to get her car from the house; they should've left it. He was worried about her driving; he was worried about her.

"How is this because of you?" he asked her. She looked at him, blocking her exit, then looked to the window. "I'm trying to understand, but I don't, Tenn. Please. Please explain it to me."

"I can't," she said, and reached around him for the doorknob. He took her face in his hands, and she shook her head hard, like she was having a seizure. So he let go. "There's something in the room; something is here with us, and I know you don't believe me—I know you don't. But it's here because of me, or it's just here and it's affecting you because of me, but either way I have to leave. I can't explain it. You're not safe with me in the room."

She looked to the kids, who were somehow sleeping through this, Anders with both arms splayed and reaching, just as Ward slept.

"Don't go," he said, though he knew she was going anyway. "This isn't your fault. I'll go back to the doctor. You can come with me. He said there's medication, if it gets bad. It's the same thing we give Gogo when she goes to the vet. I'll take dog tranquilizers, and I'll stay asleep at night. Don't leave like this."

Ward had his own terror now, the kind that blanked him out, like that morning when she'd told him she was thinking about dying. It was like that, but bigger, obliterating. In that moment, Ward was certain that if he let Tenn leave, he'd never see her again.

"Please," Tenn said, tears in her eyes. She looked like a wild animal, caught in a trap. She would gnaw off a leg if that's what it took to get free. "Please," she said again, louder this time. Aisling tossed in bed.

"Don't go," he whispered, and wrapped his hand around her wrist, the hand of the arm that wasn't killing him. His back hurt, too, like there was a knife in his spine, and his hip, which he touched.

"Are you okay?" Tenn said. She squeezed past him and got a hand on the doorknob.

"My hip hurts," he said. He didn't know what to do. He didn't know how to keep her from slipping away from him. He considered picking her up, shoving her in the car, driving her somewhere to get help, but there was no doubt in his mind—this was a woman who'd throw herself out of a moving vehicle. He didn't know what to do to keep her safe.

"Go to the doctor," she told him. She seemed a little calmer now, with her hand on the door. Maybe she would be better once she got in her car. Maybe she just needed time to calm down. "You fell so many times I lost count. I thought I was about to watch you break your neck and die in front of me. You kept doing it over and over even though every time you got hurt."

"Don't go," he said again. "I'm awake now. It's over."

"It's not over," Tenn said. She opened the door and stepped into the hall, and Ward let her. Outside the room, her terror abated by degrees—Ward could see the relief in her shoulders. "But maybe it can be for you."

Ward reached out again, and he wanted to pull her back in, but Tenn ran away fast, and she didn't look back. Behind him, the kids kicked the covers.

Aisling was awake now, her voice an alarm. "Where's Mommy?"

PART 3

Stay, illusion!

—WILLIAM SHAKESPEARE,
Hamlet

17

Tenn drove without aim, her only goal to put as much distance as possible between herself and her family. She didn't realize she was heading toward Pennsylvania until three hours into the drive. It was late afternoon by the time she neared Hawleyville, the sky clearing as the sun sparkled over a hubcap emporium. This part of Pennsylvania was similar to New York—the peeling farmhouses and rolling hills dried to pale gold—and Tenn wondered for a moment if she'd gone anywhere at all, if she'd been circling Westchester the whole time without realizing. But no, a few more miles down the interstate and there was her exit, by the diner where she and her high school friends had drunk coffee and smoked one million cigarettes, staying as late as their curfews would allow. There was the grocery store parking lot where her first boyfriend had pulled over to give her—mint in mouth—a timid, hot kiss. There was the park where she'd gone to day camp, where a wasp had stung her hand, which swelled to the size of a baseball mitt.

Tenn was near the skate park when the tug returned, and she pulled to the shoulder at the spot where Crystal died, by the tree. It hadn't been her intention to come here, but she'd been driving here the whole time. The oak tree was thick and gnarled, and the wooden cross at its base looked new, unweathered, though the polyester carnations beneath it had worn to gray. Tenn sat in her car and felt her stomach; she hadn't eaten, and it hurt, as did her legs and back, cramped from sitting. She got out of the car and let the cold consume all other sensation. She hadn't brought her coat. Her shoes were still on the wrong feet and untied.

A car sped toward her—everyone drove too fast on this road—and Tenn played out what might happen if she stepped into the street, or if, like Crystal, she drove her car into this old tree, let the tug pull her out of her body once and for all. It hadn't been her plan when she left the hotel. Her only goal was to get away, to get far enough from Ward that he'd stop hurting himself. There'd been ghosts at the hotel—she'd felt them crowding around as he toppled from the desk over and over when all he wanted was to make her happy. She was sure she could feel them. She didn't know if they'd followed her from the house or if they belonged to the hotel; all she knew was that they only affected her family when she was with them. To keep her family safe, she had to get away from them. And stay away.

Tenn watched the car pass, too close, and she stumbled back over a root and came down at the base of the oak's trunk. She remembered Crystal's grandmother's house, an evening spent sitting beneath the kitchen table at women's stockinged feet, the checkerboard floors cool and dirty like the ground here under the tree, eating sugar cookies from a tin while a little gray poodle snuffled around her for crumbs. She remembered the poodle's fur, the way it felt when it nestled against her, the way her fingers got stuck in its curls while the sounds of clinking ice and shuffling cards filtered down from above with the veil of cigarette smoke. The poodle fell asleep in her lap that night, and she stayed under the table even though her legs went numb, even though Crystal's mom told her it was past bedtime. She couldn't see Crystal in the memory, but she was there—Tenn could feel her, just as she could feel the ghosts. They'd been young, and she could no longer remember the dog's name, just the weight of its warm body, the twisted curls of its coat, the feeling of belonging, of wanting to stay. Crystal was gone, but Tenn was still there to remember. This was her work, the work of the living.

Another car drove by and slowed to see if Tenn needed help. She waved them on, got back in the car, and resumed driving.

* * *

Crystal's mom, Robin, worked in the billing department at Hawleyville General. Tenn got out in the hospital parking lot and sat on a brick wall near the entrance. She wasn't expecting to see Robin—she just needed someplace safe to sit and look for a hotel—so when Robin emerged from the hospital carrying a paper shopping bag, Tenn was surprised to see her. She stood and Robin saw her and stopped, and then a car pulled to the curb, and a man rushed from the driver's seat to escort a heavily pregnant woman inside. The man left the car running and looked back at it briefly, his hand on the small of the woman's back, unsure what to do about parking. Robin looked so much older than Tenn remembered, her face deeply creased, her short curls nearly white. Tenn wasn't sure if Robin recognized her until she said her name.

"Tennessee?" When Tenn nodded, Robin went in for a hug, her tentativeness giving way as she dug her fingers into Tenn's back. There was garlic on her breath and a slight tremor in her body. Tenn had a hard time letting go, some childlike part of her wanting to cling. "What are you doing here?"

Tenn wasn't sure how to answer. "I'm visiting someone," she said.

Tenn had tried and failed to remember the last time she'd seen Robin. Her parents had moved to a lakeside community in Virginia several years ago, so she hadn't had a reason to return to Hawleyville, other than a handful of weddings and funerals. She hadn't come back for Crystal's service, not because she hadn't wanted to but because she'd convinced herself her presence was unimportant. Crystal's life had not included Tenn for a long time—she had a family of her own, friends who were deeply grieving a version of Crystal Tenn hadn't known. Tenn's own grief was irrelevant to them. The death of someone she hadn't spoken to in years shouldn't have affected her so much.

"Oh no, dear," Robin said. "Is it your parents?"

Tenn's parents had been gone for years now, which presumably Robin knew—they'd been neighbors.

"No," Tenn said. "They're both good."

A security guard with a gray mullet and droopy bags under his eyes came out from the lobby, having noticed the car left running in the fire lane.

"Larry, it was a woman in labor," Robin told him. "He'll be back."

Larry smiled and nodded, then slid into the driver's seat to turn off the engine. "Must be their first," Larry said, closing the door. "Racing in when she'll probably be in labor for three days."

Robin's smile was polite but distracted. The paper shopping bag in her hand was faded and torn, like she'd been using it for a while. Tenn tried to imagine what was inside, but this woman who'd been a second mother was now a stranger to her.

"I was really sorry," Tenn said. She knew she had to say it even though it seemed impossible. She couldn't keep doing the same things over and over; she had to try something new. "I'm so sorry about Crystal. I know I haven't seen you in a long time . . ."

Robin looked sharply into the distance, and Tenn shut up, remembered the poodle in her lap, the greasiness of its fur. The memory was so strong, a living thing. Robin's face was unreadable, and Tenn could only guess what she felt—grief and guilt, anger that Crystal had left them. Crystal had chosen to leave, and now Robin had to live with her absence.

"She's in a better place now," Robin said, her face softening, and Tenn was so glad she had whatever comfort that thought provided. Robin looked at Tenn as if she could still see the child inside her, the person she used to be, full of promise she hadn't fulfilled. "How are you? How are your babies? Are they with you?"

"They're at home, in New York," Tenn said. "They're doing well." She didn't know that, because she'd left them, but she trusted Ward, trusted he would do what they needed. "Outgrowing their clothes at an alarming rate. I make them your spaghetti sometimes. It's my son's favorite, and he's picky."

Robin smiled mildly and nodded. It had been Tenn's favorite, too, a long time ago. She'd come to Robin's house for refuge when her parents fought, the table always set with a place for her, like she was part of the family. She never knocked, then, which seemed strange to her now. She tried to imagine inviting a child who wasn't her own into her home, letting them come and go as they pleased, letting them crash any meal, making them pie on their birthday, taking them on long weekends to visit grandparents. It was something she'd never experience again—all that was left was the memory.

Robin wiped her nose, which had reddened from the cold. Then she held Tenn again, just as tightly as the first time. "She asked about you sometimes," she said. She was giving this to Tenn, because she knew Tenn needed it. "We all watched your movie together. We made popcorn and everything. She told people about her friend the director. She was very proud of you. We all are."

"Thank you," Tenn said, and held the poodle in her memory, the comfort of its greasy fur on her fingers. "I keep thinking about something from when we were kids, one time when we were at your mom's house. There was a little gray poodle who'd sit under the table with us, but I can't remember its name. Do you know it?"

At the front of the parking lot, two cars parked side by side, and the drivers emerged, a young woman and an older one who appeared to be her mother. The young woman pulled a car seat from her back seat and swapped it to her mother's car without speaking. There was no child in the seat, no child to be seen. Robin didn't answer until the exchange had been completed.

"That was my brother's dog," Robin told her. "You remember my brother, Allen. He had a little poodle for a while. Gizmo was its name. But I don't think you ever met Gizmo."

Robin didn't remember that Tenn's parents had moved; Tenn didn't know the state of her memory. "I can remember him sleeping in my lap," she said. "It's so clear to me. I remember a gray poodle."

Robin screwed up her face and shook her head. "No, I don't think so. How old were you when you moved to the neighborhood. Eight?"

"I was seven," Tenn said. She'd been seven, and Crystal had been nine, the same ages her kids were now.

"Gizmo would've been dead for a few years by then. Crystal loved that dog so much; he followed her around like a little duckling. She would tie ribbons on his fur, and he'd let her and then run away and scratch the ribbons out. But Allen never put him on a leash, and he got hit by a car right in front of the house. It was just before Crystal started kindergarten, which I know because she drew pictures of him that whole year. Her teacher was always sending drawings of Gizmo home with little notes with sad faces on them. So you wouldn't have met him, but you're right—she'd sit with him under the table while we played cards, and he would sleep in her lap, and she would stay there half the night, even when her legs fell asleep."

Tenn could feel the poodle in her lap and the prickles in her feet, and she wondered how the memory could be so clear—if Crystal had described it to her in enough detail that she'd internalized it. But she knew that wasn't the answer; she knew now that wasn't where the memory had come from. This was Crystal's memory, which Tenn had collected from the place of her death. She didn't understand why it was so clear, free from the usual feeling of conflation. Maybe it felt real to Tenn because she'd been close to Crystal. Crystal was already with her, in a way, so it was easy to let her in. Or maybe it felt real because whatever was happening to Tenn was getting worse, her bad energy cracking her open like the house's walls.

"I won't keep you from your visit," Robin said, and kissed Tenn on the cheek. Again, Tenn felt the urge to cling, which she understood differently this time. She kissed Robin's cheek back, and Robin held her for another moment, just long enough to choke out a sob. Then she gathered herself. "Kiss your babies," she said. "Kiss your babies."

"I will," Tenn told her.

Robin's car was in a side lot, and she disappeared around the building just as the man who'd left his car ran out from the lobby. Larry was leaning against the brick, waiting.

"Boy or girl?" he asked, and handed the man, visibly relieved to find his car where he'd left it, his keys.

"We don't know yet," the man said. He was flushed, and he shook his head like he couldn't believe anything that was happening. He was wild with the joy of it, because he hadn't yet considered all that his child's life might hold, hadn't considered the possibility of anything beyond this joy. "We have no idea what it'll be!"

* * *

Tenn sat in her car in the hospital parking lot as an ambulance pulled into the bay, its lights on but its siren off. No one seemed to be in a hurry to unload it. Tenn didn't know how to confirm what she suspected. So many times in her life, she'd been visited by unplaceable memories, which she'd come to think of as processing errors on the part of her absorbent brain. She couldn't always locate her memories' origins, but she'd collected them from *somewhere*—from books, from films, from art. But what if the memories had come from somewhere else? Houses could be haunted, but a house was only a container. Maybe people could be haunted, too.

Tenn stared at her phone, thinking about what Senna had said, as Tenn watched candles flicker at the dining room table, that maybe she would experience something she couldn't on her own, implying that it had happened to Tenn before. On that day at the meeting house, Tenn had gotten a nosebleed, and a memory had preceded it—hot seats and sunscreen, the sweet burst of mango. Senna had withdrawn when Tenn told her. Tenn could still feel it, the sticky vinyl against her legs, the smell of chlorine on her skin. But she'd gone to the pool as a kid; she'd ridden in plenty of hot cars. She'd worn sunscreen and gotten sunburned anyway. This memory was different, though—the pain across her nose, the pressure in her face, the subsequent nosebleed. Tenn never got nosebleeds.

Tenn called Senna, and Senna answered like she'd been waiting for the call.

"Are you okay?" Senna asked. "I drove by your house, and no one was there."

Tenn could feel the pressure in her face again, in her sinuses. "What did I write on that notepad?"

In the background, Tenn heard a familiar voice—Eloise Borden. Senna was watching Tenn's film. Then Eloise went quiet, the television mute. "It was a song," Senna told her. "My sister made it up and sang it all the time to make me nuts. Nonsense really. A bunch of words that were fun for her to sing. Or yell, really. Mostly she yelled it at me. She wasn't singing it in the car that day, because I'd jinxed her and she had to be quiet, but maybe she was singing it in her head."

"What happened to her?" Tenn asked, though she already knew, because Senna's sister was there with her, her death at home inside Tenn's living body.

"It was a car accident," Senna said. "We were on our way home from the pool. I was giving her the finger, because she got the last mango Popsicle and she was being really smug about it. My older sister's boyfriend was driving, and some guy went through the light."

Tenn put a hand to her face. Her nose wasn't bleeding, but she could feel it, the impact.

"Are you okay?" Senna asked.

Tenn wasn't sure who she was asking—it was possible Senna wasn't asking Tenn at all, but her sister. Tenn held some part of Senna's sister, and this was as close as Senna could get.

"Not really," she said. She'd been a vessel all this time without realizing it, and what she held was impossible to comprehend. "Are you?"

Senna was quiet for a while. "I miss my sister," she said. "Can you feel her? I don't know how it works. I don't think it's like this for my aunt."

Tenn searched inside herself, but the mango and sinus pain had both dissipated. "I'm sorry," she said. "I can't feel anything right now." It wasn't true, but what she felt, she couldn't express, her fear and incomprehension so much bigger than she was.

"She was always a flighty bitch," Senna said. "Will you let me know if she comes back?"

Tenn didn't know how to answer. She didn't want to be a vessel; she wanted it to stop. "Of course," she said. Then: "It doesn't matter if I'm in the house or not. There's no getting away from it if it's me."

"Maybe you don't need to get away from it," Senna said. "Maybe it's one of those things you learn to live with, like anxiety or irritable bowel."

"But how?" Tenn said. There were medications for anxiety, but not, as far as Tenn knew, for ghosts. Outside, a man in a white jacket and tie came through the ambulance bay. The ambulance driver, who'd been smoking a cigarette, stamped it out.

"I don't know," Senna said. "I'm really only good at things like research and vandalism."

Tenn laughed despite herself. "What was her name?" she asked.

"Zinnia," Senna said. "There's a whole flower thing in our family."

"Zinnia," Tenn said, as if saying a name could be a conjuring. But still she felt nothing. She didn't know how any of it worked.

The man in the white jacket opened the back of the ambulance, so Tenn started her car, put it in reverse. "I have to go," she told Senna. It no longer felt safe to stay here, in the vicinity of a hospital, its dying and its dead.

"Drive safe," Senna told her. "And just in case Zinnia can hear: You're not jinxed anymore—I release you. You don't even have to buy me a Coke."

* * *

Ward called Tenn as she pulled into a gas station in Scranton. She didn't want to go home, but she couldn't put another hotel on their credit card.

"You're in Scranton," he said.

"I'm in Scranton," she confirmed. He was watching her location on his phone, she knew, a blue dot moving away from him. They'd driven through Scranton a lot when they were younger, coming or going from Tenn's parents' house, and every time they invented a new life for themselves, in which they lived in Scranton and were completely different people. Sometimes they raised rabbits for meat, or Ward played in a local band that Tenn despised, or they jointly founded an MLM that sold wellness products through new mothers who were desperate to feel like entrepreneurs. On their last Pennsylvania road trip, they'd opened a small theater where they put on murder mysteries that required audience participation, something both of them, in real life, would do anything to avoid.

"What are you going to do with yourself there in Scranton?" Ward asked her.

Tenn kept a cache of alternate lives in her mind for future road trips, but she was too tired now to pretend. "Make movies," she said. Maybe in Scranton she would be herself for a change. She'd already crossed a line, and though she could cross back, on the other side, she was different. Crossing back was not the only option. "Where are you right now?" she asked him.

"Bathroom," he said. "The kids are finishing their homework."

Tenn pictured Ward on the hotel bathroom floor, surrounded by towels that smelled like pool water. They'd swum for an hour before dinner, Tenn knew, because he'd texted pictures.

"I've always had a soft spot for Scranton," Ward told her. "Lots of pizza options—the kids would be in heaven. And think about the cost of living!"

They were circling too many things, but they were talking, at least. They'd been through rough patches before and survived them. You found ways to survive if you stayed with someone long enough—recalibrating as you both changed, letting one version of the relationship die to resurrect it as something new, more expansive. It was time again to shed what wasn't serving them, for their relationship to find a new shape. But Tenn was no longer sure that's what she or Ward wanted.

"I think we should go for new construction this time," Ward said. Tenn held on to his choice of language, the *we*. "I'm done with old houses."

"I don't want a house anyone has been inside before," Tenn agreed. "Not even the builders. I want a house that simply materialized out of thin air."

Ward responded, but the reception was spotty, his voice garbled.

"I'm losing you," Tenn said. The line went quiet, but neither of them hung up.

A van pulled into the space beside Tenn's, and a family spilled from the sliding door, sullen teens in hoodies, slumped and slow. Tenn watched the driver—a man—trail behind them, leaving the woman from the passenger seat to deal with a younger girl in the back who was crying.

"Tenn?" Ward said.

"I'm here," she said. "Did you say something? You cut out."

"I said, 'You haven't lost me yet.'"

The woman from the van said something to the man as he walked away, but he gestured at the teens. He was doing his part—what more did she want?

"I know you don't want to hear this," Tenn said, "but I have to tell you anyway."

"Okay," Ward said.

"I don't think moving to Scranton is going to fix things."

"Hold on," Ward said.

Tenn listened as a door opened and Ward crossed the hotel room to Anders, who was freaking out about a word problem.

"'A family is driving to a beach three hundred miles away,'" Ward read. Anders was good at math; what he needed wasn't help but Ward's attention. "'If they travel for five hours at a steady speed, how many miles per hour do they need to drive to reach their destination?'"

Aisling took advantage of the pause in conversation. "Is that Mommy? Can I talk to her?" Tenn imagined Aisling's fingers, always sticky, pressing Ward's phone to her ear. "Mommy?" she said. "Are you coming home now?"

"Not yet, baby," Tenn said. "How was your day? Did you finish all your homework?"

"I have a science test tomorrow," Aisling said.

"Are you ready for it?" Tenn asked.

"Living things have needs, but nonliving things don't," Aisling told her.

"Wonderful," Tenn said, "what else?"

"Living things need energy," Aisling said, "to grow."

Ward reclaimed his phone before Tenn could respond. "You can talk to Mommy later," he told Aisling. The bathroom door shut again. "Sorry about that," he said. "I didn't hear your answer to the question."

"What question?" Tenn asked. She was doing her own word problems now: How many ghosts could one woman carry without destroying her family? How many miles from home did she have to stay to keep them safe?

"Are you coming home?" Ward said.

Tenn tried to do the math, but she couldn't get from point A to point B in her mind.

"Something happened today," she said. She didn't know how Ward would respond, but there was no way forward if she couldn't tell him the truth. Even then, nothing was certain. "I remembered something that didn't happen to me—it happened to Crystal. I remembered it at the place where she died. It wasn't something I could have known on my own. I wasn't there. She never told me about it." Ward didn't speak; Tenn wasn't sure he could hear her but continued anyway. "I know how this sounds. I know you think I'm sick. But this isn't the first time it's happened. I think—"

"Hold on," Ward said, and got up again. A minute later, he was back. "Is it like this all the time?" he asked. "One thing after another?"

"Pretty much," Tenn said. Then: "I think I'm haunted."

"Is that a metaphor?" Ward said.

"Not really," Tenn said. "Not as much as it could be."

They were both quiet for a while, and Tenn cracked the window because the car felt stuffy, a stuffiness that didn't dissipate as cold air streamed in. The car felt crowded, because Tenn wasn't alone.

"I'm still here," Ward said, though Tenn hadn't asked. "I'm trying to think about it like a religious conversion. That happens sometimes—people who are happy atheists start believing in God, or the devout stop believing in anything. Their relationships don't all just end, right? They change. Or some of them do."

"Some of them," Tenn said.

"Do you believe in God now?" Ward asked her.

"It's not really a coherent belief system," Tenn told him. "It's more like I've seen something and my understanding of it doesn't matter. It exists, and now I can't unsee it."

"What does it entail?" Ward asked. "Being married to someone who's haunted."

"I'm not sure," Tenn said. "I'd prefer to be unhaunted, but I'm not sure that's an option. What if I'm stuck with it?" In asking the question, a raw spot inside her cooled. Whatever Ward's answer, whether a solution could or could not be found, she'd said the thing out loud and was no longer alone with it.

"I don't know," Ward said. "I don't think I can answer that right now."

"That's fair," Tenn said.

The man emerged from the gas station trailed by his rumpled children, all carrying bottles of soda. His partner was nowhere to be seen.

"I've had this feeling since we moved," Ward said, "like you're far away from me." Tenn could hear it in his voice, too, the relief of finally saying the hard thing out loud. "Because you're different now. You changed, and I don't know you anymore, and I don't know what to do about it."

"You could get to know me again," Tenn offered. There was a lot she didn't understand, but this she did: her terrible energy wouldn't improve unless they both did something about it. "I have to get to know me again, too. As someone other than the person who packs the lunches and runs the errands and picks the kids up from school."

"I never meant for you to be that person," Ward said. "That's not what I wanted."

"Neither did I," Tenn said, "but I'm not the only one who let it happen."

Ward was quiet. The woman from the van finally returned. The man had loaded the kids up and was waiting for her. Outside the van, he put an arm around her shoulder and she pulled away, but then he said something into her ear and she softened and leaned into him. They climbed back in the van together, this time with the woman in the driver's seat.

"You know, my beef with word problems is that they don't adequately prepare kids for the real problems they'll have to face," Ward said. "The GPS can do the math on driving time. How about: 'You have a mortgage, nineteen work projects, two kids, and a wife who needs your help. Which ball can you drop without fucking it all up?'"

"I've got one," Tenn said. "'Your partner makes five times as much as you ever will, but giving up your own work has turned you into a ticking time bomb. How many sandwiches can you make before the bomb destroys you?'"

"I let you down," Ward said. Somehow distance made it all easier, this long-overdue accounting. "I let you down and I keep doing it and I'm sorry. I don't know how to fix the problem, and it's killing me."

Ward couldn't find the solution to their problem, but one thing was clear: if they were going to stay together, they'd have to bridge the gap they'd allowed to grow between them. Maybe Senna was right, and there was a way for Tenn to live with what she carried, safely, now that she could recognize what was hers and what wasn't.

In childbirth, resisting the pain had only made it worse; it wasn't until she'd stopped fighting that her panic had receded and the pain, though still present, had become manageable.

Still, the image lingered in Tenn's mind: a trail of bloody footprints on a floor.

There was a knock on the bathroom door. Ward opened it to Aisling.

"I need to talk to Mommy," she said. Her voice was authoritative—she wasn't asking. "I need to talk to her. Now!"

"Okay, okay," Ward said. "I'm handing you over," he told Tenn.

Tenn heard Aisling say, "Privacy, please."

"Mommy and I were still talking," Ward told her.

"I need to pee!" Aisling said, to which Ward had no argument. Tenn listened as Aisling closed the bathroom door, then turned on the sink.

"Are you okay?" Tenn asked her. "What's with the secrecy?"

Aisling lowered her voice to a whisper. "Mommy, do you remember when we milked the cows?"

"No, sweet pea," Tenn said. They'd never gone to milk cows—Ward had promised, but Tenn hadn't been able to find a local barn that offered milking. "We pet the cows. Is that what you mean?"

"No, I remember it," Aisling said, insistent. "I know how to do it even though I didn't do it. I keep remembering things I didn't do."

"Like what?" Tenn said. Aisling, like Tenn, was absorbent when it came to movies. Maybe she'd watched a clip about milking cows at school. It was too terrifying for Tenn to consider anything else.

"Things!" Aisling said, exasperated. It was so hard to explain something you couldn't understand yourself. "Driving a tractor. Swallowing a whole bottle of medicine." Someone walked a dog past Tenn's car, and the dog stopped and barked at her. "Falling into water and staying under until I die."

Tenn held the steering wheel even though the car was off, because she felt like she was slipping sideways. "Everyone has bad dreams," Tenn told her, because she wanted so badly to believe that's what this was. "I'll have Daddy put the meditation app on his phone. Do you think doing a meditation might help?"

"It's getting worse," Aisling said, ignoring Tenn's bullshit. Maybe Tenn couldn't face it, but Aisling had no choice. "I don't like it," she said. "It hurts."

In the parking lot, everyone was smoking, staring at their phones. The dog was still barking even though its owner had dragged it away. There were ghosts here—Tenn could feel them all around her, now that she was tuned to the right station. They were everywhere all the time. And Aisling could feel them, too.

"I don't know how to stop it yet," Tenn told her. "But I'm coming home now, and we're going to figure it out."

18

Ward brought the kids home the next morning. Tenn texted when she was almost there so he'd keep his distance. She could hear the kids in the backyard, in the snow. Ward had picked up Gogo from the pet sitter on his way home, and she clawed at Tenn's shins in the foyer, making goat noises. Ward waited at the far end of the living room, giving Tenn space. She didn't want to be there, in the house with him and the kids, but it was clear now that she couldn't solve this problem by running away from it.

Tenn scooped Gogo up, and Gogo gouged her chest. The first greeting after a separation was always painful.

"I missed you, too," Tenn told her.

"What about me?" Ward said.

Tenn set Gogo down, and she rolled over Tenn's feet, then righted herself and raced out of the room. A moment later, she was back, greeting Tenn as if she'd just walked in the door.

"I'm afraid to get too close," Tenn told him.

The plan was for Tenn to quarantine upstairs in their bedroom while Ward stayed downstairs in the guest room. They would tell the kids Tenn was sick, contagious. Tenn wasn't sure it would work, but they had to try something. If the bedroom was too close, she would sleep in the yard, in a tent, in the garage, in her car. She and Ward would put the full force of their problem-solving energy into it. They would keep trying until they found something that worked.

"A quick hug probably won't hurt," Ward said.

"Maybe we should order pizza," Tenn told him. When Ward took her in his arms, she sank into his chest and wanted to stay there, locked against him. They were a unit—things were always better when they worked as a team. She hadn't realized what she'd been missing all this time, but it was this, the feeling of partnership, Tenn and Ward against the world. They could get through this, Tenn thought, if she was no longer alone. She felt good in Ward's arms, and—she had to believe—the goodness of that energy would keep them safe.

The kids ran around the house to the front yard, screeching. Through the window, Tenn saw that Ward hadn't put them in snow pants.

"Come back in," she yelled out the porch door. "Come in and get bundled, or I'll pelt you both with snowballs."

In response, Anders threw a clump of snow in her direction, and Aisling screamed as he fell onto the wings of her snow angel. She had snow in her hair, because she was hatless. The kids never registered discomfort when they were having fun.

"Listen to your mother," Ward said. "We want to keep her around."

Tenn retreated up the stairs and waited while the kids came in and Ward zipped them into their new snow gear.

"Your fingers are like ice," Ward said.

"Can you come play with us?" Aisling asked. "Can Mommy?"

Tenn was afraid to greet them, afraid to give them hugs.

"Not today," Ward told her, "but we have the whole winter ahead of us."

Tenn waited until the kids were back outside and Ward was in the guest room to come downstairs. She needed to unpack, to start the laundry. They would find a rhythm, eventually. They were hardly in the same room together most days anyway. Ward had left her luggage by the front door, but when she went for it, the door to the guest room was open, and Ward was not inside.

"Ward?" she called. It was important for her to know where he was, so she could avoid him. Through the window, she saw movement, but this time it wasn't the kids.

Tenn walked outside into the snow with no shoes on. The cold was a shock, burning her bare feet. Ward was on a ladder leaning against the tree; there were tracks in the snow where he'd dragged it. He'd climbed to the top and now grabbed at a branch like he was hanging a spider only he could see. He was in a T-shirt and socks, the socks shaggy with snow. He didn't seem aware of Tenn's presence, and she was afraid that if she spoke to him, he'd fall. He hung another spider and wobbled on the ladder. Tenn didn't know what to do to snap him out of it. Her energy had been good—optimistic, even. Ward regained his balance and resumed his task. Tenn slowly stepped into his line of sight, filled with dread that she was about to watch him fall. The snow was soft, but anything could be hidden beneath it—sharp sticks, a forgotten rake, a rock.

"Ward," Tenn said gently. She was afraid she would scare him; she was afraid. He had a brace on his elbow from his falls from the hotel desk. You could only do the same thing so many times before you got hurt. "Ward," she said again.

Ward looped an empty hand over a branch. "Yeah," he said. His voice was flat, expressionless. It was so cold—Tenn's feet were burning. At least she was here, she thought, to find him.

"Aren't you cold?" Tenn asked him. "Don't you want to come in?"

Ward wobbled on the ladder, caught his balance, hung nothing from a branch.

Gogo busted out the door and ran straight to Tenn, clawing at her shins as if she'd just gotten home. Tenn couldn't move. All she could do was watch Ward, wobbling.

"Please come down," she said. She could hear the kids in the back, shrieking. Gogo ran a lap around the yard and came back to greet Tenn.

"It'll be Halloween before you know it," Ward said, teetering. Tenn could do nothing but stand there in horror and watch him fall.

* * *

When Tenn texted Senna, Senna responded with the name of a church. Tenn had put Ward on the couch and dragged the ladder down the street, where she left it in Frankie's yard. She could explain later. When she returned to the house, Ward was on the kitchen floor, one hand on his head, the other holding an ice pack to his hip.

"Again?" he asked her. Tenn stood in the dining room, afraid to get too close, afraid there was no distance that would keep him safe from her.

"Again," she told him. "I have to go."

"Again?" he said. He pulled down his waistband to survey the damage, but it wasn't visible yet. Tenn watched the kids through the window. Anders was eating snow from his gloved hand; Aisling was doing pratfalls, sinking over and over into a clean, white grave. Tenn had barely seen them, hadn't even said hello.

"I'm coming back," she told him, though she wasn't sure this was true. "But I need help."

Ward tried to stand, but his hip didn't let him. Tenn ordered a pizza, then got in her car and fishtailed down the icy road. She'd thought Ward could help her, but he couldn't, no matter how much they both wanted it. Tenn needed to find someone who could.

The church parking lot was full, and as Tenn pulled in, a woman in a beaded wedding gown emerged through the doors, holding the hand of her tuxedoed groom. Tenn parked in a spot reserved for clergy. The church was Carpenter Gothic, the building stark white except for the steeple, which was black. Behind the bride and groom, people streamed from the church into the parking lot. Senna had a lot of sisters, and today was one's wedding day. Senna had not been looking forward to it. Tenn stepped out of the car, and her sneakers were immediately soaked with gray slush. She pulled her coat tight, hoping no one would notice her sweatpants.

When Senna saw Tenn, she rushed from the church doors and took Tenn by the forearms. "Are you alone?" Senna asked her.

Tenn looked at Senna's fingers on her skin, which scared her. Tenn was a danger to Ward, and maybe to others as well. She searched inside herself, but there was no mango to be found, no poodle fur, no hallmarks of death. "For now," she said.

Senna began walking, charging into the snow in her satin pumps. Tenn had no choice but to follow. "Cam threw a tantrum, and now the videographer is refusing to stay for the reception. My older sisters are trying to talk him down, but they're both loaded, because Cam was screaming at us for, like, three hours before the ceremony even started. Can you just, like, hold a camera and pretend you're filming shit for a few minutes? I don't even care if the camera is on, but if Cam yells at my mom again, I'm pretty sure she's going to have a nervous breakdown, and we've all had like seven breakdowns today already."

"Ward fell off a ladder in the yard," Tenn told her. "I'd only been in the house for five minutes."

Senna stopped on the path and took this in. "Fuck," she said.

"Yes," Tenn said.

An elderly woman in a too-big men's coat approached, holding the hand of a small girl in a Darth Vader costume. "Don't make me do this alone," the woman told Senna, grabbing at her wrist. "I need you."

"Right behind you, Nana," Senna told her, and kissed her on the cheek. The small girl picked her nose and wiped her finger on her costume. Senna turned to Tenn. "Your family is safe with you here? It doesn't happen when Ward's alone?"

Tenn shrugged—it hadn't yet, but it was still possible she'd go home to find him frozen under the buckeye tree.

"I don't think so," she said, "but I can't stay away forever." She could move to Scranton and parent the kids through video calls. She could stuff rocks in her pockets and walk into the sea. But if Aisling was like Tenn, she wouldn't be safer if Tenn was gone. She would just be alone.

Senna was still walking, and Tenn trailed behind her, down a narrow path lined by dense aisles of trees. They emerged in a cemetery.

"She thinks taking wedding photos in the cemetery is goth or something," Senna explained. "My sister, who looks like she walked out of a Ralph Lauren catalog."

Tenn stood still, unable to move, as visitors flooded in, as Tenn absorbed them. It was the same as when they'd arrived at the burial mounds, only now she understood what was happening. The crackling in her chest, the scent of wet leather, the sound of a warbly voice, singing a hymn—all these memories belonged to the dead. Tenn felt her self giving way as they filled her; she felt hands on her hips and smelled lilacs and ammonia and blood. She closed her eyes and tried to block more from entering, but the stream was steady, rushing inward, taking up space. As with a migraine, her vision became occluded, and an unbearable pressure crept along her scalp. She felt like an inflatable pool toy whose valve was wide open. Something essential was being emptied from her and replaced by many things that were not her own.

"Are you okay?" Senna said.

Tenn realized she was hunched over, one hand on a tombstone.

"Fuck," someone said—the woman in the wedding gown, Senna's sister, Cam. "It's one fucking thing after another today. Is she going to do it?" she asked Senna.

"She's not feeling well," Senna told her, and squeezed Tenn's arm. "Do you want to go inside the church?" she said. "Do you need to sit?"

"Just give me a minute," Tenn told her. "I'll be fine."

"Oh, okay," Cam said, "I guess I'll just take my wedding photos without anyone to document it."

"Jesus," Senna said. "The photographer is documenting it." The photographer, a woman in all black with hair slicked in a severe ponytail, adjusted her camera settings, dissociated from the drama. "Can you be happily married for five seconds without having a camera pointed at you?"

"Actually, no," Cam said. "I'm paying through the nose for this, so no."

Tenn looked at the gravestone beneath her as Cam stormed off toward her mother. The stone was part of a pair—husband and wife who'd died thirty years apart.

"Like she's the one paying for anything," Senna said under her breath. "Are you going to be okay?" she asked again. "You look like you're possessed."

"I kind of am," Tenn said, realizing for the first time what it meant, the trade-off. She could possess the dead, but not a fleet of the dead and herself at the same time. She felt like she was a sweater being unraveled one slow stitch at a time. She could almost see it—the long thread of her self unspooling.

"Here," a voice said. Tenn looked up to see Senna's aunt Dahlia, the town historian, a red velvet cape draped over her dress. She took hold of Tenn's wrist and put the videographer's camera in her hand.

Tenn could barely see, but she brought the camera to her eye anyway. Through it, she watched Cam arguing with her mother, her new husband turning away to raise an eyebrow at his best man. She panned left. The girl in the Darth Vader costume plopped in the lap of her great-grandmother, who held her tiny hands between her own and clapped. Tenn focused on their hands—one pair small and grubby, the knuckles of the other scraped raw. Behind them, a gaggle of children assembled around a statue, a bronze angel on her knees, cheeks streaked with verdigris tears. A boy in a pastel bow tie rested an elbow on the angel's head while one of the girls gave him a finger-wagging lecture. When she was finished, he bowed to a second girl, who dragged him into a waltz, as if they were the ones who'd just been married. But they were stepping on each other's feet, on purpose it seemed, and the bossy girl continued to talk and wag her finger. Finally, she gave the boy a shove and took the dancing girl as her partner, and together they twirled around until they spilled to the snowy ground. Inside of Tenn, a space began to open, as if the valve at her neck had finally closed.

"Jesus Christ," Cam said, "all I want is for someone to film the happiest day of my life. Hello?" she said to Tenn. "Remember me, the bride?"

At the sound of Cam's voice, Tenn directed the camera bride-ward.

"She's not feeling well," Senna told her.

"No," Tenn said. She trained the camera on Cam, on her thumb running over and over her new ring. "I feel better now. I really do."

* * *

There was an hour before the reception, held in the ballroom of a Victorian manor. Ward had gone to the hospital, kids in tow, to get an X-ray on his hip, so Tenn could stop worrying about him freezing to death, for now. She found Dahlia in the sitting room, a room blocked from use with a velvet rope and a sign that said *Do Not Enter.* Inside, Dahlia sat knitting with pale pink yarn. For a ghost expert, she seemed unimpressed by Tenn and her ghostly baggage. She motioned for Tenn to join her, so Tenn ducked under the rope. Senna's sisters had successfully bribed the videographer with a case of wine, relieving her of camera duty. The wooden frames of the sitting room chairs were ornately carved and upholstered with needlepoint flowers. Tenn sat gingerly, afraid she might damage the fabric. Everywhere she went, she was a threat. Senna rushed to the doorway carrying a cardboard box, then rushed away when she realized whoever she was looking for was elsewhere.

"Are you feeling better?" Dahlia asked.

Tenn's vision had cleared along with the stray memories, like a storm blowing across the sky. "I am," Tenn told her. "I'm not sure why, but filming for a while really helped me."

"You're not sure why?" Dahlia asked. "Senna told me this has happened to you before. How do you usually deal with it?"

"I don't have a way to deal with it," Tenn told her. "I didn't understand what it was, before now. I've always waited for it to pass, which it does, eventually."

Dahlia focused on her knitting, a baby blanket in progress. "Are you sure, though," she asked, "that you haven't developed a coping mechanism?"

Tenn watched Dahlia's fingers move like machinery. She understood now she'd been picking up passengers for a long time, but the way she carried them was changing. She'd never been overwhelmed by them before; they'd never affected her family.

"It was different before we moved," Tenn said. "It got worse, after. It keeps getting worse. I thought it was the house, because it's old. I understand now that it's me, but I haven't always been like this. I couldn't see them before. There weren't so many."

Dahlia continued knitting, the skein of yarn in her lap dwindling.

Outside the room, music began to play, a pop song from the '80s that elicited a few whoops. "Senna told me you're a filmmaker," she said.

"Not really," Tenn said. "I haven't made a film for a long time."

"Just because you're not making art now doesn't mean you're not an artist," Dahlia said. She was priestly in her red cape. Tenn wanted to believe her. "It doesn't always have to be profound. You were working before you moved, right?"

"It was just wedding videography," Tenn said. "Like what I did today. I wasn't actually making anything for myself."

Dahlia undid a few stitches and started again. "But it helped you."

Tenn watched Dahlia's fingers and wished she could knit, too, wished she could make a mistake and fix it with ease. She wished she had a way to occupy her hands. "I'm not sure how much it helped me," Tenn said.

Dahlia flipped the blanket to check her work. "Tell me," she said. "I've never been good with a camera. When you're filming something like a wedding and there's activity all around, how do you decide what to focus on?"

Tenn thought of the hands, young and old, and the way she'd been drawn to them. "It's hard to explain," she said. She'd always been drawn to details left of center, so much so that it alienated viewers. But Tenn couldn't fully articulate why she was drawn to hands and statues over a dramatic bride. "There's meaning in the moments that seem the most mundane," she said, which she believed, though she knew that was only part of it.

Dahlia set down her knitting. "But that's not all, is it?"

Tenn shook her head. She captured those moments because she felt a tug toward them, a tug on her attention. She could feel the tug now, her eyes drawn to the hall, where a bridesmaid dabbed at her cheeks, trying to save her makeup. Then footsteps approached, and the bridesmaid rushed away.

The feet belonged to Senna, who ducked under the rope, carrying two plates of hors d'oeuvres.

"Finally," Dahlia said. "I'm starving." She put a stuffed mushroom in her mouth and continued talking while she chewed. "Your friend," she told Senna, "is worse off than I thought."

Senna offered Tenn the second plate, and Tenn accepted it and held it in her lap but couldn't eat. In the ballroom, the '80s pop song started over, once again eliciting whoops. Tenn imagined the guests, stuck in an endless loop because of her, dancing to the same song over and over, until their feet bled.

"Can you help?" Senna asked her aunt.

Tenn looked at her plate, at the bites of beautiful food she didn't want—she didn't want any of it. She only wanted to go home, for everything to go back to the way it was before.

"In your book," she told Dahlia, "you wrote about banishment spells." Tenn was desperate; she'd do anything, no matter how ridiculous it seemed. "It said certain kinds of spirits can be banished from a house. Is that something you can apply to people?"

Dahlia shook her head, ate a puff pastry topped with jam and brie. "That's made up," she said, and closed her eyes, savoring the bite. "There's no spells." She chuckled at the thought.

Outside the room, the music got louder. People were streaming in, starting to dance. Tenn sank in her chair, devastated. She'd genuinely thought a spell might do the trick. She was, at last, actually losing it.

"Your real issue is that you think this is a problem to be solved," Dahlia told her. She ate another bite because her life was not crumbling around her. "There's nothing to fix here. I'm not telling you anything you don't already know. I'm sure you've been like this your whole life."

"But I don't want to be like this," Tenn said. A chill ran through her body. Even now, she could feel something outside her, working its way in.

"Well, too bad," Dahlia said. "There's a concept in some Eastern religions: the hungry ghost. Are you familiar?"

Tenn shook her head.

"In life, hungry ghosts were greedy. In death, they're no different. Big, round bellies, necks as thin as needles. Their hunger is insatiable, same as their thirst. This is how I think about ghosts. But what they hunger for isn't food or money or power—it's simple witness. They want to be perceived, to be remembered. And you"—Dahlia poked at Tenn's head—"have the ability to perceive them. And in turn, they affect your perception. Even if you've never realized it."

Dahlia ate a cocktail shrimp while Tenn considered this. She'd always felt a tug—toward beauty, toward tenderness, toward pain. She'd just thought that was how her mind worked. She hadn't considered the possibility that something else was directing her, that it was the dead, that it could be both her and the dead at the same time.

Senna reached over and snatched a shrimp from her plate. "I'm not letting this guy go to waste," she said.

"But why is it getting so much worse?" Tenn asked.

"It's getting worse because you stopped dissipating them," Dahlia said. "You can't let them accumulate. That's the worst thing you can do. If you don't give them somewhere to go, they pile up; they feed on you. You have to be less adherent. You have to flush them out of your system."

In the hall, two people were whispering—the conversation was tense, but Tenn couldn't make out what they were saying.

"But how does that affect my husband?" she asked Dahlia. "He keeps getting stuck. He keeps falling down." She could accept that ghosts were drawn to her but not that, through her, they could hurt Ward. It didn't make sense. Or it made sense, but she didn't like it.

Dahlia shrugged. "I promise, I've read every scrap of ghost lore I could find, and there's no one ideology that explains what I've seen. I only know what I've experienced myself. When I was young, I was exhausted all the time, but the doctors could never find anything wrong with me. Nothing got better until I started writing. I didn't expect it to change me, but it did. The ghosts had been sticking to me, to all the shit I held inside. But I can't tell you what worked for me will work for you, because you're a different person. It never affected my family, but then, I don't think I've ever been as full as you are. Maybe you're not paying enough attention, so they're trying to create a captive audience. Maybe they've been affecting your family, too, but in different ways—hunger or thirst, dreams, pain. All I know is that they're with you, like toilet paper stuck to your shoe."

"But why me?" Tenn said. She thought of her mother, an accountant who threw great parties; her father, who was much nicer to his friends than his own family. She didn't think either of them had been porous the way she was. Or if they were, they'd been better at the dissipation.

"Some people are more porous than others," Dahlia told her, "which can't be helped. And some people are more adherent, which can."

In the hall, a whisper raised into recognizability—Cam apologizing, an apology that sounded sincere.

"Don't look so miserable," Dahlia said. "It doesn't have to be a curse. You collect the dead, what's left of their energy, and that energy informs your vision. Then you have a choice: You can let that energy build up inside of you, or you can channel it into something external. I flush them out through my writing—I preserve them in my work. If you don't, they drain you. They take the place of what's alive. If you want to feel better, you have to be a conduit, not a receptacle."

Tenn sat in her ancient chair and felt what was inside of her.

Maybe she could understand it after all. If ghosts were like actors, they needed a stage. She could help them take their curtain calls and make their exits.

"But what if I don't want it?" Tenn said. "Isn't there a way to close my pores? To stop collecting them?"

"You're looking for a cure when there's no sickness," Dahlia said. "This is just how you are."

"So there's no solution," Tenn said.

In the hall, Cam laughed, and her new husband along with her. Tenn watched him kiss her ear, then her nose.

"If there's a solution to your problem, you're the only one who can find it," Dahlia said. "But it's unlikely that you're going to solve death."

19

When Tenn got home, she went straight for her camera, which she hadn't touched since the move, except to bring it down from the attic and charge it. She'd bought this camera with money left to her—unexpectedly—by Eloise Borden. Once, after the young woman who read to Eloise had gone home, after Tenn had turned off her camera, Eloise had sat Tenn down and told her to leave Ward. Tenn had been bewildered by the advice, though Eloise had spoken many times about her ambivalence over the ways in which marriage and motherhood had consumed her own career. In that moment, Tenn realized the core of the film was not Eloise or her reader but Tenn herself, her fear that Eloise's fate would be her own. The very act of making the film was Tenn's safeguard against it, her attempt to escape the trap of domesticity. But Tenn could never center herself—her own fears and ambitions. She had no desire to be on camera, to be seen. Or being behind the camera meant she could be seen without being visible.

Now Tenn was back where she was comfortable, behind the camera's lens, though she understood her vision through that lens differently. If she could be a conduit, as Dahlia said, if she gave herself over to the tug, what haunted her might move through her and disperse.

Ward and the kids were still gone, so Tenn was alone with Gogo, who hadn't run to greet Tenn, as she normally did. Instead, she panted and watched Tenn, keeping her distance. Her tail was tucked between her legs, her hackles raised, and Tenn held the camera between them and began filming. It felt different now, guided by the knowledge that her vision was not hers alone. She filmed Gogo cowering in the hall and felt a tug, turned her lens to the beam crossing the spare bedroom's ceiling, scored by the hands of a long-gone craftsman. When the tug pulled her toward the window, Tenn filmed the horse across the street, which kicked at the house, as if it could sense Tenn inside with her many guests. She felt as she filmed it as she had in the cemetery, as if inside her space was opening, a room in her body that was hers and no one else's.

Anders was the first one through the door, and when he saw Tenn with her camera, he dropped to his knees and began roaring. Tenn tried not to imagine him stuck that way, crawling the floors till his knees bled, roaring until his voice went hoarse, then mute. His tongue was stained blue, and Tenn felt the tug pulling her focus toward his mouth.

"Are you making a movie?" he asked. The question was hopeful—he liked it when Tenn worked, liked being able to brag to his teachers.

"It's a new project," Tenn told him. "Starting right now. You're going to be seeing this camera a lot."

Anders swung away from the camera and farted.

"That's it!" Tenn said. "Just be yourself."

"What's the project?" Ward asked. Tenn could hear him in the foyer, stomping snow off his boots.

"It's about us," Tenn said. "It's about our house and our family."

Ward limped into the living room, where he stalled, unsure if it was safe to come closer. He had an ice pack on his hip but no crutches. Gogo darted past Tenn and barked once at Ward, as if in warning. "It's not broken," he told Tenn. "Just soft tissue damage. They told me to stay off it if I can."

"What's about us?" Aisling asked. Her voice from the foyer was muddy, as if she'd fallen asleep on the drive and wasn't fully awake yet. But Tenn felt something as she entered the room, an unstable energy, like the buzz of fluorescent lights. She kept the camera to her eye, a barrier between her and Ward, her and the kids.

"I'm making a movie," she told Aisling. She held the camera tight, as if the camera were an amulet, because—she could now feel—the source of danger in the room was no longer her, but Aisling. Aisling was like Tenn, absorbent. And there was a cemetery across from the hospital. It was hard to find parking there—sometimes you had to circle the block.

"Can I have a snack?" Anders said.

"Eat in the kitchen, please," Tenn said, and then he was gone. She wanted to tell Ward to go, too, but he was already approaching.

"Can I kiss you?" he asked.

Ward took a step closer, and Tenn watched through the camera. She could feel Aisling, her small body brimming, follow Anders into the kitchen.

"This is going to take some getting used to," Ward said. Tenn didn't lower the camera as he wrapped her in his arms and squeezed so tightly it hurt.

He let go when Aisling screamed.

Tenn followed the sound to the kitchen, where she found Aisling pressing one hand to her cheek, which was bleeding. At her feet was a fork. Gogo whined but kept her distance, from Tenn and Aisling both.

"What happened?" Tenn asked, still holding the camera, still looking through it. She filmed Aisling's cheek, the helplessness in her eyes. Aisling didn't understand what was happening to her.

Across the room, Anders stood, fists in balls, furious. "We're out of bars!" he yelled. "She took the last one!"

"We have plenty of granola bars," Tenn said. "I just bought a whole box."

"Not the ones with chocolate chips," Anders said. His anger turned to tears, because all that anger was just a front for loneliness and fear. "I hate the other bars! The chocolate ones are mine!"

Aisling said nothing, just looked at Tenn, waiting for her to do something.

"I can buy more granola bars later," Tenn said. She crossed the room to the bin of art supplies and took out the paper and markers and paint. "We really don't need to fight over them." She knelt before Aisling, camera still to her eye. "Can you sit at the table and draw for me?"

Aisling shook her head, the tiniest of motions. Just like Ward—when she was scared, she couldn't move.

"Anders, please apologize to your sister," Tenn said. She was trying to avert too many disasters at once. "It's okay to feel frustrated, but it's not okay to take your feelings out on other people. Look at Aisling's face." The cheek continued to bleed, and Tenn did not set down the camera to attend to it. "You almost got her in the eye. One of these days you're going to hurt someone, and it won't be fixable."

"I don't care," Anders said. "No one likes me! No one wants to be friends with me anyway!" He stormed off toward his room but didn't make it far before he, too, screamed.

In the living room, Tenn found Anders curled over his foot. She didn't need to ask what had happened.

"My foot's bleeding," Anders said. "I stepped on that."

Tenn mashed the camera against her eye like a prayer. On the floor beside Anders, a nail was protruding, the same nail they'd pounded back in a thousand times. Gogo circled him, whining.

"It's okay," Tenn said. She filmed Anders's face, twisted toward bravery, the sock on his foot, darkening. "Let's get you to the bathroom and take care of this."

When she stood, Ward was beside her, leaning in. "Can I kiss you?" he said.

"What?" Tenn said. She took one step back and watched through the camera, trying to pass something through it, to make it disperse. But the problem wasn't Tenn anymore. Ward kissed her on the chin, then wrapped her in his arms so tightly it hurt.

Anders got off the floor, but instead of going to the bathroom, he returned to the kitchen, Gogo at his heels. She barked once as Tenn listened with dread.

Aisling cried out.

In the kitchen, Aisling's cheek bled, a new streak parallel to the first, two bloody tears, each on its own track. At her feet was a second fork. Across the room, Anders stood furious, his foot bleeding onto the wood. Gogo paced between the kids, back and forth, over and over.

"Anders," Tenn said, trying to stay calm. She filmed Ward, walking toward her, all desperation in the eyes, like there was nothing he wouldn't do. He was capable of anything; they all were. Anders stormed out before Tenn could stop him and howled once again as the nail impaled his foot. Ward was still approaching, arms extended.

Tenn knelt again before Aisling, who did not even move to put a hand to her cheek. Tenn took the camera from her eye and held it to Aisling's. And as she did, she could feel them. Defenseless without her camera, she could feel Aisling's ghosts, so many more than Tenn had ever held all at once.

Tenn knew what it meant to be porous now, and she let herself be a vessel, opening herself so Aisling's ghosts could stream into her instead. Tenn was more absorbent than Aisling, who had art class and music and ballet, who had a bedroom full of crayons and pipe cleaners and beads.

Tenn could feel every ghost in the room, flooding into her body. She was outnumbered. Aisling brought a hand to her bleeding cheek and began to cry. Tenn turned back toward Ward, who limped at her through his pain.

"Can I kiss you?" he said, then wrapped her in his arms so tightly it hurt.

* * *

Tenn pried the nail from the floor, removed the tray of silverware from the drawer, and took it to the pantry, where she hid from Ward. She'd taken the camera back from Aisling even though the camera was no longer helping—what Aisling had accumulated was too vast to be dispersed this way. Ward was in the kitchen, calling her name, oblivious to what was happening with the kids. Tenn didn't know what to do. She couldn't keep leaving and coming back, over and over. She had to do something different.

Ward appeared in the doorway to the pantry. "Can I kiss you?" he said.

"No," Tenn said firmly. "Not at the moment."

Ward came at her anyway, and Tenn ducked around him, back into the kitchen. She needed to get Ward away from her; his arms around her neck got tighter with every hug. She held the camera in one hand and with her other took out her phone. Ward answered on the fourth ring.

"Hello?" he said. He was looking right at Tenn but didn't register the fact that she was the one calling.

"Hello," she said. He was standing at the base of the stairs, where she'd found him many times before. There was a time when she'd been able to snap him out of it. "Can you check something?" she asked him. "For work?"

"For work," Ward repeated. He stood there for a beat, his expression blank, then nodded and said, "Of course, of course." He slipped his phone in his pocket without ending the call and ascended the stairs to his office.

From the living room, Anders yelped, and Tenn raced across the house. Anders was curled over his foot, which had been punctured by a different nail this time.

"My foot's bleeding," he said. "I stepped on that."

Tenn took Anders to the bathroom, where she bandaged his foot with an entire roll of gauze, then stuffed his feet into his snow boots. She grabbed the peroxide for Aisling's face, pried the second nail from the floor.

Back in the kitchen, Aisling was staring at the door.

"Are you okay?" Tenn asked her. Aisling was the only member of the family who seemed immune to getting stuck. If all else failed, Tenn could send Aisling to Frankie's to call for help.

Aisling walked past Tenn as if she were on a mission. A mission to the door.

"Where are you going?" Tenn said.

"Outside," Aisling said. "Where you can't find me."

There was snow on the ground, and Aisling was barefoot. For one moment, Tenn could see herself, hours or days later, finding Aisling in the doghouse, frozen in the yard. She locked the door and watched Aisling turn the knob with unseeing eyes. She turned Aisling around, and Aisling crossed the room, bumped into the wall, and started back again. They'd reached a critical mass, and now Aisling was stuck, too, attempting to run away from Tenn, from this house, over and over. Tenn turned Aisling again, like a windup toy, and this time pulled the table from across the room, with the assistance of a heavy dose of adrenaline. She shoved it against the door to block it. If Aisling was stuck, Tenn couldn't be far behind.

"Goodbye," Aisling said, and walked into the table.

Tenn heard Ward on the stairs and waited for him, but the door didn't open.

"Hello?" she said. She opened the door. On the other side, Ward stood, phone in hand. He looked up at her, surprised.

"Hey," he said. "I didn't hear you there."

"You need to be working," Tenn told him. She couldn't deal with everyone all at once. Behind her, Aisling bumped into the table; in the living room, Anders cried out in pain. Gogo entered the room with something the size of a small pine cone in her mouth. Tenn took a treat from the bag by the door, and Gogo dropped her prize—a half-eaten block of rat poison.

"I have a meeting," Ward said. He was holding his phone, but his eyes weren't focused on its screen.

"What's the meeting?" Tenn said. Maybe if she left now, she thought, all the ghosts she'd accumulated would follow her. Maybe all she needed to do was cross the street, the town, the threshold of life. She was capable of anything—she could drive her car into a tree; she could stab herself in the stomach with a knife. But she didn't want to. "Tell me what the meeting is about," she said.

"You know," Ward said. On his phone, he was watching footage of the cruise ship. A man fell from a deck, over and over, in a loop.

"Tell me," Tenn said. She knelt on the floor and forced a capful of peroxide down Gogo's throat.

Ward looked at his phone, running his fingers over its cracked screen. "A cruise ship," he said.

"What about the cruise ship?" Tenn said. Gogo rolled onto her back, playing dead—her favorite trick—in hopes of a treat. "What happened on the ship? Tell me."

Ward's eyes focused—he was watching the footage now. "Someone's falling," he said. "Someone's going to die." He was talking like a child reciting a nursery rhyme.

"Who's falling?" Tenn said. She'd asked him this before; she was worried he'd answer and she'd ask again, and again, unable to stop herself. Who's falling? Who's going to die? Gogo popped up, then flopped on her back, playing dead again. "Who's dying?" Tenn said.

"It's you," Ward said.

The faucet was running; Tenn hadn't noticed before. There was something wrong with the water, with the electricity, with the foundation. Tenn felt a tremor; the house was on jacks, suspending them above the ground. The table slid from the door, and Aisling squeezed past it, to escape, barefoot, into the snow. Tenn put one hand on the door to hold it closed.

"You're the one who's falling," Ward continued. "I keep watching you look over the edge, but I never stop you."

Aisling locked a hand around the doorknob and pulled with more strength than her small body contained. Tenn didn't know how to keep her inside, to keep her from disappearing. Gogo rolled to her back, dead, then stood and vomited rat poison on the floor.

Tenn carried Aisling away from the door, pointed her toward the dining room, and watched her walk away.

"I saw you at the edge, and I didn't stop you," Ward said. The edge of what, Tenn didn't ask—there had been too many moments. "And then I left. It was easier to go away than to stay there with my guilt. I had to leave because I couldn't face you anymore. I couldn't even face myself." His voice changed as he said this, his humanity restored.

Aisling hit a wall, turned, and headed back. Tenn stood for a moment there at her world's edge, then rammed the table against the door with all her might. When it hit, Tenn finally fell—because the house jolted out from underneath her. The floor seemed to drop; the whole room tilted sideways. Cabinet doors flung open; dishes slid off shelves and shattered against the floor. The chairs toppled, the salt spilled, the coffee maker tipped into the sink. Aisling knocked into a wall; Ward stumbled forward, onto his knees. Tenn braced herself against the dishwasher as everything broke around her.

Once the room had stilled, Aisling righted herself, then walked through the broken china, barefoot.

"What the fuck," Ward said. He was still holding his phone, and Tenn watched the footage, someone's beloved dropping from the deck into oblivion. In the blue sky, in the distance, there was a helicopter.

Aisling walked into the table, reversed through broken glass, walked into it again, leaving a trail of bloody footprints behind.

"Honey," Ward said, and took her by the hand, but she ripped it free to reach for the door. "What the fuck," Ward repeated, and Tenn watched him, amidst the rubble. If he was stuck again, she would call 911, wait for the sirens, then leave with the nugget of rat poison in her pocket.

But he wasn't stuck anymore. "What is she doing?" he asked her.

Aisling climbed atop the table like a monkey and tried to pry open the door. In the living room, Anders cried out in pain.

"She's stuck," Tenn said.

Ward took in the mess—the house had fallen off a jack, and everything was sideways. "What do we do?" he asked Tenn. He didn't look as he had that day, in their bedroom, before he left her. He was terrified but full of resolve. He still had his phone in his hand, and the footage continued playing, the helicopter crossing the surreal blue of the sky.

"I have an idea," Tenn told him.

* * *

Ward wrapped Aisling's feet in paper towels and duct tape and carried her up the stairs, while Tenn pulled Anders by the hand. Gogo had emptied the contents of her stomach and continued to vomit yellow pools of bile on the white bedroom rug. Tenn moved the dresser to block the door, sealing them in, and Aisling walked into it over and over. Anders picked up the first object he encountered—a seashell from Tenn's nightstand, collected by Ward on a long-ago trip—and threw it at Aisling's head. The seashell grazed her cheek, hit the wall, and shattered. Anders repeated the action, this time picking up nothing, throwing nothing, his arm completing the motion empty-handed. Ward pulled Aisling back from the dresser, but as soon as he let go, she walked into it again. He looked at Tenn, helpless.

"Should we leave?" he asked her.

"It's not the house," she said. She didn't say *It's me*, because she didn't have to. And though Tenn had considered, over and over, the possibility of disappearing completely, now that its inevitability was upon her, she no longer wanted to go. She wanted to throw snowballs at her kids' heads in the yard; she wanted hot chocolate piled high with marshmallows. She wanted to drink wine in the kitchen with Ward and dance, to sit with him on the porch swing in the spring, to wake next to him in the morning and listen to the horses. She wanted her hours and days with the dishwasher that always needed running because it was full of dishes from meals they'd shared together.

She pointed to Ward's phone, still open to the footage of the cruise ship, the helicopter. "Look at this," she said. "You see how the helicopter blades look stationary, like they're not even moving?"

"Because of frame rate synchronization," Ward said. "Our work cameras record thirty frames per second. If a helicopter's blades are moving at a multiple of that, like six revolutions per second, then every time the camera captures an image, the blades are in the same place, so it looks like they're not moving."

"Because you can only see the frames that are captured," Tenn said. "And not the ones that aren't."

Ward held Tenn's camera to his eye and through it watched Aisling walk into the dresser, Anders lob an invisible object at her head. Tenn wasn't sure why it hadn't occurred to her before.

"I don't think I follow," Ward said.

"What if I'm using the wrong frame rate for what I'm trying to capture?" Tenn asked him. "What if the ghosts are flickering in and out of view, so they're not visible every microsecond?"

"You mean they're coming through in the space between frames, and that's why we can't see them?"

Anders threw the dish that held Tenn's rings, and Tenn watched her wedding ring fly across the room and disappear between two floorboards. Gogo vomited yellow foam onto the rug. Ward sat on the bed—Tenn could tell he didn't get it, but he was going along with it anyway because he was determined to try. "So you think changing the frame rate might help?" he said.

Tenn pointed the camera in his hands toward the window. On the screen, she saw the window, the street, the sun. That was all the camera captured. It didn't record the ghosts that were there, too, crowded around the window frame. Tenn could feel them, but Ward and the camera couldn't pick them up at all.

"What's the current frame rate?" Ward asked her. He was already scrolling through the options menu.

"Twenty-four," she told him. She reached for the camera, but her fingers were cold and stiff. The closer she and Ward got, the more the ghosts resisted. And Tenn was so tired—what she'd accumulated had eroded her. Together they were stronger than she was. Aisling walked into the dresser, and blood soaked through the paper towels at her big toe.

Ward went through the menu and changed the frame rate: ten frames per second, then twenty, forty, eighty. Together they watched the screen, the footage unchanged—the window, the street, the sun. Aisling bled on the hardwood; Gogo vomited on the rug.

Ward scrolled again through the menu, then set the camera on the bed. Changing the frame rate hadn't worked. Tenn waited for him to say he was taking the kids away, to safety. Instead he sprung from the bed and ran to his office, then returned with his laptop. "You can only pick the frame rates from the menu," he said.

"Yes," Tenn said.

Anders found a tray of candles and threw one at Aisling's head.

"You can't just set it to whatever you want," Ward said.

"Yes," Tenn said again. She couldn't set the frame rate manually; the options were all preset.

"Right," Ward said. "I know what to do."

Ward's phone buzzed, but he ignored it and began typing. Aisling walked into the dresser; Anders threw a candle. Tenn swept the remaining candles into her underwear drawer and covered the dresser's surface with balls of socks. The faster Ward typed, the more clearly Tenn could sense her guests—the smell of their sheets hanging on the line, the taste of their deaths in her mouth. They were still gathering, drawn here by Tenn, her terrible fear.

Tenn tried to reach for the camera, but her fingers were too stiff. But she didn't need to move, not anymore. She was here, in the bedroom, to watch them. She would stay here in this house where she belonged and be their witness.

* * *

Tenn felt pressure on her arms and saw Ward in front of her. He was shaking her hard; he was terrified.

"What's wrong?" she said.

"Stay alive!" he yelled. His cheeks were red and streaked with tears, his voice broken. "All I want is for you to stay alive. I'll do anything."

"What?" Tenn said. Aisling tracked blood across the floor; Gogo heaved but nothing came out.

"You looked at me and said, 'I have to tell you something.'" Ward said it, but Tenn knew; she understood what had happened. "You said, 'I've been thinking about dying,' and then you said it again, and you said it again, and I was telling you no, but it was like you couldn't hear me."

Tenn held his forearms, which were familiar, which she'd held many times before. She knew every one of his moles; she'd given them names. "I hear you now," she said. "You got me out of it." Her hands were freezing, but they were her own again. "How did you do it?"

Ward watched her as if it might happen again, like it could happen again anytime. "I told you I wanted you to stay alive," he said. He was shaking, all adrenaline. "Which I should have said the first time, but I didn't." Anders threw a sock ball, which hit Aisling in the face and fell to the floor. "I should have said it then, but I panicked and I left, and I'm sorry. I want you alive; I'll do anything. I'll quit; I'll find a different job, even if the pay is shit. We can move; we can go anywhere. I just want you to stay alive."

"I know," she said, because she did know. She believed it now. "But we need to hurry, or it's going to happen again."

Ward nodded and slid his laptop in front of her. He couldn't see what she could see, but he'd decided to trust her vision. "I found some open-source firmware for your camera, and I've used that to modify the frame rate options in the menu. We can go pretty high with a camera of this resolution."

Ward opened the updated menu, and Tenn adjusted the frame rate, then the rest of the settings. She started with the frame rate at 120 and, keeping the camera focused on the window, began lowering the rate, one frame per second at a time, as she and Ward watched the screen. The sun poured through the window and traveled across the wall; Tenn felt ghosts gathering like a family at a reunion. Anders ran out of socks and in Tenn's dresser found a vibrator, which he threw at Aisling's head. The vibrator hit the wall and buzzed on the floor. Tenn considered taping gloves to Anders's hands, or cocooning the kids in Bubble Wrap, but she couldn't stop now. She lowered the frame rate in increments, her fingers getting stiffer and stiffer until they were no longer her own.

Then Ward was shaking her, begging her to stay alive.

"Again?" she said.

"Again," he said. He returned to his laptop, typing fast, as he'd done before.

There were more ghosts in the room now, many more than before. Tenn could feel them crowding her, seeping in through the cracks around the windows and doors. On the camera's screen—the sun, the street. "Lots of people shoot at thirty or sixty," she told him. "We're not going to capture anything new at those frame rates."

"But people don't normally shoot at odd numbers, right?" Ward asked her. "What about twenty-seven frames per second?" Tenn was losing hope, but Ward was just getting started. "What about thirteen? And we're only using whole numbers now. What if we do double prime numbers? What about seventeen point seventeen?" he said. He got back on his laptop and began writing new code.

Tenn moved through the menu while her hands were still her own, the possibilities expanding rather than dwindling. Ward updated the menu, and she began working through the new options. The ghosts weren't appearing every thirtieth of a second or every sixtieth of a second, but maybe she would see something at weirder intervals. She tried a frame rate of 17.17. She tried variants of pi. She was changing the frame rate so fast, she didn't process it at first. She'd already moved on, the camera's screen displaying a lone bird in the street.

"Did you see that?" she said.

"Typing," Ward said.

Tenn decreased the frame rate by two tenths.

Ward looked up from his laptop, and for a long moment, Tenn

thought he couldn't see them—he couldn't see what she saw because it was all in her head. Ward did nothing, said nothing. Tenn wasn't sure he was even breathing. He was stuck again, and now he'd stay that way forever, trapped in the moment when everything could have changed.

"No," he said, more breath than speech. "What's happening?"

Tenn held the camera, her hands cold but steady, her own. She was fixing them there, on video—she'd finally found a way to give them witness, to preserve their memory here so they could disperse elsewhere. The room pulsed, and Tenn felt the crowd begin to thin. Aisling walked into the dresser and said, "Ow!" She stopped and turned, looked to Tenn in confusion. Anders picked up the buzzing vibrator and studied it in his hand.

"Can we watch TV?" he asked.

"Soon," Tenn said.

"Why is the dresser here?" Aisling said. She noticed her feet. "My feet hurt."

Ward shook his head, one hand over his mouth. "We did it," he told Tenn.

They had done it, but in that moment, Tenn felt no relief. "But they're in our home because of me," she said. "Aisling, too." Ward could see them now—the crowd of ghosts they'd gathered and brought home, like strays. "I may be able to capture them now, but I'm not sure we can stop collecting them. There's no solution to that problem."

Ward considered this as Gogo stopped midheave and jumped on the bed to lick faces.

"You're not a problem to be solved," Ward told Tenn. "Neither is Aisling. And I don't want you to stop being you. I've always loved the way your mind works. That scene where Eloise is standing in front of her wall covered with calendars, turning each one to a new month, and you can hear Jerome in the next room, reading his essay about writers' reputations? I still think about that all the time. And the part where Eloise is reciting a poem on the porch, and lightning breaks across the sky behind her like she conjured it!"

Tenn had never heard Ward talk about her work like this. She hadn't thought about those scenes in years.

Ward continued, "I miss that. I miss that for you. I miss seeing you at work, like you're in the presence of something. I miss feeling like the sacred is all around, and I can see it, too, once you reveal it to me."

"I miss that, too," Tenn said. She missed it, but it didn't feel so far away now. It felt like it might still be within reach.

"Besides," Ward said, "nothing is fixed in place. We'll all be different a year from now, just like we'll be different five years from now. And I want to be there with you. Five years from now, thirty. I want to be there when you become a different person again. I want to be there through all the things that don't make sense. I can do better, if you'll let me. Can we start over?"

"Again?" Tenn said.

"Again," Ward said. "But different this time."

On the screen, a silhouette blurred at its edges, growing fainter as it became viewable, as its viewability here allowed it to disperse elsewhere. Ward took Tenn's hand, and she felt their connection like a sacrament, renewed—one version of their marriage gone and replaced by a fresh one. In this version, they would say things out loud; they would believe each other. In this version, they would sit together in thrall to this mystery.

20

Tenn sat at her desk and tabbed through the feeds. In the kitchen, a silhouette lingered by the sink; in the attic, a small party appeared to be underway. Now that Tenn could see the ghosts consistently, she knew where they liked to congregate. They were like spiders—drawn to corners and windows, as if they might spin a web or escape into the yard. It had taken a few weeks to get it right—the camera placement, the frame rates. Tenn created safe spots, put the cameras in the kids' rooms on timers to protect their privacy, but the family was already used to having cameras around the house. It was easy to forget they were there.

Traffic to the website was high today, though Tenn wasn't sure why. In Anders's room: a silhouette shaped like a dog, planted at the foot of his bed. Anders had named it Phantom and drew it in art class to impress a girl named Nell who played his favorite video game and was pretty sure she had ghosts in her bedroom, too. In Aisling's room, amongst the proliferation of art supplies: two thin silhouettes by the door, as if they were standing guard. These two were new—Tenn had picked them up last week on the train home from the city. They'd joined her as the train passed through a crossing. They stayed close together, the pair of them, listing toward one another, never apart. They already seemed to be fading at the edges.

Ward had designed the website, which Tenn had titled *Gathering Place: An Installation*. They'd kept it bare-bones, to resemble the live streams Tenn loved—the northern lights, the eagles' nest. Only Tenn's website didn't feature a nest of eggs but a haunted house where viewers could click through, room by room, and watch the ghosts. Tenn had written an artist's statement about the project and sent it with a press release to the media contacts she had left, as well as to curators and museums, other filmmakers. Within days, the traffic started to grow, and now visitors arrived at a steady clip.

At first, Tenn wasn't sure if the source of her relief was the presence of an audience or the fact that, for the first time in a long time, she woke each day with a sense of purpose. One morning, she found herself singing while she washed the dishes. One afternoon, she sat at the dining room table, helping Aisling, in tears over math homework, and instead of feeling frustrated because helping with math homework was the last way she wanted to spend her precious days, she felt the moment's sweetness, because Aisling would learn the math and feel proud of herself, and her pride would exist because this struggle had preceded it, and Tenn took a bag of jelly beans from the pantry to use as counters, and then she and the kids were swapping flavors, competing to see who could make the best mix. One day, she woke to Ward spooning her from behind, his erection against her ass, and though he had an early meeting, they fucked in near silence while Gogo snored in her crate, and Tenn did not think once about what presence might be in the room with them.

She couldn't deny it, though: the more people viewed her ghosts, the lighter she felt. She was invigorated by the energy moving through her. The ghosts were recorded, witnessed, preserved in memory—and then they were gone. But the house was never empty—in the absence of one ghost, new ones arrived to fill the space. Tenn was attuned to it now, the sensation of a new passenger joining her as she went about her day, the fleeting cold in her hands, the unmooring moment in which she felt as if she'd woken from a dream she could no longer remember. The more time she dedicated to her own work—every morning she carved out two hours that were hers alone—the more her porosity felt like a privilege rather than a burden. The project would be ongoing—it would have to be—the cameras streaming footage of the kitchen, the hall, capturing not just the ghosts but Tenn's life. Anders refusing the dinner she'd made, Gogo shitting on the rug and eating it. Aisling making bracelets, rehearsing for the school play, writing a story about a girl who is haunted. Helen coming to visit, gleefully mugging for the cameras after weeks of texting Tenn about what to wear, Tenn and Ward racing to the bedroom after a rare night out, draping a pair of shorts over the camera's watchful eye. All of it—the remnants of life and the living of life, side by side—that was Tenn's project. In order to preserve the dead, she had to engage in the act of living.

Outside, men were talking, and Tenn closed her laptop, followed the noise to the kitchen to check their progress. The foundation repairs were almost complete; the broken dishes had been replaced with ones that were less fragile. In the yard, two men smoked cigarettes, one looking up toward the attic window. Someone had left the water running—some ghosts were stubborn—so Tenn turned off the faucet. Ward had made waffles for breakfast, and the kids had left the whipped cream out on the counter. Tenn enjoyed a squirt directly from the can.

Gogo trotted in with something in her mouth, and Tenn offered her whipped cream off her finger in exchange. Gogo took the trade, releasing an old Post-it from a moving box that said *things we should throw away but will keep until we die*.

Tenn could hear Ward coming down the stairs, but it took him longer than she expected to reach the bottom. They'd spent the whole morning in near misses, one of them entering a room just as the other exited. Tenn stood by the door and waited. The sound of his footsteps stopped.

"Hello?" she said. She was waiting to tell him about her meeting. She opened the door.

On the other side, Ward stood with his phone in his hand. He lifted his eyes, then he kissed her.

"Hey," he said. "I didn't hear you there."

"I'm just taking a break," Tenn said. There was waffle batter smeared on the counter, and she left it, reached instead for the whipped cream can. "Open your mouth."

Ward opened his mouth obediently, and Tenn filled it with whipped cream. "How's your morning?" she asked.

"Meetingy," Ward said. "But I got the eye appointments scheduled, and my therapy." He crossed the room to the family calendar and began writing. "I can take the kids to the eye doctor," he told Tenn.

"What about Johann?" Tenn asked.

"I told him if it's not affecting my job performance, it's none of his fucking business." When Tenn raised an eyebrow, he added: "Not in those exact words, but I'm on it." He kissed her again, whipped cream from his mouth dissolving into hers. She pulled away, filled her mouth for another messy kiss.

Then Ward was back to business. "So, how was it?"

Tenn had been on a call that morning with a producer who thought her installation had potential. She'd decided she wanted to branch out from documentary and was pitching a limited series about a family who moves into a haunted house and is too busy pranking each other with the creepy doll they find in their yard to notice that the house is actually haunted.

"He didn't like the idea," she told him.

"Why not?" Ward said. "He only wants it if it's a documentary?"

"No," Tenn said. "He doesn't think a series is the way to go. He thinks we'll have better luck if we pitch it as a feature."

Ward reached immediately for the whipped cream can.

"I like this," Tenn said, her mouth full again. "As a way to celebrate."

Ward had a dab of whipped cream on the tip of his nose, and Tenn licked it off. "We can celebrate any time you want," he told her. "It's a new tradition."

The trash was overflowing, and Ward pulled the bag from the can. Gogo jumped up to see if there was anything she might scavenge.

"I meant to tell you," he said, "we're out of little spoons again. I don't know what the kids were doing, but the dishwasher is a real clusterfuck."

"I'll run it," Tenn said. She'd just run the dishwasher yesterday.

"Let's buy paper plates," Ward said. "We can eat off them for a week like heathens and wash nothing."

"That's the hottest thing you've ever said," Tenn told him.

He kissed her one more time, both of their mouths sticky and sweet, the camera behind them recording both the kiss and the ghosts witnessing the kiss, the ghosts that were there because they needed witnesses of their own, the ghosts that Tenn accumulated and shed like skin, a continually renewing process.

"I should get back to work," she said. She'd started accepting ads because they needed the money for all the repairs.

"I know," he said. "But can you start the dishwasher?"

Ward held the trash bag but did not move to carry it outside.

"What?" she said.

"What do you mean, *what*?" he said. "Why are you so suspicious? I just like watching you bend over."

Ward was a terrible liar, though, and, sometimes, still, Tenn could see right through him. She bent, flaunting her ass more than necessary, opened the cabinet under the sink to grab a pod of detergent. There, she found the doll, staring blankly from between bottles of cleaner.

Ward couldn't suppress his grin. He and the doll, they were in cahoots.

"Where did you find this?" Tenn asked him. She hadn't seen it in ages; she'd thought for sure Ward had destroyed it.

"I found it in the yard," Ward said. "In the ivy."

"I thought it was gone," Tenn told him.

"Me, too," Ward said.

Tenn held the doll in her hand and felt nothing—no tug, no extra presence guiding her hand. She slipped it in her pocket, mentally staging its next appearance. What she did next was all her.

Acknowledgments

This book would not exist without:

My agent, Stacia Decker, who found this book its perfect home. I will never not be grateful for your advocacy, insight, and quick responses to my anxious emails.

My editor, Daphne Durham, whose edits not only made this book better but also helped me understand how to take my own work more seriously. Thank you for meeting my exclamation points with more exclamation points!

The extraordinary team at Putnam, whose hard work brought this book to life: Brianna Fairman, Janice Barral, Dora Mak, Aja Pollock, Laura Corless, Kristen Bianco, Jess Cuate, and Molly Pieper.

Christopher Lin, for a cover that still has me dancing with joy.

Susan Egginton, former owner of my old house, for sharing her research into the house's history (and the UFO sighting in our neighborhood).

Lewisboro, New York, town historian Maureen Koehl, whose book

Lewisboro Ghosts: Strange Tales and Scary Sightings was a source of inspiration, in addition to *A History of the Town of Lewisboro* by the Lewisboro History Book Committee.

Casey Scieszka and Steven Weinberg at the Spruceton Inn, for a transformative residency that gave me time and space to revise this book. And all of my fellow Spruceton Inn artist residents, especially Molly Gillis, Jordan Mann, and Daniel Sitts, who generously answered my film-related questions.

The Provincetown Community Compact Writer Residency, where I spent a blissful week thinking and writing, especially Jay Critchley and Chip Brock for making it happen.

Tina Villaveces at Yellow Studio, for a residency that not only gave me space to work through edits on this book, but also a community that feels like family. And to the entire Yellow Studio crew: Thank you for being an unending source of inspiration and support.

Rainer and Gulliver: Thank you for not being too embarrassed by your mother (yet).

And finally, Jason: I would live in the yard with you, in a tree house, and be happy.

Discussion Guide

1. How does *Accumulation* use horror to reveal the everyday pressures women and mothers face, and the toll of being the one who keeps everything running?

2. Be honest—at what point in the book would you have packed up the family and left the house behind?

3. The house seems to feed on silence and denial. How does communication—or the lack of it—fuel both the haunting and the tension in Tenn's marriage and family life?

4. Which scene stood out to you the most, and why did it stick with you?

5. Did your opinion of any of the characters change from the beginning of the book to the end?

6. What did you make of the house's history and the lore surrounding it?

7. What was your favorite line or paragraph?

8. Did you guess any of the book's revelations as you were reading? Which one surprised you the most?

9. Tenn's sense of self frays as her roles as mother, wife, and artist collide. Which moments made you feel her unraveling most vividly?

10. No spoilers, but that finale! Were you surprised? Hopeful? Shocked? How did you interpret the ending? Does *Accumulation* offer Tenn (and us) a way out—or suggest that some types of hauntings never leave?